JAN

I love writing authentic, passionate and emotional ...
I began my first novel, a historical, when I was sixteen, but life derailed me a bit when I started suffering with Ankylosing Spondylitis, so I didn't complete a novel until after I was thirty when I put it on my to do before I'm forty list. Now I love getting caught up in the lives and traumas of my characters, and I'm so thrilled to be giving my characters life in others' imaginations, especially when readers tell me they've read the characters just as I've tried to portray them.

You can follow me on Twitter @JaneLark.

The Scandalous Love
of a Duke

JANE LARK

HarperImpulse an imprint of
HarperCollins*Publishers Ltd*
77–85 Fulham Palace Road
Hammersmith, London W6 8JB

www.harpercollins.co.uk

A Paperback Original 2014

First published in Great Britain in ebook format by HarperImpulse 2014

ISBN: 9780007591701

Automatically produced by Atomik ePublisher from Easypress

The Marlow Intrigues Series is gathering followers, and the story of Ellen's son, John, is my first step into the next generation. There is still more to come, including the prequel to The Illicit Love of a Courtesan, but for now I hope you enjoy the tale of my moody, arrogant, fractured, golden-hearted, young Duke.

If you wonder who, or what inspired John's story—it was written at the time that Prince William asked Catherine Middleton to marry him. His apparent reluctance to accept his royal status, his reliance on Catherine, and the way he is so much more relaxed with her, gave me the inspiration for John's circumstances and his own Catherine, though John's story does not follow theirs.

Prologue

Katherine's fingers grasped the pale, uneven trunk of the beech tree. Laughing, she braced her body to stop her descent down the grassy slope, her grip slipping on the thin strips of peeling bark.

She turned back to catch her friend's hand.

In fits of giggles, Margaret fell against the tree too.

"Shhh..." Eleanor whispered, her fingers pressing to her lips as she struggled to tame her own intemperate humour. "They will hear us." Eleanor was Margaret's younger cousin.

More giggles erupted from the large group of younger girls behind them. Eleanor was the most boisterous of them, though.

Looking across her shoulder, Katherine smiled.

Katherine was the outsider here. The odd one out. A Spencer. All the other girls were the Duke of Pembroke's grandchildren. Katherine was nothing compared to them. Her adopted father was a mere lowly squire. But Katherine had grown up amongst this family. These girls were more sisterly to her than her own sister. Her brother Phillip was John Harding's friend and John was another of the Duke's grandchildren, the eldest, and his heir.

One day John would own the land they stood on, and a dozen other estates. He'd be rich.

John. His name stilled Katherine's heart and slowed her breathing as a secret longing welled inside her.

1

She no longer felt like laughing, she clung to the tree, her palms pressing against the trunk as her gaze reached through the veil of branches and leaves that stirred gently on a warm summer breeze.

"Can you see them?" Caroline, one of Margaret's younger sisters, whispered.

"What are they doing?" Margaret leant forwards, looking over Katherine's shoulder.

"Swimming," Eleanor gasped with another giggle. "They're naked."

The girls about Katherine broke into fits of laughter again, their fingers pressing over their mouths.

"Hush," Heather, Margaret's older sister, who was the eldest of the girls, urged them to be silent. She was eight and ten. She had already curtsied to the Queen. Her father was an heir to a duke too. All the other girls were the daughters of dukes or earls. Katherine loved them all, but even so she wore the weight of her lower birth as prominently as her second-hand scarlet cloak. She stood out.

"We should not have followed," Heather said

"Papa, will kill me," Eleanor laughed, breathlessly pressing her fingers against her chest.

"And Grandfather will kill John," Margaret whispered.

The girls looked at one another as Katherine looked about them all. John was their pattern card. All his younger cousins followed him like shadows, emulating everything he did. They were all mesmerised by him. But Katherine's feelings were much more than just awe. She loved John, secretly, but without hope or expectation. When she was with him her heart ached and raced, and well… She did not know how to explain it.

The others whispered and giggled.

Katherine focused on the boys cavorting in the lake. They seemed oblivious to the girls obscured by the curtain of leaves.

They were splashing water at each other, shouting and baiting one another, laughing. John, pale-skinned, lean and athletic, lunged at Katherine's brother, gripped his shoulders and pushed him

2

under water. The game grew more aggressive. Phillip thrust up and retaliated, lunging back at John, and when John dodged him, Phillip dived beneath the water and pulled John under.

All the boys, a dozen or more of John's friends from Oxford, broke into an uproar then, as the game became a mêlée.

They were not boys, though, not anymore, no more than she was a girl. They were young men, and she was on the brink of womanhood. She could be married now if she wished. The problem was the only person she wished to marry was unattainable. John.

"We should go," Heather breathed beside her. "We shouldn't be here."

Katherine turned.

Eleanor made a mischievous face at her older cousin. "Killjoy."

"Give them their privacy," Heather pressed.

Eleanor pouted, she was only thirteen. "We didn't know they were going to swim—"

"And that is precisely why we should go back before we are missed," Heather caught hold of Eleanor's arm. "Come on, they will start the celebrations soon."

The other girls began peeling away.

Katherine would have to go back too, but she would rather be in the water. Her gaze returned to the lake. The day was hot, and the heat was heavy, clinging and oppressive. She understood why they'd shed their clothes and dived in.

"Kate!" Eleanor called, in an *are-you-coming* voice.

Katherine glanced back and nodded before taking an irresistible final look at the boys.

John was standing in the shallow water, near where the lake dropped over a weir into a cascade, taunting her brother.

The lake rose to the indent of muscle at his hip.

Katherine's breath caught, trapped in her lungs.

He'd lost the coltish look he'd had a few years ago when she'd first met him, he was physically magnificent now. He was over six feet tall, sinuous and muscular. She longed to touch him and her heart raced as warmth flooded her veins.

"Kate!" Eleanor called again.

John's head turned and his ice-blue eyes spun in the direction of the trees where she was hiding. His gaze reached between the leaves as they stirred into motion on the warm breeze sweeping up from the ornamental lake. Katherine felt the intensity in his eyes.

There was an aura about John, an attraction which drew everyone in.

His looks were striking and he had a presence which captured people's attention when he was in a room.

He was born to lead people, or perhaps bred to do so.

His fingers lifted and swept his damp jet-black hair off his brow, but his gaze didn't leave the trees.

He had an inherent grace too.

He was calm and silent in nature, though strong-willed. He won most arguments with her brother. But he had an instinctive awareness of others, and he'd been kind to her. John had acted like a brother to her. He was always considerate. He'd included her even when Phillip forgot to, and John had never grown tired of her dogged company as Phillip sometimes did.

At what point her feelings had changed from sisterly to something else, she couldn't say. Perhaps she'd always felt differently about John. But now it was obsession.

His gaze seemed to strike hers, though surely he had not seen her. She smiled. All the girls in his family were stunningly beautiful, it carried from their mothers. In John that beauty was breathtakingly masculine. She could not take her eyes off him when she was near him.

"John!" her brother called.

John's gaze ripped away, his awareness disengaging from the trees and returning to the lake.

"Kate!"

Katherine caught her breath, dragging air into her lungs, and turned back.

Eleanor and the others were already at the top of the slope looking down.

Katherine lifted her hand to say she was coming, and then began to climb.

~

Egypt, December, Seven years later

John let the handle of the spade rest against his midriff, set one hand on his lean waist and wiped his brow with his forearm. Then he lifted the wide-brimmed leather hat from his head and tipped his gaze to the endlessly clear, blue sky.

God, it was hot here, but it was the middle of a bloody desert.

"Water, please." He looked at one of the native men in his train. Almost instantly the water skin was in John's hand.

The warm fluid slid down his throat, relieving the dryness.

He handed the skin back.

They'd found a new tomb but it was buried beneath centuries of sand.

Dropping his hat back on his head, John then bent and began digging again. His blade slipped easily into the sand, but half of each shovel load slid back into the hole. He cursed and increased his pace.

"My Lord, I have it!" Yassah, the man who'd been John's right hand for years, called. John let his spade fall and moved to where Yassah worked, dropping to his knees to scoop sand out with his bare hands.

"It is the entrance." There was a flare of excitement in John's chest. The hours of hunting and digging were worth it for this moment of success.

Before Egypt, John had drifted, despondent. This was why he had come and this was why he stayed.

"It is open, robbed," Yassah stated. He was on his knees too.

5

Empty. *Damn.* But there would still be the paintings. John leant back, resting his buttocks on his heels. "Hand me the spade."

Later, John sat beneath the canopy before his tent, in a canvas chair, his feet resting on the sand. The sky was red, and the sun glowed on the horizon, about to fall. Then suddenly it literally dropped over the edge of the world, leaving only the blue-black darkness and a million glinting stars, the stars he'd seen painted on the ceiling of every temple.

The sun had never set like this in England.

He drew on the tip of a thin cigar and then let his hand fall when he exhaled.

The tomb they'd discovered today had been an official's. It was empty, but it wasn't treasure which excited John anyway. What thrilled him was the emotion of the search and the find.

John took another draw on his cigar.

He was in a thoughtful mood, brooding.

His gaze reached up to the darkness and the stars. The black of night was like polished jet here, not the dull pitch it was at home.

When his grandfather had packed John off on the grand tour to *sow his wild oats* abroad, the intention had been that John would return with his youthful dissipated fire burnt out. The only problem was that nothing in England drew John back.

The images from the dream he'd had last night crowded into his head. It was a dream he'd had a thousand times. This was the root of his melancholy mood. He always felt like this when he'd dreamt it.

In the dream, he was a child, looking from the window of his grandfather's grand black coach. He saw his mother, with her dress clutched in one hand as she ran behind them, reaching towards him. His stepfather was there too, behind her, his expression violent with anger. But it wasn't only a dream, it was a memory. A memory John had never asked to be explained. A memory he'd never admitted he had.

His grandfather had taken him from them, he'd never

6

understood why.

His childhood had been lonely before that.

Perhaps that was why he felt so comfortable in a desert.

He'd been given back to his mother a few weeks later. But the memory his head constantly echoed in a dream was the defining moment of his life. The point he had been torn in two, by his grandfather's will and his mother's love. One was hard, cold and aggressive, the other warm, welcoming and enchanting. But the second had been a childish need. What abided in him now was the barren land his grandfather had cultivated.

John's earliest memory was of his grandfather saying he had no mother, when John knew he did. He'd not been allowed to speak of her. He'd never known why. She'd written to him for years, and then she'd come. She'd taught him kindness and consideration, empathy and understanding, while his grandfather had encouraged restraint and harsh judgement.

Now, John was just constantly angry at the world. This was the reason he'd stayed abroad. He was his grandfather's monster. The years spent in Europe had taught John that.

He took another drag on his cigar, and then exhaled.

Good God he'd been his mother's child, naïve and foolish, when he'd arrived in Paris. Obvious prey for the she-wolves hunting those grounds. He'd been seduced by their world and fleeced. It had taken months to learn the art of disengagement. It had left him bitter. His grandfather had achieved his wish: John did not trust a soul.

The choice he'd made after that was the only one open to him – not to go back. Not going back was his defiance. The only way he could win the battle against his grandfather.

Then he'd found Egypt and a purpose, something beyond himself. Something which made him *feel* again. The only problem was this loneliness at night.

When it was dark, the isolation became stark and these memories flooded in. In his youth he'd covered them with friendships.

In his dissipated years he'd smothered them with sex. He'd had nothing to do with women since he'd come to Egypt. There was no hiding from recollections here.

He tilted his lips in a mock smile. He thought of his stepfather, and his brothers and sisters, who kept increasing in number. It was Christmas in four days. He imagined all his family together. Occasionally he wrote home to tell them he was still alive.

He took another drag on his cigar, clearing his thoughts.

He didn't wish to think of them, nor England. He thought of the tomb he'd found.

~

A brush in his hand, John lay on his stomach, cautiously sweeping sand away from the painted wall-plaster of the tomb they'd discovered four days before. The colours were so bright they could have been painted days ago not hundreds of years before.

"My Lord!" John looked back. Mustafa, his manservant, who usually stayed in camp, was at the entrance, looking in past the couple of feet of sand still filling the opening

"My Lord! This letter came from England."

Mustafa waved the thin paper as though it were something wonderful.

John glanced at Yassah. "Carry on without me." Then crawled backwards out of the tomb.

The midday sun blazed down.

John stood.

He took the letter and saw it had passed through Alexandria a month ago. He recognised the writing as his stepfather's. In England it was winter. Today was Christmas Day. His family would be on his stepfather's small estate. Sometimes he had spent it with them there. Sometimes he had been forced to spend it at his grandfather's. Either way, Christmas did not bring forward many fond memories. Perhaps a couple before his brothers and sisters had become so numerous, but after…

John wiped a hand on his trousers then broke the seal.

His grandfather would be horrified if he saw the calluses on John's hands.

Glancing up, John thanked Mustafa and then began walking towards the canopy his men used at prayer times.

He stopped in its shade and opened the letter. A second, separate folded sheet fell out. He held that aside and read.

The letter was dated months ago, in August.

His father's words were carefully couched, but the meaning was clear, the Duke of Pembroke, John's grandfather, was dying.

He could be dead.

Lord!

John's fingers covered his mouth. His lips were dry, but inside he felt like ice, even in the heat. His hand swept back his hair.

He had to go back. He'd been bred to take over his grandfather's estates. The choice was no longer his.

Then it struck him, he should feel grief. He did not. He cared nothing for the old tyrant. But he did feel strangely suspended, as though time had stopped. As though it would never start again.

John looked at the other letter and saw Mary's effervescent writing. She was his eldest sister, the first child of his mother's second marriage. She was just sixteen, approaching her first season.

She'd clearly rushed to write, scribbling a note to include in her father's letter. She told John she needed her big brother home to lead her in her first waltz. She vowed she wouldn't dance a single one unless he came.

Their grandfather's death would postpone her debut, she obviously did not know he was ill, and so perhaps the Duke had not been at death's door.

Whatever, John had to go back.

"Mustafa!" John turned.

Chapter One

London, April, four months later

John's ship docked in London just as twilight darkened into night.
A light drizzle was falling as he descended from the gangplank.

England.

It was over seven years since he'd stood on English soil. It felt
odd stepping onto the dock; like travelling back in time.

He remembered the callow youth who'd left here. He wasn't
that child anymore.

One of the crew had called a hackney carriage. It waited before
him, its oil lamp glowing into the now full darkness. He gave the
address to the driver then climbed in. A few moments after he'd
clicked the door shut, the carriage jarred into movement, rocking
over the cobbles.

He'd not sent word ahead. There'd seemed little point when
he'd arrive just as fast.

He lifted the curtain and looked at the passing streets.

They'd left the narrow backstreets of the slums near the docks
and now they were progressing into the more affluent areas of
London.

He'd had months to get used to the idea of coming home. He
had accepted it. But it did not mean he was looking forward to

it. He would be weighed down by duty here.

John's heart drummed steadily in his chest. Was his grandfather alive or dead?

The carriage turned a sharp corner and John caught hold of the leather strap.

The streets were quiet, virtually dead. Early evening in Mayfair was not a social hour. People would be dining now, before they went out. All John could hear was the sound of the carriage horses and iron-rimmed wheels on cobble.

He didn't even know if his family were here, but he was heading for his grandfather's townhouse. It seemed the best place to start.

A few minutes later, the hired carriage drew to a halt and John looked from the window at his grandfather's palatial town residence. It was set back from the road and guarded by iron railings, taking up one entire side of the square.

John had found it oppressive as a child. As a youth he'd been more impressed. As a man it simply seemed ostentatious.

John climbed out onto the pavement.

He'd left his luggage at the docks to be sent on.

The light drizzle had not eased.

He paid the driver.

The man tipped his hat.

John looked up at the house as the hackney pulled away. The knocker was in place, someone was home.

He took a deep breath and then jogged up the pale stone steps. When he reached the top he lifted the lion-head brass knocker and struck it down thrice, then stepped back a little and waited.

It was several moments before it opened.

Finch, the man who'd been his grandfather's butler for as long as John could remember, stood in the hall. John watched recognition, and then shock, dawn on the butler's face. He'd never seen Finch's upper lip show any expression before.

"Good Lord – I mean come in, my Lord. You were not expected?"

"No, I travelled at the same speed as any message; I saw no

point in sending word. My luggage will follow. Tell me, who is currently at home?" He already knew his grandfather yet survived, otherwise Finch would have said Your Grace.

"Their Graces, the Duke and Duchess, my Lord, and the Duke and Duchess of Arundel." His grandparents then, and his uncle and aunt. John's heart pounded. Finch then nodded to a footman, obviously sending him somewhere to announce John's arrival. But even as he did so there was a shout from above.

"John."

He looked up as his name echoed off the black and white marble beneath his feet and the decorative plaster all about him, and saw his Uncle Richard, the Duke of Arundel, descending the wide curving stone steps briskly. This man had been like a father to John before John's mother had come back. But he had aged. His hair was peppered with grey and his face more lined.

"Thank God. We had no idea if you had even received Edward's letter." John saw relief in his uncle's eyes as he neared and then he smiled. "It is good to have you home, John."

John met Richard at the bottom of the stairs, and took his hand to shake it, but Richard also gripped John's shoulder. An uncomfortable feeling tingled through John's nerves. He was unused to being touched. No one had touched him in four years.

"You have changed, John. Grown up, I suppose."

"Uncle—" John began, only to have his speech halted by a wave of his uncle's hand.

"No uncle, just Richard now we are both men."

John smiled, "Richard, it is good to see a familiar face. The journey was long and I've no idea of how things stand." *How is the Duke?* He didn't say the last, he didn't know how to.

"Things stand not well, John." Richard slung an arm about John's shoulders and drew him to the stairs. "I'll take you up. The family will be pleased to see you, your mother particularly."

"And my grandfather?" John had to ask.

"He is near the end," Richard answered, his arm falling as they

12

began climbing the stairs. "He has been holding on for your return, I think. He will want to speak to you at once. I'll tell him you are here. He is much changed, John. He's been ill for many months."

John nodded sharply, angry at the emptiness in his chest and the anxiety stirring in his stomach. *For God's sake, I am a man full-grown now. I need not fear him.*

"Why not wait with your grandmother and Penny. They will be overjoyed you're home. I'll come and fetch you." His uncle must have seen something of John's feelings.

John felt like the child he'd been when he'd left. The child his uncle had always seemed to pity. He nodded, though, and walked on along the familiar hall as Richard turned the other way.

John's head was suddenly full of pictures from the past. The most acute being the day his mother and his stepfather had come here to fetch him during that troubled tenth year of his life. The day he'd been returned to her after the scene which haunted him.

She'd taken John from school previously, in the middle of the night. John's stepfather had been with her then, but he'd been a stranger to John at the time. They'd travelled north for miles and then she'd married that stranger.

It was only a couple of weeks after that John's grandfather had come to take him back.

The day his mother had collected John here, his grandfather had acknowledged her for the first time.

The drawing room door was ajar. John could hear the women talking.

"I have no idea what else to do. He will see no other physician but he is so obviously in considerable pain and yet he will not take laudanum," John's grandmother was saying. Her voice sounded weak and worried.

Both she and his aunt Penny had been mothers to him until he'd been ten. His grandfather's monster wanted to roar even now, and yell at them when he entered; why had they needed to be? Why had his mother not been here? He'd never understood who to blame for his loss.

He thrust his maudlin childish thoughts aside and pushed the door wider to enter. "Grandmamma. Aunt Penny."

Both women stood, exclaiming at the sight of him then crossing the room, their eyes wide. He had shocked them.

"Grandmother," he kissed the back of her fingers, bowing, but when he rose he saw tears in her eyes, and then he hugged her gently and pressed a kiss on her temple before letting her go.

"Oh John, your grandfather will be glad. *I* am glad. It is good to have you home. You look well. Your journey was not too difficult?"

"My journey was long, and difficult, but that is travelling, and particularly in winter. It is good to see you too, Grandmother. You have not aged a day."

She smiled. "Flatterer."

"You have an air of mystery about you now, John, and I think it suits you," his aunt said.

John turned to her, smiled and opened his arms.

She hugged him. "Ellen must be overjoyed." She was crying too when she pulled away and she reached for a handkerchief.

"I have not seen Mama yet. I thought it best to come here first. Is she in town?"

"Oh John, yes, she is in town, and she will never forgive me for seeing you first."

"I shall have Finch send word," his grandmother said. "The whole family are in London…" *Because of my grandfather's illness?* "I shall have him contact them all."

"John."

John turned to face Richard, who stood at the open door.

"His Grace wishes to see you."

A moment later, John was walking back along the statue-lined hall beside his uncle.

"How long is he likely to live?"

His uncle glanced sideways. "It could be hours or days or weeks, John. There is no certainty. He has defied a hundred predictions

14

already."

John nodded, feeling his anxiety rise again.

"You have nothing to fear," his uncle stated more quietly.

John was thrown back into the position of a ten-year-old child. Richard rested a palm on his shoulder.

John shrugged it off. He was not that child anymore, and if his grandfather was so close to death, he needed to earn respect not pity. "I am half his age and in my prime. He is on his deathbed. He can hardly dominate me now."

"I was not challenging you, John," his uncle answered with a smile. "I know you are capable, but I also know how cutting his words can be, pay no mind to them. I have never done so."

John tried to recognise Richard's good intent but only felt discomfort. He felt emotionally naked here. He was not used to the feeling. He was no longer used to people who knew him so well. He did not like it.

Richard knocked on the door of the state bedchamber and waited to be called in.

John's heart raced when Richard turned the handle.

The red and gold decoration in the room was subdued by the low light. Just two candles were burning: one on either side of the bed, casting shadows. The canopy towered above them, and long curtains fell to the floor at either side, screening his grandfather from view. But John could hear his laboured breathing, and the chamber had the putrid smell of sickness.

His grandfather's valet stood across the room and another man was beside the bed. The physician?

"Your Grace, I have brought John." Richard moved forwards.

John followed.

The Duke of Pembroke was propped up on pillows and his head lay back, as though he could not lift it. He was extremely thin, a ghost compared to the statuesque giant who'd intimidated John as a child. He *was* unrecognisable. His skin was grey and his cheeks sunken. His hands, which rested on the red cover, were skeletal.

The old man took a breath, which looked painful, and lifted his hand an inch from the bed. He breathed John's name and then it fell.

John passed his uncle, moving to take his grandfather's hand. He pressed a kiss upon the bony knuckles. "Your Grace."

"My... boy." The words were barely audible as he fought for breath.

"John."

John turned to see Richard had brought a chair for him. He sat, still holding his grandfather's hand, and rested an elbow on the bed, leaning forwards.

"Grandfather, I was sorry to hear your situation."

A condemnatory sound escaped the old man's lips "Because... it... meant... you... must... come... home... Sayle." The Duke was the only one who called him by his token title, the Marquess of Sayle.

"Because it meant you were dying," John corrected. "I do not relish that, Your Grace. True, I do not hunger for the reins of the dukedom, but nor do I wish to see you gone; you are my grandfather." It was probably the most honest statement he'd ever made to the old man. It was about bloody time he spoke truthfully.

"Unlikely... But... now... you... are... back... I... may... go... in... peace."

"And that is equally unlikely." John smiled as he met his grandfather's gaze. The old man's body may have been weakened, but his direct gaze and the mind behind it had not.

"Enough... of... your... cheek."

John smiled more broadly. "So do you wish to know what I have been up to in my absence?"

"I-know... your... mother... has... read... your... letters... to... me—" the Duke's words were cut off by a painful-sounding cough.

John rose and pressed a hand on his grandfather's shoulder. "Perhaps I ought not disturb you."

The Duke's fingers lifted from the bed. "Stay," he breathed.

John sat again.

"I... have... waited... for-you. You-must... speak-to... Harvey... about... business—"

"I am sure I shall manage, Grandfather."

"I... know... you... shall."

John smiled again. That was possibly the only compliment he'd ever heard from this man.

"I'll leave you to it," Richard said. The Duke's gaze reached across John's shoulder, then John heard the door open and shut.

As soon as it did, the Duke's hand moved and touched John's forearm, which rested on the bed. "But... you... must... promise-me... *one... thing*. You... will... not... wed... beneath... you. You... must... choose... a... wife... to... preserve... the... bloodline."

John felt his face twist in disgust. Even now, even on his deathbed, the old man sought to cast orders and manipulate John's life. Still, when the time came to set up a nursery, John would have plenty of choice from those in his own class. With a self-deprecating smile, he nodded. What did he care, it would not matter who he picked.

"*You swear*," his grandfather pressed on a single breath.

"I swear," John answered, his smile falling. He knew the old man's game but chose to play.

"Now... talk... to... me... of... what... you... have... done. I... will... listen."

John smiled again and leant back in the chair, folding his arms over his chest and stretching out his legs.

He spoke of Europe, of what he'd made of it, the things he'd seen and done, and he made his stories humorous and even caused the old man to express a muted laugh. It ended in another visibly painful coughing fit, at which point the old man's valet stepped forward to plump the pillows and make the Duke more comfortable. John would have left, but his grandfather once more bid him stay.

John changed his subject to his true passion, to Egypt, and began talking about the place and people, about the amazing artefacts and architecture of that ancient world. He talked of the finds he was shipping home.

While John spoke, the old man smiled and shut his eyes, his chest rising and falling with each rasping breath.

It was strange watching him thus – this ogre who'd dominated John's life – as a man and not a child. His grandfather was just a man too, with human frailty.

John felt a heavy sense of regret as he continued recounting a pointless search he'd set out upon once.

A sound of humour escaped the Duke's lips.

If John had returned in better circumstances, he wondered if they'd had more time, man to man, whether the past could be put straight between them.

His grandsire's physician stepped forward a while later, advising His Grace to rest.

John rose and laid a hand on his grandfather's shoulder. The old man opened his eyes.

"I… do-not… want… your… pity… Sayle."

John laughed. "You'll not have it, Grandfather. But you will have my admiration." He bowed, slightly. "Your Grace, I'll leave you to recoup." He had never spoken so openly to the old man in his younger days.

John's hands slid into his pockets as he walked back along the hall, his head was full of drifting thoughts. He wondered now if the perceptions he'd held as a child would have changed with an adult's view. Possibly? Probably. But it was too late to know now.

"John!"

Looking forward, he saw a slender, strikingly beautiful young woman. She had ebony hair and pale-blue eyes, like his own. A beam of joy lit her face, and then she caught up her skirt and ran at him.

Good God, was this Mary-Rose, his sister, all grown up?

She hugged him fiercely, her arms about his neck, and he held her loosely. "John! Oh John! I am so glad you're back." His baby sister was not even a child anymore. She'd been about ten years old and not much taller than his midriff when he'd left. Now she was as tall as his shoulder.

He lifted her off her feet and twirled her once, smiling, before pressing a kiss against her temple. "Mary-Rose, my *not-so-little-anymore* sister."

Her fingers gripped his coat sleeves and she leant back, grinning as she looked him over. "You are no different, other than a little older, and no one calls me Mary-Rose anymore, it is just Mary now. That is a childish name."

"And more worldly," another female voice reached along the hall.

John looked beyond Mary and saw his mother had stepped out from the drawing room. She was also still strikingly beautiful, their colouring was hers. But there were now two wings of grey in her hair at her temples. His smile softened. "Mama."

"John." She swept towards him as Mary moved aside, and she was in his arms in a moment and pressed a kiss on his cheek. "You have been away too long. I've missed you." There were tears in her eyes.

"And I have missed you too, Mama."

"Liar," she whispered before she drew away, low enough so Mary could not hear. It was not a malicious word, just the truth, and they both knew she was right.

Tapping her beneath the chin, he made a face. "I am home now, anyway."

"And I am glad. Come and meet everyone else." She slipped her arm through his as she turned back towards the drawing room. Mary occupied his other arm, and both women questioned him eagerly as they walked.

He felt very strange and disorientated to be so besieged.

When they reached the drawing room, though, all hell broke

loose. He was mobbed by his various aunts and elder female cousins.

Once they finally pulled away, hankies in their hands, John was then greeted by the men, his uncle's by marriage first, and then his male cousins. His stepfather, Edward, held back.

When the pandemonium ceased, John looked at his stepfather. He stood across the room with a youth beside him. *Robbie*, John's eldest brother, he looked so like his father it was unmistakable. Robbie was fifteen; the age when awkwardness set in. He seemed to deliberately not look at John. That must be why Edward stayed back, torn between welcoming his stepson and supporting his own son.

John smiled and approached them. He greeted his brother first. Robbie was already over shoulder height when compared with his father. "Robbie."

The boy coloured up with palpable self-consciousness. John's smile broadened. Robbie had idolised John as a child, but he'd only been eight when John had left. The gap between them was too wide for any real relationship.

"John." Robbie took the hand John had offered and shook it limply. But John used the grip to draw his brother into a brief embrace and patted his shoulder.

"You've grown," John stated the obvious as he let Robbie go. "Would you like me to take you to Tats with me when I look for a carriage and horses?"

"*Yes.*" The enthusiasm thrust into that one word was completely at odds to the demeanour of his welcome and the boy's face lit up as Mary's had done earlier. "God, John. Will you really take me?"

"If you're good." He lifted a closed fist to press to his brother's jaw, in a masculine gesture of affection, but the lad ducked away laughing.

"I'm always good. You've just not been here to know it," the cocky brat responded, and John laughed. Then his stepfather interrupted.

"Perhaps you ought to ask *me* if he's been good. I think his masters at Eton may have some tales to tell if they were asked."

John turned.

"John." His name was spoken with warmth and layered with hidden emotion.

John smiled again. Edward's hair was still a dark brown, untainted by age. He was younger than John's mother and yet there were definitely more lines about his eyes, marking John's absent years. "Father."

A twinkle in his eye, Edward said, "Son," and gripped John's shoulders firmly. The man had always treated John as a real son, no different to Mary or Robbie or the rest. "I'm glad you are back." Edward's grip fell away.

Robbie then began urging his father for agreement on their outing to Tats.

~

John was woken by a sharp rap on his bedchamber door. He sat up and threw the sheet aside from where it had lain across his hips.

"My Lord," a low voice called.

"Yes, what is it?" John was already swinging his legs from the bed and rising.

"His Grace, my Lord. The physician believes there is not much time. He sent me to fetch you."

"I'll be there in a moment," John called back, instantly shifting to search for his clothes in the dark room.

It felt bizarre to be here. It had felt odd to see his grandfather ill, and now… It was like a dream, not a nightmare though. He only felt emptiness inside, not fear.

Finding his trousers, he slid them on now his eyes had adjusted to the dark.

The family had taken supper together before they'd left, sitting at the long dining table en masse in an impromptu, informal meal. It had felt like a celebration. The only quiet person was his grandmother, who'd sat at the far end of the table as John was encouraged to take his grandfather's place.

Perhaps it was wrong to have held such a gathering while his grandfather lay on his deathbed, but John had appreciated the gesture and the jovial conversation, even though at times he kept feeling the axis within him shift as though he was poorly balanced.

He pulled his shirt over his head.

He'd said goodnight to his grandfather, as had the others before they'd left, one by one, and he'd wondered then, how long.

Hours.

He sat and pulled on his stockings.

God, this world felt strange to him – strange and a little surreal.

When John left his room, the hall was morbidly silent and the statues seemed like sombre mourners.

John gently knocked on the door of his grandfather's chambers. "It is the Marquess of Sayle."

The door opened and a footman bowed. "My Lord."

His grandmother sat in the chair John had occupied earlier, her hand resting over his grandfather's. She looked across her shoulder at John. "John." Her voice was heavy with emotion, though he knew their marriage had never been a love match. For her it had been more like endurance.

John stood behind her and laid his hands on her shoulders.

There were three footmen in the room, his grandfather's valet and the physician.

"His Grace's heartbeat is very weak," the physician said quietly. "He is unconscious."

John nodded acceptance and then his eyes fell to the bed – to the man who'd always been a significant figure in John's life. Even during the years he'd hidden from that influence abroad, he'd still been the Duke's heir. He'd never been able to escape that.

The old man was barely breathing, weak and wraith-like.

John took a deep breath, stepped about his grandmother, leant forwards and rested a hand on his grandfather's shoulder, then pressed a kiss on his cold brow.

"Goodbye. I never thought I would miss you, but I shall," John whispered, before rising.

The Duke had probably not been able to hear it, there was no sign that he did, yet John felt better for saying those words. They were true.

The old man passed away in moments, as John stood with his grandmother, watching.

The room fell completely silent when the Duke of Pembroke took his last breath.

John's grandmother rose and leant to kiss the Duke's cheek, tears slipping from her eyes.

John felt only emptiness, oddness, a lacking…

When she drew back, the physician walked past them both and lifted John's grandfather's wrist, checking for a pulse. Then he bent and listened for breath, before finally rising and drawing the sheet up and over the old man's face.

John's grandmother turned sharply and John opened his arms to her.

While he held her, the men about the room bowed and his grandfather's valet said, "Your Grace."

John felt the ground shift sideways beneath his feet. He'd known this day would come. But *God*, it was strange now it was here. *I am the Duke of Pembroke*. This house, everything in it, and several more like it, acres and acres of land and the tenants living and working upon that land were all his to manage and care for.

Chapter Two

Standing on the lea beside Westminster Abbey, Katherine watched as the procession neared.

The coffin was displayed in a black hearse pulled by six jet horses, with black dyed ostrich feathers bobbing on their heads as they trotted with high, precise, perfect steps. Their manes and tails were plaited and tied with black ribbon.

Gripping her reticule with both hands and holding it more tightly, Katherine took a deep breath. Her heart was pounding.

As the hearse drew to a halt, she lifted to her toes to see over the gathered crowd. She would swear half of London was in attendance to view the pomp and ceremony of the old Duke of Pembroke's funeral. All she could see of John, as he climbed from his open carriage behind the hearse, was his head and shoulders.

Her heart ached.

She watched him move alongside his uncles to release and lift the coffin.

A rush of pain and longing spilled from her heart into her limbs. It was so long since she'd seen him but her reaction was the same as it had been more than half a dozen years before. The rhythm of her heart rang like a hammer against her ribs.

Her brother, Phillip, gripped her elbow, to stop her being knocked off balance by the crowd. He could have gone into the

Abbey, but women were not to attend funerals and he'd promised to stay with her.

Katherine's heart continued to thump hard as John and his uncle's passed them.

The crowd swelled then as people moved in a crush to enter the Abbey and stand at the back.

Katherine waited outside with Phillip, her heart racing, so very aware of the chasm which stood between her and John. Yet she'd snatched at the chance to see him when Phillip had said he was going to come to the funeral. She'd read of the old Duke's death and John's return in the paper only days ago and she could hardly believe John had finally come back. She was still hopelessly in love with him, or rather with her dreams of him. She could hardly claim to know him now. She hadn't seen him in years.

When his family filed back out of the Abbey, John was at the front and she could see his face as many of the crowd were still inside. He looked different. He'd matured. He'd travelled the world and seen things she would never see, experienced things she could never imagine. She was an inane, provincial nobody compared to him.

She felt as though she stood in a tragedy, and she mourned. But it was not for the loss of the former Duke, it was for the loss of any hope. Her feelings would never be reciprocated. She would never have John. It had just been a childish dream she couldn't shake off. She had always known who he was – and what he was.

He walked past them. Though there were three or four people standing in front of her, she still had a clear view.

He looked unbearably, breathtakingly handsome, with his pitch-black hair and pale crystalline gaze, and there was strength in his sculpted features which drew the eye. Behind her, a dozen female whispers concurred with her view.

Katherine dropped her head and hid beneath the brim of her bonnet when John's gaze passed across the crowd. Not that he would remember her, or even care that she was here.

Phillip gripped her arm.

He thought she'd come because John had been a close friend for a number of years and she wished to support him. It was why Phillip was here.

She'd come only to put flesh back on the bones of her foolish dreams.

It had been ludicrous of Phillip to think John needed their support. John was surrounded by people of his own class.

We are fools, the pair of us, harping back to a relationship that no longer exists. This was not the boy, nor the young man, who'd treated her as an equal. This man was an entirely different beast, influential, dominant and superior. Way beyond her.

She glanced at Phillip. He was watching John's progress with a slight smile on his face as if he thought John might acknowledge them and smile too.

Katherine had no expectation.

She looked at John again. He was climbing back up into his carriage, lithe and athletic.

Oh God, I love him, I cannot help it. I just do.

She'd hoped to end her silly infatuation by coming here. She'd hoped she would feel nothing when she saw him. But she did, she still did.

When he was seated, he glanced out at the crowd once more, and she sensed a moment of vulnerability in him.

She could not justify the feeling; it was just a sixth sense she could not explain. She longed to hold him and tell him all would be well.

How absurd; he would probably push her away if she attempted it. Why would he choose plain Katherine Spencer to confide in?

Phillip's fingers squeezed her arm.

"We will go to John's for a little while, before I run you home."

She looked up. "Phillip? We cannot. We will not be welcome."

"We can and we are. We may not be aristocracy but we are gentry. Come, we'll be mingling with half of the House of Lords.

I'm not missing a chance like this. Just think about the tales you'll be able to tell at your little Sunday school."

"Phillip, we will be turned away."

"We will not. John would never throw us out. He'll remember us and we'll be welcome, you'll see." Phillip smiled.

"We'll look ridiculous if you are wrong," she said as she let him lead her on.

Half an hour later, Katherine rose onto her toes to whisper in her brother's ear, "This is folly." A second later they crossed the threshold of John's opulent townhouse.

Her gaze swept the massive hall with its black and white chequered floor and gilded marble pilasters. It was intimidating, and it all belonged to John. It only underscored how many miles he was beyond her reach.

The butler bowed slightly, plainly waiting on their names. He was the gatekeeper and this was the moment of success or failure.

The hall was crowded. Katherine could barely breathe.

"Master Phillip Spencer and Miss Katherine Spencer," Phillip stated.

The butler's eyes widened. "*Master Spencer?*" The stately butler looked hard at Phillip.

Katherine let her breath out. She'd forgotten Phillip had stayed in town at John's grandfather's house. This man remembered Phillip.

Oh, she wished she'd paid more attention to John's life when she was young. She would not have fallen in love if she'd truly realised how different they were. She'd been deceived. She had played with him in the grounds of his grandfather's estate, as though it was nothing, forgetting all the areas she was excluded from, she had never even been in the house there, only Phillip had been welcome.

"Refreshment is being served in the library, sir."

"Where is the Duke, Finch?"

"I cannot say for sure, sir. I believe His Grace is in the state

27

drawing room, yet I may be wrong."

Phillip nodded his thanks, and then his grip on Katherine's arm steered her on again.

They were absorbed in the crowd of elite society.

"I told you so," he bent sideways to whisper.

As Phillip looked for John, Katherine felt her hands trembling and her throat dry.

The drawing room was as ostentatious as the hall. The high ceiling had plaques of painted images, scenes of the Greek gods sprawled on clouds and semi-clad. She had never seen anything so beautiful and so opulent.

John should have been easy to spot, he was so tall, but she could not see him. "Where is he?" she asked Phillip, her heart racing at the prospect of actually speaking to John.

"He's not in here, but the girls are. We'll wait. He'll come back this way. You can catch up with Margaret and Eleanor."

Her heart was pounding a deafening rhythm as Phillip led her across the room towards John's family.

John's eldest sister, Mary-Rose, spotted them first. She was dressed in black, as they all were, but with her colouring the black only made her look more beautiful. All John's family were beautiful. Katherine had never compared.

She pinned a smile on her face. She felt more certain of a welcome from the girls, but she did not wish to appear gauche.

"I cannot believe it!" Mary exclaimed as they neared. "Phillip! Katherine!" Her exclamation drew the attention of the others.

Mary had been a young girl when Katherine had seen her last; she was grown up now.

"I have not seen you for an age," Mary hugged Katherine.

They had never been friends, Mary had been too young, and yet the younger girl had admired her brother's playmate and had a desire to join in. Katherine knew Mary had challenged John as a child over why Kate was allowed to play the boys' games, when Mary was not. But the young woman's exuberance was open and honest as Mary gripped Phillip's offered hand.

Of course, again, Katherine had forgotten how much better Phillip had known John. She had been welcomed into their circle for an hour here or there in the grounds of Pembroke Place. Phillip had lived with John in the way of a brother, both at school and during the holidays.

Phillip gallantly kissed the back of Mary's fingers.

"John will be beside himself to know you have come. I'm sure he never expected to see you. I shall find him." Lifting to her toes, she looked across the room. "Oh I cannot see him, I'll go and look."

"No," Katherine stated firmly, as she felt a sudden panic. "Please, do not disturb him. I'm sure he has more important people to speak with than us."

Mary's pale-blue eyes, the image of John's, met Katherine's. "Well, if he has time later I'm sure he will come over and speak."

Katherine gave Mary a grateful smile and then looked at Eleanor and Margaret, who stepped forward. "You are both married. I saw the announcements. Are you happy?" It was probably an impertinent question but she could think of nothing else to say.

They looked at one another and then their eyes looked beyond Katherine.

"They are together, across the room, there," Eleanor said, pointing, suddenly a smile in her eyes.

Katherine turned.

"Harry is the blonde-haired gentleman, my dashing heir to an Earl," Eleanor stated. "Is he not handsome? And Margaret's husband, George, is the brown-haired man. He is a little older than Harry—"

"But distinguished, don't you think?" Margaret interjected. "It is lovely to see you."

When Katherine turned to face Margaret, she was hugged again, but this time with restraint.

Then Eleanor hugged Katherine too, but that was not superficial. "It is *wonderful* to see you. What do you think of them?"

Her fingers gripped Katherine's arm as Katherine looked back at their husbands.

"They are *both* exceedingly handsome."

"We know." Eleanor laughed. "We'll introduce you later. Oh I cannot believe you are here. Now tell us what you have been up to?"

"Nothing exciting."

"She is being modest," Phillip cut in. "She will not sing her own praises. Kate has set up a Sunday School at home, for the local children who can neither read nor write."

It was hardly comparable. They would not be interested. These were glamorous women who fitted in here. Katherine did not.

"I always said she was too virtuous. You are a saint, Kate," Eleanor stated.

Katherine felt her colour rise. "Hardly." She felt both false and fragile, and tried to hide it.

"Phillip is right," Margaret smiled. "You should not feel embarrassed to admit good deeds."

Katherine felt ashamed. She was not what they were portraying her as. "Well, I have good reason to give something back, do I not?" They all, possibly bar Mary, knew of her birth, but perhaps she had raised it a little too bluntly. The conversation dried.

Phillip's hand rested on Katherine's waist and the grip gently pulled her closer for a moment, then he let go. Even he did not usually broach the subject.

"I do it because I enjoy it," she said to clear the air.

"That is true," Phillip stated. "They adore her, every last one of them."

The conversation then slipped into questions and answers as they all explored the years of each other's lives that had been missed.

~

When John entered the state drawing room he felt exhausted. The days since his grandfather's death had slipped past in a whirl of activity. First there had been the wider family to inform and the state acknowledgements to manage, then the funeral to prepare, and, on top of it, getting to grips with all his grandfather's business affairs. The mantle of a duke was lying heavy on his shoulders.

He sighed.

Richard had said several times that it would feel normal after a while. John could not imagine it. Even though the house was straining at the seams with people today, he felt as isolated as he had been in Egypt, and incapable of relaxing. That was not due to the responsibility, though. It was just who he was – a buzzard among peacocks.

John doubted any of them had really cared for the old man. He had returned to a world of farce.

A glass of red wine balanced in one hand, the stem dangling between his fingers, he joined another group of guests, fulfilling his duty. He trusted no one here.

God, this was his life now: duty and falsehood. He missed Egypt, he missed adventure and peace and simplicity. He was already bored by people's endless supplication. Everyone seemed to want something from him. They sought to attach themselves to either his wealth or his power.

His grandfather had warned of this.

John had had enough. He was seeking his family to escape it for a little while, and he was looking for Mary particularly. He knew his vibrant sister would bring him back from the cold darkness crowding in on him.

He'd passed his mother and Edward in the hall, they'd been speaking with Richard and Penny and they'd directed him in here.

His gaze swept about the room then stopped.

There was a young woman standing amidst his family, like a blonde beacon of light amongst his dark-haired black-clad cousins. She was an angel in her pale-mauve dress.

Lust gripped hard and firm in his stomach, an intense physical attraction. He'd never experienced anything so instant before. But it was a long time since he'd bedded a woman – far too long.

Her figure was a sublime balance of curves and narrow waist. Her spine had a beautiful arch as it curved into the point where her dress opened onto a full skirt.

Wheat-blonde hair escaped a dull dove-grey bonnet, caressing her neck and drawing his eyes to a place he'd like to kiss.

She was speaking with animation, her hands moving.

He moved closer, and as if she sensed his gaze, the stranger turned and looked at him. In answer, a lightening need struck his groin; a sharp sudden pain. She was an English rose among orchids, the sort of woman he had seen nothing of abroad. Her skin was pale, with roses blooming in her cheeks, and her eyes were a vivid beautiful blue, like the bluebells which bloomed in spring, in the woods at Pembroke Place.

She was what he had longed for abroad and not even known he'd been lacking.

His attention wholly captured, he felt desire slip into his blood as his groin grew heavy with hunger.

This was what came from abstinence he supposed. He'd never had a fancy for fair, fey women before. He did now.

She did not look the sort for a fling though, certainly not the she-wolf type who stalked the foreign fields. His mind began rattling through his guest list, but no name fit her, and her dull grey bonnet and shawl did not speak of affluence. Who was she?

He smiled as he grew nearer, then realised he was staring and shifted his gaze to the others in the group. It was then he noticed Phillip as they turned to towards him. "My God."

"Your Grace."

"Phillip." Lord, John hoped Phillip had not come here with a motive. John did not wish to hear oily grovelling from an old friend. His heart thumped in cold anger, not gladness. Then he looked at the blonde and his breath caught as recognition whispered in his head. *Kate.*

Her gaze soaked him up, wide and bright, and then her eyelids fell and red roses coloured her cheeks.

Katherine Spencer, Phillip's shy little sister, full grown. *Good God, she had blossomed.* John felt his heartbeat stutter into warm longing again. Wanting Phillip's little sister was not a good thing.

John gritted his teeth, forced a smile and lifted his hand to shake Phillip's. He was not looking at Katherine but he was thinking of her, trying to remember how old she would be now. She must be married. *Shame.*

Or perhaps it was better she was, maybe she had tired of her husband already and she'd be tempted by a little dalliance after all. Better to play with a woman who had no need to be grasping, there would be no ties. "I did not expect to see you here," John said to Phillip.

"Our condolences, Your Grace."

John shrugged. Phillip knew the true nature of John's volatile relationship with his grandfather; there was hardly any point in pretending to be sad. But the word "our" gave John the opportunity to turn to Katherine.

A sharp pain pierced his chest like a stitch when he saw those blue eyes up close. Her turquoise gaze was framed by pale-brown lashes. Her beauty was delicate – subtle. He was unused to that, compared to his family.

He had an urge to touch her face. He did not, but he did take her hand and lift it to his lips as she dropped a low curtsy.

Her kid-leather gloves were warm from the heat of her skin beneath.

He brushed a finger across her wrist accidentally and felt her shiver. She smelt of rosewater.

She was blushing deeply when she straightened.

When had he last known a woman who could blush?

"Your Grace."

"Katherine." He'd more often called her Kate when they'd been young but Katherine seemed to suit her so much more now. "You look well." Her husband, whoever he was, was a lucky man. John doubted she was the sort to stray. *A pity.*

With a gentle tug, she pulled her fingers free of his.

"H… how are you?" she stuttered, her gaze descending to his cravat pin.

"Well enough." He could not take his eyes off her and it clearly made her feel uncomfortable. "A little dumbfounded by the speed of things, I suppose. I only returned to England a fortnight ago, my grandfather died that night."

Her gaze lifted momentarily and compassion burned there before it fell away again. "I'm sorry, Your Grace."

"Don't be, he was old, he had to die eventually and I doubt he shall be much missed."

"Hear, hear," Eleanor stated. "He was a bully, Mama always says so, and John shall make a far better duke."

"Tell me what you have been up to then," John asked, only wishing to know if she was wed, but he threw a look at Phillip, extending the question to hide his interest.

"Studying," Phillip answered. "I'm a qualified barrister now."

John's attention turned. He was so well trained to play ducal host it was instinctual. "Congratulations." He met Phillip's gaze. This must be Phillip's reason for attending, to use their old friendship to increase his clientele. Everyone here had a reason. *God, I have become a cynic.*

"My firm is Boscombe and Parkin."

And you hope I'll use them so you'll progress… Aloud John said, "Parkin? I have heard of them."

John had been close to Phillip long ago. Their friendship had made life bearable in John's later childhood and youth, Phillip's company had been the one concession allowed when John had visited his grandfather. Beyond their friendship, life had been all about learning discipline and developing the mind. "Do you live in town?"

Phillip nodded. "Perhaps we could meet? I'll give Finch my

address."

John was not inclined to socialise with men who thought to gain something by it. He was tired to the bones of this ingratiating behaviour already and he had a lifetime of it to live. "Perhaps..." John echoed with no commitment.

"I'd like to hear your travelling tales," Phillip continued, chatting as though their friendship had not ended seven years before.

"I have thousands but I would not wish to bore you." John's gaze strayed to Kate again. "And you Katherine?"

She reddened and opened her mouth as if to reply but said nothing.

John felt like laughing, she looked so unsettled by him. Yet her discomfort gave him hope that his attraction might be reciprocated?

"She's been busy. Katherine has started a Sunday School in Ashford," Mary answered for her.

Katherine's blush deepened.

He was certain it was his presence which was making her colour up so beautifully. "That is noble of you, Katherine. Is there a husband who supports this venture?"

Her cheeks flushed with even brighter colour. Then she said in a low voice, "I am not wed." Her pitch said the idea was absurd.

John felt a flare light inside him. Hope. But that was ridiculous, what it meant was she was innocent and untouchable. *Hands off you villain*. He felt like laughing again, at his own arrogant desire.

Playing the gallant, he took her hand once more and pressed another kiss upon it. "More fool the men who have passed you by."

"She has had numerous offers. She turns them all away," Phillip interjected, apparently oblivious to John's flirtation.

John did not think Katherine was so blind. Her eyes held his as he let her hand fall, full of questions.

The girl was a mile beneath his rank. She would know there was nothing serious in it, which meant she was wondering why. "There is nothing wrong with being choosy, Katherine. I commend you." He smiled, telling her without words she need not fear him.

She smiled suddenly, in reply, and it glimmered in her azure-blue eyes.

"Are you staying in town?" Mary asked.

Katherine's gaze swung to his sister and John realised he had forgotten the others were even there for a moment.

"No. Phillip brought me into town. And we should be going. Phillip?" She glanced at her brother, who nodded agreement.

"But you have not met Harry and George," Eleanor cried. "You must meet them..." In barely a moment all the women were gone, and John was left alone with Phillip.

John felt as though the world had grown colder, but instinctively he filled the quietness with words, setting his glass down on a side table. "How come she is not wed?"

He and Phillip both looked at Katherine.

John could see her awkwardness again.

She was out of place amongst his guests and she felt it. But her self-awareness was refreshing.

It seemed his taste had not only turned to blonde, but timid too. He was interested despite himself, even though he really should not be, yet there was nothing wrong with indulging curiosity.

"The right offer has never come along, or rather the right man, I think. My mother's patience is wearing thin, and my father wishes her settled, after all there is Jennifer waiting in the wings. I believe Kate does not know what to do with herself. She does not wish to simply take anyone."

John looked at Phillip. Jennifer was Phillip's youngest sister. She was six years younger than Katherine. But Katherine was adopted. She was no blood relation to Phillip.

"Katherine is not happy then?" As children, Katherine had invariably seemed insecure, while Jennifer was simply spoilt.

Phillip glanced at John. "The schooling brings her happiness, but I do not think she is content. You knew Kate as well as I did. She has not changed."

36

John's gaze returned to her and he sensed untapped depths trapped within that timid shell. Depths it would be a pleasure exploring.

"There is something I'd hoped to ask you… if we…" Phillip's pitch had dropped and the tone implied begging.

John felt his body stiffen in denial as he looked across. "Go on, ask me now?" *Devil take it*, he would have preferred to be proven wrong about Phillip's intentions. Was there no one in London who did not want something from him?

Phillip turned fully and his gaze ran over John's expression, showing uncertainty. "This is a bit distasteful to discuss at a funeral…"

John felt himself scowl. "*Nevertheless…*" His voice was hard and deep. *Just have out with it and let's be done.*

"Boscombe did some business for the old Duke a while ago and, well, it was unsuccessful, but the thing is Boscombe was never paid."

"So you have come here to chase me for it?" John's voice turned gruff.

"No, *no*. I decided to come and told Boscombe I would need the time. He asked if I would mention it…"

John swallowed, fighting impatience. What he wished to do was toss his former friend out for this audacity. "Why not simply contact Harvey?" Harvey was the Duke of Pembroke's man of business, everything was done through him.

"The business did not come from Harvey. It came from Mr Wareham, from Pembroke Place."

"Wareham?" John's surprise sounded in his voice. "Why would Wareham…?" Wareham was the Estate manager at Pembroke Place. "But he should refer everything through Harvey…" And Harvey had managed John's grandfather's affairs for decades?

"I thought it strange too. I haven't a clue. Even more odd is that the job was reclaiming a loan. Boscombe couldn't get it back. That's the only reason I agreed to ask you. Anyway, I'm sure you don't really wish to talk of this today. I'll send the details to Harvey. He can look at it and advise you."

"Yes," John searched Phillip's gaze for ill-intent but could see nothing false.

"I've put you out of sorts by asking." He had. "I really did not come to ask you that, John, I only came to see you…"

John shrugged, his judgement was still undecided, but the fact that Phillip had read that expression only aggravated further.

Too many people here knew John too well. He really ought to learn his grandfather's lessons and cease showing any emotion at all. "Let Harvey have the details and your address."

"Yes," Phillip held John's gaze as though he might say more, like making another foolish suggestion they meet, but he did not. "I ought to take Kate home."

John merely nodded and then Phillip walked away.

John's eyes returned to Katherine.

She must have felt his gaze as she'd done earlier, because she looked back.

He smiled.

She coloured up, smiling uncertainly, and then looked away.

~

Katherine clung to the edge of Phillip's curricle with one hand, as her other held the warm rug over her lap while he drove like a madman to get her home before dark.

The first thing he'd said to her after leaving John's was, "*I told you we'd be welcome.*" The second was, "*And he was pleased to see you*". She'd conceded the first, but she'd made no comment on the second point.

Her heart still hammered.

John had kissed her hand, twice, and she could still feel those kisses burning through her glove. But he had changed. She was certain he'd felt the chasm between them as much as she had, there was no easy camaraderie now. There had been an edge of steel instead, one that warned, *do not come too close.*

Her heart ached as she remembered his gaze boring into her.

Seven years had not changed her. She was still fool enough to crave a man who could never be hers. She was frail, as her adoptive mother said. It was in Katherine's blood, inherited from her natural mother. Katherine was flawed, *wicked* and full of sin. It was true. She had an unnatural need for John.

When they arrived home, Phillip walked about the carriage to help Katherine down with a broad smile.

She accepted his hand and made a decision never to see John again. If she never saw him she could forget this human desire.

Phillip gripped her arm and guided her towards the house.

"If you want to come up to Town, to pay a visit on Eleanor or Margaret, write."

She shook her head. "I am sure the last thing they would want is for me to actually call. I know they made the offer and their husbands were charming, but it was just politeness, Phillip."

"You are too self-deprecating, Kate. They meant it."

She looked up at him, "They were merely being charitable, Phillip. I am happy as I am."

Phillip's gaze held hers. "Are you?"

"*Yes.*" She pulled her arm free from his grip as they reached the door.

"You do not convince me of it, Kate, you hardly ever smile, and I cannot remember the last time I heard you laugh."

He was speaking out of concern, she knew that, but she had no intention of talking to him about how things stood for her, it would not be fair, and she would never speak to anyone of her redundant feelings for John.

The door opened, "Castle," Phillip acknowledged the middle-aged butler.

Katherine untied the ribbons of her bonnet as Phillip encouraged her to enter first.

"Phillip! You are back!" Their mother's voice came from the drawing room, and then she was in the hall, holding her hands out to Phillip. "You must stay for tea."

"I need to get back to town, Mama."

Katherine clung on to her bonnet and gloves.

"But, Phillip, I barely see you."

He gave their mother an understanding smile, and took her hands. "I'll come on Sunday next, Mama"

All eyes for Phillip, their mother nodded. "I shall look forward to seeing you then."

"We spoke to John," Katherine stated, feeling uncomfortable.

Ignoring Katherine, their mother said to Phillip, "Is he in good health?"

"Well enough. Eleanor and Margaret were pleased to see Kate. They have asked her to call." Phillip was trying to push their mother's attention to Katherine; it was pointless.

"Well, one can understand why they would be polite."

Katherine threw Phillip a look to say, see, she agrees. He smiled. Katherine poked out her tongue, without her mother seeing, and then turned to take her bonnet and gloves upstairs.

"I will see you next Sunday, Mama," Phillip began to take his leave.

"Kate. Phillip."

Her father.

Her hand on the newel post, Katherine looked back and smiled.

He was standing in the doorway of his study, smiling too, his affection genuine.

"And how does John fare?" he asked of Katherine.

"Like he was born to it," Katherine quipped, smiling more openly. Her father's eyes glowed, catching a hold of her humour.

"He's as rich as Croesus." Phillip added, "I hardly think we need worry about John."

Their father nodded, but his posture had stiffened. There was always tension between herself and her mother, and the same between Phillip and their father. They had never been a happy family.

"Phillip!" Jennifer erupted from the drawing room. "You must tell me all about it, you cannot go yet…"

Phillip looked back. "Kate will tell you." That was the height of insult to Jenny, to be reliant on Katherine for anything. She was spoilt and selfish. But Katherine did not blame her sister. Jenny had been brought up by their mother to exclude Katherine.

Jennifer's nose tipped up. "I can live without knowing, if you are going to be so mean. Mama, may we go into Maidstone tomorrow…?"

Phillip sighed.

Katherine turned and began climbing the stairs, but Phillip caught her hand and held her back. "Say goodbye before you go up."

He'd always been protective. It was why she'd had the chance to grow so close to John, because Phillip had taken pity on her in the holidays when he was home, and given her opportunity to escape from their mother and Jenny.

She turned back and hugged him, standing on the first step so that she was taller and her arms more easily reached about his neck.

He hugged her too, as their mother and Jenny looked on with jealousy in their eyes.

He would say goodbye to them also. It was just that they wanted Katherine to have no love. Yet Phillip loved her, and her father did too.

She wondered sometimes if jealousy caused her mother's hatred, because her father was kinder to Katherine than his wife. But Katherine had never really understood. Why had her mother adopted her, if she didn't want her?

"If I hear that Eleanor or Margaret have written and you have refused an invitation, be prepared for a scold," Phillip whispered.

"Scold all you like," Katherine whispered back, "I'll still say, no."

He laughed as he let her go. "I'll see you soon."

As she climbed the stairs, he said his other goodbyes, and then,

41

when she reached the landing, she heard the door close. He was gone.

"Katherine, fetch my shawl would you, and my embroidery, they are on the chair in my chamber, oh and fetch Jennifer's shawl also?" It immediately began – the behaviour which set Katherine back in her place. She was little higher than a servant when Phillip was not at home and her father did nothing to prevent it. He hid away and avoided the arguments and bitterness. It was only different when Phillip called because their mother doted on Phillip and did not wish to upset him.

"Yes, Mother," Katherine called back downstairs.

"And once you have done that Kate, you may help with the tea. You know I prefer it when you make it."

"Yes, Mother," she called again.

"And do not get any silly notions in your head about visiting the Pembrokes. You would only shame yourself in that company."

"Yes, Mother." *I know my place, even if Phillip does not.*

Chapter Three

John leant back in his seat and flicked the reins, stirring his matching pair of chestnut-coloured horses into a gallop and letting the animals run.

The air rushed past him. It was hot. One of England's rare truly summer days. It felt good, and he liked the sound of thundering hoof beats, tack and creaking springs, and the jolting of the carriage as it raced along the track.

Robbie had spent the last two months bragging about the day they'd bought this matching pair and curricle.

Thinking of Robbie made John remember the money he'd settled on his brothers. He'd told Edward it was to ensure his brothers would live in a fashion which would not embarrass a duke. The truth was it eased John's conscience, because he'd had little to do with any of them since the day he'd taken Robbie to Tattersalls.

He did not feel a part of his family anymore. There was too much of a gap in years, and status. So he'd traded genuine affection for cold hard coin. He'd agreed to enhance his sisters' dowries too.

Mary had hugged him when he'd told her and John had warned her of fortune hunters.

As he thought of marriage, his mind turned to Eleanor and Nettleton. They'd made an announcement before he'd left town. Their first child was due next year. A new generation. A generation John would play patriarch to.

It only added to his sense of isolation.

Life was busy setting him on a pedestal so others might not reach him. His grandfather had warned him it would be so, now he understood.

He sighed. He'd been too busy for family or friendships the last few months anyway. He'd spent them sorting out the old man's estate and making his name in the House of Lords, fulfilling his duty as he'd been bred to do.

Yet, since leaving London and coming out to Pembroke Place, he'd been avoiding duty.

John saw a woman walking along the road in the distance. He did not slow his horses.

He'd come here to meet the estate manager, Mr Wareham, who not only managed Pembroke Place but also oversaw the stewards at all John's properties. None of which explained why Wareham had approached an external lawyer, as Phillip had advised at the funeral.

The carriage drew nearer the lone woman.

Wareham was supposed to refer any legal issue to Harvey, who'd sworn he knew nothing of this. John believed him.

If there was one thing the old Duke had done well, it was manage his estate, and he'd have said something to Harvey if he'd known of this loan. So Harvey should know of it, if it was legitimate. Which meant – as Harvey did not – it was not.

John had reiterated to Wareham during their first meeting, on his arrival, that all business should be done through Harvey, without giving any indication he knew of the deal with Boscombe. There had not even been a flicker in Wareham's eyelids, but his belligerence had put John out of sorts.

Since then, he'd evaded duty. He ought to be visiting tenants not racing about the country lanes.

John sighed.

He'd focus again tomorrow. Today he'd continue letting the weight slip from his shoulders.

The woman was yet nearer. He eased up a little, pulling on the reins.

Half his trouble was the bad memories haunting him here. They hung around him like shadows in the Palladian mansion. He'd already started changing things in town now his grandmother had retired to one of the smaller estates, redecorating the townhouse to dispense with the memories of his childhood. He was going to do the same here, to chase off the bloody desperate child who still lived in his head. He hated the house. He'd felt it the minute he'd returned and known in the same moment it was irrational. But no matter how many years he'd come here with his mother, the memories which pervaded were the dreadful years of longing he'd lived here without her.

The emotion made him feel weak, and then angry at himself for weakness.

He should just be getting on with his duty and visiting tenants and sorting out Wareham. What he was doing instead was running from the demons in his head.

The woman was now a couple of hundred yards away.

The other half of his trouble was that John was really beginning to understand his grandfather. The burdens of duty and expectation were making John more and more withdrawn. He hated the parasitical nature of people. No matter how much he did not wish to be like the old man, John could see no other way to cope with the barrage of falsehood and make a path through it. The only way was to shut it out.

The darkness which had always haunted him abroad had set its hood over him again.

He tightened his grip on the reins as he drew near the woman, slowing the horses to a trot, then realised he'd over-pushed them. The animals' coats were slick with sweat. It was too hot for them really.

He was used to Egypt's desert heat. His animals were not.

He decided to go back at the same moment he realised who the woman was. *Katherine*. He'd not seen her since the funeral, at least not in person; he'd seen her in his dreams. Vivid dreams, which would certainly make her blush if she knew of them.

Perhaps his guilt over those dreams was why he'd given Phillip the benefit of doubt and used him to develop the contracts for a business deal between John and his Uncle Robert; or rather the guilt John *should* feel. In fact, he felt only longing.

That longing returned now, in full measure.

He'd asked after her when he'd seen Phillip. Phillip only smiled and said she was the same as ever.

John had also heard Eleanor say Katherine had declined an invitation to stay. He hadn't known if he was relieved or angry at the time. It was dangerous this obsession he was developing for her. But obsession it was beginning to be, the number of times he thought of her. Her image had become a sanctuary from the burden of duty. There was no harm in imagining. But here was the real Kate.

"Katherine!"

The girl jumped half out of her skin and spun about. She must have been completely lost in a world of thought.

God. He'd been craving air and sky, and nature, in his desire for escape the last couple of days, and here was his quintessential English rose, a woman with modesty who could still blush, *for heaven's sake.*

The she-wolves had begun stalking him again in town, and he'd even been moderately tempted, knowing he needed some form of release from his burdens. But his dream was for Katherine, simplicity and innocence, and *they* were not that, *they* would not assuage his hunger. Katherine would.

His gaze clung to her, sweeping over her figure. She wore a thin muslin dress beneath a faded light-blue spencer. Her arms were slender. His gaze trailed upwards from her narrow waist to see her bosom lift and fall as though she was short of breath.

Her face was in the shadow of a broad-rimmed poke straw-bonnet, while her hands were covered by the same kid leather gloves she'd worn in London, which must feel excruciatingly hot in this heat.

He halted the animals, set the brake, looped the ribbons across the rail and jumped down.

He had come out in unseemly dress; he'd not intended speaking to anyone. His black waistcoat hung open and his shirtsleeves were rolled up. He probably looked like a labourer, but he had wished to be the man from Egypt again today and not a duke.

"Katherine?" he said again, approaching her.

She hadn't said a thing, or even moved since she'd turned, but as he neared, she took a step back.

She looked as though any minute she might turn and run.

He reached out and caught her forearm to stop her.

"What on earth were you wool-gathering over?"

Those wide blue eyes, which did not show their true colour when hidden in the shadow of her bonnet, questioned his existence.

His hand slid down her slender arm and felt her muscle judder from the intimacy. Then he gripped her fingers and lifted them to his lips.

He would rather have kissed her skin than her worn leather glove.

He let her hand fall.

"You should have heard the horses yards back."

She was blushing again, and her eyes glittered with a starry look, as though she was shocked, or…

The air left his lungs.

Or…

He knew that look of want. He'd seen it in a hundred women's eyes.

Without thought, one hand released the bow securing the

ribbons of her bonnet, while the other cupped her nape. Then as her bonnet tumbled down her back and fell into the dust, he kissed her mouth.

He burned for her, and the uncertain pressure of her fingers gripping his shoulders was sublime as she opened her mouth under the pressure of his lips. His tongue invaded, taking as she gave, claiming what he suddenly desperately wanted to be his.

She arched against him and his other arm came about her waist to pull her body nearer.

A tender, desperate and shocked sound came from her mouth and then she was pulling away, and pushing him back. An instant later she gave him a stinging slap across the cheek.

Damn!

His hand covered his cheek, but instead of feeling regret or guilt it was laughter which rose inside him and a feeling of relief, as though a cork had just blown from an effervescent bottle and let emotion spew out.

She was clearly not amused by his laughter and her cheeks flamed red, while her eyes burned a bright turquoise. It was a look of insulted pride.

Yet, a moment ago, her eyes had said quite clearly "kiss me", and far more, and she'd been pliant and willing when he'd accepted that unspoken offer.

His heart thumped steadily. He had been too long without a woman.

He dragged in a deep breath and smiled, genuinely. He could not remember the last time he had smiled from emotion and not merely made the correct face.

The horses whickered behind him.

Both his hands gripped her waist.

She stepped back, out of his reach, almost treading on her bonnet.

He bent and picked it up.

Katherine's heart raced. What had she done? What had she let *him* do? Why had he done it?

She had not even known John was there. She had not even known he was in the county. His only greeting had been her name.

She took another step back, longing to distance herself from the tug she felt towards him as he stood straight again, gripping her bonnet in his hand.

Why had he kissed her? She was mute with anger and embarrassment. She felt appalled. Why would he do that? Why had she let him?

"John!" she said as his hand reached out towards her again, while his other gripped her bonnet. She stepped back once more, avoiding him, but at the same time lifted her hand to claim her bonnet.

He pulled it out of reach.

"What did you think you were you doing?" she thrust accusingly at him.

"Saying hello." He laughed again, as though kissing her on a public highway was a joke.

There was warmth in his eyes, though, which had not been there on the day of the funeral, and her heart ached to see it, no matter that she was angry. She saw a glimpse of the old John there.

"Let me have my bonnet!"

He lifted his arm so she would never be able to reach it, and merely smiled.

"John! Do not be a brute!" She didn't understand what was going on, and she lifted her hand to slap him again, but his free hand caught her wrist. "The weather has touched you in the head, John!"

"Not the weather, Katherine." He grinned. But then his smile slipped away and an austere look came over him.

Her heartbeat rang like a hammer on an anvil. Did he think it was acceptable to kiss a woman like that?

A dark light suddenly glowed at the heart of his pale eyes.

Her hand shook as she reached out for her bonnet again. She felt sick.

When he lifted it away once more, she said, "Let me have it, John," feeling suddenly desperate and a little afraid of him.

"So you can cover up that pretty face. These things are a crime. Someone ought to make a law against poke bonnets. Perhaps I shall propose it in the house – every woman's bonnet must let a man see her face."

He was being ridiculous. "John!"

"*Katherine*," he mocked.

She could not believe he was doing this. Nor that he had kissed her so crudely.

She had done nothing but worship him for nearly a decade and he was busy ridiculing her. She hated him suddenly. "Give me back my bonnet, John, and let me go, and you are not to come near me again. I am not something for you to play with, Your Grace." *Fool. You fool, Katherine.*

His manor changed almost instantly and his hand let her arm go, as his other fell to offer her bonnet.

"It was not an insult, Katherine," he said as she gripped it.

"Then you kiss every woman you see walking alone on a road, I suppose?" Of course he would not. Only the ones who were foolish enough to love him, and only the ones who had no family to protect them.

His fingers tightened on her bonnet again, crushing it, before she could free it from his hand.

"Not every woman, Katherine, just the ones who look at me with azure-blue eyes that say they long for it – just you, Kate."

She felt herself turn pink but refused to play tug of war for her bonnet and let it go again.

"Give it to me," she stated gruffly.

"No, not until you admit you wished it so."

"No!"

"I'll not beg your forgiveness," he answered in a hard pitch.

"You wished for it."

"And you've grown arrogant, John Harding."

"Perhaps so," he said in a low harsh voice. "But you wished for it. You did. I know."

"You cannot know." There was anguish in her voice and, in answer, his eyes softened again and he held forth her bonnet once more.

"Katherine, you held me and kissed me back, you cannot deny it." The words were gentle but they cut into her heart. She still craved him. It was almost desperation which she felt.

Tears rushed into her eyes. She *had* longed for it. But not like this.

His pitch softened further. "Your eyes expressed desire before I even kissed you."

She lifted her hand to slap him again, but he caught it once more and raised his eyebrows.

She felt ashamed. They both knew what he'd said was true. She had turned and faced him, and her heart had leapt into her throat. His attraction was fierce today. He was half undressed, unshaven and he wore no hat, and he was simply, essentially, masculine – tall, strong, agile and assertive.

Was this what her natural mother had felt for her father, this desperation?

Katherine had wanted to be kissed, and if that desire was to be fulfilled, how else might it be done if not like this? He would hardly choose to marry her. There was a world between them, not simply miles. If she wanted kisses from him, they would have to be kisses like this.

She did not try to pull either her arm free, or her bonnet from his hand, she felt calm suddenly. "Give me back my bonnet, Your Grace. *Please?*"

"Say that you wished for it?" There was a cold hard look back in his eyes.

"No."

"Say it."

When she did not, his grip firmed on her arm, though it was not painful. "Say it!"

His voice rang with determination.

"*No, John.*"

His hand suddenly left her arm and then it was back at her nape bracing her neck and holding her firm as he pulled her mouth to his.

His kiss was a hard pressure against her lips. She had not imagined kissing to be like this. Her heart raced, and her fingers clawed into the muscle of his arms to steady herself. She felt faint and hot and liquid-boned.

It was brief, barely an instant long, but when he pulled away his pale eyes shone like glass with triumph. "You wished for it," he whispered over her lips. "Say it."

"Yes," she answered, knowing she turned crimson as she did so. She felt the provincial idiot she was; gauche, weak and base-born.

He said nothing, his eyes boring deep into her soul.

What must he think of her?

"Here," he said, letting go of her nape and her bonnet at the same moment. "I'll give you a lift home."

She felt disorientated and dizzy. She shook her bonnet, trying to get it to recover its shape, while she also tried to recall who and where she was.

Her hands trembled as she tied the ribbons and her legs felt weak, too weak to walk home.

She hadn't looked at him since he'd let her take her bonnet. She looked at him now and saw questions in his eyes as he lifted his hand to take hers.

She accepted it, to climb up into his curricle, and said nothing. He climbed up beside her once she had slid across the seat.

Her throat was dry.

He released the brake and flicked the reins, setting his fashionable, expensive horses into a trot.

She hated herself.

His gaze turned to her.

She looked at him.

"I'm sorry, Katherine, I should not have kissed you, no matter that you wished for it."

She felt like crying. Had he not even really wished to do it? Had he only done it because he'd realised he could?

A dark humour suddenly shone in his eyes once more. "But, then again, maybe I am not really sorry." He looked back at the road.

"You have changed," she answered, staring at him, not understanding him at all, and yet loving him.

His eyes turned back to her, a look of granite in them. "*Life* has changed me, Katherine. But you are not changed. Perhaps you can make me remember who I was?"

What did she say to that? What did she say to this stranger?

He looked back at the road ahead and flicked the reins again.

She gripped the side of his curricle and hung on.

Chapter Four

John steered his chestnut thoroughbreds through the gates of the courtyard leading into the stables.

His blood was still boiling with a mix of desire and anger.

He had made Katherine admit she had wanted to kiss him but, nevertheless, she'd accused him of arrogance and being changed.

She was right, of course.

He had not spoken to her for the rest of the drive as bitter thoughts had bounced about his head. It had been wrong to kiss her. But he did not regret it. She made him remember the past, she made him remember what it was like to be warm-blooded and feel. He wanted to feel with her.

His heart thumped as he set the brake. God, he felt better even for having had that one kiss. It had been the way she'd pressed so innocently against him, with tenderness, not with a grabbing, greedy lust. She could wash his soul clean; that was how he felt.

A weight had lifted from his shoulders when he dropped to the ground.

His grooms rushed forwards to free the horses and put away the carriage.

John strode towards the servants' entrance to the house. He had something he ought to do. He had put it off long enough.

The flagstone-floored hall was busy with numerous maids and

footmen scurrying through it. The house bells lined one wall of the passage, the side the women occupied, while the men walked along the opposite side.

They carried a variety of items: linen, copper pans, silver, candles, coal scuttles…

One of the young maids jumped when she saw him and dropped an armful of linen. When she bent to pick it up, others began noticing his presence. It swept along the hall like a wave as they dropped into curtsies or bowed. He was invading their territory and making them feel uncomfortable – the arrogant duke.

Well he had not been arrogant abroad, he had laboured with his men in Egypt and he would go wherever he wished in his own home.

He carried on.

"Your Grace?" Finch appeared from a doorway a little ahead of John and bowed.

"Is Wareham somewhere, Finch?" John heard the maids and footmen shifting back into movement behind him.

"He is in his rooms I believe, Your Grace."

"Then send for him. Have him come to his office. I shall wait there."

"Your Grace," Finch bowed again then disappeared.

The estate manager's office was at the end of the hall, away from the main thoroughfare.

The door was shut and when John tried the handle, he discovered it locked.

"Does someone have the key?" he asked, looking back along the busy hall.

One of the footmen stopped and bowed. "Mr Wareham keeps it on his person, Your Grace, but there's a copy of every key in Mrs East's office. Shall I fetch it?"

"Please, do."

The young footman bowed again and then rushed off to the housekeeper's room. A moment later he was running back with the key.

John took it and thanked him, remembering that his grandfather had never said thank you to a soul. John felt the tug of war inside him pull. This was an instant of the old John, his mother's child, but these instants were getting rarer. He had changed, and he was changing even more.

When John unlocked the door, he felt a cold shiver grip him.

This was another room brimful of ill memories. The whitewashed walls and flagstone floor made it feel cold despite the sun pouring through the windows on two sides, which looked out across the park.

Shelves full of ledgers lined the other walls, while the middle of the room was dominated by Wareham's large oak desk.

John had spent numerous hours sitting at it as a child, learning the art of bookkeeping.

He crossed to the shelves and scanned the dates on the spines of the ledgers. Wareham began a new one each year and recorded every expenditure and income for the house and the tenancies in these books.

Finding the current year's, John slid it off the shelf and carried it to the desk.

He sat and opened the broad record book.

Columns of transactions ran down each page, all totalled at the bottom.

His memories turned to his childhood, when he'd sat here beside Wareham scanning these books. The old Duke had schooled John to manage the estates from the age of thirteen. John had spent hours studying such things, to learn how to achieve profit, when to take risks and when to be prudent. Wareham had been the man who'd explained it all.

If Wareham is fleecing me, he's fleeced the old man. What did that mean?

The old Duke had trusted Wareham implicitly; he was one of few the old man had. Wareham had been here years; like many of his grandfather's staff. People who'd earned his trust had been kept. If Phillip had not raised this situation, John would never have considered doubting Wareham.

John's index finger followed lines of figures on the first page. There was nothing abnormal listed, no unusual purchases or amounts.

Remembering the date of the loan Phillip had queried, John rose to find last year's ledger.

He pulled it from the shelf and then, at the desk, began flicking through the pages, searching for the date.

There were no unexpected sums. Nothing was recorded which would suggest the reason for giving out a loan.

"Your Grace?"

John looked up.

Wareham was standing in the doorway, his fingers on the handle of the open door.

John smiled the smile he'd taught himself in London in the last few weeks, the one which screened out all other expression, his grandfather's smile, and straightened but did not stand.

There was an insolent, angry glint in Wareham's light blue-grey eyes. He did not defer. He neither bowed nor even nodded his head. It had been the same on John's arrival.

The old man's monster roared to life as John waited, imparting the cold condemning glare he had also learned from his grandfather. Silence stretched across the room while Wareham stared back.

"Your Grace." Wareham finally allowed, nodding slightly and showing more defiance than deference.

The bastard. What is this?

John wished to make him do it over, but that would be churlish. It was far better to let it pass. Wareham must surely realise his days were numbered if he continued this. He must know John would not be lenient or soft. He ought to know the old man had drilled this detachment into John. Sentimentality had been thrashed out of him as a child, and Wareham had watched.

"Is there something I may help you with?" Wareham closed the door, his whole demeanour challenging John's presence in the room.

John felt anger burn deep. He was entirely his grandfather's monster now.

"Take a seat." John deliberately indicated the chair on the far side, refusing to vacate Wareham's. John owned this house, this office and the money passing through these ledgers – let Wareham remember that.

When Wareham sat, John held every muscle in his face steady. Thank God he'd learned how easily read he'd been in town and mastered that. Now he expressed only a mask of indifference.

"I would have thought, if Your Grace wished to view the ledgers, you would have asked me to bring them to you?" Wareham's tone was tipped with steel.

You? It was an unforgivable insult not to use John's title. *You!*

"Who owns the estates you manage, Wareham?" John felt as though a sandstorm had swept over him, his vision blurred and his skin prickled with anger.

"You do, Your Grace."

Even when Wareham did use John's title, he made it offensive.

"And please tell me then, Wareham, therefore, who owns this office and these ledgers?"

The man's eyes momentarily showed a questioning thought, but then he stated, "Your Grace," the challenge slipping from his voice.

"And pray, who employs you?"

"Your Grace." There was darkness at the heart of Wareham's eyes. A darkness which said this would not be the last of this conversation.

John smiled his grandfather's vicious smile. "We have that straight then. Let us move on."

John did not mention the loan after that minor mutiny. He did not wish to give Wareham any chance to cover his tracks.

"I have decided to review every aspect of my estate. I shall take these accounts now to help me do so and I wish to see all the supporting receipts and invoices. You may begin a new ledger."

Wareham finally showed an element of emotion as his eyebrows lifted.

He'd clearly not anticipated John's direct interference, and that meant, hopefully, the reason for the loan was still hidden somewhere in these books.

The older man's icy gaze met John's across the desk.

When John had sat here with him as a boy, the man had been brash, intolerant and rude. John had thought it a lack of patience for a youth. Now he presumed it was more. Wareham had never acted this way with his grandfather.

John did not move…

"*Now*, Your Grace?" The man finally understood.

"I am here, am I not Wareham, so now would be a good time."

"But…"

"I shall begin reading these ledgers, while you find everything out." Of course Wareham would wish for more time if he wanted to hide evidence.

He stood.

John looked down at the ledgers.

A few minutes later, Wareham set two thick leather pouches tied with string and stuffed with papers on the desk. "Your Grace."

"Everything is here?" John asked, rising, ignoring the subtle insult in Wareham's voice. "All I need to review these two years?"

"Yes, Your Grace."

"Any omissions I may assume errors on your part then?"

Wareham's jaw set and a muscle flickered in his cheek. "Your Grace."

"Call a footman to carry them up." John could have shouted himself, but he did not, to remind Wareham of his place.

Another ten minutes and the ledgers and packets of receipts and papers were all secured in John's personal safe, in his rooms.

Chapter Five

Katherine picked up the Bibles the children had been working with and set them aside. Then she turned towards the small altar in the chancel chapel where she'd led the Sunday school.

She was looking for something to do to pass the time while the congregation dispersed and she waited for Reverend Barker to drive her home. Her gaze caught on the open side door. John stood there watching her, his athletic silhouette framed in the arch of sunlight.

She had not forgiven him for kissing her, nor for forcing her to admit she had wished him to do it. Neither was a gentlemanly act. He had changed.

Ignoring him, she turned to the storage cupboard. She felt his presence so keenly she could sense him smiling behind her. She'd heard him singing amidst the congregation as she'd worked with the children. He had a beautiful voice. It rose above that of everyone else with perfect clarity.

How could a man who was now so steely hard and disgracefully arrogant still sing like an angel?

She pressed a palm against the slates to make them straight when they were already perfectly aligned.

"Are you hiding, Katherine?"

Her heart thumped. "Working, John."

His boot heels rang on the glazed medieval tiles and she spun about when she heard him get too close.

He was two feet away, his pale eyes gleaming yet unfathomable. "I was waiting to speak with you, your parents have left. I thought… You are not hiding from me, are you?"

"No," she breathed, knowing she coloured.

His gaze swept across her face clearly assessing her as she had not been able to assess him because his features were set like marble.

"There is no need for you to fear me, Katherine."

She lifted her chin. "I am not afraid of you, John." *I am afraid of myself.*

"I would never hurt you."

Her chin lifted another notch. She hurt for him anyway. She had ached for him for seven years. Hiding was the only way to escape more pain.

He did not move, his pale gaze holding hers as though he could hear the words she did not speak.

"I have thought about you since the funeral." His voice whispered, bouncing off the cold bare stone. "I know I said sorry to you yesterday, Katherine, but I really do not think I am. I wanted to kiss you, too. Why should either of us feel regret?"

She dragged a deep breath into her lungs. "John, do not do this." She stepped back and collided with the shelves.

He caught her arm to stop her fall, but did not let go.

"Do what? Admit I am attracted to you. I am, as you are to me." His head was bowing before he'd even finished speaking.

Their lips touched.

It was different from yesterday, it was gentle, hesitant and reassuring, and without conscious thought her hands slid over his shoulders, one settling behind his neck, half holding his mouth to hers.

When his lips opened and his tongue slid across the seam of hers, she could not help but part hers and kiss him back as he was kissing her.

Their tongues weaved an intricate dance and she felt her body press against his, as the shelves dug into her back.

His hand supported her, slipping to the first curve of her lower back and her shoulder, but then his kiss became more ardent and his tongue pressed deep into her mouth.

"Katherine!"

They flew apart and she knew she must be crimson. The back of her hand pressed to her mouth, wondering how swollen her lips must look and then her palms pressed to her hot cheeks before trying to tuck wisps of her hair back beneath her bonnet.

Reverend Barker's long, confident footsteps could be heard as he walked briskly up the aisle.

Her hands ran quickly over her gown, smoothing out creases which were not there. She felt dishevelled but it was not an outward turmoil, it was an inward one.

She looked at John. He did not look contrite at all.

Oh John, what are you trying to do to me?

She turned her back on him, presuming he would leave by the side door, and walked into the aisle. Her hands were shaking. She clasped them together.

She felt as though she'd played with fire and been burned. She was left charred and smouldering.

The suddenness of their separation had left John feeling bereft. All his senses were smarting at her loss as his gaze followed her departure.

The Reverend approached. John could see him through the ornate grid separating off the little chapel and his stomach clenched in a sharp spasm.

The vicar no longer wore his robes. He had changed somewhere and come back for her.

"Katherine!" The man's voice echoed about the church.

Not, Miss Spencer.

John felt icy cold. The reverend was around the same age as

himself. John's grandfather had helped appoint him three years ago. John walked into the church as Katherine had done, a moment before she met the reverend in the aisle.

"Richard, I'm here."

When John entered the square of four arches beneath the church tower, he felt like a cockerel in a pit, bitter hatred running into his blood. He wished to fight this man whose name she used. Had John walked in on a tryst *they* had planned?

He forced a smile. "I enjoyed your sermon, Reverend. I was just offering to take Miss Spencer home."

She looked back, appearing to have not known he'd followed.

She gave him an uncertain look. "Thank you, Your Grace, but Reverend Barker usually drives me home."

Ah, so she had not been hiding. She had been waiting for the vicar. She was embarrassed, blushing again, and John could feel the awareness running between Katherine and the reverend. But moments ago she had been kissing *him*.

"Forgive me, I thought Your Grace had gone." The vicar gave John a deferential bow but John could see the man was prickling. There was a stand-off here. Two men interested in one woman.

The vicar sent Katherine a conciliatory and questioning smile. He obviously did not trust a duke near his prim Sunday-school teacher.

John laughed internally but it was a bitter sound which rung in his head. He felt a desperate need to cling to Katherine, to keep her for himself. He felt so much better in her presence – human.

He'd watched her during the service, moving about beyond the metal screen speaking with the children, sitting beside them and whispering to them.

He'd forgotten Wareham, the account books and the tenants he'd yet to meet. He'd forgotten the two halves of his whole. He was one person in her presence, a man who could feel warmth. He was only John.

Setting a false smile – all the old Duke's grandson – John met the vicar's gaze. "I saw Miss Spencer's parents leave, I had not realised you had an arrangement." His eyebrows lifted. Was the vicar her beau? Was Katherine inclined towards him?

"If you'll excuse us then, Your Grace?" The vicar dismissed John and looked at Katherine. "Are you ready?"

She nodded.

John seethed, nobody routed him. Katherine was his and he was going to damn well have her. This bloody nothing of a vicar would have to step aside.

"Your Grace." She turned to him and dropped a deep curtsy as though he was a stranger and they had not been kissing but moments ago.

I want you.

If she was playing games, well he'd learnt them from the she-wolves abroad, he knew how to play.

"Katherine," he stated, in a deep warm pitch, reminding her they were not strangers.

She blushed intensely, but John had let her vicar know he was not the only one who had permission to call her by her given name. But then she had never actually given John permission, he had assumed the right based on their childhood friendship.

He turned to the vicar. "Reverend Barker."

Then he left.

~

It had been three days since John had felt Katherine's kiss slip into complete abandon in the chancel chapel. Since then his mind had been full of her.

Oh but that was a lie, his mind had been full of her since the funeral, only now it was becoming even more of an obsession.

His whole body ached with need for her and at night she occupied his dreams.

It irritated him immensely whenever he thought of her with her Godly priest.

64

She had kissed John back in the church and admitted she had wanted him to kiss her in the road. She could not therefore wish for a pious bloody vicar. John strode on along Maidstone's pavement and shoved his thoughts of Kate aside. He had a job to do. He'd scoured the accounts and found nothing unusual, so now he was resorting to asking Pembroke Place's suppliers about Wareham's business practices.

He'd also visited tenants over the last two days and asked them if they'd had any problems with the management of their tenancies. No one had complained.

As John walked, he received bows and curtsies in acknowledgement. He nodded at the people noting his presence, though his now habitual *lack of* patience was wearing thin. He knew why his grandfather had never walked anywhere. John set his jaw and kept going. But then his gaze alighted on one person he was pleased to see.

Warmth and light suddenly swept into the cold, arid darkness inside him.

Katherine! He shouted her name, though not aloud.

She was on the far side of the street, standing outside a hat shop, looking in through the window. She held a pile of parcels.

A primal hunger roared inside him.

Her profile was perfect and dainty, with her round-tipped nose, and her rose-coloured lips were slightly parted. He imagined her in a black silhouette portrait, as they'd cut images in Naples. He crossed the cobbled street, now entirely ignoring other passers-by.

"Katherine." He took the last step and touched her elbow.

She started and spun around, her eyes wide. "Y-your Grace."

"It seems I surprise you every time," he whispered.

She was blushing again.

"I-I'm sorry."

He looked to where she had been looking and saw a pretty bonnet dressed with ornamental cherries and a cerise-pink ribbon. Mary thought the mode for fruit on a bonnet absurd. Katherine

65

obviously did not.

"Your Grace?" he queried. "If the vicar is Richard, Katherine, I think I might remain, John, privately? We have known each other years!" Her wide turquoise-blue eyes stared back, but she said nothing. "What is going on between the two of you anyway?" The question had been rattling about in John's head for days.

"N-nothing, I…" She did not continue.

"Nothing? He drives you home every Sunday? Have you an agreement with him?"

"An agreement?" Her eyes kept glancing beyond him, into the shop.

"Are you promised to him?"

She turned a deeper pink. "*No.*"

He suddenly remembered she was holding parcels and took them from her.

Where was her groom or maid? Phillip's family were not high society but nor were they low. Her father was the local squire.

"Who is with you?" The question probably sounded impertinent. He was still angry over the bloody vicar.

"My mother is in the shop." She looked embarrassed. She had not been embarrassed with her vicar. John wished she'd feel as comfortable with him.

He glanced through the shop window and saw her mother and her younger sister, sifting through a drawer of ribbons. Why was she not in the shop with them?

"You are not shopping?" She flushed bright red, but said nothing. It was obvious she was not. "Where is your groom?" That was who should be carrying her parcels.

"He is in the livery stable—"

"Leaving you playing maid." John turned back, looking for his own man and waved him forwards. "There's no need for you to stand here looking to all and sundry like a pack mule, Katherine, I'll have my groom take these to yours."

Her fingers hovered at her waist as though she wished to take the parcels back, but he would not allow it.

"Katherine, is something wrong?"

Her eyes widened. "No."

"And you and the vicar?" he pressed again.

"Please, Your Grace, John, do not…"

Her lack of an answer said there was something. Yet if there was something, why had she let him kiss her, and kissed him back. Her company gave John peace, and peace was a much-vaunted thing in his current life, he was not willing to relinquish it.

"Do not what, Kate?"

Her mother chose that moment to leave the shop, and his question was answered only by a ringing bell. "Your Grace."

John had never liked Phillip's mother.

"Your Grace." Nor his youngest sister.

John's innards hardened to stone at their fawning pitch. They were money-grabbing, scheming females; he'd never had the same sense from Katherine.

"Katherine, you should have called us." Her mother, and then her sister, rose from their curtsies.

Conveniently, John's groom arrived and, ignoring the women, John passed off the parcels. "Take these to the Spencers' groom at the livery."

John's groom bowed and then turned away, but Mrs Spencer stopped him. "There is another here."

John felt a rush of irritation again. She was taking his assistance for granted, as if it was her given right to have his help. It was not. But then this is what came of showing any preference when you were a duke. He had once favoured her son.

"Your Grace, you will not have met Jennifer since she was young."

His eyes turned to the youngest sister. Like John's siblings, Jenny was much younger.

"Your Grace," Jenny stated again, offering her hand as though he would want to take it.

He accepted it – only because she was Katherine's and Phillip's little sister – held it for a moment and then let go.

"Are you in town for long, Your Grace?" the girl asked as if she knew him.

"We were just on our way to the inn for refreshments if you would care to join us?" Mrs Spencer added.

He did not care. Had it been Katherine alone however… But she remained mute, and when he glanced at her she was staring at the pavement, her face largely hidden by the broad rim of her bonnet.

"I'm busy, I'm afraid."

"That is a shame, Your Grace, but you must come to Jenny's party. It is her coming-out ball, here, at the assembly rooms. It is two weeks today. You will attend, Your Grace? Shall I send an invitation?"

"Mama, John is still in mourning," Katherine whispered. She had used his given name.

"I had not forgotten." The woman thrust at Katherine. "It will do no harm if he does not dance."

Anger struck him again over Mrs Spencer's presumption. He did not appreciate being told what he may do.

"Phillip will be there of course."

Phillip could go hang, but John would attend for Katherine. It would give him a chance to have another hour or so in her company.

"I shall come. Send the invitation. But now I must be getting on." He bowed slightly to Katherine's mother. "Mrs Spencer."

She curtsied.

"Miss Jennifer." He nodded again as the girl dropped another deep curtsy, trying to please.

Then he looked at Katherine. "Katherine." She curtsied, but he caught her hand before she dropped too deep and lifted it to his lips. His kiss pressed onto the same pair of kid leather gloves she had worn at the funeral and in the road the other day.

She blushed again.

"Good day ladies." He let Katherine's hand go.

"Your Grace," her mother and sister replied.

But she said, "John." Before he turned and walked away.

He returned to the shop an hour later, though – frustration niggling after none of his suppliers had expressed any inkling of error in Wareham's work – and did what he should not do. He had seen the longing in her eyes before she'd turned and he could simply not resist the urge.

~

"Miss, this came an hour ago." Hetty, the housemaid, bustled into Katherine's bedchamber, carrying a large round box, excitement in her voice. "Mr Castle put it in the scullery and forgot to bring it up. I said to him, how could you forget it when 'tis for Miss Katherine, she never gets nothin', do you Miss?"

Katherine's eyebrows lifted. "Are you certain it is not for Jenny? She and Mama ordered all sorts in Maidstone yesterday."

"No, Miss, 'tis addressed to Miss *Katherine* Spencer, clear as day."

Katherine set down the darning she was working on and rose from her chair by the window.

The weather had turned chillier today, although it was still sunny, and several white fluffy clouds flew across the sky on a brisk summer breeze.

Her mother and sister were out calling on those they were inviting to the ball. Katherine had not been asked to join them. Her mother never treated her as part of the family. But that was an ancient fact, and the pain it caused so old now it was dulled.

Yet perhaps there was still tallow to keep her hurt burning, because she had stayed in her room to hide her exclusion from the house servants.

"Leave it on the bed, Hetty, and bring the tea up to my room as no one else is in."

Katherine's gaze fell to the box when Hetty put it down. Perhaps

Phillip had bought it? Whatever it was.

"I'll fetch it now, Miss."

The maid disappeared as Katherine walked over to the parcel.

It was tied with string and she pulled it free, feeling excited despite her current melancholy mood. Hetty had been right, Katherine was rarely given anything new.

When she lifted the lid her heart pounded. It was the bonnet she'd admired in Maidstone the day before. It lay nestled in a bed of tissue paper.

She lifted it out with shaking fingers. It was beautiful, but it could not be from Phillip.

There was a card beneath it.

I saw you staring and wish to give you what you desire.
J

He had not! No! He could not have done. How could he?
John!

Oh he was so arrogant.

Without any care for the fashionable creation, she stuffed it back in its box, furious. She may be provincial, but she knew a woman should not accept gifts from a man.

If her mother had seen it…

If her father had!

Did John think she did not know the connotation? Or did he mean to buy her favour? He'd kissed her twice.

He'd risked her reputation by sending this.

Oh the arrogant, selfish man.

Angry, she turned to her small travelling desk and withdrew a quill and paper.

No thank you, Your Grace. On all accounts, I am afraid I may not accept.
K

~

John stared at the rows of facts and figures in annoyance. There were no anomalies in the ledgers. He could find nothing wrong. Yet something did not make sense. There was the inexplicable loan and then there was the way Wareham behaved.

This morning the man had come to John with a taunting smile on his face, as if he wished to know if anything had been found in the books and then had been gloating over the fact it had not.

He'd asked John if he wished to ride along one of the estate's boundaries. John had accepted and so he'd had the pleasure of Wareham's insolent company for three hours.

They had ridden mostly in silence but when they'd met tenants, John had had to correct Wareham's words on two occasions. It obviously infuriated the man, but John could hardly let things slip when Wareham was deliberately being facetious. Wareham needed ruling with an iron hand. This could be a powder keg if John let any spark be lit. The man had influence in every one of John's estates.

The morning had merely made John decide to ask Harvey to employ an investigator and track the loan Wareham had made from the other end, to investigate why it had been given.

A light knock hit the sitting room door.

"Come in," John called, glad of the interruption and sick of the accounts.

"Your Grace," Finch's deep tone echoed into the room, as a footman entered bearing a parcel.

John's brow furrowed and he rose as the footman set it down, then undid the string and lifted the lid.

It was the bonnet he'd sent to Katherine, carelessly thrown atop its wrapping with a scrawled note cast on top of it.

He laughed when he read it. *No* indeed. God, the girl amused him. She had not said no to his kisses, and he was not inclined to accept it now. She had liked the bonnet. He wished her to have it.

He wanted her to favour him over her vicar. Perhaps the cherries ought to be apples and her, Eve, because Katherine Spencer was temptation.

"Finch!" John called.

"Your Grace?" The door opened again.

"I am going out. Have my curricle made ready."

Half an hour or so later, John drew his curricle to a halt before the Spencers' small manor house and then looked back at the groom who'd accompanied him.

The man jumped down and ran about the curricle to hold the horses.

John climbed down and then lifted the hatbox from the seat.

His heels crunched on the gravel as he crossed the drive to the door.

He felt light-hearted, glad to be escaping his duty for a brief interlude.

The door opened immediately and Castle, their butler, greeted John with recognition. "Your Grace?" He bowed. "I am afraid Mr and Mrs Spencer are not at home."

Excellent. John smiled. "I have come to call on Miss Katherine Spencer, Castle, is *she* home?"

The man's eyebrows lifted and he glanced at the box John carried. Of course, he'd probably seen it before.

Well, let the man speculate, Katherine was Phillip's sister, the gift could be explained away.

"Will you wait in the parlour, Your Grace?"

John walked along the hall, glancing up the stairs. If she was not in the parlour, she must be up there. He would much rather be going to her chamber to visit her. A sudden imagined vision of Katherine, hair tussled, half asleep and languid-eyed, came into his mind.

The butler left John in the small receiving room at the back of the house, with a look of disapproval as he went to fetch Katherine.

John set the hatbox down in an armchair, took off his hat and gloves, and then tossed them there too.

The room was decorated in light blue and cream, and was probably the size of Wareham's office.

A large portrait hung on one wall: Phillip in his wig. John smiled, looking at the miniatures on another wall: Jennifer, Phillip and Katherine's parents. There was a later miniature of Jennifer too, probably painted recently. There were no images of Katherine.

John walked across the room, his hands settling behind his back, and looked through the French door out into the garden.

A sharp breeze swept at the flower heads.

He felt uncharacteristically nervous.

After a few moments, he heard her footsteps on the stairs and then in the hall.

He turned.

She looked beautiful when she came in. Her cheeks were pink and her bright-blue eyes wide. Her blonde hair was loosely held in a topknot, with wisps of it falling to her shoulders and about her face; a mix of bright-yellow sunshine shades, and duller damp-wheat hues. She wore a faded blue short-sleeved summer dress, which moulded to her figure. His eyes were drawn to her arms. It was the first time he had seen her without a pelisse or a spencer and her bare, slender arms were exquisite pure pale, milk-white skin.

His English rose. His, not her vicar's.

He crossed the room, took her hand and bore it to his lips.

Thank God those tired kid leather gloves were not on them. Her skin was beautifully cool and soft and he let his thumb run over her palm as he breathed in the scent of her soap.

Clearly uncomfortable and colouring up again, she pulled her hand free.

"I brought your bonnet back," he whispered, without preamble. "I am afraid I was offended by its return."

Blue fire flashed in her eyes instantly, as it had done on the road the other day. There was a hidden zeal tucked away within Katherine. He wondered how many others saw it or if it was just him she showed it to. She wanted more from her life, he could tell. He longed to give it to her. He knew she could give him what he wished – release, freedom, moments of escape.

Varying shades of blue warred in her eyes. "What do you think you are doing, John?" It was a harsh, accusing whisper. "You cannot buy me gifts. What if my mother saw it?"

"You are Phillip's sister, why should I not buy you something you wish for. No one need think it odd!" He smiled. He wanted to laugh. Not because she was funny, but because the passion in her outburst struck him so intensely. She was not the shy quiet person she portrayed herself to be, not in the least.

"Did you wish me to send for tea, Miss Katherine?" Castle asked from the open door, having followed her.

Katherine turned bright pink, but John grasped the opportunity to stay longer. "That would be welcome, Castle, thank you."

Katherine's gaze bored into John when the butler turned away.

"You should not be here," she whispered once the man had gone.

She was right. John only hoped Castle could be discreet, but John did not admit it. "If you are afraid of this being misconstrued, say I brought the gift from Phillip."

"And when Mama writes to him and asks why he bought me it, and Jenny nothing, what then? Besides Phillip does not have money to waste on bonnets."

Still disinclined to accept refusal, John picked the box up and held it out.

It was suddenly extremely important to him that she accept it. If she accepted it, she accepted him. She could save him from the darkness. "I shall not take it back, say what you wish. Hide it away, if you will. But I imagine you will look well in it, and if you wear it, I will know you have kept something from me, and you will know it too, but no one else need know a thing."

Her gaze struck his and then fell to the box. She appeared tempted.

"Take it," he said more gently.

"But what does it mean, John?" she whispered, her gaze lifting to his again. "What do you want from me?"

He could see there was no anger left in her now, only questions.

"I don't know." It was the truth. She deserved honesty from him if nothing else. She had been honest with him on the road and admitted she had wished to be kissed. "I am attracted to you, as you are to me, I can say no more than that. I wish to give you this, Katherine. I wish you to take it. That is all for now."

"John?"

"You give me ease, Katherine. Let me give you this. Let me think of you wearing it and know you think of me. Perhaps one day I might see you in it."

Her hands finally reached to accept it and her bare fingers touched his, they melted the feeling of cold ice in his stomach to water, the reaction disturbed him, and suddenly vulnerable, he turned away and crossed to the French door.

"What is going on, John?" she whispered behind him.

He turned back. "Nothing."

"I don't understand you."

Nor do I understand myself. Perhaps that was half his problem! Who was he, his mother's son or his grandfather's dark, cold, unfeeling monster? Far more the latter lately. But he didn't wish to be, and Katherine could make him feel warmth.

He walked back towards her, his gaze holding hers as physical and emotional desire burned inside him like an inferno. "You are beautiful, Katherine."

"You are beautiful, John. I am not."

"You are to me. I like your hair, and your eyes. I like *you*." — *And I want you.*

He took the box from her hands then discarded it in the chair, before lifting her chin. She did not turn her head away, her gaze held his, bright with the knowledge that he intended kissing her. "Katherine." He kissed her gently, unable to comprehend the level of feeling in his chest. How could she have come to mean so much to him in such a short time?

His kiss travelled to brush her cheek, her nose, her temple, as her face tilted towards him like a flower to the sun. "I like your skin too," he whispered.

She shivered and her fingers clasped his coat at his sides, as though her legs could no longer hold her up.

He liked affecting her like this. She was nothing like the women he'd known before. She was everything he craved.

Castle's heels rung on the floorboards in the hall.

They pulled apart sharply and John turned and walked back to the window, looking out once more as his heart pounded and his groin ached with the need for fulfilment.

He clasped his hands behind his back, only to stop them shaking.

He wanted to touch her.

Katherine thanked the butler and he heard her take the tea tray and set it down.

It was not tea he was thirsty for.

When she brought him a full cup, he turned and met her gaze again, very aware of the door which still stood open.

She could not shut it. It would be the height of impropriety to do so, but at this moment, it was only that open door which saved her chastity. He wished to do wicked things with her, very wicked things, and he didn't know if it was his monster roaring or just the boy who desperately longed to be loved.

"Katherine…" John's pale eyes shone as he looked at her.

She had thought him vulnerable at the funeral months ago, with no evidence to pin the thought against. But today she could see it clearly.

There had been a desperate desire for acceptance in his eyes when he had pressed the bonnet on her, and there was insecurity in them now. She could see nothing of the arrogant man who'd jumped down from his curricle less than a week ago. This was a different person. The boy she had known and the young man who had left for the continent, grown up.

"John," she said in a low voice, "I do not understand what is happening? I can be no one to you."

He took the full cup she held out. "You are wrong. You can be everything to me, Katherine."

She felt the earth shift beneath her feet but she did not know what to do. So she turned away and sought her cup.

"I have never felt this way for anyone before, Katherine," he said behind her. "I have no idea what it is, or how to progress, all I know is, I wish to be in your company constantly... "

Her heart pounded. It was John saying this to her.

She was about to turn back, when she heard the front door open. Her cup wobbled in its saucer as she jumped.

"Sir, the Duke of Pembroke is here."

Her father.

She set her cup aside and moved before the hatbox, her heart thumping even harder.

"The Duke of Pembroke?" Her father's voice rang along the hall. Then his brisk footsteps could be heard.

She did not look at John.

"Your Grace." Her father appeared at the open parlour door.

"Papa." She moved forwards, knowing she must look guilty as she tried to ensure he would not be able to see the box resting in the chair.

There was a question in his eyes.

John set his cup down and crossed the room, offering his hand. "Good day, sir."

Her father accepted it and shook it briefly, before letting go.

"I called to accept Mrs Spencer's invitation to your gathering for Jenny, sir," John progressed. It was a lie of course.

Her father was stiff and silent. He looked at Katherine again. "I am sure your mother will be pleased, Kate." *He* did not sound pleased.

Katherine bit her lip. He seemed to have sensed there was

something odd going on, but then she was acting as though she had something to hide. Did she? There was the bonnet, but... what else...

Her heart thumped as her father's gaze passed back to her.

"Katherine?"

"John also brought word from Phillip, father." Now she had lied too.

Her father's eyebrows lifted and then he looked back at John. "I was sorry to hear of your grandfather's passing."

John nodded. "Your son does well in town, sir."

"He does..."

Their stilted conversation passed over Katherine's head as she watched John change back into the Duke – untouchable, unreachable, distant and withheld.

When it ran dry, John turned to her, his eyes cold and direct. "As we still have the sunshine, even though it's a little blustery, I wondered if you would care to walk in the garden with me."

She looked at her father. There was still a question in his eyes which said he was unsure what to do. "Shall I leave you two young people to stroll then, Kate, and retire to my study?"

She nodded.

"Your Grace," he said to John, bowing.

"Sir," John responded.

Once he'd gone, Katherine turned to John. "You are shameless, the way you manipulate people."

He merely laughed as she moved to ring the bell for Hetty to collect the hatbox.

She turned back and faced him. "I cannot believe you have persuaded me to accept your gift against my better judgement, and I still do not know what you wish in return for it."

"A moment of freedom, Katherine, or however many you will give me."

"Miss Kate?"

Katherine spun about to face Hetty, certain she was entirely pink. "Take this up to my room please, and would you fetch my spencer and bonnet, and my gloves."

"No," John interrupted.

Katherine turned.

"Hetty, is it? Your mistress needs none of that, it is cooler today, she need not fear the sun."

"I have a fair complexion, Your Grace." His boorishness annoyed her.

"Then a parasol will suffice." His pale eyes glowed, daring her to challenge him.

She did not, and once the maid had gone, he whispered, "I want to touch your skin."

Was this the price of her bonnet?

Her heartbeat thundered, as she realised she wished to be touched. She had always known she was base and sinful and weak, John was only proving what she knew, and if any man were to touch her, then let it be John.

Hetty was back in a moment, bearing the promised parasol, and Katherine accepted it with a brief thank you, realising her hands shook when she did so.

John smiled when she turned. His eyes said he needed her.

Her bare arm trembled when he took it.

He opened the French door and together they stepped outside. His grip was gentle. She felt cared for.

There was a little wilderness of wild flowers to the right of the garden, and he led her there as she opened her parasol and rested it on her shoulder. The chill summer breeze caught at her skirt and wrapped it against John's leg.

He let go of her arm and instead raised his so she could lay her fingers on it. She felt firm muscle beneath the cloth of his morning coat. There was strength, security and support.

"You say you wish for freedom," she said quietly, "but I still do not understand what you mean, John." She was being gauche and provincial again.

79

"Just your company, Katherine, and perhaps your kisses." His other hand covered hers as it lay on his arm. "We will be discreet."

Discreet? Was she agreeing to an assignation then? "You make it sound as though you wish for an affair."

He stopped and looked down at her, vulnerability and need burning in his eyes again. "An affair of sorts, an intrigue. But I shall not take your innocence. I'll not hurt you."

His gaze said, *please do not deny me.*

A rush of yearning swamped her heart.

He began walking again, looking ahead and not at her.

Oh John. John! She remembered that day long ago when she had watched him in the lake and felt desperate to touch him. If she did this, she could touch him and she could kiss him. If she did it, the pain buried in her soul for years would have ease.

John! She ached for him. How could she say no? She had always known he could never offer her marriage, but he could offer her *this* and she could take it. It was what she'd longed for. Why say no?

As they neared an ancient oak, John's arm slipped from beneath her hand and then he caught a hold of her arm again and drew her behind the broad trunk, then pressed her back against it.

Her parasol fell and tumbled across the lawn, blown on the wind, as his lips covered hers, gently at first, but then the kiss became more insistent.

His body was barely an inch from hers.

One of his long-fingered hands braced against her cheek.

John!

She kissed him back, her tongue dancing with his, learning from his.

His other hand pressed against her lower back. While hers gripped his morning coat, clinging to him.

The storm of emotion she could feel in him was bitter need.

His mouth left hers and he began nipping beneath her chin in soft little bites. "I want you Katherine." His breath was hot. "I can show and teach you things you will enjoy, but I swear I shall not take your virginity. I know you want me, too."

I do!

His hand cupped her breast through her bodice, kneading it gently. It ached for him.

"Say yes, Katherine," he whispered urgently.

His lips nipped at her neck and his hand rubbed her breast while his hips pressed against hers.

She wanted him, there, between her legs, she wanted to do the indecent things her mother had done to beget her. He was the only thing she had ever really wanted. Why hold back?

Her breath was shallow, and his hard and rasping.

His hand left her breast and moved to the place where she wanted him to be.

John!

He pressed her through the layers of her gown and petticoats, and her arms rose to his neck as he kissed her lips again, more passionately.

"Katherine," he said into her mouth, sounding as breathless and desperate as her as his fingers rubbed her intimately between her legs through the layers of clothing.

She was so in need. This is what she had spent so many years craving. It was just the two of them in the world. It was wrong, she knew it was, but it felt so right and she did not care. She was like her mother. She had always been told it. This had been inevitable since her birth. The sins of the parent visited on the child.

Her body pressed against his, arching with its need.

It was so perfect what he did, how could it be wrong?

The feelings inside her whirled in a spiral of heated delight, rising up and overwhelming her, and then they seemed to break on a high tide that swept through her body, leaving her panting and weak-limbed.

His fingers braced against her cheek again as he kissed her more urgently for a moment.

She could no longer kiss him back.

Then he ceased, and when she opened her eyes he was looking into them, beautiful and all John.

He sighed, appearing to look right into her soul, the pale blue in his eyes glittering like melting ice.

Her fingers stroked through his soft, dark hair.

"*That* is what I can give you, Katherine," he said quietly, as if that was everything. It was his love she wished for. "Will you meet me in my grandfather's tower tomorrow at two?"

"Yes," her answer was caught on the breeze and swept away. *Yes.*

Chapter Six

Thoughts of Katherine hovering in his mind, John strode along the bare flagstone of the servants' hall, ready to ride out to meet her. The image of her had hung in his mind since yesterday, along with a subconscious feeling of companionship.

The beauty of her submission had been a revelation.

She'd ceased fighting her desire yesterday, giving him her trust, and a hundred times last night he'd vowed to honour it.

He was so hungry for her he'd hardly slept, burning with restless frustration. He itched to have her, but he had made her a promise. He would temper his lust. Yet there were many things a man could do without taking a woman's virginity and his mind had dwelled on all of them last night. He was impatient to see her.

He'd visited tenants earlier, alone, and then returned to look at the ledgers again over luncheon. There was still nothing there. Now he was searching for Wareham, who apparently kept the key to the folly. John had come himself because it gave him another opportunity to try and discover what Wareham was up to.

The office door was shut. John gripped the handle and turned it without knocking. It was locked.

Ill temper flared. John was too tired and impatient. He rapped on the door harshly, angry at being excluded from a room in his own property.

A chair scraped within, and a moment later the lock turned. Then the door opened.

Wareham's expression was insolent – antagonising. Like the other day, there was no deference.

John had an urge to grip the man by the throat and shove him up against a wall. "Must I remind you of your place again…"

Wareham turned his back and crossed the room, returning to his desk. "You need not remind me. I am well aware of it."

John wished to hold him with one fist and punch him with the other. He'd not used John's title, again.

Wareham looked at John and barely bent his head, as though that would suffice. "Your Grace, pray, to what do I owe this honour?" Then he sat.

It was insupportable for him to do so. John's servants should always be standing in his presence. Wareham was deliberately insulting. His entire manner expressed rebellion, and his expression said he wished to make John angry. He had. Was John a damned bull to be pulled by a nose ring?

"I have come for the key to the tower." John held out his hand. Let the man bring it to him.

"And why would you want that, Your Grace?"

"That is none of your business. *The key,* Wareham."

The man rose again and moved to fetch it from a tall narrow cupboard.

John waited, but when Wareham held the large iron key out and came towards John, when John reached for it, Wareham pulled it back.

John's façade of calm evaporated. "Give me the key and stop these games!" His loss of control made him even angrier.

"Games, Your Grace?" Wareham taunted with a gleam in eyes. "I am a bit old for games. It is not a game I am playing."

"The key, Wareham." John's voice was bitterly hard, his patience having fled. Blast the missing money, he wasn't short of that. Let Wareham have it. He would rather be rid of this problem and rid of Wareham.

Wareham lifted the key and John snatched it from his hand.

"Did you truly think I would tolerate these insults?" John was calmer now, back under control. His voice was no longer angry. This would be an end to it. "You are dismissed. You will leave immediately. I will have you escorted."

For a moment, Wareham just stared at John. There was not a single flicker of emotion which showed in his eyes or on his face. He was far better at holding his emotion in than John.

"*Now*," John pressed.

"Do you think I *wish* to serve you?"

"You need not. Go."

"While you have idled abroad, I have built up these estates." Wareham sounded as though he thought he had a right over John.

John glanced back towards the hall and yelled. "Finch!" He had seen the butler a moment ago.

"Your Grace?" He was there in an instant.

"Mr Wareham is leaving. Immediately. I wish him escorted from the grounds. You may pack his things and send them on, but he is to take nothing which belongs to *my* estates. Have some of the grooms escort him."

John looked at Wareham. "You may send Finch your address when you have found somewhere to stay." Then John turned away and left the room.

The key cut into his palm as his fist clenched, while the maids and footmen bowed and curtsied as he walked along the corridor. John would be known as a tyrant now, for dismissing his steward simply because it took too long to find a key. John felt his prison cell slam shut. He was trapped in this life, he had not chosen it. Darkness and isolation engulfed him as he stepped into the courtyard and felt sunshine on his skin.

I want Katherine.

At least he could have her, and she was his choice.

~

John was breathless with exhilaration when he reached the tower, having ridden hard to get there.

It was a square, red-bricked building, which stood in a clearing, on the brow of a shallow hill, and it reached fifty feet upwards, stretching towards the sky like the tower of Babel.

He'd come here often as a child, though he was sworn never to play in it. He'd stolen the key to come in secret and be alone. He would climb up to the square room at the very top and look down onto the world like God, imagining what he would do if he could rule and order it as he wished: he'd turn back time and know his mother from his birth, he'd long to change fate and stop his father dying. No one had known he'd come here, not even Phillip; he'd never shared this space.

As he climbed the slope towards the entrance, Katherine emerged from the other side. His heart struck harder in his chest. She was wearing the bonnet he'd given her.

A deep sense of place filled him, as though he'd waited for this moment all his life. His anger dissipated. His loneliness was gone.

When he drew closer, she smiled. The warmth of it filled him.

"You're late," she accused, her eyes searching his.

He took her hand and kissed the back of her shabby kid leather glove. "I got caught up in business."

"I thought it was some horrid joke you were playing on me, like Phillip used to do. I thought you would not come and then laugh over the fact I was fool enough to think you serious."

"That was never me." He felt suddenly grave again.

Her blue eyes were in shadow beneath the brim of her bonnet and she looked nervous although she was smiling.

He was desperate to make this good for her, to prove to himself he was neither a monster nor a tyrant. She could see into him, he knew she could, he'd seen it in her eyes. Let her reach into him and find the youth she'd known. "I'll not hurt you, Katherine."

86

The bonnet suited her, the cerise ribbon contrasted perfectly with the colour of her eyes and her pale skin. She was breathtaking.

He set the key in the lock and turned it. The stiff door creaked open.

His hand still gripping hers, he drew her in and then locked the door behind them. The stairs were steep and numerous.

Her fingers clung to his as they climbed, small, delicate, fragile fingers.

She wore the same tired spencer he'd seen twice before.

When they reached the top of the stairs he let go of her hand, opened the door and then let her enter first. His heart thudded like the hoof beats of a galloping horse.

Once inside, she turned to him, breathless from the climb, and smiled.

The room had windows along all four sides. It was flooded with light and the view looked across four counties.

Impatient, he caught her about the waist, drew her into his arms then kissed her gently, his lips brushing against hers. He felt in awe of her.

Her arms reached about his neck, and when he ended the kiss she hung onto him, laughing and lifting her feet from the floor, letting him bear her weight.

He did not mind bearing it.

He swung her in a circle.

She was only a light burden. A precious burden.

What was he to do about this, about her?

He shoved the thought aside. He wished to just live for this moment, to shut the world outside and let only her in.

A single table stood against one wall. He carried her there and sat her on it. Then tugged loose the ribbon tying her bonnet, it fell down her back onto the table behind her.

Her arms were still about his neck, loosely holding on, and he lowered his mouth to hers again but this time his kiss was searing. He wanted her to know how desperate he was for her.

She kissed him back without reservation and his heart swelled with a soul-deep satisfaction.

Her body arching against him, her fingers slid into his hair. She had no modesty today. The demure girl he'd met on the road and in the church had slipped away.

He ended the kiss and smiled at her. "You are a contradiction."

She blushed as he straightened.

His hands fell to his sides.

She did not jump down but instead leant back onto her hands, and watched him, crossing her ankles and then swinging her legs forward and back.

He was charmed. She was an antidote to every other woman he'd known.

His hand lifted and he began tugging pins from her hair. He had an urge to see it loose. Most women he'd known abroad wore their hair short. It was the fashion.

The jet orbs at the heart of her eyes flared, and her feet stopped swinging.

Loose blonde curls fell to her shoulders and then tumbled down her back.

"You can be so prim when you wish, shy, like a quiet church mouse. And then there is *this* you…"

Her lips pouted and her breasts pressed against her bodice when she took a breath, while her feet uncrossed. So he might step between her parted thighs if he chose. He chose. She let him, her knees parting until they brushed the outer surfaces of his thighs.

"I think this is the real you, this reckless girl who has come to tryst with me."

He bent and kissed her again, and her mouth opened to his, not denying his words. Emotion stirred in his chest as an ache. It was a very long time since he'd felt emotion when he'd kissed a woman. He'd thought himself in love once, as a youth, when he had first gone abroad. It had not been love. He no longer believed in that – or the romantic kind anyway. That was a fiction crafted by poets.

When he'd pulled the last pin free, he buried his fingers in her soft hair, held her scalp and kissed her more deeply. She responded equally.

Lust was what a man felt for a woman, and a woman felt for a man. There was nothing romantic in that, and there was a strong intuitive passionate streak in Katherine. He had known it without knowing, but now there was evidence, she was here, trysting with him, and returning his kisses.

Her fingers clasped his open coat at his waist in fists and then they released and moved beneath his coat instead.

He wished to be without the barrier of clothes.

He broke the kiss, showing her the intensity of his desire in his eyes. He hoped it did not scare her but he refused to hide it, or himself. Let her see who he was and know all of him. He prayed she would still want him. He could not bear her rejection.

She leant back again, and watched as he stripped off his coat.

He smiled at her. "Have you no modesty anymore?"

She blushed – beautifully.

He loved her blushes, but it meant the church mouse had returned.

She shrank back into her shyness. "You cannot ask me here to do this and then chide me for being immodest, John." There was insecurity in her eyes.

He set his coat aside and cupped her cheek. His thumb brushed across it. Her eyes closed, probably to hide from him.

He did not wish her to withdraw. He wanted to be the only one who knew the real Katherine. He wished her to be the only one who really knew him. Let this be a bond between them no one else could ever break or share. Let it be something just for them.

He brushed her hair back across her shoulder. "I was not complaining, Katherine." Her eyes opened. "I like your shyness and your blushes. I treasure them. But I equally like the brash girl who will willingly kiss me back."

89

Her gaze gave him her trust again.

"I hate this thing," he whispered, beginning to release the buttons securing her spencer. "You wear it every day, no matter the heat. It's as though you hide behind it."

Her brow furrowed. "We are not all wealthy, John." She seemed insulted. "I have only one spencer, I do not have a choice, unless it is not to wear it and be freckled."

"I think just a few freckles might be fun." He smiled, brushing her comment off, though it had cut into his thoughts. Did she have so little then? Phillip's family were hardly poor, surely.

"Take it off." The order was probably too harsh as his mind turned over her words, but she did his bidding.

He took off his waistcoat and his neckcloth too, then kissed her once more, banishing their conversation, denying the differences in their status. Here she was only Katherine and he was only John. That was all he wished to think about.

His fingers undid the buttons which secured her bodice, opening it all the way down to her stomach. It gaped, revealing milk-white breasts spilling over the top of her corset.

There was a catch in her breath as his fingers slid inside her underwear. He lifted one breast free. It was soft and warm, and moulded to his touch.

He ceased kissing her.

She bit her lip, but she did not demur, she leant back on her hands once more and offered herself as his sacrifice.

She was beautiful.

He kissed her breast, gently, honouring that tender flesh.

When he lifted his head and looked at her again, her eyes were darker. They were not really blue at all, merely greys which deceived the eye and portrayed blue.

His thumb ran over her nipple and made her shiver.

"Touch me in return." He wanted to feel her hands on him. He wanted her participation not only her acceptance. This had to be equal or it was nothing at all.

She sat upright, and her eyes fell to his stomach as her palms braced the muscle at his waist, over the thin cotton of his shirt.

He took a deep breath as she began lifting it, drawing it from his waistband. He let her take it off.

She was biting her lip again once he'd freed it from his head and arms, her eyes and hands skimming over his torso. His heart thumped and his groin was heavy with need.

Leaning forwards, he bent over her to unlace her stays.

Her hands gripped his bare skin as he continued to undress her.

"John?" she whispered uncertainly when she was naked to the waist, her gaze meeting his.

She was afraid now, he could see that.

"I'll not hurt you, I swear it. I'll do nothing you do not wish."

Her skin was beautiful, unblemished and milk-white. So English – his English rose.

His hands cupped her breasts and he kissed her again.

She kissed him back, her arms innocently reaching about his neck even though he was naked to the waist and she might touch him more intimately.

Katherine revelled in everything John did as her fingers sifted through his black hair.

He was touching her with exquisite gentleness and adoration. His fingers kneaded her breasts and trailed across her bare skin.

She dared herself to touch him too, and let her hands fall to his shoulders.

He was hot and his skin felt like velvet. The muscles across his abdomen were rigid slopes and hollows.

Her thighs rested open about his as he kissed and touched her. Her heart pounded. She craved him with something that was painful misery and blissful hunger, as the tension he had taught her body the day before rose.

The things he did were wicked and wrong, her conscience shouted it, but she did not listen. *I think this you is the real you, this reckless girl who has come to tryst with me.* She'd known it for a long time.

His head dropped and his mouth claimed her breast again, tugging on her nipple as he sucked her gently. Her fingers rested in his hair once more as the place where he'd touched her yesterday begged for attention.

"John, please." His name came out as a tortured sound.

His head lifted and he smiled as his fingers slid her skirt and petticoats upwards. Her fingers shook as she held his bright crystalline gaze and her hands fell to the waistband of his trousers. He did not stop her. She did not stop him. But her heart pounded.

His hands slipped beneath her petticoats and brushed her inner thighs. Shivering, she instinctively moved forward to sit flush against his body.

She did not dare touch him where she wished to. But as his trousers and underwear slid down, she gripped his hips, her fingers pressing into the first curve of his buttocks as he kissed her deeply, his tongue penetrating her mouth, as her breasts crushed against his chest. It was the most beautiful feeling in the world to be so close to him physically.

When his thumbs skimmed over her, she arched against him, longing for him to do the things he should not. "John." Her voice gave another plea.

He kissed her cheek, her chin, her neck. "I'll not take your virginity."

She did not care if he did, she longed for him to do it.

He touched her, there, between her legs, his thumbs gently caressing, and she widened her thighs, urging him closer.

"Let me take off all your clothes."

Her eyes flew open. She hadn't even known she'd shut them.

She nodded and then he helped her stand.

Her body trembled as he stripped her garments from her hips, letting them pool on the floor.

This was utter madness and yet it was complete heaven too.

"Cold?" he asked, as his fingers gripped her waist and then he gently pressed a kiss against her temple.

"No." Her arms lifted about his neck.

He kissed her again and his hands gripped her buttocks, his fingertips pressing into her flesh.

When he ended the kiss, his hands slid down her thighs and then lifted her back onto the table. In a moment he was between her parted thighs again, naked skin against naked skin. He could do anything now, but she trusted him not to break his promise. She wished he would.

She looked down.

"Touch me," he whispered as his hands pressed her legs wider and he set himself against her. When she did not, he took her hand. "Like this."

It had not been cowardice preventing her, just a lack of knowledge. Now she knew.

He moved his hips, sliding against her as he came through her hand.

The movement was like a chant, or a charm, repetitive and mesmerising. He was watching what he did.

She watched too, aware that she was blushing. Then her gaze lifted to his face. His expression was deep concentration. She was not sure who she was doing this with, John or the Duke. But she did not care.

Sunshine poured through the windows, illuminating the room and warming her skin.

She felt as if she stood on the very top of the world. She never wished to come down. Her fingers clung more tightly and his breathing changed, then his thumb moved across her thigh and rubbed and pressed.

"John." She only said his name because she needed to make some sound. Her free hand clawed into his shoulder.

Was it only yesterday she had refused the bonnet he gave her and sent it back for fear he was buying her favours? Today she was giving them freely, wantonly, desperately.

His gaze lifted and despite his stiff expression she saw need in his eyes – hunger.

"John," she said again, pulling his mouth to hers.

He kissed her aggressively as the pace of his movements quickened. She felt his urgent determination, and as though he refused to leave her behind, his thumb pressed harder.

An ache inside her swelled and overflowed, submerging her in a wave so she could no longer kiss him, and her fingers clung in his hair, while he worked through the grip of her other hand, until he cried out, and then stilled. She felt him throb and his release was warm and liquid.

Her muscles trembled when their kiss ended, and she hugged him close.

He was trembling too.

Surely they had just shared the most intimate thing it was possible to share.

Even the soft triangle of hair at the apex of Katherine's thighs was pale, not blonde but a very light brown, and her nipples were the same rose hue as her lips, both upper and lower.

He picked up his coat and found a handkerchief to wipe her hand. It still shook.

Her skin felt so soft, and yet he supposed it could be no different to any other woman's. Yet every other woman was gone from his mind. There was only this *one* woman.

Meeting her gaze, he then picked her up, bracing her legs about his waist as he carried her to the only chair in the room, a single leather armchair.

John knew his grandfather used to come up here and just sit in silence. Now he understood his grandfather more, John guessed the old man had built this and come here for the same reason John was here, to escape the dukedom for a while.

"God, you are beautiful," he said, sitting down with her exotically placed astride his lap. "I ought to put you in a box and keep you. I could take you wherever I needed you then."

"And when I am in need of you?"

"You may put me on a chain about your neck and I shall be your servant."

"You are talking nonsense." Her eyes looked a little intoxicated.

"Being *here* is nonsense." His afternoon of dalliance suddenly soured. Doing this was beyond foolish. It was ridiculous escaping and hiding here with a woman who could never be anything to him beyond this. She was no courtesan, nor was she one of the she-wolves of elite society. She had been his childhood friend.

He cast the thought aside. He refused to rationalise this, and he refused to think of consequence, or future. This was about escaping. He would not face the truth. Let the truth live outside this tower.

"Being here is folly." She smiled, and yet he could see his words had let reality encroach in the room. She knew as well as he did she should not be here. "Did you choose the location for that reason?"

If she was trying to make him laugh, she did not succeed. He kissed her instead, his fingers gripping her upper thighs. He was hot again and aroused in moments.

He liked the way her lithe, slim body curved and undulated against him when he kissed her. There was no falsehood or façade with her. Every motion was instinctive and a natural need.

Her slender fingers braced the sides of his head as she kissed him back, while the apex of her thighs pressed against his groin.

It would be so easy to bury himself inside her and take her completely. He would not, but he broke the kiss and said across her lips, "Shall we go for a second round?"

She nodded, her teeth biting her lower lip again. Then she said, "You are very bad, now, aren't you?" as though she was confused by the thought.

"My grandfather taught me. He was a very good teacher." It was self-mockery, but he hid his emotions now too well for her

95

to see. "But if I was really bad, Katherine, you would no longer be a virgin."

Her eyes shone. "I am bad too. I shouldn't be here. But I choose to be…"

"You should be. I have wanted you like this since the day of the funeral."

"And I have wanted *you* like this since I saw you swimming in the lake before you even went abroad." The words were obviously spoken without thought, and regretted the moment they were said. She turned pink and the colour stained her whole body.

My God, how beautiful.

But then he realised she was moving to rise, and his grip on her thighs firmed, holding her still as he digested her words. Had she just said she had wanted him before he'd gone?

"But you have probably had a hundred women like this anyway…" There was jealousy and anger in her pitch.

What was this? Her revelation had somehow turned the steady ground beneath his feet to shifting sand. He felt a bitter, hard barrier of denial slip over him, covering the emotion which gripped his stomach and his chest. He did not know how to feel anymore – how to respond. "Are you fishing for compliments, Katherine?" His voice had turned cold. He could not force warmth back into it. All his emotions were shuttered away, out of reach. He could speak the truth though. "In fact, the number of women I've probably had is far more, but none like this, Katherine, and none like you."

"Flattery will win you nothing," she taunted, clearly trying to cover her tracks and hide the vulnerability she obviously felt. She could not hide her emotion, though.

"It has won me this tryst with you."

"You did not win it!" Her response spoke of bitter hurt. "I am giving it to you."

She tried moving again, but once more he stopped her. "Wait." She had wanted him when he was one and twenty, little Katherine Spencer.

"You watched me swimming, in the lake?"

He felt as though his innards were tangled up somehow. He could remember that day. His grandfather had held a ball in his honour, before packing John off abroad. All his friends had come to stay for the house party, and they'd swum naked in the lake because it was so hot.

John had been preoccupied that day, engrossed in himself as he'd dealt with the changes planned for his life. If he was honest, he had not even noticed her, and of course she had not been invited to the ball. She had not yet come out, even though she'd been of age. Phillip had come, though, with his parents, but not Katherine.

She was blushing harder.

"I am flattered."

"Don't be, it was just a childish infatuation." Her gaze had dropped to his throat.

His fingers lifted her chin. "You don't convince me. Have you carried a torch for me since then?" He was suddenly desperate to know, though he knew his voice only implied the merest interest.

"No!"

But the answer was yes, he was sure it was yes. Her voice lied but her body said it, soft and moulded to his, warm and wet between her thighs.

I am giving it to you. That was why this innocent young woman had agreed to this immoral liaison. She was right, she should not be here, but she was, and she was because she cared for him, because she had cared for him for years, for the all the years while he had isolated himself and thought himself superfluous. For all the years he had held people away because of the false affection he'd been barraged with abroad. All that time she had been here longing and waiting for him. If only he had come back earlier.

Life was bizarre.

"I think you have. All this time. Am I the reason you have never married, Katherine?" It was an arrogant, selfish thought, but somehow he knew it was true. He could remember her blushes when she'd seen him at the wake, particularly when he'd spoken of a husband. She'd been standing there that day wanting him as much as he'd wanted her, only with a loyalty which had lasted years.

"No!" she said again, pulling away more aggressively. He let her go.

She climbed from his lap.

He felt in chaos.

John had thought the ground beneath him hard as rock, he had thought his foundations as solid as granite, built upon the bitter, cold, isolated ground his grandfather had lain inside him. But now he stood on quicksand.

She moved away, collected her clothes and then began dressing.

He rose, feeling like a fool, unsure what to say. "Well that explains you making this *choice* of yours."

That of course had been the wrong thing to say.

She threw him a sideways look which called him a bastard for his mockery.

But he was *not* mocking, merely trying to adjust his head to this. He did not believe in romantic love but Katherine clearly did, and she thought herself in love with *him*.

He did not deserve it.

Anyway, what was romantic love? Lust. But, *God*, it was more than lust surely, and more than nothing if she had carried a torch of strong emotion for all these years. Lust he understood, he felt that for her, but it was short-lived. He wished suddenly that he understood what people called love between a man and a woman, and that he was capable of it. He also wished he was worthy of receiving it. But such tenderness had been forced out of him long ago.

"It doesn't matter." He reached out a hand to her, but she knocked it away.

"It does matter, when your choice to ask me here was made in a moment." Ah, so she knew the truth of his affection, too, then.

"Well, you said I was bad." He laughed, not knowing what else

98

to say or do.

"I take it back. You are not bad, just spoilt." She was half-dressed already and she turned her back to him, wordlessly asking him to re-lace her corset.

"Spoilt?" He began pulling at the threads.

"You've always had everything you want. You wish for it and you get it, John, including me."

Her assessment stung, and he pulled her corset over-tight and felt her wince. "I have not always had everything I want, Katherine."

She bent to pick up her dress.

He reached for his own clothing and began dressing too. He had not had a mother for the first ten years of his life. He was hardly spoilt.

She did not reply.

His heart beat steadily.

It was so strange to know she had cared for him all this time. The only time he had thought a woman loved him she had made him look a fool. Naïve and gullible, he had fallen hard and she'd cut him loose in a month. He'd been torn in half. He'd thought his heart broken. But then time had taught him it was only his pride which had been wounded. His feelings *had* merely been lust. He'd fallen in *lust* with numerous women since. Women whose names he could not even remember and whose faces had become a blur.

Katherine's feelings were probably just lust.

He tucked his shirt into the waistband of his trousers and then began tying his cravat.

But others cared for him: his mother, Mary, his stepfather. The error was in John. *Because I do not believe in the fanciful notion of poetry!* If "love" was real, his mother would have been there for the first ten years of his life! The crushing despondency which always came on the back of his recurring dream flooded in.

He reached for his waistcoat and put it on. It had not looked like lust in Katherine's eyes, though. Her eyes had shone like his mother's and his sister's did when they looked at him. Affection.

Yes, there was affection, like, regard.

She was dressed, he saw, when he turned about, lifting his coat to put it on.

She stood near the door, wearing the bonnet he'd bought, looking beautiful and utterly bereft.

He'd hurt her.

His arms slipped into his sleeves.

"I should not have come here."

That grasped hold of his attention.

"I am just amusement to you."

"You are not!" He crossed the room in an instant and gripped her hands, which hovered before her waist. "Truly, Katherine."

Then his hands lifted and braced against her cheeks. "I am touched that you have cared for me for so long. I cannot say the same to you. You know it would be a lie if I did. I did not notice you before, Katherine, but I have seen you now."

Her eyes held his, shining with questions she did not speak.

Did she want promises from him, declarations and vows he would never be able to speak? He wasn't that person. He did not know how to love. But he was willing to let her try and prove to him that it was real for her, that she felt for him what the poets spoke of. Did she know how to love?

"Will you meet me again tomorrow, Katherine, here, at the same hour?"

She nodded, but she looked as though she did not wish to.

Chapter Seven

John leant back in the armchair, his elbows resting on the arms. He had a glass of port balanced in one hand, and one ankle rested on the opposite knee.

The house was silent, and as there was no one here to care but himself, he'd lit a thin cigar.

He was sitting in the library, looking up at the life-size portrait of his grandfather, digesting the events of the day.

He could not fathom why his pragmatic, intolerant grandfather had kept a man like Wareham on all these years.

John drew on the cigar, let his head fall back, and blew the smoke upwards.

Wareham had left without a word of complaint, according to Finch. No one here knew why Wareham had gone. John had not even told Finch the details. It was no one's concern but his.

He'd written to Harvey the minute he'd returned from seeing Katherine, informing him Wareham had been dismissed, and asking Harvey to advise all the other stewards that Wareham had gone and to find a replacement.

John had a feeling he'd missed something, though. He sipped his port and his mind swung to childhood memories. Ghosts always haunted him at night here, just as they'd done in Egypt. But tonight he called them forward. He was so sure there was something he'd forgotten.

The problem with memories was that they came with the feelings which supported them. Feelings he was not allowed as a child but had had none the less: loneliness, isolation, emptiness and hurt.

He stared at his grandfather's image and took another drag on the cigar.

John had been intensely glad of his capacity to hide and bury his feelings today. *Perhaps I ought to thank you.*

He lifted his glass in a mocking toast.

Now he was in the old man's place, it seemed he was learning to understand the method behind the old man's madness.

Neither Wareham nor Katherine can have known quite how much they disturbed him.

It was a blessing.

But John pushed that thought aside, it was not what he wished to consider. He wanted to know what he was forgetting. There was something… it was on the very edge of his conscious thought.

Wareham had always hovered when John had reviewed the books in his youth, leaning over John's shoulder in an ominous, almost threatening, way. Wareham had never once left John alone, and when John had reached the end of each page, Wareham would check the lines John had written and total them.

"Bloody hell!"

John stood. He'd checked none of the totals.

He threw the remainder of the cigar into the empty hearth and put down his glass, then left the room.

The clever bastard.

Wareham had never once taught John to add up the columns or check the totals. He had not wanted John to consider them.

How long had Wareham's fraud been running? It was years ago that he'd shown John the books.

John's heart beat harder as he jogged upstairs. He was certain this was it.

In his private sitting room, he withdrew the key to his safe from his waistcoat pocket.

He had the ledgers on the desk in a moment and ran his finger down the first page, mentally calculating quickly. His count and the figure did not match. He checked it. It still did not.

Turning the page, he checked another total, no match, and the next, still no match. He looked at several and none of them tallied.

Oh my God. Wareham had been fleecing the old man for years. *The bastard.* The old man would be rolling in his grave.

The differences in the sums were miniscule, but add every page together, and times that by years, it must be hundreds, perhaps thousands.

John's fingers swept back his fallen fringe, and he remembered Katherine's fingers sweeping it back from his brow earlier as she'd said goodbye.

It was strange thinking of her. Why this moment? *And I have wanted you like this since I saw you swimming in the lake before you even went abroad.* Perhaps it was the thought of the length of time.

Wareham had secretly hated John all this time, while Katherine had secretly loved, or lusted, or whatever it was she felt.

John pushed the thought of her aside, and sat down to write another letter to Harvey, certain there must be copies of these ledgers somewhere. Wareham would have needed to keep track of how much he stole.

There must be an account somewhere, too, an account from which Wareham must have made the loan that had never been repaid.

Of course, he could not have asked Harvey to manage the issue of the defaulted loan when it had been made from stolen money. It must have been paid from his own account not the duke's.

Now all the detail slotted into place.

~

When Katherine entered the room at the top of the tower, John was sitting in the armchair. He'd already removed his coat, waist-coat and neckcloth.

"I thought you weren't coming," he charged. His eyes were like bright diamonds as he glared at her, and his fingers were toying with a long, jet-black rook's feather, twirling it in the air.

John said no more, clearly waiting for her to speak.

He was in an ill mood she could see, and his ill moods obvi-ously intensified his arrogant and spoilt nature. He didn't smile and there was no welcome in his eyes as there had been yesterday.

She had only come back because when he'd asked her to yesterday, and said that he had noticed her now, she had seen the old John in his eyes, the youth she'd tumbled head-over-heels in love with, and he'd looked vulnerable. Yet that vulnerability was hidden, buried deep beneath the stance he held now.

She undid the ribbons of her bonnet.

Yet vulnerability was probably the reason he was sulking over her lateness – and why his posture was like stone. He obviously did not like people seeing it.

He looked detached and austere as she faced him. She guessed he was not. He had become hollow and heartless, to her eyes. But her soul said he was lonely and sorrowful. This is just what life had made him while he'd been abroad.

He'd brought a bottle of wine. It stood open on the table, with a single glass beside it. He'd clearly been here long enough to have a drink.

She hadn't realised she was so late.

"My mother had errands she wished me to run." Katherine felt angry with herself for giving excuses. What did it matter? It was her choice to come or not. She was not a servant to be ordered to attend him at a given time.

She set her bonnet aside and removed her gloves.

"I see," he answered bitterly.

Oh, he was infuriating today.

She undid her spencer and slid it off, remembering him saying he hated it. It was that comment which had made her call him spoilt. Let him live her life and see how he felt about someone insulting the coat he wore each day. But of course that would never happen, his were cut and tailored on Savile Row, and he probably had three dozen.

"I thought you'd changed your mind, after yesterday."

It *was* vulnerability then. She looked back at him and tried to see it beneath his hard exterior. She could not. He was sliding the tip of the feather down one cheek and across his chin, watching her.

"Obviously not." If he was going to act like a child, she would treat him like one. "But you are sulking because I'm late."

"I'm not sulking. I do not sulk, Kate. If I wished to sulk, I would pay someone to sulk for me."

She poked her tongue out at him, knowing he was referring back to her accusation that he was spoilt. She put her spencer down, then crossed the room and bent to kiss his brow, smoothing back his hair. He still didn't move.

"May I have some wine?" she asked, drawing away.

"If you wish."

She did. She poured it for herself and said, with her back to him, "If you are not sulking, then you are angry with me."

"No."

"What are you then?" She turned back, gripping the full glass.

"Hungry for you. Take off your dress."

"A ducal command. How romantic." He was in such a strange mood today – studying her – uncommunicative. Had something happened which he was taking out on her? He genuinely seemed upset.

"I am not romantic. Do not expect it of me."

She had not. But she was not stripping on his whim.

She turned and looked out through the window, sipping her wine. The only house visible was Pembroke Place. The pale-stone Palladian mansion reminded her of how far apart their worlds were. It felt as though she was living in fiction. She could not really be here.

"So are you going to undress?" he asked, behind her.

Ignoring his petulant tone, and his order, she sipped her wine again.

"Do you still want me?" There was an odd note to his voice now, one that did sound like a child. His ducal shield was slipping.

She turned back and met his hard, judging gaze. "I was not late on purpose, John."

"No?"

"No." Indignant anger tightened like a knot in her chest. "I had things to do. My absence would have been noted if I had not done them first."

"Is it some lesson to me?"

"Of course it must be to do with you, it can be nothing to do with me, because everyone knows even the sun only circles the earth to pass about you." She sipped her wine and hoped the jab hurt him as he'd hurt her yesterday.

He had not taken his eyes off her, but nothing in his expression showed a response to her words. She had said it to make him angrier. She wished for some reaction from him. At least let him prove he was human.

She drank the last of her wine, set the glass down and went to him. Then she leant forward and kissed his lips, her fingers bracing her weight on his shoulders. He did not kiss her back.

She pulled away and still faced his chilly look, but behind it she knew there was insecurity and need, though she was sure he would never admit it openly.

She kissed him again and this time his hand came up and braced the back of her head as his lips opened and he kissed her in return. It was a stubborn and demanding kiss. It didn't matter, she had needs too, and they pulsed into life, exhilarated by the anticipation which clutched in her stomach.

When she ended the kiss because it was too awkward bending down, he said again, "Take off your dress."

She might be a bastard by birth but John Harding had become a bastard in nature.

However, she chose to comply, because beneath the skin of the duke was the young man she had adored, and *he* needed her. She began undoing her dress.

That young man had been kind and thoughtful towards her, as much of a brother as Phillip had been. This man, she didn't know. He was a stranger in John's body, really, and yet she knew the boy and the youth were within him. He needed her to help him find who he was again. This was not John.

The black feather still brushing his cheek, John watched her, feeling control slipping through his fingers like sand. She undid her buttons and then slid her arms free so her dress hung from her waist, before pushing it off over her petticoats. His heart pounded so loud he heard it in his ears.

"And the rest," he prompted, waving the feather in her direction, *because everyone knows even the sun only circles the earth to pass about you.* Her words had cut again. Why did she think him spoilt? He was not.

Once she'd undone the tapes of her petticoats they slid to the floor, and then she walked towards him and turned so he could help with her corset. His mouth dried at the defiant look he saw in her eyes. He liked her timidity, but he rather liked her in a defiant mood too. It made her blue eyes glow and her skin flush pinker.

He unlaced her in a trice and she needed no prompting to continue. She slipped off her chemise, baring her breasts before removing her underwear and revealing all. He'd seen her yesterday, yet today he still felt awed, and heat pulsed into his groin. She had long, slender limbs and her curves were beautifully slight, yet perfectly formed.

When he looked from her body back up to her face, she was watching him.

"Come here." The heat in his blood had warmed his voice.

She came and stood between his parted thighs.

He began playing with the feather he'd found where he'd left his horse, drawing circles on her tummy.

She shivered.

He brushed it across her hip, then down her outer thigh, before running it back up her inner thigh.

He saw her muscle jolt.

When he looked up, her eyes were closed, but then they opened and her hands cupped his cheeks so he could not look down again.

He did not cease his caresses but let the tip of the feather touch her intimately. The reaction on her face was shock, but then her body relaxed and she bit her lip.

She could hide nothing from him, this girl, she did not even try, and there was that fierce burning look of love in her eyes.

Katherine.

He ran the feather in and out between her legs, testing her. He had a desire to make her hate him today, to prove that love was wrong – to fail him, because he did not deserve to be loved. If love was what she truly felt.

He'd had the dream again last night.

He set out to torture her, and perhaps it was cruel, perhaps he was spoilt, but he didn't care. He'd thought she wasn't going to come and he'd not been able to bear the thought, and so it was better the truth was out and she let him down now rather than in the future.

"Touch me," she pleaded after a while, as he danced the very tip of the feather about the point where she was most sensitive.

He did not comply but carried on, holding her gaze with his eyes and her mind with his wicked game. Let her see how bad he was, let her know and then decide if she could love him.

He tormented her for a little longer, just to prove the point that he would not be told. If anyone was the master it would be him. But then he did a thing he knew would shock her virginal soul and used his mouth and tongue, bracing and kneading her buttocks while he pleasured her and himself, and her fingers clasped in demure shock clutching fistfuls of his hair.

He made her climax like that, teaching her just how base her passion could be, and she did so on a fractured cry, her muscle quaking in his hands.

Without words, he brought her down onto his lap, as they'd been seated yesterday, with her straddled across his groin, yet today she was naked and he clothed. He braced against her face and kissed her, deeply, devotedly, forgetting all his plans to make her hate him, *let her love me – let this be real*, it would be the only damned real thing he'd ever had in his life. Spoilt for things, he might be, but he had never been spoilt by love.

He touched her then and whispered, "Ride them," into her ear, he dare not undo his trousers, he did not quite trust himself today, if she was that close to him he might just be tempted to take it all.

She reached another peak like this, with a beautiful broken cry after many little gasps. She was a swift learner. As she'd rubbed against him she had not been doing it for his benefit but her own, and yet still it was nothing like the she-wolves he'd shared beds with abroad. She was so natural. There was no vicious hunger and hard edge.

But the climax was addictive, he more than anyone knew that, after he'd learned love was really only lust he had fed it with just as greedy selfishness as the women he'd hated. He'd had anyone he wished, if they'd said no initially, he'd cajoled and flattered until the answer became yes, and he'd slept with women daily, sometimes two in one day, sometimes two at once. Until he'd woken one morning and seen with bitter clarity how cold, shallow and empty his life was. Then he'd run to Egypt, to escape, seeking isolation and survival.

"You have not had your own release," she said, looking down at him flushed and panting, her small breasts wobbling.

She was not selfish. She was *selfless*.

He suddenly knew she had only come here to do this for him,

not for herself, she might enjoy the climax, she might even have raced to reach it today, but for her this was about him, not herself.

Was that love? Doing things for others had only ever been duty to him.

He kissed her hard, his hand in her hair. She was throwing him off his natural axis again today. His good intentions scattered to the wind, rising, he lifted her and turned so she was then sitting, or rather half-lying in the chair, naked legs about his waist as she slumped back, her back curved and hunched in a way which scrunched up her stomach. Her hands gripped the arms of the chair as he undid his trousers and then he set himself between the open flesh at the apex of her thighs. Her lips were as soft as petals damp with dew.

Something hard and firm gripped in his stomach and tightened in his chest and he felt excruciatingly desperate to baptise himself in her warmth. He did not. He had made her a promise, but his hands gripped the very tops of her thighs, his fingers clasping at the first curve of her buttocks, and he simply ravished her, working hard and fast towards his own end without deference for her need. *I am selfish.*

"I want you inside me," she whispered after a while, clearly enchanted by his onslaught, whether it was his intent or not. Her blue eyes glowed up at him, her pupils wide with lust, but even now, even now, the look was not hard-edged need, it was soft adoration.

"You do not," he answered, denying them both, but the words had come out with a sour note because it was what he wanted too, and he saw the pain hit her eyes in response. He gathered her up then and held her against him, this precious gift he'd found.

Her nude body was flush to his and her arms gripped about his neck, while his hands pressed against her shoulder and her back. He finished it thus, but not before she had come again as hot fluid over his groin.

"You would have regretted it, Katherine," he whispered afterwards as she clung to him and he brushed his fingers through her hair.

"I would not," she answered stubbornly against his shoulder, her muscles trembling.

"You would." Again his voice was cold, because his mind and body were reeling with emotion too hard to tame.

He stood and turned away to re-secure his clothes. Then picked up her underwear and threw it to her. "Get dressed."

God, it seemed he could not stop himself from casting orders and sounding cold, no matter that he no longer wished to push her away.

"You have two sides," Katherine said, without thought, as he threw her clothes at her as though she was dirty linen.

"Do I?" his answer was dismissive.

He was so cold most of the time, and yet when they'd done what they'd done she had seen that look again, deep in his eyes, the one which questioned life, and looked almost desperate. He'd looked afraid. "The Duke who shuts me out and John who lets me in."

"I am one person, the Duke and John, Katherine." He reached for his waistcoat then turned to look at her again. "And besides, I can say the same of you; shy church mouse, Miss Spencer, and passionate Katherine. You have barely blushed in this room when we have done indecent things, while outside it you colour up even when I look at you or speak."

He was stabbing at her, because she was daring to try and penetrate beneath his granite skin. She blushed. She felt it. He could be so cruel. Was he casting shame on her because she'd enjoyed what they'd done? If it was only her timidity he appreci-ated, he should not have asked her here. But then it couldn't be her beauty he was interested in. She was not beautiful compared to him. Perhaps he was only attracted to her because he'd known she would allow these things. Had his expectation been that only he should enjoy it and she should merely allow it?

Buttoning up his waistcoat, he said, "Get dressed, sweetheart."

It was in a warmer voice, but it seemed belittling to be ordered to undress and then dress.

"Now that you are done with me." She felt betrayed as she rose.

"Now that *you* are done with me." He reached for his cravat.

She *was* done with him. She was never doing this again. It obviously meant nothing to him. *It means everything to me.*

She dressed silently, as he did, turning her back to ask him to re-secure her lacing.

Once he'd done so, he leant his buttocks back against the table and poured himself a glass of wine as she put on her dress.

He was drinking from the glass she had drunk from; there felt something very spiritual in that.

He sighed behind her as she picked up her spencer. She turned to look at him, "Are you tired?" He looked tired; he looked worn out.

His gaze lifted and met hers. He had been looking into the wine but now his gaze shuttered, locking her out of his thoughts. "I had a late night."

She lifted her chin at his defiant, dismissive tone. "I am not going to hurt you, John, you do not have to push me away."

"Do I not, Kate?"

He was in such a strange mood, she could not understand him. "No, and you need not answer me with questions whenever I get close to the truth."

"Is that what I am doing?" He set down the glass and walked forward, then began securing her buttons.

She pushed his hands away and did them herself. She wanted to help him, but he was not letting her close enough to help.

"I cannot easily trust, Katherine, you do not understand, it is the nature—"

"You do not trust me? Yet you asked me here to do this and trust you."

"A duke cannot trust anyone, even family." His voice was impatient. He spoke as though she was too naïve to know.

Perhaps she was. She had been foolish enough to agree to this.

112

But she was not unintelligent. She was not the imbecile he implied. "You mean you *choose* not to trust anyone."

"I do not trust people for a reason, Kate. People associate with me for a purpose."

"And what purpose do I have, John? Or your family?"

He said nothing, merely looked at her, in his unapproachable *do-not-come-too-close-to-me* way.

She picked up her bonnet, the bonnet he had bought, and looked away, putting it on and tying the ribbons beneath her chin. She loved the bonnet, she had loved the gesture, it was a frivolous thing which she would never have been allowed to have, and never had the money to purchase. But had it only been a trade to secure her trust when he would not give his?

He spoke again then, his voice a little softer, as though he had been questioning himself. "I am different from the others in my family. I am different from everyone. My title sets me apart, yes, but in my family it is not *just* that. I am the eldest and the only one not of my stepfather, and I am so much older than the others I cannot be a part of them." He sounded as though he wished he was.

She understood that – she understood that more than anyone.

He sipped his wine but would not look at her. Perhaps he realised sometimes his vulnerability showed in his eyes and this was part of his lack of trust. It was an insult when she had trusted him completely and let him do indecent things.

"*I* am different, John." Her tone was indignant again. "I was born out of wedlock. My natural mother took her own life. The entire village are waiting for me to fall as my mother did. I do not even know who my father is. *I* have to fight against these things—"

"And I am spoilt. So you have said."

Belligerence. "*Yes. You are.* Especially if you think you must treat the world with mistrust and indifference."

He set the glass down and stared at her.

"I could wallow in misery, but I get on with my life, John. I am thankful I have a home and my father and Phillip. I chose a path to seek happiness. It seems you have chosen to wallow. Is that what you've done all those years abroad? You do not have my pity, John."

His face screwed up in a disgusted sudden frown, "I do not wish for it!"

"Good." Walking forward, she picked up the glass and took a sip to clear her dry throat then set it back and turned to leave. He grasped her wrist and turned her back, his pale eyes boring into hers.

"You would understand if you lived my life, Katherine. My grandfather spent a dozen years teaching me it would be like this. Like it or not, my position sets me apart from people."

She did understand. She knew what it was to be isolated and lonely. But that was not what he was pointing out to her now. He was saying everyone was below him. "Including me?"

"I did not say that."

"You said it earlier. You admitted I am a risk you are taking."

"What you are, Katherine, is a novelty, and one I am grateful for."

To me it is just love.

For the first time, she understood how risky this was for her.

She was going to be hurt. He was not.

His hand came up and braced against her nape and then he kissed her, gently at first, and then more forcefully, as though making a point that the only thing between them was this, kisses and physical attraction.

It was not what she had wished for with him; she had wished for a Cinderella story, even though it had been an empty hope. When she had longed for him, for all the years he'd been abroad and more, she had longed for love, not for this emotionally detached bodily bond between them.

It was not enough.

"I cannot meet you tomorrow, I shall be busy. But on Sunday I'll drive you home from church." It was not a request, as his invitation had been yesterday or the day before, it was an assumption.

Katherine's brow furrowed. "Reverend Barker drives me home, John."

"The vicar can go to hell. *I* am driving you."

"John…"

His fingers tightened at the back of her neck. "It is non-negotiable, Katherine. I will drive you home."

"And risk my reputation." She shook her head. Had she not just mentioned all the women who wished to see her fall? She had already fallen, but they need not know.

"Our connection is well known, people will not question it, and I will take a groom. But you are riding with me, not with him."

"I am not your servant to be ordered, John."

His intense gaze held hers, and then for an instant only she saw the full force of his true feelings. "Can I help it if I am jealous of the man?"

Her stomach flip-flopped with a sudden desperate longing, for love though, not lust. "You have nothing to be jealous of." Her fingers touched his cheek and a deep pain pierced her heart. He did need her, no matter how deep he sought to hide it. He needed someone who would fight through his armour.

"Don't I? He can give you what I cannot. He can offer you a future."

It was the first time he'd admitted they had none. She had known it. But it still hurt to hear it said.

"Are you tempted by him? Has he offered you marriage?" John felt his emotion like lacerations. She had been busy cutting him to shreds.

He was prideful and spoilt, lonely, childish, because he sulked, and weak because he chose to wallow in self-pity. Such a commendable assessment. But yet again it only proved she was not here to curry his favour. She was here because, for some strange reason, despite thinking so many ill things of him, *she cared*. Bizarre thought.

No, he did not trust her, not yet, but she was making him question his lack of trust, she was making him want to trust.

Why was she here when she thought him everything ill, and she had her perfect vicar to compare him to? He would swear she had not even kissed the saintly man.

John had no right to claim her. No right to do these things with her. Yet he could not stand the thought she might be another man's. He never wished to let her slip through his fingers. But how could he keep her when he could offer nothing more than this, not even trust.

"I am not having that conversation with you, John."

The fact that she did not answer him only made John more concerned. "Would you accept him, if he asked?"

"I don't know. I do not even know if he would ask."

God, he was in an acerbic mood today, but he could not help himself. It was due to having the dream last night and facing Wareham yesterday, and she had set him off balance with her harsh judgements. Yet no matter, he was not relinquishing her to the bloody vicar, even though he could offer her nothing himself.

"How long have you been courting?"

"Is this an interrogation, John?" Her voice sounded as though she had shifted from anger to exasperation. It was the thing he liked most about her; that she showed every emotion without care. It was so damned refreshing to speak to an honest woman. Then why did he not trust her?

Because caution had been bred and beaten into him as a child and later relearned in his youth, it was too instinctual, he no more knew how to trust than he knew how to love.

"If you must know, we are not courting. He is not even looking for a wife. He is just a friend." *And what she had with him was just sex.* The comparison hit John hard.

"Do you want to be his wife?"

"Stop this, John."

He sighed, then realised his fingers were running through his hair. Yes, then. If she would not answer, the answer must be yes.

He felt sick. He did not wish any other man to steal away this precious woman. No other man must find out about her secret passion, nor know her love – if it was love. He wanted her to keep it all for him.

He *was* selfish.

But he was not spoilt; all the most important things he'd wanted in his life he'd not had, and now she was added to that list.

He turned away to put his coat on, trying to get a grip on the obsession he felt for her. He felt angry and annoyed, and betrayed again. Could no woman hold by him? And yet his subconscious shouted that barely moments ago he had sought to push her away.

Her hands slipped about his midriff without warning, he had not heard her move, and then her cheek pressed to the back of his shoulder.

Ridiculously, he felt like weeping, and then he realised he had not shed a single tear over his grandfather's death, he'd barely mourned at all. But he wanted to cry over this woman, who'd been waiting here for him for a quarter of his life when he had not even known she was waiting. Not only was she passionate, selfless and giving, but she was also a survivor, as he was, and lonely, as he was. In so many ways they were the same, and yet in so many others they were entirely opposite and poles apart.

"You may drive me if it is so important to you," she whispered against his back.

He felt something warm and fluid in his chest. The emotion constricted his lungs and stole his breath.

He said nothing but let her hold him and let himself feel the reassurance she offered. This woman he'd assumed was a fragile English rose had more courage than him.

"If you wish it, Katherine," he said without turning.

His gaze looked outwards, across the land that was his. It stretched for miles. He had everything except what he most wished for, the ability to love this woman and make her his companion for life.

He was not spoilt.

"I wish it."

God alone knew why.

~

Loitering among the standing gravestones and crypts in the church-yard, suffering inane conversation, John waited on Katherine's appearance.

Her parents had already gone, as had half the village. The other half, it seemed, only stayed to indulge him.

John had initially waited beside the clergyman, with hands clasped behind his back so he would not be tempted to throttle the man. But then, those left had huddled into groups and drawn him into conversations.

He was not in the mood to talk. He was too distracted, and not only by thoughts of Katherine. Wareham had turned up. Late. To make an entrance. The whole congregation had turned when the door had opened to let him in. Then the whole congregation had turned to look at John. Clearly Wareham had made no secret of his dismissal.

John had ignored them and looked back to the front, very aware of Katherine talking quietly with the children in the small chapel at the side of the church.

When Wareham had left, he'd smiled at John, with hatred in his eyes.

The look reminded John of his grandfather. It was an image which was seared into his memory like a brand. His grandfather had given John's mother that look the day which was immortalised in John's recurring dream.

Of course, Wareham had had far more years to capture the old man's image than John. Yet despite Wareham's ability to hide his thoughts, John sensed Wareham had come to find out if his fraud had been discovered.

John had smiled back just as viciously, giving not a single hint of the answer. Let the man fret and squirm, John was not ready to move yet, he wanted more evidence to ensure Wareham could not claim that the incorrect totals were just errors.

However, after Wareham had walked away, John sent his grooms to follow, and to go and fetch others to watch Wareham once they knew where he was staying. John wanted to be able to find the man when the time came to make the charge. John trusted the grooms. He'd discovered Wareham was unpopular among the servants.

God, since his conversation with Katherine, John noticed each time he made a decision to trust.

The groom he'd asked to return was already back.

John sighed.

He longed to go into the church and drag Katherine out. He was bored of the obsequious company of local society, and her vicar.

When she finally did appear, though, John was a little shocked to face the paragon of virtue again.

Last time he'd seen her she'd allowed him indecent privileges, now she looked as pure as snow once more. It seemed she *was* capable of hiding her emotions when she wished.

She smiled at her vicar, before even looking at John. Contempt and envy filled him, only proving her poor assessments of him right. How had she got so beneath his skin?

He'd watched her during the service, moving behind the iron-work screen closing off the chancel chapel. She had grace, and she showed compassion and gentleness to the children.

Damn, he was so bloody intrigued and infatuated by her. She shone a light into the barren darkness inside him. If Egypt had been his arid desert, *she* was his oasis.

When she did turn to face him, he smiled and felt a lightning bolt of recognition. He knew her naked body.

His gaze swept over her. She wore the same tired blue dress she'd worn last week. God, when had he seen his sister, his mother or

119

his cousins wear a dress twice within a month? Never. No wonder she thought him spoilt.

"Your Grace." She dropped a formal curtsy.

God, he had forgotten she even should, he'd become so unaware of the difference in their status.

"Miss Spencer."

"I'm sorry I took so long."

"Are you, ready?"

She nodded.

He offered his arm.

When she laid her fingers on it, he felt a rush of overwhelming warmth as the ground rocked beneath his feet. It was a mix of gratitude, protectiveness and a deep-seated respect, which hit him like a fist to the stomach.

Behind her, her vicar said, "If you will wait a moment, Miss Spencer, I shall be free to run you home."

So the vicar played barely known among local society too. It only made John seethe with jealousy again. Her vicar had something to hide if he used her given name in private only. She may not know her vicar wanted her, but he did.

"There is no need, Reverend Barker," Katherine said. John knew she had felt his arm stiffen and sensed his anger. "His Grace has offered and I accepted."

That routed the bloody man.

The vicar's gaze turned to John.

John smiled, the stiff taut smile which had been his grandfather's. Let the good reverend know the truth, John was claiming his ground and he was never stepping back. *He* was not saintly.

"Excuse us," John said.

"Of course." What else could the man say? But then he looked at Katherine meaningfully, communicating concern. He and Katherine must be close if they spoke in looks. She must share her thoughts with him. John's envy hit him harder.

"I shall look forward to seeing you at Miss Jennifer's come-out then, Miss Spencer."

She nodded and bobbed a lesser curtsy for the vicar, blushing.

In a moment she was up in John's curricle beside him, her thigh pressing along the side of his, while one hand clung to the edge and the other held her reticule in her lap.

Behind them, John's groom perched on the step at the back, bracing himself by gripping the frame, as John flicked the ribbons again and lifted the animal's pace from a trot to a canter.

He felt a burning pride to have her up beside him and the vicar left behind.

She did not speak, nor did he, unsure of what to say with his groom in earshot, he was sensitive of making some *faux pas*. When they reached her home, he slowed the horses and steered them onto the crescent drive. Once he'd stopped, he jumped down at the same moment as his groom, who moved forwards to hold the animals while John walked about to the other side.

As he handed her down, he heard the door open behind him.

"Katherine?" It was her father. "If Reverend Barker was busy you should have spoken up, we would have waited."

Her fingers were still in John's hand when she turned to her father, but then she tugged them free.

"John offered, Papa."

"I am sure His Grace has better things to do, Kate. You should have said."

The censure in his voice struck John and he saw it hit Katherine too. She turned an exquisite pink and her gaze dropped suddenly to the level of her father's shoes.

"It was no trouble," John said, speaking up before her father could hurt her anymore. "I was coming past your door."

"We are hardly en route to Pembroke Place, Your Grace."

"True, but I am going to London, sir."

The man visibly bristled. Apparently her father was as suspicious as her vicar. He had been so the other day but John had soothed things with a little flattery. Katherine had accused him of

121

manipulating people that day. He could, he'd learned that power from his grandfather too. John merely gave people what they longed for, his attention. He was about to try the trick again but Katherine turned to him.

"You are going to town, today?"

He had intended telling her when they'd walked to the door. Her father had stolen that opportunity. But John needed to speak to Harvey and sort out this mess Wareham had created.

"I will be back on Wednesday, for your sister's celebration."

Her eyes were shimmering as she looked at him, full of uncertainty again.

"Go indoors, Katherine," her father said.

Damn, had her father seen her lost look? Had she given them away?

She sent John a quick, swift apologetic smile full of insecurity, the Katherine he had met in town again, before bobbing a curtsy. "Your Grace. Thank you for driving me home," she added more quietly.

"You're welcome."

She was gone in an instant.

He felt her loss as though the sun had dropped beyond the horizon as it did in Egypt.

"May I speak with you privately." Her father's words sent a chill running down John's spine. He nodded, and then followed the man inside. Katherine had already disappeared.

There was a sense of the absurd in this moment. Katherine's father was a meaningless nothing of a man in John's world and John was at least three inches taller than Mr Spencer. Yet he was treating John like a schoolboy about to get a scolding. John felt like laughing. Spencer could never stand against John if it came down to a battle of wills.

He was led into Spencer's study and the door was shut behind him.

"I am no fool, Your Grace," her father opened, standing before the window.

John stared at him.

"You may leave my daughter alone after today. I do not wish to see you speaking with her privately nor showing her particular attention. You will leave her be, do you understand."

An order. The foolish man. John did not like be told what he could and could not do. He was more likely to do anything he was asked not to. Yet speaking against him took courage, and John gave Spencer a grudging respect, even though John would not back down. "You of all people, sir, are aware of my longstanding connection with Katherine. She values my friendship and I hers."

"And do you take advantage of that friendship, Your Grace?"

There was bitter challenge in Spencer's voice. *He knew.* Yet John denied it. "No." *Yes.* His internal admission brought guilt.

"My daughter is judged enough for her birth, Your Grace. She does not need vultures circling over her to add to her pain. If you have any conscience, cease preying on her and leave her be."

"I would not hurt her," John answered instinctively.

"Then is it marriage you are thinking of?"

A painful fist seemed to clench John's heart, winding him and preventing him from answer. Of course it was not marriage. She could never be his wife.

"I thought not," Spencer answered, looking at John as though *he* was carrion. "Then I ask again. Please leave my daughter alone."

No. He was not letting her go, her father and her vicar be damned. "If Katherine wishes for my friendship, sir, she shall have it." His answer was bitter with defiance. Then John turned away.

"Then you are not welcome in my home." Her father clipped out behind him.

John smiled, a vicious smile, and looked back, feeling his grandfather's monster roar inside him. "As you wish."

Chapter Eight

Katherine looked at the door of the assembly rooms for the umpteenth time. Neither Phillip nor John had arrived. Her mother, father and sister had stopped receiving guests an hour ago and the clock on the mantle said it was already nearly ten.

Gentlemen and their town hours. She felt an internal smile.

But, oh, where were they?

She had been on tenterhooks all day thinking about seeing John again, and Phillip too. She was looking forward to seeing her brother as much as John.

Yet it was John she longed for.

She glanced at the clock and then the door again. She'd missed him dreadfully. She'd not even realised how precious those hours with him had been until he'd gone. He had left a gaping hole in her life and in her chest.

She was standing to one side of the room, alone, a little apart from everyone else, playing wallflower. Her fingers were clasped at her waist to stop them shaking.

Her mother was excluding Katherine as usual, ignoring her presence whenever possible. Currently, she and Jenny were with Mrs Ellis and her daughters, across the room.

At least, earlier, when people had been dancing, Katherine's omission had been less obvious, but now the music had ceased and supper was being served, and she had no friends to sit with.

"Katherine? Shall we sit together?" Except Richard.

She turned to him with a broad smile, thanking heaven for his rescue. He had been talking with the Dawkins, another family her mother did not approve Katherine speaking to, and so she had not dared join him.

Reverend Barker had always been kind to her since his arrival. She knew that riled her mother too, but Richard was one of the few who dared to ignore her mother's disparaging words. Everyone else in the village gave the Spencer's little orphan a wide berth in case the baseness of her origin might be infectious. Richard had never believed it and he'd told her bluntly early on, she was to ignore her mother's cutting words. "God does not judge any child by its parents' sins," he'd said.

Oh, how wrong he was. She had proved her mother right now. She had given herself to John in a way she should not have done and she had enjoyed every moment of it. She *was* like her natural mother.

When her gaze met Richard's she felt her smile fall, as guilt struck. Her actions had let him down. "Thank you, Richard."

Despite her denial to John, Richard probably did like her as more than a friend. He'd never given any verbal indication, though, but sometimes there was an appreciative look in his eyes, a look she had seen before in others' eyes, when a man was building up towards an offer.

When she'd seen it before, she'd actively discouraged them. John had always occupied her heart. But Richard's kindness seduced her soul a little, and at one point she had seriously thought that if he asked she might say yes. But how could she now? She could never evict John from her heart.

Richard seated her at a table in the corner and then went to fill them both a plate. Yet his expression was stiff and serious when he returned. "The Duke of Pembroke and your brother have arrived."

"Oh," she felt instantly ashamed that for all his kindness she wished to leave him and go to John. Why had they come, now, when she was already seated?

She looked over her shoulder and saw John being greeted by her mother and Lady Ellis. Then Mrs Bishop, Miss Elizabeth, the Listers, the Dawkins and others all moved forward for introductions.

She remembered his complaints about people pressuring him and toadying. She stayed where she was. Her mother would not wish her there anyway.

Katherine turned back and faced Richard's intuitive eyes. "I shall wait and greet them later, my mother will only be angry if I interfere. His Grace has more important people to greet than me."

"And yet I have seen him single you out twice at church."

She knew she coloured up.

"Why do you think that is, Katherine?" the question was spoken with implication and her pulse suddenly raced, but she refused to drop her gaze and admit her guilt. Perhaps she was learning things from John, how to be brash and bold for a start, when she did not feel it.

"I have known him since I was a child, Richard. He is a friend."

"A friend? Can a man in his position be your friend, Katherine? Have you heard that he laid Mr Wareham off without any explanation?"

She had not heard. "When?" Mr Wareham had been at Pembroke Place for as long as she could remember. Even her mother looked upon him with respect. People treated him like a lord because he managed such a large estate. Why would John have dismissed him?

"A week ago."

When she had been meeting John.

Why had he not said?

"Do not trust him, Katherine. A man in his position would not align himself with the adopted daughter of a local squire?"

She felt cut. It was cruel of Richard to point out how unworthy she was of John. He was implying her chastity was at risk, but

John had preserved it. "He is Phillip's friend. He is merely being kind. You need not be concerned."

"I hope that you are right."

Was she arguing with Richard? The most placid and considerate man she had ever known. She *was* becoming more like John.

They fell into silence and ate, but when John and Phillip arrived at their table a quarter-hour later, Richard glanced at her meaningfully, as if suggesting John had sought her out.

She and Richard stood, but Richard did not stay, he gave John a curt bow and then walked away.

She knew her cheeks were pink when she met John's gaze. "I thought you weren't coming," she said breathlessly.

Both men carried plates and John waved her to sit down again while Phillip drew up a third chair.

"Our business took a little longer than expected today," John answered as he sat.

"But then John gave me a lift home. His curricle is much faster than mine," her brother added.

John had not said he'd gone to London to see Phillip.

"Why did you not sit with Mama or Jenny, or at least Papa?" Phillip asked, before he took a bite of a pastry.

She smiled at him, feeling overwhelmingly glad to see them both. She felt as she'd done as a child when they came home from school or college – visible and human. "You know very well why not, she does not wish me anywhere near her."

"That is absurd." John's expression showed rare emotion, shock and disbelief.

"That is my mother," Katherine responded, her smile dropping, but she was not bitter. This was her life, she knew nothing else. "What business did you have in town?"

"Nothing of any importance," John answered, dismissively.

"Merely some issue John has asked me to help resolve," Phillip added.

She was surprised by the camaraderie flowing between them.

"Are you sure it is business that made you late, and nothing to do with avoiding the number of times you shall have to dance." She smiled again, teasing Phillip.

"You wound me, would I be so calculating?"

"Yes."

"You know me too well, Kate." He gave her a fond smile.

She loved her brother. He was the reason she was so untroubled by her lot in life, he'd always been there to cheer her up. "Well, you shall have to make up for it after supper. Mama will be throwing every eligible woman your way."

"But I shall dance the first with you."

Her smile lifted, and it came from a warm glow in her heart as she reached out and captured his hand to say thank you.

When she let go, he turned and looked at John. "See what a blessing it is to be in mourning. No one can throw the women at you."

When Katherine looked at John too, his eyes were on her, crystalline and bright. "Yet I shall regret not being able to take Katherine onto the floor."

There was a hard edge to his words which made Phillip look askance. But then Phillip turned and smiled at her, appearing to dismiss the undercurrent as being John's now-natural coldness, and began bantering with her again.

John watched their interaction with captivated amusement.

Katherine was different again with her brother. She smiled and laughed in a way he had not seen her do before, her eyes shining.

Heavens, he had missed her. He'd missed her glowing honesty. He'd been reminded in town of just how precious she was when he'd faced the ennui of the women of his class. She had permeated his hard exterior as no other woman ever had.

He'd not appreciated seeing her seated beside her vicar though.

She was the first person he had seen when he walked through the door, even though her back had been to him, and the instant he'd seen her, a desire to cleave the other man in two had roared through John's head.

The sound of instruments being tuned stretched from the hall next door.

"Phillip!" Phillip's mother's voice rose behind them.

"Damn," Phillip said, throwing a conspiratorial, amused look at Katherine.

She smiled in return, sharing a private joke.

"My summons, I'm afraid," Phillip said apologetically, glancing at John. Then he looked at his sister and shrugged his shoulders. "Sorry, you shall have to take second place again."

She nodded, smiling still.

But when Phillip turned, John saw pain touch her eyes and her smile fell a notch.

"She will make him lead Jennifer out first," Katherine said, answering a question John had not yet asked.

My daughter is judged enough for her birth... She does not need vultures circling over her to add to her pain. Her father's warning replayed in John's mind. He'd heard the same words over and over for the last three days.

But he refused to believe he'd hurt her. He had taught her a few things she ought not know, but they could cause her no lasting harm.

"Richard said you have dismissed Mr Wareham."

John's gaze focused. So her vicar had been telling tales. "Yes. Although I cannot see why that is your vicar's concern."

"People talk, John. Why did you dismiss him?"

"And that is none of your concern." He had no intention of involving Katherine in his dispute with Wareham, and John did not wish to even think of that tonight. He'd spent three days in London with Phillip and Harvey seeking further evidence, and today he'd interviewed potential replacements. Tonight he wished to concentrate on her.

"How will you replace him? He was there for years."

"I'm sure you are not really interested, Katherine. Tell me why your mother is excluding you, have you fallen out?"

She bit her lip, but then laughed, as though it was a foolish question.

He noticed she wore no jewellery, not even a pretty ornament in her hair. She did not even wear flowers. Her dress was pale pink and again it looked as though it had been owned and worn for years, and before he'd gone abroad he remembered her always wearing the same outdated scarlet cloak. He looked over at Jenny, she'd taken Phillip's arm across the room and she laughed at some comment.

Phillip must be teasing her in the same way he had teased Katherine. But the difference between the sisters shouted itself across the room. Jenny had a string of glossy pearls about her neck, and her hair had been curled and coiffed and decorated with small pale-yellow rosebuds and sparkled with what looked like a small diamond comb. Katherine's hair was scraped back in a chignon she had clearly secured herself. John had seen her do it in the tower room.

Equally, there was a difference in attire. Katherine's dress was old and plain muslin. Jenny's was a luscious striped yellow-and-cream silk and obviously new.

Katherine smiled as he looked back at her.

John smiled in return, feeling thrown off balance again.

He thought of her gazing longingly into the milliner's window in Maidstone, looking at the bonnet he had later bought. Her mother and her sister had been shopping inside while she'd carried parcels. He remembered looking at the portraits in her parents' parlour. There had been none of Katherine.

What of that foul old spencer she wore every day and her tired kid leather gloves, when most women wore lace ones in the summer?

She was Phillip's sister, but she was *not* Phillip's sister. John had always known she was adopted, everyone knew it. But why on earth would the Spencers adopt her only to treat her with disdain? *She does not need vultures circling over her to add to her pain...* Her father knew the distinction between the sisters hurt her, yet he allowed it.

"Why?" John asked without explanation, but she clearly understood.

"Why does the sun rise and set. I am base-born, John. I am the daughter of a milkmaid." He had known that, but he had never heard her say it before, and suddenly just how low her birth was hit him. "I am an embarrassment to her."

"Then why did she take you in?" He felt angry on her behalf. How could anybody wish to hurt her?

She shrugged, as though it was a question she had asked herself all her life and never found the answer to. Perhaps it was. He, more than anyone, knew about questions like that.

"Do not say anything to Phillip," she whispered suddenly.

"How can he not know? Does he not have eyes?"

"He knows she does not treat me the same, but Mama is not so bad when he is there because he would speak up for me and she does not wish to lose his affection, and I will not destroy his closeness with her. He may jest, but he loves her. She is his mother."

"While you are ignored."

"I am fed and clothed, John, and I have a father and brother who love me and even Mama does not ill-treat me, not really. She does not beat me."

"Just ignores you, or treats you like a servant." He was appalled.

"Come on." Standing, he held out his arm.

She did not rise.

"I said come on," he repeated, knowing there was a thread of steel in his voice. "She can hardly deny me, and I am not going to let any of them continue cutting you, Katherine."

"John, I cannot."

"You can and you will. Get up, and that is an order."

She rose.

"Right, to whom shall I introduce you first? Lord and Lady Ellis. Let us start with the most toplofty of our neighbours and work our way down."

"My mother will be furious," she whispered, but he heard the note of laughter in her voice. Perhaps she would judge him a little less harshly after this. Sometimes power and influence paid off, and sometimes he was not selfish.

An hour later, occupying a chair in the refreshment room, which faced the archway into the assembly hall, John watched the dancing while he played cards. Or rather he watched Katherine dance.

He'd frequently heard her trill laugh and every time he looked up she was smiling.

All the sons of local society had stepped up to the mark since he had done the pretty and made the introductions, and he had done them with ruthless insistence, calling her a particularly close friend from his childhood whom he was shocked to discover no one knew. He had implied in both voice and stance that if anyone continued cutting her he would cut them.

After each introduction he had remained for fifteen minutes, managing the conversation by asking Katherine questions and ensuring their neighbours engaged. Her mother would never get away with treating her badly in public again, he had ended that, and the girl was having the time of her life. He did not even begrudge watching her dance with others, including her vicar. She shone with a beauty brighter than her sister's, no matter that she wore no jewels.

"Thank you," Phillip said, drawing John's attention back to the table.

"For what?"

"For getting Kate accepted. I've not seen her smile so much for years."

"I have never been able to abide snobbery," John answered, looking at his cards. Then he selected one and laid it against Phillip.

"Still, you had no need to do it."

John met Phillip's gaze.

In London, John had found himself becoming less affected by Phillip. They'd met twice in the last two days, to discuss business and obviously travelled back together. Phillip was like his sister, he hid nothing of himself.

"No, but how could I sit here and not. They will never dare snub her again now my favour relies on it."

Phillip laughed, retrieving John's discarded card and then looking at his own. "What it is to have the power of a duke…" He'd been like this at school, full of satiric humour. John had never been conscious of the difference in their standing then. But now…"I believe the cliché you missed was in your pocket and that I am not, Phillip."

"Which is why I did not say it," Phillip grinned, tossing a card on the table, before looking at Katherine himself. "I think there is a chance she might say yes to the reverend."

John followed Phillip's gaze. She was certainly smiling warmly at the man as they promenaded during a country dance. John's green devil stirred.

"I have never seen her form such an attachment before," Phillip said. "He has been solicitous towards her for months. If he asks her to marry him, I hope she says yes. Her life would be so much better if she was not tied to the history of her birth."

John's eyes narrowed. "Do you know more of it?" It had sounded as though Phillip did.

"No more than you."

John would swear Phillip was lying. He knew more. But John could hardly press. What business should it be of his? *My daughter is judged enough for her birth… She does not need vultures circling over her to add to her pain.*

A pang of guilt struck John and he looked back at Katherine as he reached to take a card from the pile between him and Phillip.

She looked younger when she danced and smiled.

He should leave her alone.

I should never have touched her. The yell of conscience rang in his thoughts. She should belong to her vicar. John had no place playing with this woman's life. He had no right to be jealous, yet he was. She was the only one who could see inside him and had the courage to challenge him. She was the only woman who had cared what he was and, in answer, when he had nothing to give her in return, he'd stolen her innocence. *My God, John Harding, what have you become?*

He would leave her to her vicar. He must. He could be selfless too.

He laughed.

Phillip looked at him but John ignored it.

He was not like his grandfather, not yet. He would let her go, no matter how much it cut him with envy, it was the right thing to do.

John threw away the card he'd picked up.

The decision sickened him, and he felt bereft already, but it was the right one.

"Phillip." They both looked up as Katherine approached. "You have not danced with me once. You cannot evade me any longer."

Her expression was bright and happy. Phillip stood and threw his hand of cards onto the table. "I was one away."

John smiled. "Then you win. Enjoy your dance."

As they walked away John had a sudden idea, and as soon as it came into his mind it germinated like a planted seed.

His grandfather had always had a celebration at the end of the harvest before returning to town. It would not look at all odd.

Katherine had never even seen inside John's home, and now he understood why he was going to change that.

It would be his last indulgence as far as she was concerned. He would ask his family down. His mother could plan it and Katherine could come and solidify her new standing in this community.

Then that would be an end to it and John would return to town.

~

"Have you seen this?" Phillip walked into the drawing room, waving a card in his hand, which he gripped between his index and forefingers.

"What is it?" Jenny asked, as both Jenny and Katherine looked up.

Jenny had been reading, while Katherine was darning a pair of her father's stockings.

"An invitation, that is what, for a week Friday, from Pembroke Place."

"From John?" Katherine stood, feeling her insides tumble to her feet. She had heard nothing from him since Jenny's ball and she could not understand why when he'd been so solicitous there. She feared he had finally seen how wide the chasm between them was. He'd seemed shocked by her exclusion.

She'd been equally stunned to see how easily he filled his grandfather's shoes. He had manipulated both conversation and people to bring her to the fore. She was in awe of him all over again, and since the ball all her thoughts had centred on the aristocratic, authoritative and attractive duke, not memories of John Harding.

"Patience," Phillip stated, laughing at her and pulling the card away when she tried to reach for it.

"Is it a ball?" Jenny questioned excitedly, on her feet too.

"It would not be a ball," Katherine looked back at her sister, "he is still in mourning."

"No, but it is a dinner party," Phillip smiled, "and we are all invited, along with half of local society mind you, so do not think yourselves particularly favoured."

Phillip let Jenny take the invitation and looked at Kate. "His family will all be there, Eleanor and Margaret too. You shall be mixing with a quarter of the House of Lords again."

Katherine's smile fell. "I shall not. I cannot go." Her words were spoken in a bitter whisper so Jenny would not hear. "I have nothing to wear."

"How exciting!" Jenny cried, beside them, "He has a dozen

135

eligible cousins too, doesn't he? Oh, I am going to tell Mama."

Phillip gave Jenny a tolerant, adoring look as she left the room, but when he looked back at Katherine there was concern in his eyes. "He will take it as an insult if you are not there, Kate."

"Then do you have the money to buy me a dress?" she said cruelly. It was entirely out of character for her to be petulant, and yet this was not fair. How could she stay at home when everyone else went to see John?

"You know I do not." His voice said he wished he did. "Wear the dress you wore at Jenny's party."

"This is not a local assembly, Phillip, I cannot wear a dress which is little more than a day gown. I would stand out as ridiculous." Tears burned in her eyes.

He held her gaze but clearly did not know what to say.

She could not remember ever getting angry with him before, nor begging for anything, nor even crying over things she lacked. Yet she refused to stand among John's family and look so horribly out of place. She could never bear such embarrassment.

She sat back down and covered her face as the tears overflowed.

"Kate?" Phillip had squatted down beside her, and his palm settled on her shoulder.

"I cannot go," she said into her hands, in bitter complaint.

"Kate, I am sure John's family will not care what you wear, and everyone else knows how things stand anyway."

"And you think that makes it better," she said, looking up, flashing anger at him when it was not his fault. "I care!" In the hall she could hear Jenny's excited outpouring of enthusiasm as she told their mother.

"If I could buy you a dress I would."

She hugged him, her arms about his neck, but cried again.

He held her in return, hesitantly, as though unsure of what to do.

She had never been like this before.

When she heard Jenny returning with their mother, she pulled away and wiped the tears from her face. Forcing herself to stop being so silly. This was her life. She could not reorder it, merely live it, and she had always done that well enough before. She must *not* feel sorry for herself.

"I'm sorry," she whispered to Phillip, forcing a smile before they came in. "I know you do your best to help me. I am just having a selfish moment, that is all. It hardly matters, it is just one party."

Phillip's eyebrows lifted. "People do not cry over things which hardly matter, Katherine."

"I'm just tired," she answered dismissively, rising. He stood too. "When you see John, please tell him I am sorry I cannot come."

"Katherine, just go, let people think what they like about your dress."

She shook her head. She could not appear so insignificant before John. The embarrassment would be a physical pain when she knew what she had let him do to her.

~

"Miss Katherine?" Hetty appeared with a light scratch on Katherine's chamber door. "There's another parcel come for you, Miss."

Katherine looked up. She had retreated to her room to escape the excitement which still raged downstairs. Jenny had talked of nothing but John's party since this morning.

"Hetty?" Katherine saw a large flat box in her hands.

The girl bobbed a curtsy.

"Who sent it?" Katherine stood and then crossed the room, feeling both shocked and anxious.

"They did not say, Miss. It came from the dressmakers in Maidstone."

An ice-cold chill raced through her veins. He would not have done this? But she took the box and pulled the string loose, before setting it on the bed. When she lifted the lid, there was another knock on the open door.

Phillip stepped in as she looked back.

"I was going to drive over to John's and I... What's that?"

"I don't know yet," she turned back to the parcel and tipped the lid on to the bed.

Phillip looked over her shoulder when she lifted the tissue paper.

She glimpsed bright-blue satin, and then saw an expanse of glossy, shimmering fabric. "Gracious, it's beautiful," she whispered as she touched it.

John had picked the colour to match her eyes.

She lifted it a little and saw that the skirt sparkled with little glass beads, but the dress was not flamboyant, it was simply cut. She would blend in without appearing to overstate her position in society. *Oh John.* He should not have done this, and yet she loved him still more for knowing she'd need a dress to accept his invitation.

Phillip touched the fabric too, and then he picked up the card which lay in the box. "It is from Eleanor. She says it is a gift to ensure you will have no excuse not to come to John's gathering. She used the Maidstone dressmaker because the woman had your measurements."

He let Katherine have the card, smiling. "I take it you will be going now."

Katherine felt herself glow with happiness. "Yes."

"Good girl. Now put your bonnet on and we'll drive over to John's and accept."

"Really?" She felt breathless at the prospect of seeing John. She knew the dress was from him, not Eleanor.

"Yes, really. Hurry then."

She laid the dress back in its box, carefully. It was the most precious thing she had ever owned. "I won't be long."

Phillip left the room with Hetty, but as Katherine hurried to put on her spencer and a bonnet, she heard a cry from downstairs.

"A dress!"

Katherine's heart beat harder, as she swiftly tied the ribbons of her bonnet.

"From where?"

Oh, why must her mother always spoil everything.

"It is a gift," Katherine heard Phillip say as she rushed out into the hall.

"From whom?" The voice was her father's now, and Katherine saw them all gathered in the hall as she came downstairs. Jenny was there too, hovering beside their mother.

"From Eleanor, Papa," Katherine said, still walking downstairs. "She knew I would have nothing to wear to John's party."

"From Eleanor?" her father repeated doubtfully.

"Yes, Papa." He had good reason to doubt, she knew it was not from Eleanor.

"I read the card," Phillip stated. "I think it kind of her."

"To make Katherine a charity case," their mother bit back.

"To give her less-fortunate friend a gift," Phillip replied.

Please, do not make me send it back. If they did, Katherine might die. She wanted to go to John's party.

Her father was staring at her, a question in his eyes.

"I think it kind of her too," Jenny said suddenly.

Katherine looked at her, it was probably the nicest thing Jenny had ever said, and catching Katherine entirely off guard, Jenny rushed to hug her when she stepped off the bottom step. "I am glad you shall have a pretty dress."

"Thank you," Katherine said, uncertain what to do, waiting on the condemnation of their mother. If she insisted Katherine send it back, it would go back.

Her mother's eyes glowed with malice, but there was doubt there too. After John had so publically taken up Katherine's cause last week perhaps her mother feared offending him.

"You may keep it," she announced, in imperious judgement. "You must write and thank the Countess."

"Thank you," Katherine breathed, wishing to hug her mother for the first time in her life

"May I see it," Jennifer asked, her face glowing with excitement.

"Kate and I were just going out, Jenny," Phillip said. "We shall be back for dinner, Mama. We are going to Pembroke Place to accept our invitations."

"Can I come?" Jenny asked.

But at the same moment Katherine's father said in a savage voice, "Katherine has no need to go. Go alone, the girls should stay here."

Oh why must there be family disputes today? Katherine wanted to feel happy.

"Kate wishes to come, Papa. John is her friend also. And you may come if you wish, Jenny, but you shall have to squeeze into my curricle." He looked back at their father. "I cannot see why you question it."

"I question it, Phillip, because is it not odd for a duke to pursue a friendship with Kate?"

She felt struck. He may as well have slapped her, and she could see Phillip was equally shocked. Her father was usually the one to support her.

"Go and get ready, Jenny," Phillip said. Then he looked at their father. "Let us speak in the study." He'd said it to take the conversation out of her hearing, but Katherine heard it through the door anyway as her mother walked away.

"Do not judge him by yourself, Papa. John has known Kate years. He is merely being kind. He saw how things were last week and he changed them; something you have never done."

"And why should he have done that?" She heard her father answer. "He is singling her out. He is not just being kind, Phillip." *Her father knew what she had done.* She hoped Phillip never did. There would be no one who loved her then.

~

Katherine was nervous when Phillip drew his curricle to a halt before Pembroke Place. She had never been inside and she was feeling vulnerable after her father's tirade.

Half a dozen grooms raced forward to greet them and one of them handed her down before turning to help Jenny.

Katherine's heart thumped.

Phillip offered them an arm each to walk in.

There was a row of broad, shallow, pale-yellow stone steps ascending to the portico of the Palladian mansion, and four giant columns rose upwards. Her eyes followed them and saw palm leaves carved at the top. While the triangular stone decorating the head of the portico bore roundels of some sort of sculpted flowers.

It was overwhelmingly grand.

Her heart beat even harder.

Her father had a point, he really did, what on earth could John want with a woman who had come from nothing when he had all of this?

"Is the Duke at home, Mr Finch?" It was the same man who'd let Phillip in, in London, who opened the door.

"His Grace is, Master Spencer, will you wait in the hall a moment."

It was huge and Katherine saw Jenny's eyes were just as wide as hers felt. Jenny had never been here before either.

It was lined in a mottled beige marble, the whole thing, on the floor and rising in columns, with fireplaces at either side of the room. And it stood two storeys high, flooded with light from two long windows which reached the height of the room either side of the door. Above the door was another window, but the other walls were decorated with paintings of nymphs and gods, and on the ceiling above was a massive circular painting of all the gods of Olympus reclining on their clouds.

She could not believe the audacity she had to even come here.

Phillip removed his gloves and his hat, so Katherine did the same, as did Jenny, passing all their outdoor articles to a footman.

"If you will follow me." Looking up, she saw the butler had reappeared.

They were led through doors at the back of the hall to a room beyond which contained the most beautiful staircase she had ever seen. It was pale carved stone, like the house, and it seemed to hang in the air as it climbed upwards about the square walls. The banister struts were glossy metal with elements of gilding and the rail was polished mahogany. She was truly awed as they climbed, surrounded by stunning pictures of foreign lands. She spotted images of Venice and Rome.

It is another world.

At the top of the stairs, the butler carried on along a hall lined with busts and portraits. She presumed them John's ancestors, but there were artefacts from foreign lands too.

Then they stopped before a carved wooden door.

The butler opened it and stepped inside, leaving them outside unseen.

"Master Spencer, Miss Spencer and Miss Jennifer Spencer, Your Grace." Katherine watched the man bow deeply but then he stepped aside.

As they entered, Katherine's eyes spun about the room.

John was not alone. It was full of people. His family were already here.

"Kate! How wonderful!" It was Mary who shouted and rose. Then she rushed across the room.

Behind Mary, Katherine saw John rise too.

He moved to welcome Phillip, as Mary took Katherine's hands. "Oh it is so lovely to see you."

Katherine curtsied blindly, as Mary then turned to Jenny and introduced herself. Katherine took over and formally gave Jennifer's name.

John's stepfather had risen and greeted Phillip.

John's grandmother and mother were also among the group.

Katherine and Jennifer bobbed curtsies at them all.

Oh, Katherine felt such an interloper here, as though she had been deceiving them and trying to steal John.

Several of the younger children were in the room too; some were sitting around one table playing a card game and others were lying on the floor about a wooden ark with numerous painted animals. It was a family scene that would never have been portrayed in Katherine's home.

Katherine looked sideways at John and found him looking at her but she had no idea what he was thinking; his gaze was completely masked. She was thrilled to see him though.

"We thought we would come in person and accept your invitation…" Phillip was saying.

"Oh I am so glad you did," Mary extolled, as John held Katherine's gaze a moment more. "Mama and Grandmamma are managing it all."

I love you, Katherine thought the moment before John turned away, and she longed for him to know.

Having said something to Mary in response, and then Jenny, John came to Katherine and took her hand. Her heart beat wildly and she felt herself flush pink as she lowered in a deep formal curtsy, incredibly aware of his light hold on her fingers.

"You are coming I hope, Katherine," he said as she rose. "Did you receive Eleanor's gift?"

It was from him, she *knew* it was from him. She nodded, "She is very kind. I am grateful. You must tell her thank you."

"I shall, and I know she will be very pleased you like it."

"I love it," she answered.

He smiled and it warmed her soul right down to her toes.

He turned to speak to Jenny again, who his stepfather was also talking to. Mary grasped Katherine's arm and led her to a sofa, where they both then perched amidst his family.

Katherine felt like a fraud as she acknowledged John's grandmother, the Duchess, and sick, as she smiled at his mother too. But they spoke to Katherine pleasantly with no reproach for her status.

"Is Eleanor here?" Katherine asked of Mary when the conversation fractured into pockets about the room.

"Not yet." Mary smiled. "She and the others are coming to stay the day before the dinner. Everyone is coming, and I know we are not to be exuberant because we are still in half-mourning, but even so I am excited. It will be the most fun I have had in an age. And Grandmamma approves wholeheartedly. She…"

Katherine did not listen beyond hearing Eleanor was not here. How had he engineered the card from her when she was not here?

Katherine looked at him. He was looking at her. He smiled. She smiled back before looking away, longing to speak to him privately.

"…And I am trying to persuade John to at least let us dance after dinner, after all we are only in half-mourning."

There was to be dancing then as well as dinner.

"Where would you like the refreshments served, Your Grace?" the butler asked of the Duchess.

"We shall take them on the terrace, I think, Finch," she said, rising, "as it is a nice day. So the children might play. And we shall have lemonade for them and tea for us."

"That's a lovely idea, Mama." John's mother stood too.

Mary rose also and began rounding up the younger children.

There was suddenly a mass of motion and noise as the children excitedly packed up their games.

"Katherine."

John.

She looked up. He was standing beside her chair, holding out a hand towards her. She gripped his fingers and rose, then let go, though she longed to cling.

"Will you walk with me?" He offered his arm as the others began leaving the room.

Jennifer had gripped Phillip's arm. He was walking beside John's stepfather, and Mary was minding the children with her mother and grandmother.

Katherine nodded and laid her hand on his sleeve. The muscle in her abdomen clasped with a spasm of longing as she remembered all of their wicked games in the tower room.

"How are you?" he asked, quietly as the distance between them and the others grew.

She looked up and smiled, meeting his pale gaze.

"Well. Thank you for the dress. But how on earth did you involve Eleanor, does she not suspect something?"

He slowed their steps, creating even more distance between themselves and everyone else ahead of them, and laughed quietly. "Possibly, yet she said herself you would not come unless you were given something to wear. You have refused every invitation from her, after all."

She held his gaze and saw him looking deep into her eyes as if he sought answers.

Had he feared she'd refuse it?

"I would feel out of place with Eleanor on my own, but at your party Phillip will be there and… you…"

His fingers covered hers as they lay on his arm.

"I would not have let you send it back or say no, you know. The whole damned thing has been planned for you."

She heat flushed her cheeks.

"I am not allowing people to treat you as they have been anymore, Katherine. This party will secure the ground we claimed the other night."

"When can we meet again, John?" she asked as they reached the top of the stairs. The others were at the bottom.

He stopped and turned to her, his eyes welling with an emotion she did not understand, although his expression was still hard. "I think *never*, Katherine." The words took her completely off guard. "I have been unfair to you." There was warmth in his voice which denied the rejection he was speaking. "We both know our little intrigue can go no further. It is over. It should never have begun. I'm sorry."

Her smile died. She had known it was folly. *She had known.*

"Katherine?" he prompted. "You do understand? After the party I shall be going back to London. The House of Lords is due to reconvene soon."

145

No. She refused to understand. While she had been falling more deeply in love with him, he had just been entertaining himself during the summer break.

I am a fool. He has offered me nothing other than a bonnet and a dress. How had she expected it to end?

Her father had asked Phillip why John would be interested in her. Well here was the answer: just to play immoral games when he was bored. *Why must I love him? Why can't I love someone who will love me back?*

"Katherine?" His fingers came up and touched her cheek. "I am truly sorry. I should not have asked you to do what we did. I offer no excuses. I merely ask you to forgive me. At least there can be no lasting harm."

No lasting harm! He was tearing her heart to shreds and he thought there would be no lasting harm. She would be in agony for the rest of her life.

Footsteps rang on the marble below.

"Katherine!" shouted Phillip. "Are you coming?"

John drew away.

She turned and went on ahead, hearing John follow.

She was so glad to see Phillip when he approached the bottom of the stairs that when he offered his hand, she hugged him instead.

"Katherine?" he whispered against her hair before she let him go.

She forced a smile as his gaze met hers, visibly wondering what was wrong.

"Mary has suggested we play badminton, in pairs. Will you play?"

She bit her lip, feeling tears in her eyes.

Phillip looked up at John, who must have stopped on the stairs.

"I have estate business to review," John stated. "I shall see you a week on Friday."

Phillip nodded, but he looked confused when his eyes returned to Katherine.

Deliberately smiling brightly, she looked back at John, infusing

146

happiness into her voice, acting as though he had not just cast her off. She did not wish him to know how much he'd hurt her. "Yes, we shall see you then."

He just looked at her, his eyes blank and his expression granite. "Enjoy your game."

She turned away, wishing to leave immediately, but she could hardly do that. Instead her smile ached as she went outside, but she'd learned many things from John during their dalliance and the most significant was how to hide how she felt. She even laughed when she played badminton with Jenny, Phillip and Mary, desperately hoping John would hear and think she had not been hurt at all.

Yet John's family did not hide their disappointment that John had stayed indoors. When the game had finished, they took lemonade with his parents on the terrace and Mary complained that John had become a bore.

"He is busy with the estate," John's stepfather said.

His mother spoke then. "I admit though, Mary, I had hoped, as he asked us here, he would keep us company some of the time." She sounded disappointed.

"Give him time," his stepfather answered.

John had said he did not feel a part of his family, but by the sound of their conversation, he kept himself apart from them.

When eventually Phillip handed Katherine back up into his curricle, after Jenny, he said in a low voice, "Are you well? You look pale, Kate."

Perhaps she had not hidden her pain as well as she'd thought. *I am merely heartsore and silly, pining for a man who will never love nor want me.* "I did not eat much luncheon."

Chapter Nine

John slid his hands into his trouser pockets and watched Katherine bid farewell to her vicar. At least it was Phillip who was driving her home and not that man. Her parents had already gone on ahead, while his stood behind him.

He'd had little opportunity to watch Katherine in the church, with the Pembroke pew packed to the brim with his fidgeting brothers and sisters.

Phillip approached Katherine and took her arm.

Jealousy and longing shot through John. He wished to be able to touch her. He wanted to hear her voice and feel her touch on him. But he was doing the right thing. He had to let her go. Yet it was not only his sacrifice, but hers. He had seen her eyes when he'd told her it was over.

What must she think of him?

Had he killed whatever it was in her she called love?

Sometimes he thought some sort of madness had overcome him as far as Katherine was concerned. How had he ever thought it had been the right thing to do, to steal her innocence when he had nothing to offer in return? *She is right – I am spoilt and selfish.*

He was going to change.

"Are you coming, John?" his mother called behind him.

John turned. What was he, a child to be called back to her?

"You are brooding about something," she said, walking towards him.

He shook his head. He did not wish her encroaching into his thoughts. This party had been an awful idea. He was tired of his brothers and sisters in the house already, and his father and mother, and his grandmother, seemed to watch him constantly and question him all the time, without using words. Consequently he'd spent little time with them.

When he walked towards her without answering, she said, "We are all proud of you. You know that don't you, John?" It was the sort of thing she would have said when he was ten.

He still did not answer, but as he reached her, she gripped his arm adding, "But you are not alone in this. If you need us, we are all here for you – Edward, your uncles, your grandmother, your aunts and I. You need not isolate yourself."

"I am hardly doing that, you are here, Mama." His pitch was irritable as they walked on towards the carriages.

His stepfather was watching, waiting for them.

John set his expression to avoid Edward reading it.

His parents had discussed this conversation. John knew how close they were. His mother would have told Edward she was concerned, before speaking.

"That is just it though, John. We are here, but you are not. You spend more time in the library and in your chambers than with us," she took a breath. "Mary and Robbie would like to know you better. You built up Robbie's expectations when you took him to Tattersalls and you have barely spoken to him since, and Mary has missed you for so many years…"

And?

"If there is anything I have done," she said suddenly.

He looked down and met her gaze but continued walking.

"Your solitude concerns me, John? It concerns Edward too. I know you deliberately stayed abroad. If I, or we, have done something to upset you, you would tell us?"

Why were you not there before I was ten? The question shot through his mind but he would not ask it. He would not appear such a fragile fool.

Her eyes shone brightly as they held his gaze.

"You need not fret over me, Mama."

She gave him a tremulous smile. "A part of me knows that, and yet another part of me senses there is something wrong, John."

"I will take Robbie driving this afternoon, if it pleases you."

"John, this is not about simply spending more time with your brother, although he will be overjoyed if you do. It is about you. I wish you to be happy, and I do not think you are."

Happiness? His life had always been about duty. He'd escaped it for a few years in Egypt, but he'd always known, even then, he was only buying time. "I have everything I need, Mama." *Except the feelings Grandfather beat out of me.* Surely he should feel some compassion towards her, not this annoyance.

"But you are not happy."

John looked up as they neared the carriages, at his stepfather, and took a deep breath.

"Life is not only about responsibility, John, happiness outweighs it," she whispered finally before they could no longer talk.

~

Katherine tried to hurry, weaving between the people in the busy high street in Maidstone.

The weather had turned as miserable as her mood and a very light drizzle of rain had been falling for hours, making everything damp and the sky dreary.

She was tired, exhausted by the thoughts running around her head in circles.

The pain had gone and now she only felt numb and hollow inside. But she still wished to look her best tonight. She did not want John to know how he'd affected her. Let him think her as

150

unaffected as him.

She'd hoped to spend the afternoon bathing and finding a prettier way to style her hair but her mother was being her usual obnoxious self and ensuring Katherine had no time to do so. It was already past two and here she was in Maidstone with a groom, running the fourth errand of the day and this time it was to find a paler ribbon for Jenny's hair to show off the colour of her eyes better.

Phillip was due back soon at least.

Her gaze reached ahead to the milliner's shop. She was almost there.

She wished she did not have to go to John's party but she was no coward. She would face him and hold her head high no matter that she felt as small as the church mouse he kept calling her.

What a dreadful idiot she had been. He must think her no different than any woman of the gutter to have asked her to do those things – *and I agreed*. That had only taught her how little she thought of herself.

Yet this dinner party made no sense. If he wished nothing more to do with her, he need have nothing more to do with her. There was no reason at all for him to hold a party and say he had done it for her.

"Miss Spencer?" a gentleman uttered as she virtually collided with him.

"Mr Wareham."

A fellow victim of John's cold heart.

She bobbed a brief curtsy.

He bowed slightly, clutching the brim of his tall hat.

"I would say good day, but this weather makes it less so, does it not? Where are you off to in such a hurry?" His tone was friendly, if a little hollow, like John's.

She blushed and met his pale, measuring gaze.

She had spoken to him at church a few times. He'd never ignored her, but he'd not made any particular effort to associate with her either.

She chose to smile and give him a little time. After all, she of all people could understand how he must be feeling as John's cast-off.

"I am in search of ribbons." She forced a light tone into her voice, as he had. "I heard you have left the Duke's service, Mr Wareham. I was sorry to hear it."

His expression darkened and his tone turned sour. "Yes, well, life is not fair is it, Miss Spencer? One does not always have what one ought." Then he smiled suddenly, although there was hardness behind his eyes. "Would you care to join me for tea at the inn? We could perhaps mourn the hand of fate together? I know you suffer from gossip."

Oh. She had not expected that, but he probably lacked company. Sympathy struck her. She knew he had no family locally and no friends. He rarely socialised in the community, even though they all held him a little in awe. But she could not stop, she had to get home.

"I am in a hurry, Mr Wareham, perhaps another time."

"Yes, indeed then, another time," he stated, his eyes on her face. "Good day, Miss Spencer." He bowed slightly again and lifted his hat.

"Good day," she bobbed another brief curtsy and then they parted, but she could feel his gaze follow her as she carried on along the street.

~

"Is this all we have?" John asked with frustration, leaning back.

Harvey just smiled lightly.

Did he think this was amusing? John was not amused.

Harvey had gathered numerous pieces of information but the key to finding the lost money was missing. He knew where Wareham had been born, to some actress, in London, as an illegitimate child with no named father. John knew where Wareham

152

had been raised and schooled too. He'd been to Eton and then Oxford. So they also knew there was some wealthy benefactor in Wareham's life. Probably the unnamed father. And John now knew Wareham had been in his grandfather's service ever since leaving Oxford. But what good were those facts?

John wondered if Wareham had been stealing from the old man off since the beginning. If so, there might be thousands stored away. Certainly, money had been dripping out of the estate's income in every ledger John had reviewed.

He had brought them all up to town now so Harvey's staff could start calculating the loss.

Wareham was probably currently living a merry life on it too. He'd made no attempt to disappear. He was still in Ashford and John was still having him watched.

Hell and the devil.

Phillip was having more luck working on the loan however. He'd discovered it was an investment rather than a loan.

Wareham had been stung by a man of his own ilk. He'd invested in a canal-building scam. The rogue who'd promoted it had apparently disappeared with Wareham's funds. Wareham had tried to use the Duke's name to get it back.

"My solicitors are still searching for an account in Wareham's name, Your Grace. We know the investment was not made in cash, so the account must exist."

John's fingers covered his mouth. He wished this over with and sorted. His eyes shut for a moment.

"Is Your Grace worried he will make some other move?" Harvey asked.

John's eyes flew open. He had let himself relax too much and Harvey had seen through his guard. John had not previously thought to hide his thoughts and emotions from Harvey, but since this situation with Wareham, John's trust had grown even less, he could not even rely upon the people his grandfather had relied on.

The word "trust" spun John's thoughts to Katherine, and

whenever she came to mind, it was her eyes he saw – bright-blue eyes burning into him as they accused him of lacking trust, being spoilt and shutting himself away.

She had called him two people, the two people he knew he was, but he was fast becoming just the one. The one he had never wanted to be. His grandfather's monster, who did indeed shut everything and everyone out.

He had shut her out.

His thoughts and feelings for her were shoved aside with vicious denial. He had a duty to fulfil and a public life to lead.

"Your Grace," Harvey prompted.

"I don't know what to expect from him," John answered. "He knows all of my grandfather's business. Is that not risk enough?"

Harvey nodded, looking serious now, and steepled his fingers. "I have warned all the stewards to be cautious, Your Grace. We can also move your accounts if you wish?"

"Yes," John agreed. "Please move them." He was sure Wareham would be capable of faking signatures and getting access, it would be best to be safe. God, he did not need these added burdens in his life.

He'd done the right thing in ending his affair with Katherine, for her sake and for his. Nothing could have come of it and it would just have been another thing battering at his conscience. And yet, when he'd been with her in the tower room it was the only time he had been able to feel like himself since leaving Egypt. A deep longing opened like a wide empty hole in his chest.

He pushed the feeling aside and faced Harvey again. "Agree some code with the other stewards too, so they will know when communications come from you. When does the new man start?"

~

"You are coming, Katherine," Eleanor urged. "We are not taking no for an answer, are we Margaret?"

Katherine looked from one to the other, feeling blown on a storm. They had been waiting for her when she returned from Maidstone, sitting in the parlour suffering her mother's company until she came home. They had come to steal her away to Pembroke Place so she might ready herself there.

"Aunt Ellen and Grandmamma have agreed. You are to stay the night. You are coming," Eleanor pressed.

Katherine was certain John could not have agreed to this. He would surely not want her there.

"Pack up her things," Margaret said, looking at Hetty.

Hetty looked uncertain about responding to orders from a visitor but then Katherine's mother apparently accepted that they would not leave without Katherine.

"Go, Hetty, do as the Countess asks."

Jenny, who Katherine was fast realising had started growing up at last, smiled across the room as if to say you must go.

"Katherine," Eleanor urged again. "You are not refusing. You will not come and visit me in town, so I wish your company here. I shall sit here until you accept and Harry will not be happy with you if I do, he's grown terribly protective now I'm with child."

Katherine's heart thumped. "It is John's home, and you've made no mention of an invitation from him, I should not come unless he has agreed."

"Poppycock! He has not even been there all week, his mama is organising it all, I doubt he even cares who is coming, all he appears to think about is business. Now, get ready."

"Yes do, Kate," Margaret added, "I really do not think John will mind, Pembroke Place is so big he'll probably never even realise you are there."

"It will be like old times," Eleanor pressed.

Katherine looked from Eleanor to Margaret and back again. She was never going to persuade them to go without her. "Very well."

"Wonderful," Eleanor said, rushing to hug her. "I am so glad. We shall have so much fun."

Less exuberantly, Margaret kissed Katherine's cheek and whispered, "It is good to see you once more."

This must be Eleanor's idea. She must have dragged Margaret along, just as Eleanor always used to when they'd been children. They were not children anymore. Life had changed completely, and Katherine knew her place now, and if she had been a little confused about it recently, John had made it plain again the other day.

Half an hour later, Katherine arrived at Pembroke Place in Eleanor's carriage, with her small holdall, which contained the evening dress John had bought her.

Even that ridiculously worn bag was an embarrassment to her.

John was nowhere in sight when they entered but Katherine's heart pounded when she heard Eleanor say to the stiff butler, "Has His Grace returned?"

"Not yet, Ma'am."

"At this rate he shall not even be here for his own dinner party," Margaret complained.

"Papa cannot believe he asked us all and then was not here when we arrived," Eleanor responded. "When I see John I am going to give him a talking to. I swear he avoids us all in town. Harry says he has a reputation as a boor."

"I do not think him dull..." Margaret responded, taking Katherine's arm.

Eleanor held the other and they led Katherine towards the stairs.

"...He always strikes me as elemental," Margaret continued, "but he has that brooding, haunted look, like Grandpapa, he glowers at people in town and scares them all off. George says he tried befriending John in the House of Lords but gave up because John is so standoffish."

"Precisely, I did not mean boring, I meant *boorish*. Harry says he is always irritable and sharp with people."

"Mama said we should be patient with him," Margaret progressed. "And Papa said he was always more silent as a boy because he never had a father to turn to."

"He had Uncle Edward."

"Not until he was ten…"

Drawn along between them, Katherine did not know what to make of their conversation. She'd never heard them disparage John before. When they'd been young, they'd idolised him. She knew he'd changed, but it seemed strange to her that he would keep himself distant from a family she'd dream of having. She did not understand him any more than Eleanor or Margaret seemed to.

But then he'd admitted to her he trusted no one, perhaps he did not want anyone to understand him. It was probably the shield he used to hide himself behind so no one would see the vulnerability she kept sensing. Perhaps she knew him more than she thought she did. Perhaps he had not hidden himself well enough from her.

Katherine was taken to the drawing room first and found it bursting at the seams with John's family and full of noise.

All his extended family were here. But not John.

After being reintroduced by Eleanor and Margaret, who ensured the whole family recognised Katherine and made her welcome, Eleanor then drew Katherine away and insisted she dress in her rooms. "My maid shall do your hair and make you look ravishing tonight in *that* dress, it was such a good idea of John's to ensure you have something to wear. At least the brute can still show the occasional kindness."

~

As John entered the hall of Pembroke Place, Finch followed his welcome by announcing the receipt of an urgent letter.

John instantly knew who it was from when a footman passed it to him on a silver tray. He had spent enough hours studying this writing in the last few weeks to recognise Wareham's hand.

"Has everyone arrived, Finch?"

"They have, Your Grace, your guests are in their rooms, dressing."

After his mother's little *tête-à-tête*, John had left the house to his family and gone back to town to avoid them, though he had fulfilled his promise and let Robbie drive the curricle before leaving. That afternoon had been amusing, although it had only stood to prove to John how distant and different he was to his brother.

Robbie laughed frequently, chatted constantly and smiled readily, as John could never remembering doing, but then Robbie had been raised by two loving parents and did not bear the weight of any anticipated title. John's stepfather was the *second son* of an Earl. Robbie could do what he wished with his life.

Glad his family were out of the way, John went to his rooms to read the letter, anger boiling in his blood as he jogged upstairs and then strode along the grand hall. There was a cold hard knot in his stomach and a sick feeling in his throat as he opened it in the privacy of his sitting room.

It said very little, it was just two lines, but the words struck John like a fist to the jaw.

If you do not wish the world to know of your mother's shameful past, you will give me the sum of fifty thousand pounds.

His mother's shameful past? She had no secrets... But then... *Where was she before I was ten?*

John's hand shook as he swept back his fringe. What did Wareham know that he did not? God, it made him angrier to think Wareham knew her secrets than it did to suffer the threat.

The letter fell from his fingers and spiralled to the floor. But then John realised he would not wish his servants to see it. Instinct bid him destroy it, but that would be foolish; even though it bore no signature it was still evidence. Snatching up the note again, John then secured it in his personal safe, locking away his anger with it. But then he turned and strode out of the room, every muscle in his body tense.

Now was the time to ask the question he had denied himself all these years.

The heels of his boots hit heavily as he strode along the hall, announcing his arrival as he stopped before the door of his parents' rooms. There was noise within, children's voices, and Mary's.

He knocked.

"Come," his mother called, humour and happiness in her voice.

The sitting room adjoining his parents' bedchamber was full of his siblings. The girls were excitedly looking over his mother's and Mary's evening clothes, while the boys were playing a rough and tumble game with his stepfather.

"John!" It was Robbie's bright voice which greeted John.

John could remember these hours before a ball. His parents had always spent time with their children before they went out for an evening, so he, *they*, would not feel so excluded by the adult world.

"John?" his stepfather said, his expression changing as he swung David, one of the younger boys, from his shoulders down to the ground. The very youngest must already be in their cots.

"I didn't know you were home," his mother stated, rising too.

"I have just returned. May I speak with you privately, Mama?"

"Did you have bad news in town?" Mary asked from across the room. "You look like thunder. In fact you look like Grandpapa."

John cast his gaze at her and felt cold darkness swamp him, he felt like stone inside, like a statue, unable to live or breathe anymore.

"Come on children, out," his stepfather said. "I'll walk you back upstairs. Dress in your room, Mary, and Robbie, you must go and get ready too."

Immediately the exodus began, as his siblings fell silent and were herded from the room by his stepfather.

Carrying her dress over one arm, Mary smiled as she passed, and gently, briefly, gripped his arm. Robbie looked at John more uncertainly but smiled anyway as though he did not know how else to react. However, Harry, John's third sibling, who'd been born when John was already at Eton, gave his older brother a

159

suspicious, guarded look.

Most of them looked at him like that, especially the girls, and they gave him a wide berth as they left.

When John looked at his mother, a crushing disappointment swept over him. He was in turmoil internally, and he felt revulsion for her. He felt betrayed. What shameful thing had she done that would give his enemy the power of blackmail.

"John? What is wrong?" she said, walking towards him, as she reached to touch his arm. He moved it back.

He did not want her touching him. She had deserted him and now deceived him.

"Sit down," he stated, without preamble.

She looked hurt but she moved away and occupied one of a pair of chairs before the window, perching on the edge of it, sitting stiffly with her hands clasped together on her lap. Perhaps she hoped he'd sit in the other. He did not. "How can I help, John?"

"You may tell me where you were before I was ten?" His pitch was deep with accusation, his emotion overwhelming, although he knew his face was set like granite. "Where did you live? What did you do?"

Stunned shock froze her expression, and her porcelain skin paled to a sickly grey. "I am not having this conversation," was her answer as she rose and crossed the room.

Something like a knife-blow thrust into his chest, but he was not going to let her escape this; he had waited long enough to ask, he wanted the answer. "Then it is true," he growled at her, moving to stand before the door so she could not leave. "You have something to hide! Are you not going to tell me what it is, Mama?"

"John? Do not bully me," her eyes held his, defiant and horrified as he gripped her arm.

A bitter feeling of dislike bit at John, not of her, but of himself. He loosened his grip and let her go, but he did not want her to leave.

Her fingers rubbed her arm where he'd held it. He'd hurt her.

"I'm sorry," he forced out. He hated himself. He hated himself

for being weak and angry. He hated himself for caring about this –
but I do. "Just tell me where you were and why you were not here?"

"No, John." Her eyes shimmered with tears. "You are my son."

Surely his being her child should be even greater reason to
speak. He should have been the most important thing in her life
then. She should have been with him.

"Mary is right," she whispered then. "Every day you grow more
and more like your grandfather. Whatever this is about, John, I am
sure my past can have no bearing on it. I'll not talk of it to you."

"Why would it have no bearing? Why do I not know where
you were? Why were you not with me?"

His questions were not about the blackmail note. He hardly
cared about it anymore. Why would she not speak? It had never
occurred to him in all the years he had questioned why, that, if
he did dare show his weakness and ask, she would refuse to speak.

His hand lifted and swept back his hair. "And I am not like *him*."
For a start he was never going to trust anyone again; he was never
going to be stung by any man like Wareham. He didn't bloody
need people, he had proved that he could live alone in Egypt, he
could do it here. After tonight he would have nothing more to do
with her – with any of them.

"You are sounding like him, now." His stepfather had opened
the door behind John without John knowing.

John turned.

"Son, what is this about?"

"I am not your son, and I asked to speak with my mother,
alone, not with you." The words that came out of John's mouth
surprised even John, but he was too lost in anger and pain to care
who he hurt. They had hurt him. They had betrayed and deceived
him. He did not doubt Edward knew the truth; they told each
other everything.

John watched his words sting, and felt glad, and then hated
himself still more. His stepfather had never treated him differently to the others, or been unkind – *but he had lied*, and he had

helped John's mother lie. He shared her secrets, secrets which even Wareham knew and John did not – secrets which had fractured John's life in his youth and made him half a man.

"John," Edward's hand lifted, reaching out to reassure, regardless of John's cutting words.

"I wish to know where she was and what she did before you two were wed, before the night you came to Eton to collect me." John ground out. "Will you tell me? *She will not.*"

"It is not my story to tell," Edward stated, before glancing at John's mother.

She rushed into Edward's arms then, sobbing.

John stared at them in silence for a moment, feeling the monster he'd become, but then he turned and left, knowing he'd learn nothing from them.

Through the open door he heard his mother sob. "I told you this day would come. How can I tell him, Edward?"

Whatever secret she was keeping, it could not be good.

John felt icy cold and cut in half, and in a couple of hours he had to face a house full of people. *Damnation!* He was not in the mood. He had no allies left. He could not trust his staff, or his family. He had no one but himself. Katherine's bright eyes came back into his head as he thought of trust.

It was no longer his choice. Too many people had let him down. He'd not try again.

Damn, he had to face her tonight too, at this bloody foolish dinner party.

He went down late, in no mood to socialise, and set his face with a false, hard, closed-lip smile as he greeted guests.

Katherine did not come over to him and he did not go to her, but he saw her, he had seen her the moment he entered, clothed in the light-blue satin he'd chosen for her. Her hair had been curled and beautifully piled, and the cut of the dress showed off her slender neck and pale-skinned shoulders. He was conscious of her presence constantly. At any moment he could have said

162

exactly where she was in the room, no matter that it was full of people, even if she was behind him.

When dinner was announced, he wished to partner Katherine and bathe in the consolation of her company for an hour, but that was impossible; he could not single her out so blatantly.

Instead, he led his grandmother into the grand stately dining room which glittered with silver, cut glass and pure-white linen. The table was forty feet in length and he left his grandmother at one end then walked to the other. Aunt Penny was to occupy the seat on one side of him while Aunt Sylvia sat on the other.

At least with his family positioned in order of importance, his mother was further down the table and so he need not speak to her.

She had not looked his way since he'd come down. However, Edward kept glancing at him.

John saw Katherine enter much further back, on the arm of her vicar.

What damned idiotic benevolent mood had overtaken John to invite that bloody man?

The vicar was seated beside her too, while Phillip was on her other side, but they were right at the far end of the table.

John wished he was there, among them, not seated at the head – irrelevant – without duty, merely himself as a young man, laughing with Phillip and teasing Katherine as if the world was not carried on his shoulders.

As dinner progressed John spoke with his aunts and uncles on shallow subjects which did not interest him. But he regularly glanced at the far end of the table.

With her blonde hair and effervescent smile, Katherine stood out amongst his family like champagne amidst the red wine of the dark-haired Pembroke women.

She spoke animatedly with Phillip, the saintly reverend, her sister and the two Dawkins sons, who sat across from her.

John could not hear her voice, he was too far away, and yet he could in his head, and he felt her presence in the region of his chest also.

She was light in his darkness, even from this distance. Just to be able to look at her warmed the coldness in his soul.

He did not want to give her up.

She must have sensed his gaze, because she looked his way, then blushed and turned away again, looking at her vicar.

He'd hurt her. He had pushed her away now. It was better things remained as they were. He returned his attention to his aunts and his thoughts to the debacle of his own life. That was what he should focus on, resolving this damned issue with Wareham, and now, if he was to do it, he also needed to find out the answer to the question he had been asking all his life and never actually spoken until today.

Once the ladies had left the table, John decided to progress that aim and he leaned towards his uncle, Richard, "I was recently asked something about my past which I couldn't answer. I know my mother is closer to Aunt Penny than anyone else. Do you know how I came to live with my grandfather? I cannot recall, I was obviously too young to remember."

His voice had been as nonchalant as he could make it and yet he saw his hand shaking when he moved to lift the glass of port Finch had poured.

Richard's eyes widened as he looked back at John and there was a hint of wariness in his expression.

How many of the family knew John's mother's secret? He would guess Richard did.

"You know your mother and father eloped?"

No, he had not even known that.

"You did not," Richard clarified, looking harder at John as John felt his stomach fall like a heavy stone.

He had not locked his expression hard enough, Richard had seen the response. All John's facial muscles stiffened.

"It is not my place to tell you," Richard continued, sounding uncomfortable. "The story must come from your mother not me, John."

But Richard knew it. Who else then?

John's eyes scanned the men left in the room as Richard progressed. "But I will tell you that your grandfather disowned her when she ran away to marry your father. Of course, it was before I married your aunt, but I know the Duke went to fetch you after your birth. He wished to protect you, John."

"From what?"

"I cannot say. This is your mother's story. Ask her."

John's gaze fell to his glass of port. "I have done. She will not speak."

"Well, that is her choice. But remind her you are not a child anymore."

When John looked at his uncle, Richard continued, "It was not a good time, John. It will take courage for her to recall it. And you will have to show her some understanding if you expect her to talk to you about it, and that is a quality I do not think comes naturally to you now."

John's eyes narrowed. His uncle laughed. "If you glared at her like that, I am not at all surprised she did not speak. Have some sympathy, John."

Sympathy? And who had bloody sympathy for him? It was his life which had been affected and everyone seemed to know the truth but him.

Looking back along the table, John caught his stepfather watching, several places away, with disapproval in his eyes.

John lifted his glass, feeling utterly vicious, and sipped the blood-red liquid. *Fuck you.* The granite inside him hardened by another degree, he just couldn't seem to help himself anymore.

Once he had finished his port, he rose, which meant all the other men must too, and then he led them out to join the women.

Dark, callous anger rolling through his head as he went in search of his mother to share what little he'd learned. But he did not seek her out immediately, instead he bided his time and waited until

165

Edward had stopped watching.

With his guests spread about the room playing cards or dancing in a small set where space had been cleared near the pianoforte, or merely hovering in small groups conversing quietly, he waited, silently watching until the perfect moment came.

She broke from the knot of her sisters to collect a glass of fruit punch from a footman and he moved to intercept her, casually standing in her path, a few feet away from anyone else.

With his glass of dessert wine half covering his lips so no one else could see his words, John asked, "Why did you not tell me that you and my father eloped?"

Her gaze flew up to his, and her skin paled, if that were possible, because it was already alabaster.

"Who told you that?"

"Richard. There is no harm in me knowing it, surely?"

"No, John, there is no harm, but it is also unimportant. What difference does it make?"

"Then why not tell me?"

"Because—"

"Richard also told me Grandfather took me from you after I was born. Why would he do that?"

Her gaze skimmed across John's face. "John…" She took a breath.

"Why did you never tell me?"

"Because you knew it, you were with him and you knew I wanted you with me."

"Did I?"

Her forehead furrowed. "John? I loved you. Do you not remember me writing to you? I wanted you back but your grandfather would not let you go…"

"Why?"

Her expression fell.

"Let it be, John," she whispered after a moment. "Please. It does not matter. It is in the past."

"It matters to me."

Ever protective, his stepfather arrived and his hand slipped about her waist. "Are you stirring up a wasps' nest again, John? Leave it, or someone *will* get stung."

John's gaze locked with Edward's. "Who?"

"The people you are supposed to care about," Edward answered, looking both exasperated and condescending if that were possible. "Your family."

John looked back at his mother, burning to know the truth and not knowing what to say to get it from her, but her pale eyes merely looked right back into his as though they searched for something she could not see, and then she said, "I am not sure that he does care anymore. You seem to wish to hurt us, John." And then she turned from him and walked away.

"What did Richard tell you?" Edward asked when the two of them were left to talk alone.

"That they eloped and my grandfather took me from her." John stiffened his spine.

"And I helped her fight to get you back. You were all she lived for before I met her. Do you ever remember not knowing your mother existed?"

John shook his head.

"Because she refused to simply melt away. Your grandfather disowned her, but she still managed to keep in contact with you despite that. You should think of that, and nothing else. I witnessed yours and her happiness when you were reunited. I *know* you care, and I know your mother cares for you. Stop this, John."

"Why?"

"Because it will hurt your mother if you know. It is not important."

John just looked at him, hard.

"You cannot manipulate or threaten me, John. I did not let your grandfather do it and I will certainly not tolerate it from you. And I will not let you hurt your mother either. If you are

167

modelling yourself on your grandfather, you will be lonely, John. He was a hated man. Is that what you wish for yourself? No one has ever doubted your ability to take his place. You do not need to shut us all out to prove you can."

John glowered at him.

"And you *are* my son in all but blood, whether you think it so or not." With that, Edward turned and walked away.

John set down his half-empty glass and then left the room, crossing it with brisk strides to reach the open French doors. He needed air. He needed space.

The sky was cloudy and the night, therefore, pitch black, the only light outside was spilling from the windows.

~

Katherine watched John walk from the room through the corner of her eye. She knew he'd been looking at her several times during the evening, but when the men rejoined them after dinner his attention was focused on his mother.

There was something wrong. His posture had seemed hostile and guarded, and now he'd left his guests again and no one apart from John's father seemed to even notice.

But John's father did not follow. He turned his back and joined the conversation John's mother had engaged in.

What was going on?

The family scene was perfect, cosy and homely. Every group was conversing and laughing occasionally. It was the typical picture of society life as Katherine had always imagined it. Yet John was not included in it.

Pity gripped her heart. Something was wrong, she knew it, something had made him exile himself, and she instinctively knew it was nothing to do with her.

Biting her lip, she looked about the room again. Everyone was talking; no one would notice if she followed. No matter how much he'd hurt her, she couldn't leave him suffering. She wanted to help him.

Phillip was speaking to Eleanor and Lord Nettleton; Katherine's mother was engaged in conversation with Lady Ellis and the Earl of Harding, one of John's uncles and his eldest son; Jennifer and Mary were dancing; and Katherine's father was sitting in a chair among other local gentleman, talking. None of them appeared to see her slip out into the darkness.

The terrace was shrouded in black, the moon invisible, and a tepid breeze stirred the trees in the park beyond it, filling the air with the sound of rustling leaves.

She couldn't see John as she walked tentatively into the dark. But then her eyes adjusted and his tall, athletically lean silhouette came into view.

He was leaning on the balustrade looking outward into the inky darkness, apparently self-absorbed. He did not even seem to notice her presence as she walked closer.

"What is wrong?" she whispered, laying a hand on his shoulder.

His muscle jolted and then he turned so her hand slipped off. "Go away, Katherine."

"Is there a problem? Is something—?"

"Nothing, Katherine. Go back in. You should not be out here." His posture was stiff and straight, both defensive and dismissive, but yet again she sensed his vulnerability.

"John?"

"Just go, Katherine, I am only likely to hurt you more if you stay out here. I am not in the best of moods."

She looked at him and took a deep breath but couldn't decide what to do. Something was not right. How could she leave him alone?

His shoulders dropped then suddenly he reached into an inside pocket of his evening coat to withdraw a slender silver box. "Seeing as you will not go away, you shall forgive me if I do the unthinkable and smoke."

She said nothing as he took out a single slim cigar and then put the box away again. He lit a flint on the stone balustrade to light it.

Her heart was thumping. John was so statuesque in his height, and his movements were always graceful. She remembered how his long, slender fingers had felt when they touched her, warmth and longing flowering inside her again as he leant his buttocks onto the balustrade and looked back towards the house, legs outstretched and crossed at the ankles, with one arm across his chest.

"John?"

"Do not try to pry, Katherine. I do not wish to speak."

She sighed. "Very well, I shan't. But seeing as you said you planned this all for me, I am sorry it seems to be like torture for you."

He laughed, but it was hollow, almost as though he laughed at himself. "I told you I do not get on with them, didn't I? Now you have seen it for yourself. And I cannot blame it on them, can I? They are all perfectly *nice*. Which means the fault must lie with me. By the way, you look beautiful; that dress suits you, and I like you hair. Did you do it?"

"No, Eleanor's maid did. You don't know I'm staying here do you? Your mother and Eleanor organised it."

He took a draw on his cigar.

She moved closer and touched his arm again. "I can understand, John."

"Can you?"

"Yes. Stop pushing me away."

"Is that what I am doing? And there was I thinking I was protecting you." His hard gaze turned to her, diamonds in the darkness, cutting and sharp. "You cannot understand, Katherine. I know you have felt alone, you said so, but you have a very good reason for it, your mother is horrible. The fault is not yours."

"But she is not my mother. I had no parents, as you had no father. There are things in your life I can understand more than anyone else, John."

He sighed, and then suddenly there was that soul-deep window in his eyes again. "I had no mother either, Katherine, not until I was ten, and no one will tell me where she was." But then, almost instantly, as though he regretted saying it, his gaze shuttered and his body stiffened, and he sucked on his cigar before rising and turning and throwing the thing out into the darkness.

"You can trust me, John," she whispered. "I promise."

"Can I?" he answered, standing with his back to her and looking outwards into the dark.

"Yes, John, you can, and stop hiding from me by answering with questions. I am here for you if you need me."

"I don't need anyone, Katherine. I am a duke."

She sighed, feeling exasperated and hurt, hating the invisible distance he was setting between them. "I survive without bitterness, John, because I have Phillip and Papa. You need someone, John."

"Do I?"

"Kate! Kate! You are damned well going to dance at least one with me, seeing as I have been dragged into the fray."

Katherine turned to see her brother stepping out of the French door. "I'll come, I'll be happy to partner you!" Her heart thumped.

Phillip stopped and looked at them. "John."

"Phillip."

"I'm coming," Katherine called again, and then she turned back to John, met his gaze and whispered, "You do, John, you need someone." With that, she spun away and walked briskly towards Phillip.

"What were you speaking to John about?" he asked, when she reached him.

"Oh, he is just in a bad mood. He's argued with his family. But do not say anything to him, Phillip, he will not thank me for telling you."

~

171

Katherine could not believe how smoothly John could manipulate people. He had returned to his guests an hour after leaving them and managed to charm his way out of giving any explanation for his absence. They fawned over him and he merely smiled or nodded. She would swear even if he showed his contempt for their company they would suffer his rudeness.

His family were more reticent, however, and she had watched them watching him with questions in their eyes. They knew something was wrong, as she did, but she also guessed he would not accept their help any more than he would accept hers.

Sitting up in bed, Katherine thumped her pillow to fluff up the feathers, before lying back down on her other side. She couldn't sleep. John was in a room barely yards from where she lay and his stark look as he'd stood on the terrace in splendid isolation kept haunting her thoughts.

She could not balance the John she saw now with the young man who'd romped with Phillip in the lake years ago.

Then she thought of the tower room. He'd promised not to take her virginity. He had not. Not even when she'd urged him to. The John she'd known as a child was inside the other – in pain. But why?

Sitting up in bed again, she knew she could not sleep unless she tried to speak to him once more. He had no one else.

The room was so dark, she had to feel her way about the edge of it to find the door, and then she progressed along the hall still using touch, her fingertips brushing across statues and doors, which she counted to find her way.

~

A cry of pain escaping his lips, John woke and sat up, feeling the weight of horror in his chest. The sheet was tangled and twisted about his waist and sweat made him feel clammy. The single candle he'd left burning at his bedside was flickering wildly, reduced to a stub.

For a minute John had no idea where he was, but then his mind escaped the web of his hated dream and his fingers lifted and swept back his hair as he regained his breath. Why would his mind not let this go? He was not a child anymore. His father was right, it didn't matter. And yet it did, deep down, it did.

God. Why would they not tell him, though? What could be so bloody secret? "Forget it," he growled at himself, his voice echoing in his bedchamber.

Then he slid his legs over the edge of the bed and rested his elbows on his thighs and his head in his hands as he felt the despair which always came after his dream.

God, he no longer gave a damn about the blackmail. Wareham could do what he wished. John's power was too great for any scandal to touch him. People wouldn't care. They had not even challenged his absence tonight. People didn't dare judge a duke.

The air in his room felt thick and hot as he breathed steadily, trying to get control of his mind. It was no use, no matter what he wished, he couldn't let the question go.

Why had she not been there?

Clarity suddenly gripped his thoughts like ice gripping shifting water and solidifying it. If his family would say nothing, then there was only one choice. He had to find out for himself. It was easily done. Harvey could use the same influence he was using to discover Wareham's history. Then once John knew, this would be over. There would be no more uncertainty and no more dreams.

He felt a sudden longing for Katherine; it was a warm sharp ache in his chest as his hands fell to his thighs and his back straightened, but before he could even qualify it, he heard movement outside his room.

Bloody-hell, had someone heard him cry out like a child?

The door handle turned without a knock and his breath caught as he watched the door open, though he didn't move.

Katherine.

She slipped in when there was a wide enough gap and then closed the door behind her. Her eyes were instantly on his as he sat facing her with only a slither of sheet across his hips covering his nakedness.

Clothed in her white nightgown from neck to toe, she looked like a damned angel come to dispel his darkness. Her hair fell about her shoulders, tumbling down her back, glowing gold in the flickering candlelight.

He had just thought of her, and here she was, as though he was truly some dominion of the Devil who could conjure her up. She hesitated by the door.

"What are you doing here?" he said, before taking a deep breath as he felt desire sweep away all his previous thoughts, he wanted her physically and emotionally with every fibre of his body. He needed her to ease all else. He knew she could. She was the only one who could.

"I came to see you."

"Obviously. Why?"

"I… you need someone, John."

I need you, Katherine. "Katherine," he said, in a deep heavy voice, weighted with the hunger and pain he felt, "if you stay in this room I cannot say what I'll do. I told you earlier I am not in a good mood. I am in no mood for restraint. Get out if you wish to preserve your chastity." It was a cold and callous thing to say but maybe it would chase her off and save her from herself, and him. "Go away, Katherine," he said more gently. He did not really wish to hurt her.

But instead of leaving, she came across the room in swift strides which stirred the white linen covering her, filling the air with the gentle sound of fabric moving. Then her hands were in his hair, brushing through it, and she pulled his head against her breasts, he could feel them soft and warm beneath her nightgown.

Ah God, her touch was such gentle agony.

"John."

He closed his eyes, already reaching for her and clinging to the cloth by her hips. "Leave, please, Katherine. It is what you ought to do. I have nothing to give you. You know it as well as I do."

"You have yourself," she whispered, her fingers stroking through his hair, "and I have myself to give you. Trust me. You needn't hide from me."

He felt like crying; he felt like that damned child driving away in the carriage with his grandfather and fighting tears because he knew if he let them fall he would be beaten. He couldn't cry, he couldn't ever trust a sole with the truth inside him. But he could have her. He could have her and feel eased as he used to feel eased even by the she-wolves he used to devour abroad. Except she would be giving generously, not taking in return, and she was full of light he wanted to bathe in. He wanted to be free of this darkness.

Lifting his head away from her breasts, he looked up and met her gaze.

Her eyes were shining with that look he thought might be love. The fairy tale glowed there for him to read, and he wanted to believe it could be true. "If you do not want to consummate what is between us, Katherine, *go*."

"I can't." Her fingers touched his cheek as her gaze held his. "You were right, I love you. I have loved you for as long as I remember and I cannot walk away knowing you need me. I can help you, John."

He shut his eyes. He couldn't say I love you back. He felt horribly inadequate here. "I need you," he answered, his eyes still shut as he took a deep breath and lust roared through his veins. He needed to feel in control again. He opened his eyes and looked up at her. "I need you. Don't go. Stay." *I want to feel desired and wanted for who I am and not what I have. I feel human with you.*

His hands gripped her hips through the cloth, taking a firm hold, and her fingers splayed across the top of his head like a benediction. She was going to let him do this. He pressed his lips to the cloth covering her stomach and then took a breath as he pulled back, lifting his gaze to meet hers again. "Take off your nightgown."

If he was decent and honest and good, he wouldn't do this – if he was not so bitterly cold, lonely and in pain, he wouldn't do this.

As she unbuttoned her prim and proper nightgown, he lay back on the bed, his weight on one elbow, while his other hand lifted the sheet for her to join him, and once she was naked she did, lying down next to him.

His heart pounded as he leant over and kissed her, his hand covering her breast.

He'd said he had no restraint but he had, his desire was to take her fast and swift in a desperate race towards escape but this was her first time so he held back.

She was so very precious and special to him. Her soft body was like silk as his fingers skimmed over her, arousing her, while he kissed her with a deep slow adoration. Let her know what he felt. Let her know how much he longed for her, how she seemed to capture something in his chest and hold on to it in her gentle grip.

Katherine.

His hand slipped between her thighs and stroked her there; her legs opening and letting him touch. She was gorgeous and beautiful and so giving.

When he slipped his fingers into her wetness and her warmth it was like heaven being opened to him.

Her fingers ran over his shoulders and her lips answered his kiss, her tongue dancing hungrily with his as he felt her breath turn to panting desperation, and then she could no longer kiss him but just cling as she toppled into ecstasy and he moved across her.

Treasuring the moment, fixing every detail of her in his head to keep forever, he settled between her legs, parting them wider with his own and positioning himself to enter her before she came back down to earth.

With a swift sharp stroke, he was baptised, dropped into the water and lost beneath it. He had died and now he was about to

176

rise again, like a phoenix, out of darkness and into light. She was so warm and soft and generous in her giving, even though he knew he'd caused her pain. When her eyes flew open and met his gaze they were full of that look he thought was love.

Was it love? Could she love him? Him, who did not deserve love. Him, whose own mother could not do it well enough to have stayed by his side when he was young.

He moved and discarded the thought by burying himself in her. He did not wish to think of the past, just Katherine.

He moved slowly and carefully, adoring the woman with her pale glowing skin, which was orange in the candlelight, and her gold hair which spilled all about her as she lay beneath him.

Katherine.

Her hips lifted and pressed back against him and he saw her fingers claw in the sheet.

Katherine.

She bit her lip and shut her eyes, her chest rising and falling more quickly.

His buttocks worked harder, his hips moving in stronger, longer strokes as he felt lust take a hold of him, gripping him by the back of the neck and urging him to hurry, to get to the end – to simply take and not give.

But she seemed to like his stronger movement and, with a cry, after a while, her hands clasped his hips and he felt her break about him with a gasp, as though she could not quite believe how it felt.

It felt good for him too. It had never felt quite like this. It was her honesty and openness. It was because he had known her for years and knew who she was and that she loved him. Did he know that? *Yes, I know that.* He believed it in her.

He let his own reins go, feeling thoroughly relaxed and absorbed by her, giving her the honesty she gave him as he panted, sighed and growled while he claimed her over and over again.

Katherine.

Her fingers were moving all over his body, on his buttocks, at his sides, on his biceps and in his hair, as they shared this escape, shared this special act which could tie a man and woman together for a moment in time.

It felt so much more intimate with her. She was in his head, his heart and his soul while he was so physically inside her. He could tell she knew he'd let go. It had become a mutual abandonment.

He held her gaze and clung to it as he drew towards the end. Staring into her precious look of love, bathing in it, until the moment he broke and cried out. He could neither breathe nor think as release swamped him.

He shut his eyes.

God. God. That had felt good. He felt so relaxed, sated and tired. He rolled to his back and pulled her over him.

Her head pillowed on his shoulder and her leg and arm came over him. He was utterly humbled by her.

"I love you," she said again.

He ought to say it back, even if it weren't true, he felt callous not doing so, and yet he couldn't lie, he had always loathed lying. *Have I not told you, your mother is dead.* Those were his grandfather's words the day he had taken John back. That had been a lie, a lie John had been forced to live.

The feelings of childhood crashed in on him again.

This reprieve had only been momentary, but, *God,* what a gift.

Still physically sated, if not now mentally relieved, he fell asleep.

~

When John woke, the grey half-light of morning was seeping about the curtains, filling his room with an eerie partial illumination. It took a matter of moments for the memories of Katherine beneath him to return.

It had been the sweetest night he'd spent with any woman. He'd never been given the gift of virginity before. A surge of masculine need to protect raced in his blood even now, pure instinct in

178

response to the utter humbleness he'd felt entering her.

He'd worship the ground she walked on for the rest of his life. There was a deep feeling of self-satisfaction within him, too, no matter that he'd had the dream last night. He felt whole and normal.

His eyes turned from the canopy of his ostentatious bed to look at Katherine and then he rolled onto his side. She was lying on her back, one hand resting backwards on the pillow while the other lay over her midriff. Her breasts rose with her breathing and her face was turned towards him. Her brow was clear of creases and her skin had not one single blemish even though it was so fair. Her nose, her cheekbones and her jaw were all perfect fragile feminine lines.

His fingers itched to touch.

With her eyes closed, her delicate light-brown lashes rested on her cheeks, while her rose-pink lips were slightly parted, as though waiting for his kiss.

A sharp pain pierced his chest, a need and longing which was, again, more than physical.

He swallowed back his want. She would be sore and he could be patient and wait for the next time to come.

God, how different it was for a woman to lose her virginity. When he'd lost his the woman had kept him up an entire night and taught him everything there was to learn. At the time it had been a young man's paradise, now he thought the whole thing sordid.

Wishing to set that memory aside, he stroked Katherine's cheek and then ran his finger along her nose and watched her eyelids flutter open.

Katherine met John's pale-blue gaze. It was filled with a tender appreciation. This was simply John, there was nothing of the duke in his eyes. It had been that way last night as they'd made love too.

His gentle touch slid lower, over her covered breast, and then it brushed along her forearm, running back and forth as her arm lay across her middle. "How are you?"

"A little achy," she answered.

He smiled, "Shall I kiss it away?" She nodded and then he leant forwards and did so, pressing his lips to hers. Warmth slipped into her blood, even though the kiss was ridiculously gentle and had no intent at all. "Better?" he asked when he pulled away.

"Yes."

She felt as though she could burst with love. His fingers skimmed across her skin again.

What he'd done last night had been so unbearably beautiful. She knew why she had been born now. She knew why her mother had craved the perfect bliss of lying with a man. Katherine did not blame her anymore. She did not even curse the wanton blood she'd inherited in her veins. She was glad of it, glad because it could make her feel like this, so cherished and attractive.

"I have to go back to London..." he said, still holding her gaze. She had known it, he'd said so before. "...The House of Lords will open soon. Come with me..." His gravelly words spilled into the air as though he'd not even thought about them and his pale earnest gaze burned into hers. "...I will buy you a house, a smart one somewhere close to Mayfair. I'll take you to the theatre and I'll buy you jewels, Katherine, and dresses, and bonnets, as many as you wish. You'll have everything you've ever dreamed of. I'll look after you."

His words threw her back into reality, and she felt as though he'd pushed her beneath the water in the lake all those years ago.

He was serious. He really thought she would wish to become his mistress in town. She felt sick and dirty, and foolish again. *Oh God, so foolish.* She had told him she loved him and he offered her this insult in return. Yet she had given her body to him as any fallen woman might for the price of a dress and a bonnet, of course he would now think this of her – he didn't understand love.

But she understood immorality. She would be looked down upon and rejected. She rolled away, rising. "I don't want those

180

things." She collected her nightgown from the floor and then slid it back on. "The only thing I have ever wanted is you."

"You'd have me."

She sighed, hearing him follow her, as her nightgown fell to sheathe her body.

Then she turned to face him. "No, John, I wouldn't have *you*. I would have the Duke."

His hand lifted. "Katherine…" She stepped back.

"I'm not for sale, John."

His brow furrowed, "I'm not buying you. I want you with me."

"You want," she echoed, angrily. "We cannot always have what we *want*, John."

His hand moved once more before she could step away again and he caught her wrist. "You wanted this. You came to me!"

Because you needed me! "I did, because I am frail like my mother. It does not mean I wish to publicly prostitute myself. Last night I told you how important Phillip and Papa are to me, and you would take them from me by suggesting *this*."

"They are not even your real family. You cannot care what they think."

Truly, he did not understand love. "I shall not be your mistress, John. It matters what they think, and to ask such a thing, you can have no respect for me."

His expression changed and closed as the bridges he'd put down last night were raised again, excluding her and not allowing her through.

"You do not want me?"

Not at the cost of herself. "Not like that, John."

His gaze held hers, his hand still gripping her wrist. "I'd not cast you off. You can trust me. I will keep you for the rest of your life if you'll let me?"

Katherine felt the bitter taste of his words. It was a vile thought. *I am not a whore. Am I?*

She was in his room, she'd come to him.

Cold crept through her.

"Let me go, John." She tugged against his grip.

His eyes were diamond-hard but his hand released her. "When may I see you then? When I am here next?"

Her heart thundered. No. It could not continue. She had learned her lesson. He thought her a whore, while she had offered love. She took a step back and then another, her pace increasing with each one. She was ready to run. "No, John. I think now it is over, as it should have been. You were right, there is nowhere this can go."

"Katherine?" His hand lifted as though he'd reach for her again. She turned and fled, racing out of his door as she heard him call again. "Katherine, wait!"

When she reached her room she threw herself on the bed and cried her heart out. Was this how her mother felt, too, when it was all over? Was this why she had taken her own life?

John dropped back to sit on the edge of the bed and his hand swept through his hair. What the hell had just happened and what on earth did she mean about being frail like her mother?

But her words had made him see with intense clarity what a blind idiot he'd been. He'd just offered a gently bred, innocent woman probably the biggest insult of her life.

Spoilt was not the half of it. He'd treated her like the women he'd learned to abhor on the continent. At that moment, he despised himself.

He got up, dressed, and went out to the stables, catching the grooms off-guard, but his stallion was ready in moments anyway and he took the animal out for a long hard ride. It was not the sport he would have chosen this morning but he could not be idle.

By the time he returned to The Place, the breakfast table was only half-full of guests. Most had already left, including Katherine, who Eleanor complained was very quiet.

Katherine had slipped away as quickly as possible to avoid him, no doubt.

182

What the hell did she think of him? He should have turned the bloody woman out last night. Still, what had been done could not be undone.

He thought of writing to her but what could he say? The word sorry would hardly suffice. Of course a marriage offer would put it all to rights, but she was the natural daughter of a milkmaid with an unknown father and he was a duke, the two did not mix. And he'd promised his grandfather on his deathbed to marry a woman of his own class. Besides, she would never cope with the public responsibilities of a duchess. She would be too out of place.

He realised then as he walked through the hall into the privacy of the library that he was actually weighing the idea up and considering it. But he couldn't do it. Looking up, he faced his grandfather's portrait, the old man's barbs were too deep in his blood. Even John's contrary nature could not quite go that far – just as becoming his mistress was a step too far for her.

They were at an impasse, then.

There was no going forward and no going back.

He stared at the portrait, holding the old man's unmoving gaze.

John would go to London today. There was no point in staying here. Let his mother close up the house. He'd leave.

Chapter Ten

John was bored in town, despite being constantly busy, and the issue with Wareham still irritated him. No new evidence had come to light and Wareham had left Ashford within hours of John. It seemed Wareham was following John, while John still had men following him.

John had former soldiers on Wareham's heels now, arranged by Harvey, because he feared Wareham might be more dangerous than anticipated. The man had made no further blackmail threats though, not yet. But why would Wareham publish whatever secret he held? The instant he did, it would lose its value. It was only valuable unsaid.

He'd taken rooms in the Oxford Hotel in Park Lane. No doubt spending John's stolen inheritance. John was impatient to trap him, yet he was not ready to move. He refused to be blackmailed, but he wanted to trace this damned invisible account before he confronted Wareham.

There was another thing John was impatient for, too – to know Wareham's secret. Harvey had sent scouts out to trace John's mother's absent history, but again, so far, there was no news.

John sighed.

While he waited for it, and for Harvey to discover Wareham's bank account, his thoughts kept turning to something else.

Katherine. She was always in his mind. She would not be forgotten. Often, even at the oddest moments, when he was speaking in the House of Lords, dining with his peers at White's, or attending some formal dinner or dance, she would spring into his thoughts. A single image or a sudden memory; Kate smiling or dancing at her sister's assembly; her touch on him; the sound of her voice; her sigh of impatience or her cry of pleasure – *her eyes*.

There were so many memories of her he would rather savour than forget. At night in bed, alone, he could feel her, visualise her. He would relive every moment of the night they'd spent together. She haunted his waking and his sleeping thoughts. He could barely manage more than ten minutes without thinking of her. He could concentrate on nothing but her. He wanted and needed Katherine Spencer with a physical and mental obsession that dulled his appetite and caused insomnia.

But with their impasse it was impossible. He had to conquer this craving. Yet that was easier said than done. It was as though Katherine had infected him. He felt empty inside, hollow, as though she'd taken something from him, and it hurt like hell.

I miss her. He was standing at the edge of Lady De Clare's long ballroom, watching the dancers, without watching them at all, after all Katherine was not among them. His world seemed so damned meaningless without her company to look forward to, no matter that he had power and circumstance to wield like a God, and hundreds of people reliant on him.

"The Duke of Pembroke, how novel…"

The feminine purr had John's head turning in recognition.

He'd not noticed Lady Ponsonby was here. If he had noticed, he would have left.

He could of course cut her, but the woman's hand intimately touched his arm before he had the chance. His muscle clenched in revulsion but he refused to show her any weakness.

"You're back. It's been a long time since I saw you"

It had not been long enough.

The contrast between this woman and Katherine could not be vaster. Lady Elizabeth Ponsonby was brash, ribald and risqué. She'd coaxed numerous men into cuckolding Lord Ponsonby, and regrettably John was among them.

He'd fallen hard for her in Paris and she'd taken his innocence, then discarded him and hurt him irreparably, with her cold-blooded nature and shallow affection. He'd thought his feelings returned, until one night he'd found another man with her. They'd laughed at his anger.

To his shame, during the brief affair John had never thought of her husband. He'd been drawn into the web of her world and been fighting to escape it ever since.

Her fingers brushed his shaven cheek. He pulled his head back.

"What? You're testy, John?"

"I am not testy, Elizabeth. I simply have no desire for your company. Is your husband here?" He looked across her shoulder, searching the gathering.

"He is here but as you know it hardly matters."

No, he remembered that, Ponsonby had his heirs so he turned a blind eye, as did most of society. These intrigues were rife. Elizabeth was no exception. And that was the cause of his real disengagement, why he'd never escaped her web, because since Elizabeth had opened his eyes he'd never been able not to see. For a while he'd lived that debauched life abroad, playing their games until he'd woken up and been disgusted by what he'd become. He hated the falseness of elite society.

Elizabeth gripped his arm and her touch made him feel unclean but he didn't shake her off. They were being observed by speculating eyes about the room.

He'd been stupidly naïve and indiscreet in his youth and stories had spread, not widely, but there were those in the room who knew of their past.

"You've matured, John. Dukedom suits you. You have a cut-throat edge." Laughing, she leaned closer. "It's alluring."

"I'm not interested, Elizabeth." He unwrapped her fingers from his arm.

"You do not convince me, John. They say love never dies. You must still carry a small flame for me." She was laughing at him, he knew, and her fingers just gripped lower down his arm.

"My infatuation with you was the error of youth. I see nothing of interest in you now. In fact, I find you revolting. So pray, go away." His tone was cold hatred and perhaps it finally convinced her, because her hand fell away and her expression briefly showed shock.

But with the skill of people of his class, she swiftly repaired her social mask and smiled. Then shook her head and turned away.

He'd probably never even been that attracted to her, he'd just been flattered by her ardent attentions and at an impressionable age. He wished it was a mistake he could undo.

As she walked away, John's mind turned back to Katherine and he remembered her saying she had watched him swimming in the lake before he'd gone to France. When he'd been caught in Elizabeth's net there had been a woman at home of much greater worth who had genuinely loved him.

If he'd have known then he could have loved her in return...

My God. For the first time he found a new truth in his thoughts. It came to him with blinding clarity. His susceptibility to Elizabeth stemmed from his upbringing. He'd wanted to be special to someone. Even then he'd been searching for someone to fill the aching hole inside him. His family's love had been too diluted by his brothers and sisters. They'd come along too quickly and he had not had enough time with his mother to banish the isolation of his younger days.

He'd thought he'd found that someone in Elizabeth. Her betrayal had just ripped open the old wound his mother had cut long before.

Katherine filled that void.

There was a sour taste in his mouth.

Elizabeth had broken his trust, he'd broken Katherine's. He'd taken her into his bed and left her behind, unloved. Just as Elizabeth had done to him.

He felt sick as he left the ball.

At home, if one could call the giant opulent villa in St James', home, John sat at the desk in the library and gripped a quill in his fingers. Ink dripped onto the page. No words would come.

He understood himself completely now. He longed for affection, for someone he would be upmost to. Elizabeth had destroyed that hope and Katherine had revived it.

But it was too late, he could not surmount their impasse. Yet he was beginning to think he felt love, despite the scorched ground of his barren soul.

The quill tip touched the paper and began to move as words flowed from his thoughts onto the page.

Katherine,

I cannot say too much in writing. I know you must be cursing my name, but I wanted you to know how I feel. That I feel. I have not stopped thinking of you. I cannot forget you. I am sorry things must be as they are. If it could be any other way, I would make it so.

You mean much to me, I will not forget you. I treasure the memories of us.

Do not hate me, Katherine. Love me still. Please. If I know that you do, I will always be able to feel you with me.

Yours completely, forever.

J

He felt drained as he applied the blotter to dry the ink, and then he folded the letter and used a blank seal, before addressing it. He would post it in the common mail to further hide its origin.

~

Accepting the letter from the tray which Mr Castle held forth, Katherine looked at the writing and frowned. Castle disappeared as she broke the seal.

Her father was seated at the head of the breakfast table, opening his own letters. Her mother and Jenny were busy discussing some call they were going to make.

Katherine's gaze fell to her half-eaten eggs and her stomach revolted. She gritted her teeth and held back the instinct to purge as she rose, whispering, "Excuse me, Papa," before leaving the room with hidden haste.

Once outside, though, she ran, racing upstairs in search of the chamber-pot in her room.

She threw up her accounts thrice before she dared sit up and as she did so she felt overwhelming despair.

Oh, what had she done? She wiped her mouth on the linen cloth used to cover the pot and knelt back on her heels.

What was she to do? She was such a fool, and fate was cruel, she had only taken one risk.

For the first two weeks she had tried to convince herself it was not true, but this was the end of the fourth week and she'd still had no blood, and now the sickness. She could no longer pretend.

She was carrying John's child.

It would be a bastard like her.

What would happen to them both?

If she told John, he'd support her. He had already offered, without even knowing of the child. But she had her pride. She did not wish the child to wear the label she had. She wanted her child to have a father and bear his name.

With her buttocks on her heels and the linen cloth in one hand, she remembered the letter which now lay on the floor. She picked it up and saw the signature, *J*. Him.

Her heart thumped.

The single page was the essence of the Duke of Pembroke, etched in a bold, ostentatious, swiftly written, graceful hand.

She read the words. They were John's.

She read it half a dozen times then let it fall to the floor again as tears ran down her cheeks. So, he was sorry and he cared. What did it matter? *If things could be any other way…* That was just it though – there was not another way – he would not offer her marriage, a Cinderella story was an impossible fiction. He had a duty to marry well and he was miles above her in status.

But she was still hurt by his cold denial. Setting reason aside, if he loved her, surely nothing would stand in the way. He simply did not feel enough for her.

Do not hate me, Katherine. Love me. It was a selfish request. She was to continue in pain so he might live with unblemished memories.

And what of our child? If she told him, he might take it from her.

That thought chilled her utterly.

For one night he'd loved her in the only way he knew how, she'd treasure the memory, as he'd said he would, but that was an end to it. She did not regret it, but she would not go to him. Let him do what he wished. She would give her love to her child now, not him.

~

John was surprised when Wareham played his next card in the game of "cut John down". He had not expected Wareham to approach him in person.

In an attempt to distract his thoughts from Katherine, he'd spurned ducal pomp and chosen to walk home from White's after luncheon and sent his carriage and footmen on. But when he turned into Regent Street, John saw Wareham immediately, approaching him among a crush of people.

John swore on his breath as the man grew nearer, hoping one of the men trailing Wareham was close enough to bear witness.

Wareham closed the distance, his gaze implying he was intent on waylaying John.

John kept walking, refusing to avoid Wareham, feeling certain now Wareham had watchers too.

"You look tired, Your Grace, does something disturb your sleep...?" Wareham stopped in John's path.

Unless he wished to step around Wareham, John had to stop too, and he felt as though he was on an island in a river of humanity as people kept walking either side of them.

John said nothing, merely held the man's gaze. His lack of sleep was due to Katherine anyway, not this man.

"I've not heard from you. Are you gathering the funds? If you do not, I shall share your mother's past"

John's jaw stiffened. "Any information is useless if you publish."

"That depends upon my reasons for publishing. Perhaps I would take pleasure in telling the world the truth about your mother."

And what the hell is it? Perhaps John should let Wareham do it, at least he'd know then. "If that was your aim, why write and warn me, just *publish*."

The man smiled.

Hatred filled John.

Wareham leaned closer, "Because I like playing with you, and the price has just doubled, Your Grace."

Angry beyond tolerance, John moved past him and walked on, blind to all the people swelling about him.

What did Wareham know?

John refused to look back and let Wareham see how much his words had kicked.

God, he needed this resolved, but he would not give the man money.

John's destination changed.

"Your Grace." The clerk said as John entered Harvey's offices. Then Harvey appeared.

"I was not expecting, Your Grace. To what do I owe the honour?"

"You owe it to Wareham..."

In Harvey's office, John expanded. "I had the unfortunate pleasure of walking into him just now. I doubt it was an accident, which means he is definitely watching my movements, as I am watching his, and he has upped his price to keep his silence over whatever information he holds on Lady Edward."

"Ah." Wareham sighed, leaning forward and resting his elbows on his desk.

"Ah, indeed," John mimicked, "but from what I gleaned, I doubt he is interested in the money, it's revenge. Although what he has to be vengeful over I have no idea. Yet it is clear he feels animosity towards me."

"Because Your Grace has spotted the error in his figures no doubt?"

John was not convinced of that, and Wareham did not even know he'd found out about it yet. No, there was something else.

"Have you any conclusions on either my mother or the money?"

"I'm sorry, Your Grace, no. I am still working on both topics."

John gritted his teeth and closed his eyes. He just wished this done with.

He opened his eyes again. "I want more men put on this. I want it resolved, Harvey."

The businessman smiled.

John did not.

"Forgive me," Harvey leant back in his chair. "There are many times Your Grace has the look of the old Duke, and it catches me unawares. I understand. Of course, I will increase our resources as Your Grace desires."

A prickle ran up John's spine when he heard Harvey's reference to the old man. John did feel more and more like him, yet he was feeling less and less in control of his life.

John stood, moved to the window, and then looked out onto the street.

There was a young lad hovering by the railings outside the property next door, staring up at Harvey's offices.

Well at least John knew who his shadow was, just a boy.

Hell. I want this over.

Still facing the street, he said, "I wish you to write to all of my stewards, and all those managing my business ventures. They know Wareham has gone and that I gave him notice but I have not shared why." John turned back. "Tell them… No. Warn them. I expect to be dealt with openly and honestly and in return I will manage them and my affairs fairly and with integrity. But disloyal service will bring equal rewards."

Harvey reached for paper, quill and ink and began to make a brief note. He understood, John knew, but there was no harm in underlining the point.

"I am *not* my grandfather. They will have to learn to deal with me, and you may tell them that in the coming months I will be visiting all my properties and reviewing in detail all my investments. I expect to find them in good order, but I shall not give notice of my arrival."

Mr Harvey's head lifted and he smiled. "I said Your Grace has the *look* of the old Duke not that Your Grace is like him, they will not have mistaken it, but I shall happily make it clear."

John valued this man. Harvey was one of the few he felt safe letting his guard down with. Perhaps that was why he was here. Seeing Wareham had been disturbing. Yet John realised then that Harvey was one of his older staff, there would come a day soon when John would lose Harvey, and then what? John sighed and then admitted, "I would be lost without you, Harvey…" He picked his words with care then. "…But one day I suppose I shall have to manage… I … I wonder if you have ever thought of working with anyone to prepare them to take over, when the time comes…"

Harvey's eyebrow's lifted but John could see he'd taken no offence. "My clerks know most of my affairs, but you are right, as ever, Your Grace, I will put some time into finding a suitable replacement and set about ensuring he is capable."

John nodded. "Thank you."

A knock on the door punctuated the conclusion of their conversation as a clerk entered.

When John walked home, he thought of Phillip, and the thought germinated.

Phillip had already shown his loyalty by raising the issue of Wareham's loan. Perhaps Phillip could be the one to play understudy to Harvey? Now there was a thought. That would surely throw Katherine into John's path again at some point.

A pain gripped in his chest as images of Katherine filled his thoughts once more.

God, he was seeking men of integrity, when he'd shown none to Katherine. If she ever did see him again she would mostly likely cut him dead.

When John reached home, he let Finch take his hat and gloves and then walked into the library.

He was a liar. He was perfectly capable of feeling. He felt anger, gratitude, disgust *and loss*. He'd been taught not to. He'd sought to pretend he did not, then failed in France and then hidden away in Egypt so he might have no stimulation. But emotions were there.

There was one of his sketchbooks from Egypt lying on the desk; he'd been glancing through it last evening, trying to distract his thoughts.

He sat and began flicking through the images of pyramids and temples, then reached the sketches he'd started last night. Katherine. He picked up his charcoal and began refining them.

"Your Grace, may I fetch you anything?"

John turned the page back and lifted his gaze to Finch who stood at the open door, and nodded. "Yes, a brandy, please, Finch."

When Finch left, John's eyes caught on his grandfather's portrait. "I am not you," he whispered harshly at the portrait. "I feel."

When his gaze fell, it stuck on the pile of invitations discarded on his desk.

His mother and father had come to town five days ago. They were planning to bring Mary out during the autumn. They were staying with Edward's brother, Robert.

John sighed. He should be hurt that they'd chosen to stay in his uncle's smaller residence. He was not. He'd not wished them here. Yet it was another line drawn between them.

They had sent him an open invitation to call. He had not gone.

Suddenly he longed for Katherine again. He felt as though he was dying internally without her.

Pushing aside the sketchbook, he picked up paper and a quill and then dipped the quill in ink. He had to say something more. He wished her here. Perhaps if he asked again?

I miss you still. I wish you were here. Have you thought about my offer? If you have changed your mind? Well, just write to me, whenever you wish, whenever you decide. My feelings are unchanged, my offer is not withdrawn.

Remember me,

J

Once the words were blotted and the letter sealed, he felt better. He would see it posted and then call on his parents and try to build a bridge between them.

He walked again, because he would not give Wareham a victory and let the man think he controlled any aspect of John's life.

His uncle's townhouse was in Bloomsbury Square.

Jenkins, the butler, opened the door and immediately grinned. "Your Grace, it is good to see you."

John had not called here since his return. His family always came to him.

The butler bowed and then took John's outdoor articles.

"Is my mother in?"

"Lady Edward is in the drawing room with Lady Barrington, the Duchess of Arundel and Miss Marlow. Shall I introduce Your Grace?"

"No, I'll surprise her." And it would be a surprise.

He climbed the stairs at a jog, knowing he had an apology to make. He had unfairly hounded her at Pembroke Place.

When he reached the drawing room, the door was ajar so pushing it wider he walked straight in.

The women were huddled on the sofas near the hearth, and they turned as one, his mother, Aunt Jane, Aunt Penny and Mary.

His mother stood, blushing, and her chin lifted. She was obviously prepared to defend herself. She'd responded the same way when his grandfather called. John felt his stomach tighten in disgust. Was that what he had done to her, made her fear him?

"John," she uttered, "we did not expect you."

"I had nothing else to do. I hope I am not intruding." He forced a smile and walked towards her.

She curtsied.

He took her hand and drew her up, then kissed her cheek. "Mama," his inflection spoke his apology, without saying the words.

A hesitant smile then formed on her lips but he could see forgiveness and gratitude in her eyes. She hugged him then and whispered to his ear, "I am glad you came." He was glad too. "You are interrupting nothing," she said more loudly, drawing away and keeping a hold of his hand for a moment. He sat beside her. "But our conversation may bore you. We are planning Mary's come-out. Will you stay for refreshments?"

He nodded, feeling another punch of guilt as he realised he ought to be sponsoring Mary. Edward had no title.

John offered up his townhouse for the ball and made a promise to escort Mary to a number of events. His name would give her opportunities Edward's would not.

In return he received joyous gratitude from his sister and approval from his mother and his aunts.

~

Katherine lay back on the bed, her stomach churning. The morning

196

sickness had not eased and she'd not taken breakfast for days. It seemed better to simply stay away from the table.

It was a good thing then that her family paid so little attention to her. None of them said a word.

With one hand on her stomach, she thought of John's child growing there.

There was a feeling of awe to think of a child, a part of John, developing in her womb, and yet there was fear too. She didn't know what to do. Pain gripped in her chest, constricting her throat, and tears tumbled from her eyes.

For days now she had been building up her courage to ask Richard for help. He'd helped other women in the parish find somewhere safe. But she would lose his respect and his friendship, and she would lose Phillip and her father when she left.

She sighed.

At the beginning of this dreadful folly, she'd longed to know how her mother had felt. Now Katherine knew. Alone and ashamed. No wonder her mother had taken her own life.

Tears ran again.

Katherine was her mother's perfect legacy – frail and naïve. But she would not follow her mother to the grave. She wished the child to live and have its mother.

A slight knock struck her bedchamber door.

Katherine rose, ignoring the lurch of her stomach. She had dressed, in case anyone came.

She crossed to the window seat and picked up her mending. Then she called, "Come in," and set a smile on her face, belying her inner despair.

Hetty entered, waving a letter. "'Aven't you eaten, Miss? This letter was left on the table. You've barely touched a thing in days. Still, here you are, I brought it up so you'd 'ave it, Miss."

Hetty had noted Katherine's absence then, even if her family had not.

"Thank you," she accepted the letter and ignored everything else.

Hetty bobbed a superficial curtsy, then left.

Katherine felt faint when she saw the bold script. John's. She took a deep breath and broke the seal.

He'd written just three lines, which spoke his lack of respect for her. He repeated the offer he'd made in the summer and said again, *remember me*. She did not wish to, not anymore. She wished to forget him. She would not live in sin with him. Her child would not grow up being called his bastard. The letter only spurred her to speak to Richard. She could trust Richard.

Angry, she crossed to her small travelling desk and then wrote a letter back.

~

When John spotted Katherine's writing amidst his post his heart stuttered to a sharper pace and his lungs felt as though there was no air in the room. His hand shook as he broke the seal.

It was addressed formally to the Duke of Pembroke. He knew without reading a word it was a rebuff.

I'm sure you think your contacting me is kindness. It is not. It is, as usual, selfish. "Remember me." "Love me." Do you ever not think of yourself?

I do not wish to remember you anymore. I wish to forget you, and that dreadful mistake.

Then you renew your offer, as though I should be honoured, when it is entirely lacking honour. My answer is no, and will always be, no! Pray, if you have an ounce of human feeling, as you claimed to in your last letter, leave me alone. I do not want to hear from you. What was between us is over. All you are doing is hurting me more because I did love you and you did not love me.

Have a heart, John.

It was not even signed.

John felt a chasm rip open in his chest, a sharp pain that cut him in two.

She'd said she *did* love him – loved – she did not love him now.

The letter fell from his fingers and slipped to the floor. A footman bent and picked it up before refilling John's coffee cup.

John felt sick and empty. He'd lost Katherine.

But then anger came in a rush. *Fool, I never had her. She was never mine to have.*

He stood, with an urge to run. But where would he run to.

He picked the letter up from the table, folded it and then put it in his pocket, forcing himself to have some control. Then he picked the others up too and left the table.

In his private sitting room upstairs, he dropped the rest of the post on a small table and then walked to the hearth, where the embers still glowed. He tossed Katherine's letter into them and watched it catch alight and burn.

Hell. He needed to get over her. She had gotten over him.

What foolhardy notion had possessed him to make that offer again? *Need. Desperate, bloody need.* His fingers curled into fists, then released.

He longed to go to Pembroke Place and see her, yet it would hardly be worth doing so now. But he was the Duke of Pembroke, he could do anything he wished. He could go there and steal her away if he chose. He could force her into accepting by threatening to destroy her father.

God, you are an ass, John.

He'd not do that. He'd do what she asked and leave her alone. His gaze caught his reflection in the mirror and he snarled. He didn't like that man. His fingers lifted and swept back his fringe.

But how do I let her go? It was an anguished thought.

Pray, if you have an ounce of human feeling in your heart, leave me alone.

Did he? Could he?

Tomorrow was Sunday. She would be with her vicar.

John felt as though she had been the glue which held him together and now he was falling apart. He forced himself to sit down and read his other letters.

The clock chimed eleven behind him. He remembered promising to call on his mother so she could bring him up to date on their plans.

He rose, and leaving the letters there, left the room.

Inside him was dry, barren sand again. Any doubt left in him that he could feel was dispelled. He felt. He hurt like hell.

Calling for his curricle, John strode downstairs, pain eating at his innards with harsh, unrelenting bites.

He drove through the streets absent-mindedly, nearly running over people at a crossing.

By the time he reached his uncle's, he'd realised the truth. It had hit him like a fist. He loved Katherine. He'd loved her for months. This infatuation, which was far beyond lust or any physical need, it had to be love. He'd never felt like this for any woman before.

"John!" Mary called from across the hall as he stepped over the threshold. She had their youngest sister balanced on her hip. "You're early."

He nodded, without saying a word, feeling too much pain in his chest to speak as he passed everything off to Jenkins.

He had pushed his family away too, and yet *they* had hung on, *because they loved him*. He should try and return that love from now on.

"Mama is upstairs in the nursery, playing spillikins with the little ones. Jemima kept destroying the game so I brought her down." As she spoke Mary crossed the room, and when she reached him she held the little girl out towards him, smiling brightly.

"Here, take her. I'll go and fetch Mama."

Unwilling to refuse and show his discomfort with the younger ones, John took his youngest half-sister, bracing her weight in his hands as he lifted the child to his chest.

"I will not be long," Mary breathed. "Take her up to the drawing room. I'll be there in a moment." Mary turned away, and lifting her skirt with one hand, ran upstairs, with her other hand brushing over the banister.

John followed, cradling the little girl on one forearm, his hand bracing her leg, while his other palm splayed over her back.

He'd held Mary like this when he'd been eleven or twelve. He climbed the stairs with care while Jemima played with the knot of his cravat.

More memories of Mary and Robbie stirred. Although by the time Robbie had come along John had tired of the novelty of having young siblings. He'd lost interest in them soon after. He'd preferred Phillip's company, so Phillip had been invited to stay for most of the holidays, and in general they'd ignored John's siblings, only Katherine had been allowed to intrude on their camaraderie, if they were at Pembroke Place.

The possibility of Phillip replacing Harvey occurred to John again. If Katherine would let him have nothing to do with her, he could at least favour her family. He'd hire Phillip.

As John neared the drawing room, Jemima stretched out her legs and her chubby little fingers gripped at the shoulders of his morning coat. It was a silent request to be put down. *God*, he remembered Mary doing the same.

He leant down and set the child on her feet but she couldn't walk yet and so she gripped his fingers, bouncing on unsteady legs. Thus they crossed the room.

What would it be like to sire a child with Katherine?

A blonde-haired girl, like her mother, with shining blue eyes and a bright smile.

His little sister led him to the window seat, and there she let him go and gripped the cushion instead. He sat down and then lifted her up and instantly the little girl pressed her nose to the pane and looked down at the passing traffic and his curricle in the street below.

He withdrew a shiny sixpence from his pocket and steadying

her with one hand, began spinning the coin through his fingers. His Uncle Robert had taught him the trick when John was a child.

Jemima watched and then squealed and tried to catch it just at the moment his mother, Mary, and his aunt Jane arrived.

John caught hold of Jemima before she fell, and slipped the coin into his pocket.

His Aunt Jane's figure was expanding again.

No one could question his family's ability to breed.

It would have irritated him a couple of months ago but today it made him feel jealous. All his family were in love matches.

"Are you well, John?"

His gaze lifted and met Mary's questioning look.

He blanked his expression, as his mother moved to collect Jemima.

"I'm well," he stated, rising. "And you?"

She nodded, smiling broadly. "I am ridiculously excited, I cannot sleep." John kissed her cheek. "You are still coming tonight, to Aunt Jane's supper party?"

He nodded then smiled, deliberately letting his guard down. "Come then, tell me all your plans and my role in them." This would take his mind off his own troubles anyway.

Chapter Eleven

"Are you ready, Katherine?"

Katherine turned as Richard called. They'd slipped back into the old routine since John had left, but it had never felt quite the same. She nodded when he came into the chapel and then took his offered arm.

When he handed her up into his horse and trap a few moments later, she met his gaze for the first time. She had not been able to look him in the eye; now she blushed. He smiled.

As he drove, she sat in silence. It was cold and the autumn breeze swept at her bonnet and brought jewel-coloured leaves spinning down from the trees – amber, ruby and gold.

"Here, put this rug over your lap."

She glanced at him, accepted the blanket and spread it over her legs.

This was the time to speak but the words would not come. She sensed him look across at her. She did not look back.

Richard sighed, then he said, "What is bothering you, Kate? There is something…"

She still did not look at him, as her hands gripped the rug to stop them shaking.

He slowed the horses from a trot to a walk. "You may trust me, Katherine. I am your friend."

She turned and faced him. She just had to say the words... "I have made a terrible mistake, Richard... I am with child."

A look of shock struck his face and he pulled the horses to a halt then tied the reins off.

"It is—"

"Pembroke's." His voice was steady but there was a pitch of judgement in it. "I warned you against him. Did he force you?"

"No! No. It was not like that."

"Just seduced you and then left."

Tears brimmed in her eyes. Yes, she supposed she had been seduced by the idea of John, not by John.

Richard's hand lay over hers. "Do not worry. We shall sort it out."

She shivered. "How?"

His arm came about her shoulders then and he held her. He'd never held her before, but she needed comfort and she held him too, burying her face in his neckcloth and hugging his midriff. But he was not John. He did not have John's physique or strength. He did not make her feel secure. But what was secure about John?

He was silent for a while, then he said, "Katherine... I...I need a wife. I have wished to ask you anyway... and now... Now... Well, it would seem to be the best answer." Drawing from his hold, she met his gaze. "I would bring the child up as my own. We will have to change parish of course. We cannot raise it here, people may realise if it were to look like Pembroke. But I swear I shall take care of you both." She saw sincerity in his eyes and felt steadier.

What choice did she have? She liked Richard. He would do everything he promised.

But he is not John.

"If you agree, we shan't delay, I will call the banns immediately, and once we are married I'll give notice here. Will you accept me, Katherine? Will you be my wife?" He caught her fingers up, then kissed them.

What choice did she have? This would solve everything. Her child would have a father. "Yes, Richard." Her heart beat hard.

"You must know, though, Katherine…" His fingers still gripped hers. "…My offer is purely selfish. I am in love with you."

"Oh, Richard." She hugged him again. He was good and kind, it was not selfish to willingly take on John's child. Richard could have despised her. He did not.

"I lay no blame on you."

He should, though, she had let this happen, she had said yes in the beginning, and in the end she was the one who had gone to John. It was her fault. "I do bear blame," she whispered, looking forwards again. "It was my fault. I loved him, Richard. I'm sorry if it changes how you feel…"

"It does not." His hand gripped hers harder. "I know what you felt for him, I could see that, and I saw him take advantage of it."

Richard was painting John as cruel. He was selfish and spoilt, but she did not think him cruel. She still loved John. *Yet I will be Richard's wife…*

~

John walked into the narrow hall of what was basically a brothel. He was with his Harding cousins, the twins, Harry and Oliver. His cousins from his father's side were more of an age with him and he'd been close to them at Oxford.

The house was packed to the brim with men of his class.

John had only come because, when Oliver had recommended a night at the opera, and later a party, John had seen an opportunity to cure his apathy. He'd never associated with courtesans before. He hadn't needed to. Other men's wives and widows had been more than willing to satisfy his need. But his cousins did associate with courtesans. They'd watched the opera in the courtesans' theatre box, with others who sought the attention of the birds of paradise. John had stood at the back and listened to their idle flirtation but had not participated.

The women had made much of him, teasing him for his silence.

205

It amused his cousins. It only annoyed John. He found the women's make-up and their forced high-pitched giggles and low bodices simply crass. Yet he had not been able to just take himself away, because he was bored of his own company and hunting for something tonight, a woman to ease his pain.

They had accompanied the diamonds of the demi-monde home for an open house, but when the invitation had been extended he'd foolishly assumed it would only be the occupants of the theatre box here; no, there were three dozen more men massaging the egos of the whores. There was no space in the hall, or air.

He followed his cousins.

He needed a mistress, some woman who'd dispel Katherine from his mind.

Oliver and Harry led him into a packed salon where men stood talking in groups.

The liquor was flowing and one of the women played a pianoforte in the far corner. Four men stood about her. Another woman was sitting in an alcove with a companion, and at the far end of the room two more were playing three-card loo with other men. A crowd was gathering about them.

Oliver pressed a glass into John's hand and John caught the eye of the woman at the pianoforte.

She smiled.

Her hair was a similar colour to Katherine's and her smile was guileless.

John left his cousins and crossed the room. When she came to the end of her tune, she stood and picked up a glass of champagne, then sipped from it. When her gaze caught his, she dropped a curtsy.

John smiled, well aware she was posturing to capture his interest. He knew these women were favouring him. He would be a coup because he did not normally enter their circles. He was not put off by it. But perhaps that was merely because she reminded him of Katherine.

"The Duke of Pembroke, if I am not mistaken. This is the first time I have seen you here, Your Grace." Her voice was sweet. It did not have the urging lilt of a harlot.

"That would be because it is the first time I have wished for such relief."

"I am happy to oblige." She smiled at his careless innuendo, anticipation suddenly shining in her eyes.

He felt revulsion.

"Your Grace." She touched his arm.

His distaste sharpened.

She was not Katherine. She was nothing like Katherine. And it was Katherine he wanted.

He set his glass down on the pianoforte and turned away, then left without even finding his cousins and saying goodnight.

Lord, how much longer would this pain endure? He couldn't bear it.

When he reached the street, he breathed in the cold night air and gathered his thoughts as he began walking home. What would it matter if he wed the girl? His blood was not really blue, it was as red as hers, no matter that his family were descendants of medieval royalty.

A breeze caught the tails of his evening coat; he had no outer coat.

Was he really contemplating marrying her, then?

Yes.

If she accepted, it would be hard on her. Society would not easily accept her. But it was fickle, and people would forget.

His family would support her, though. She could weather the storm. He'd carry her through it.

The old man would turn in his grave. Perhaps he'd even come back to haunt them.

Did that put John off?

No.

With the thought hanging in his mind, John kept walking. It

was not a decision he should make hastily. There would be no going back. He needed to be certain.

But already the weight in his chest seemed lighter, merely at the thought.

~

John strolled about the crowded ballroom.

Mary's debut ball was crushed full of people. She and his mother were overjoyed.

His grandmother was here, too, of course. She'd been glowing with pride ever since Mary had come downstairs.

His sister looked magnificent in gleaming cream silk with her dark hair pinned high and secured with diamond-tipped pins. They glistened in the light thrown from the chandeliers, and she was illuminated by joy.

John had been the first to take her onto the floor and as they'd danced he'd noted numerous appreciative male eyes following her. He doubted it would be long before she settled.

He watched her now. She was dancing with their father, and Edward's gaze shone brightly with admiration.

John saw his mother watching, too, across the room. Her eyes glinted with tears.

His parents had been emotional all evening, watching Mary make her mark on society. He knew now his mother had never had her debut. She'd eloped with his father before her time. His Aunt Penny had mentioned it during their planning.

Yet beyond that he still knew very little about her life.

She'd spent the year before his birth as an army wife, on the edge of battlefields, but he knew nothing about what had happened afterwards. Well, not until she'd returned when he was ten.

Mary laughed as the dance drew to a close.

Then the notes of a waltz began, John found himself moving towards his mother without thought. When he reached her, he held out his hand, asking without words.

She looked surprised but accepted, gripping his white-gloved fingers.

He smiled as he led her to the floor, trying to relax and let down his guard a little.

She smiled too as they formed the frame of the waltz. "Thank you. I cannot believe you are both so grown up."

Her eyes looked past his shoulder for a moment as he turned her. John saw his stepfather watching. He looked pleased.

"The years have passed so quickly." She met his gaze.

"Yes."

Mary was dancing with Lord Griffin, a young man with immense charm, who John had seen courting the attentions of a harlot last week.

John was going to have to give Mary, and Edward, a list of the men she should avoid.

John thought of Katherine, sweet innocent Katherine. The tender bud of an English rose he'd plucked. *God,* if someone treated Mary as he'd treated Katherine, he'd kill them. He'd call them out and press the tip of a pistol or a sword into their chest.

Guilt was a heavy sensation, and it was becoming a common feeling since he'd received Katherine's terse note telling him to leave her alone.

"I know you're angry, John…" his mother said. She must have misunderstood the surge of emotion in him. "…Because you did not have the life the young ones have, but I love you equally."

John's gaze turned back to her. "I do not begrudge them your love, Mama."

Her gaze held his but the conversation ended. She probably did not believe him, and she certainly did not understand the mixed-up emotions which tormented him. He had never understood them himself.

Last night, the feelings of loss he suffered over Katherine had somehow got tangled up in it all and his dream had come again, but this time it was not his mother left behind running after the carriage, it was Katherine.

Tears had shone in her eyes as she'd cried out to him, heartbroken.

He'd been shaking when he woke. He wished to have Katherine in his life in a permanent capacity, and the only option now was marriage. Yet he was bound by a stupid deathbed promise to marry someone of his own class.

The music drew to a close with a flourish, and when John stopped dancing, his mother's hand braced against his cheek. "I wish I knew how to reach you, John, you hold yourself so distant, and sometimes I see so much pain in your eyes."

His stare hardened in answer. He did not wish her seeing into him. "I am trying my best, Mama. I cannot be what I am not."

"I know, John. I only say it because I care, it is not a reprimand."

"I know."

He led her back to Edward then and saw Finch move in the same direction.

"Your Grace, may I speak with you?" Finch said as John let his mother go. John nodded and then excused himself from his parents.

As he followed Finch from the room, John guessed it was not about the entertainment.

In the hall, Finch stopped and turned. "Forgive me, Your Grace, Mr Harvey has called. He believed you would wish to see him."

"Where is he?" John's heart raced. Did Harvey finally have something more on Wareham?

"In the library, Your Grace."

"Thank you."

A footman opened the library door and John passed through it. It closed behind him.

Harvey was standing at the hearth, warming one outstretched hand. He turned. His other hand held a glass of brandy. He had obviously been waiting a little while.

"Your Grace, I apologise, I did not realise you were entertaining. Had I known, I would not have come, but I knew Your Grace would wish to see this…"

"What?" John asked, crossing to the decanters. He poured himself a drink, watching Harvey collect a file from the desk.

"This."

John looked at the leather folder Harvey held out.

"Lady Edward's history, Your Grace. I have not read it. I did not like to. The statements were drawn from a colleague in Captain Harding's regiment, and also the former owner of a London gambling-house."

John felt his eyebrows lift and his blood ran cold. Half of him did not want to know. The other half could not endure not knowing.

The brandy burned his throat as he drank from the glass and took the file. Then he moved to sit behind his desk.

Harvey stood in silence as John opened it. Anger and disgust rose with every word John read. He knew they were true. They explained so much of what he'd known and not understood.

From his father's death, his mother had lived as a mistress – *a whore*. She'd belonged to four men, passing from one to another. It was noted that on two occasions she'd been passed on via a hand of cards. The second time – the last time she had changed protector – Lord Edward Marlow, John's stepfather, had won.

John let the last paper fall and picked up his glass again. His teeth were clenched hard against a desire to annihilate the men who'd treated her so badly. By these accounts, although they were scarce on detail, his mother had neither been willing nor content, but used.

John's hand covered his mouth for a moment, and then his fingers swept through his hair.

This was not a burden lifted but another to bear.

His gaze rose to the portrait of his grandfather. The old man had fetched John. The old man had come to France and taken John away and left *her* there, *his daughter*.

211

John drank the dregs in his glass, closed the folder and then stood.

Harvey was watching, so John schooled his expression.

"Thank you, Mr Harvey. I appreciate you bringing it here. You may go now."

"You're welcome, Your Grace. Contact me if there is anything I may do." With that, Harvey bowed and left.

John took a deep breath, and then went to ask the footman outside to fetch his mother. "Please tell Lady Edward I wish to speak to her here. She may wish to bring Lord Edward."

The footman bowed before disappearing.

John shut the door then returned to the desk to collect and refill his glass.

When the door opened again, he turned to see his mother slip into the room, Edward was not with her.

"Mama, sit down." He tried not to sound bitter but he probably failed.

"What is it?" she asked uncertainly, sitting in an armchair opposite his desk. She swept the skirts of her pale-blue gown beneath her as she did so, with her usual effortless grace.

She was the daughter of a duke. To him she'd always seemed so perfect, sparkling and beautiful – it was like looking up at the sun. "I know," he said, with neither explanation nor emotion.

She just stared at him, clearly not comprehending. But then her chin tipped upwards and her posture straightened, fractionally. "What?"

"Everything," John answered as he rested his buttocks on the lip of the desk and crossed his feet and arms.

Her eyes widened.

"As you would not tell me, I had Harvey find out. I have it all here." He threw a glance at the file on his desk. "A statement drawn from a man in my father's regiment, and a madam who ran a club in London you used to attend with Lord Gainsborough."

Her skin paled and her hand pressed to her chest. "Why did

you do that, John?" Her voice carried disappointment and pain as she stood.

"I thought *why* was my question, Mama."

Her fingers were shaking.

John moved. He poured her a brandy and took it to her.

"I am not talking to you about it," she whispered harshly, shaking her head and refusing the brandy. "I will not, John."

"I am not accusing you, Mama. I can see from the statements it was not your choice. I merely want to know why Grandfather took me back and not you? Why you lived like that? You are the daughter of a duke. How did you end up a common whore?"

Her eyes suddenly shone with tears.

He set the glass down on his desk.

She backed away, walking behind the chair, as though seeking refuge, and gripped its back.

The door opened.

They both looked across as Edward entered. "What is it?" he asked jovially, looking at John. "Mary is wondering where you've gone. The supper dance is next and you'd promised it…" He stopped speaking when his gaze passed to John's mother. "Ellen, what is it? What's wrong?" Edward crossed the room.

In the next moment she was sobbing into Edward's cravat.

John felt guilty. But why should he? He had the right to know this. While he'd endured a lonely childhood, she'd been earning her living on her back. He'd not even been Jemima's age when this had all begun.

"He knows," his mother whispered. "He had Mr Harvey investigate my past."

Edward's brow furrowed and he glared his accusation.

John stared back. Why should he explain himself? He had a right to know.

"Why would you do that?" Edward challenged.

John leant his buttocks back against the desk and folded his arms again. There was no point in them holding back the rest,

213

but just to make that clear, he said, "I know about the card game you had with Lord Gainsborough."

Edward's eyes suddenly glowed hot and dark with anger, and letting John's mother go, he stepped forwards.

John thought Edward would hit him. He did not, though.

Refusing to be pressured, John merely said, "All I want to know is, why?"

Edward's hands fisted. "Why do this tonight, John? It's Mary's evening. She's waited years for this." Bitterness and disgust burned in Edward's voice.

John straightened. "While I have waited *all my life*… I have not planned this to happen tonight. Harvey just turned up."

Turning away, John picked up the glass his mother had not touched, then handed it to Edward, before picking up his own. "I've sacked Wareham."

Edward sighed. "And what has that to do with anything?"

"He'd been fleecing Grandfather for years, he's stolen thousands." John met Edward's gaze. "Harvey hasn't found the money yet, so Wareham has not been charged. Yet the man's greedy, he's been threatening me with Mama's past. How would you rather I found out the truth, from you or from the broadsheets?" John looked at his mother. "I admit, I was hurt by the fact he could threaten me with something you hadn't cared to share. And you would not even tell me when I asked." He looked back to his father. "But I did not *choose* tonight to tell you. Harvey just happened to obtain the information today. I'm sorry, but having read it, I could not go back in that room and pretend I had not seen it." He looked back at his mother.

Her gaze softened, and instead of anger and disappointment he saw pity. But when she approached him to offer comfort, he leant away.

"I just want to know *why*, Mama?"

Her hands dropped to her sides and she looked pained by the need to speak, yet she did speak. "He didn't give me a choice, John.

214

When your father died, I was stranded on the continent. I had no money to bring you home. Your grandfather had disowned me. I wrote, begging him and your father's family for help. My father came. But by then a man was supporting me. I hadn't realised there was a price. I couldn't let us starve. My father took you away from me and told everyone I was dead. But you knew I was not, John. I ensured you knew. I had my old maid bring you to visit me, and I wrote to you, John."

John finished his drink and set the glass down, then opened his arms to her. She came to him. He held her tightly, giving comfort and receiving it. His grandfather would think this weakness. John did not care. He felt like that child again, the boy who had been driftwood and always felt as though he was about to drown.

Her fingers ran through John's hair as she pulled away.

He took a deep breath. "I'm sorry," he stated in a low, husky voice, which was forced past a lump in his throat.

She smiled tentatively, tears on her cheeks. "It was not your fault, John. I never wished to speak of this with you. But it was not your fault."

He kissed her cheek. "I would rather know, Mama, so I understand."

She nodded, her tears spilling over again. She wiped them away with the wrist of her evening glove. "I shall go and refresh and then return to Mary. I will not have her know something is wrong."

John nodded.

She looked at Edward.

"I'll be with you in a moment, I wish to speak with John first."

When the door closed behind her, Edward stared at John.

"Will she be well?" John asked.

"Yes, I'll make sure she is." Edward pressed a hand on John's shoulder. "I know this news must be hard for you to hear, son, I understand your anger, but it is hard for your mother to speak of it. She feels shame."

His hand fell away.

"How long was it after you met her that you came to fetch me? I remember you married as soon as we reached Uncle Robert's."

Edward smiled. "A month or so, not long. I didn't even know you existed until that night. She would not leave Gainsborough. It was not until I saw you that I understood why. What your report probably does not tell you is that Gainsborough kept her by threat. He'd told her he'd abduct you if she ran away, and blackmailed your Grandfather with the threat of revealing her existence."

John's eyebrows lifted as he felt shock lance through him.

"Gainsborough beat her, too. But she was too afraid to run and she had nowhere to run to until I met her. She'd felt trapped." Edward glanced up at the old man's portrait then. "We fought hard to get you back." He looked at John and drained his glass of brandy, then added, "For God's sake stop modelling yourself on him. And take that bloody picture down. I have too many awful memories of both him and this room." Then his voice firmed, and the muscle in his cheeks set hard. "Now you may tell me where to find Wareham, and I'll settle this. I presume you know."

John nodded, smiling slightly as he watched the change from amiable family man, to formidable leader. No wonder Edward had won out against John's grandfather. Edward was well respected by his tenants for his firm but caring hand.

John had been forced to follow his grandfather's education, but surely the better role model stood before him. "I'll come with you."

"No," Edward stated, bluntly. "You'd be missed, go back to your guests, keep Mary smiling." Accepting it without argument, feeling too wrung out to care, John gave Edward the address.

Edward looked back before he left, though. "If your mother asks, don't tell her where I've gone. I'll be back as quick as I can." Then he added, as though on an afterthought, "Would you ask your Uncle Robert to meet me in the hall, I'll take him with me."

John agreed, but before Edward could turn away again, he asked, "What happened to Lord Gainsborough?"

Edward smiled. "Your Uncle Robert killed him. It was

216

self-defence. He tried to kill your mother."

With that, Edward turned and left.

John looked up at the old man's portrait.

His father was right, John would take it down and the one at The Place, too.

"You bastard!" John felt no commitment to his deathbed promise now. It was void. If John wished to marry Katherine, he would marry Katherine. Sod the old man and sod the opinion of the world. She was what mattered. Everyone else could go to hell.

Chapter Twelve

John ran up the steps to the house and smiled at Finch as he passed through the door.

The special licence he'd recently obtained was burning a hole in his breast pocket and every fibre of his being wanted to be gone and en route to Ashford. But he couldn't leave until tomorrow. He needed to speak with Harvey before he left.

John was in such a benevolent mood he'd even kissed Mary and his mother when he'd greeted them at the breakfast table.

Edward had smiled at him as he did it.

His family had stayed the night following the ball to make things easier and he'd asked them to stay on this morning, feeling in charity with his mother.

He'd not yet had the chance to ask Edward what had happened with Wareham last night. He'd been too emotionally bruised to care, and this morning he'd focused on getting the licence. But now Edward was in the hall.

John gave his hat to Finch. "Do you have a moment, Papa?"

"Son. Mr Harvey called for you earlier. He left a note on your desk in the library."

"Thank you. Will you tell me about last night?"

Edward gave him a sudden, quick smile and set his arm about John's shoulders, turning him to the library. It reminded John of the camaraderie he'd felt with Edward when he'd been young, and love, yes, he had loved Edward as a boy. He probably still did.

"Yes, and I have something to say, too." Edward's voice became confidential. "There is nothing wrong in asking for help. Stop isolating yourself. Sharing burdens is sensible, not weak, but wise, John."

Edward's arm fell as they entered the room, and then he shut the door.

When he faced John again, he said, "And I have an apology to make to you."

John frowned.

"I saw you were not happy before your grandfather came for you at Farnborough, when you were a boy. I was going to talk to you, but once we had you back, I did not care to open old wounds. I should have spoken and helped you put the past into perspective. I'm sorry I did not, and sorry I let your grandfather misguide you. However, I cannot change that, but I can and I will tell you when you are in the wrong, John. Listen to me – argue with me if you will – but do not keep things hidden."

"I am not ten now," John mockingly replied.

Edward laughed. "No, but I am still your father and you are still my son."

John turned and picked up Harvey's letter then broke the seal before turning back, smiling. "Very well, I'll listen, if you have something sensible to say. If not, expect to be ignored."

Edward smiled. "You may ignore me, but if I'm proven right, I will gloat."

John smiled, too. "Tell me about Wareham."

"We made it clear he does not wish to publish anything regarding your mother's history. I think he heard the message."

While Edward spoke, John scanned the letter, and then looked up.

"Well, you obviously scared him. He hired a coach to Dover this morning. We finally have enough evidence against him too.

219

He withdrew money from the account we've been trying to trace before he left. Harvey's sent the runners to arrest him. Thank you for your help."

Edward smiled. "You're welcome. Now, have you any other problems I may fix?"

John thought of Katherine. "None you can fix for me."

"I'll leave you then?" Edward smiled.

John could go to Ashford now Harvey had written. But first he wished to speak to Phillip.

When John reached Boscombe and Parkin's offices, though, Phillip was out on some errand, and they advised he would not be free until five.

John thought about racing off to Ashford, but decided not to. He wanted to tell Phillip about his intentions first. It felt the right thing to do. So John called on Harvey instead and discussed the role Phillip would play if he took the post John was about to offer, while the marriage licence in John's pocket continued to whisper its presence. And as he spoke to Harvey and learned nothing new, John felt a constant concern that Katherine might say no. But why would she? He'd be lifting her miles above her station.

When John left Harvey's offices, it was still too early to look for Phillip, so John headed to White's. It was dusk when he left there, and the autumn air had chilled.

An elderly matron let John into the building where Phillip rented rooms. John jogged upstairs feeling jubilant and excited.

Tomorrow he would see Katherine again, and secure her. He'd insist she say yes. He had an arsenal of experience and resources with which to persuade her after all. If he had to court her for a bit, he would, the girl deserved to be spoilt anyway. He could ply her with his undivided attention, as well as gifts, now Wareham was out of the way.

Phillip's door was left ajar and John could hear him moving about inside.

He knocked. "Phillip?"

220

"Good God. John! Come in." Phillip was standing across the room. He had linens across his arm. "This is a bloody honour. I did not expect a duke to call on a clerk?"

"Hardly a clerk, you're qualified." John laid his hat on a chest near the door.

Phillip smiled. "But still a lackey, for the moment at least. One day I hope to be more."

"Actually, that is why I called," John opened, pulling off his gloves and then letting them drop into his upturned hat. "I have an offer for you. A position has arisen in Harvey's offices. He will retire in a few years and I want someone I can trust to replace him. He oversees everything, my estates and investments. Would you be interested?"

"Would I!" Phillip's eyebrows lifted, "I'd intended progressing a career in the courts, but this…" He stopped, looking flabbergasted, and took a breath. "It's an opportunity I would be a fool not to take. Yes, John, thank you, I gladly accept."

John smiled, pleased that he could progress his friend. In truth it was only fitting if Phillip was to be his brother-in-law.

"Do you want a drink?" Phillip asked, still looking as though he was in shock.

"No, thank you, I've just come from White's."

"Well forgive me then, because I need one after that news."

As Phillip turned to a corked bottle of wine on a nearby chest, John glanced about the room. Phillip's trunk was half-packed and there were clothes on the chair beside it.

"Are you going somewhere?"

John heard the wine pouring. Then Phillip turned, smiling broadly. "Home. Kate is getting married at last. She has accepted the vicar."

The blood drained from John's head and something sharp sliced through his gut. He couldn't find any words to answer.

Phillip sipped his wine. "I know, it stunned me too when I heard. I never thought she'd settle, but it's true. They're getting married in three days. They only announced it three weeks ago."

John hardly heard Phillip's words.

I will not let the vicar have her.

"I'm leaving at first light," Phillip continued, oblivious to John's turmoil. "The wedding is a small affair, so there's no reason you would have heard, I suppose. They're not having a wedding breakfast." The enthusiasm suddenly dropped from his voice. "I doubt mother would've agreed to fund it. Anyway, I'm sure you'll wish me to pass on your congratulations."

The hell I do, "I'll tell her myself, when I see her." His voice sounded as though it belonged to someone else.

Giving John an odd look, Phillip offered a drink again, the wine or coffee, but John refused once more and made an excuse to leave. He felt as though he was in a stupor as he returned home.

Within two hours, notes written to those who needed to know of his sudden absence, including Harvey, excuses made to his family for deserting them in town, and bags quickly packed by his valet, John was on the road, driving his phaeton.

He rode through the night, which, thank God, was clear, hurtling home to Pembroke Place.

He rested once he'd reached there, not sleeping but just waiting for light.

It was nine o'clock in the morning when he stood before the door of the Spencer's little manor house, tired and anxious. The special licence he'd acquired only yesterday still rested in his breast pocket, but now he was not sure it would ever be used.

The clear blue sky above him reminded John of Katherine's eyes, as he waited for the door to open.

Behind him, he heard his horses whinny as his groom held their heads.

John took off his hat. *God*, he could not remember ever feeling so desperate. He'd beg her to take him if he must.

The door finally opened and John's heart pounded as Castle greeted him with surprise.

Katherine looked at the clock when the door knocker struck, it was only nine. Richard had formed the habit of calling each morning since they'd announced their engagement. But this was early even for him.

Thank goodness her stomach was not too ill at ease this morning.

She checked her hair in the mirror and smiled at herself. There were only two more days to go. Two more days and her conscience would have to cease whispering that she should tell John.

She went into the hall. Usually Richard took her for a drive so that they might talk privately. But when she entered the hall she stopped.

"Katherine."

"What are you doing here?"

"I need to speak to you."

She turned her back and swept into the parlour, leaving John where he stood.

He followed her. She had not invited him in. She didn't want him here.

"Katherine…"

"Go away, John." She shut her eyes, as if just not seeing him could make him go. *Why did he have to come now?*

"You must listen to me."

Opening her eyes, she met his gaze in the mirror. He was a few feet behind her, and the door stood wide open beyond him. "You can have nothing to say I want to hear." She didn't turn.

"Katherine." His hand lifted and he moved forward with earnest eyes. Not the Duke, *John.* Her traitorous heart leapt out to him. But there was no future with him. He did not love her. He'd insulted her.

The rage which had consumed her weeks ago flared back to life and she spun to face him, certain her anger burned in her eyes though she restrained her voice to a harsh whisper so her family would not hear. They were eating breakfast. They must have assumed the visitor was Richard too. "I am marrying Richard in two days, John. Go away. You will destroy everything."

"Let me speak, Katherine, please? That is all I ask."

She hated John suddenly, with a force which overwhelmed her, and yet she loved him too. His striking pale-blue eyes held hers, lined by long black lashes, and his hand slipped through his ebony hair. She remembered the same gesture from watching him in the lake years ago. *Oh John, go away. Go away before I cannot let you go again.*

He stepped closer, and she couldn't step away. "I love you, Katherine. I can't forget you. I want to marry you." She shook her head. He was mad. Mere weeks ago he had offered her the position of mistress once more. "You have to take me."

"No. You do not love me, and I'm *already promised.*"

"I'm serious. Listen to me." His whisper carried on the air and she hoped Castle had not hovered outside the door. "I need you. You are not his. You're mine. I cannot live without you."

"*His...*"

"Your saintly reverend..." She'd known who he'd meant. "... Do not marry him. *I* want *you*. Marry me."

Good God. He was selfish to the last. He begrudged her even the possibility of happiness. "And I suppose what I want does not matter."

"What you want is me. You said you loved me, Katherine."

He was so arrogant. Why must he do this now? And why did her foolish heart have to listen? She had never seen him so emotional, not even when he'd been young, his eyes glinted with need. But she could not trust him. She would be secure with Richard. Richard loved her. "Not anymore, John." It was a lie. There was unbearable pain in her heart. "Go away." Her whisper lowered, "I am marrying Richard."

He gripped her hand. "No, marry me. Why would you choose

him?"

Because you weren't here, and you didn't offer, and... "You do not love me, John."

"I do, Katherine. I swear it. Listen to me. I thought I couldn't, but now I know I was wrong. I will fight for you if I must. I shall not give you up. Let him find someone else. You would be a duchess, not a vicar's wife."

She tugged against his grip. "Three weeks ago you wanted me as your mistress. What has changed? Nothing, this is just jealousy." He looked as though her words had pierced him and his grip became over-tight.

"You're hurting me, John."

His eyes clouding with confusion, he let her hand go and took a breath. "I... I can't lose you. It has taken me too long to make this offer, yes. I was an idiot before. But accept me now and have done. I beg you." He dropped to one knee.

"Get up, John, I do not wish you to beg. I wish you to go. Richard will be here in a moment. Don't ruin this for me... "

"It cannot be too late, Katherine." His hand gripped hers again.

Her heart bled to see him so humble, but how could she believe him when she knew his pride and possessiveness? He'd always had what he wished, and now it seemed he wanted her. But what was his motivation? And how could she step into his world? She could not become a duchess.

Looking through tears, she shook her head as she whispered her denial. "It's too late, John." It terrified her. "Just go. Please."

She freed her hand and wiped her tears away.

He stood. She could see he'd given in. "I have made a fool of myself then. I've lost you." His voice was husky.

She said nothing. If she tried to speak again she would only cry. Yet she longed to hold him and be held by him. Richard's physical comfort had never felt the same as John's. John was a hope she had clung to in her dreams for years, yet her hope had never been real.

His eyes, which were normally hard diamonds, were melted ice. "Katherine, don't send me away?"

She shook her head, fearing that if she spoke she might lose her strength and say yes. She turned and looked at the hearth. She couldn't bear to face him anymore. He had been unreachable all her life and now if she wanted him, she only had to say. She did not say.

She heard him sigh and then he left the room, his boot heels striking the floorboards in the hall, growing more distant. Her heart beat in time with his steps.

She heard the front door open and Castle say, "Your Grace." It closed.

John was gone.

Katherine collapsed into a chair and wept, with her hands covering her face and her heart pouring pain into her blood. She ached everywhere for him. It was in every muscle and bone in her body, in her lips, in her eyes and in her hands.

Richard arrived barely a quarter-hour later.

By then she had composed herself, and she stood to go and greet him as she always did. Yet she could not deceive nor use him anymore – nor deceive herself. She could never let Richard touch her in a marriage bed. She could not marry him. She still loved John.

Her father was in the hall, challenging Castle, having clearly realised it was not Richard who'd called previously. "Why did the Duke of Pembroke pay his call?"

"What is it?" Richard was beside her in a moment and his arm was about her.

He guided her back into the parlour. "Katherine, what has happened?"

She hugged him briefly; he had been her defender and her sanctuary for the last two years. What was she going to do without him?

When she let him go, his fingers brushed a stray lock of hair behind her ear.

He did not deserve what she was going to do to him.

"Shut the door," she whispered, meeting his gaze.

"Katherine?"

It was improper but they were due to be married in two days.

"Ask Castle to send for tea if you wish some, and then close the door. I need to speak to you."

"What did Pembroke have to say? He upset you." Richard didn't move. "Tell me!" he whispered, his fingers gently grasping hers.

The gesture only reminded her that moments before John had held her hand.

Tears spilled over again.

"Tell me."

She had to. She had to be honest with him. "I cannot marry you. I still love him." Anger flashed in his eyes and she felt deceitful and false, as though she'd tricked him.

He did not let go of her hand. "I suppose he came to buy you back. What has he promised you? Do not cheapen yourself, Katherine…"

"He asked me to be his wife."

"*His wife?*"

"He begged me, Richard. But I cannot do it. He does not love me. He is just jealous of you. But, I'm sorry, he made me realise I cannot accept you either. You are a good man and a good friend, but I love John…"

His gaze narrowed to a glare but, unlike John, Richard did not argue. He let go of her hands. "Very well, Katherine, as you wish." If he argued, she would not change her mind. He probably simply knew her better than John. "I shall say goodbye then." She nodded, not knowing what to say. She was hurting him as John had hurt her.

Why can I not love where it is sensible to love? "I'm sorry," she said again as he turned.

He looked back. "I understand how you feel for him; it is how I feel for you." She was crushing this good, open-hearted man.

227

She was as cruel as John. "I shall resign the parish today. I can no more stay now than we could have stayed together." He turned again and left, and for the second time that morning she listened to a man's angry footfalls in the hall.

Her legs felt unsteady as she went into the hall, longing for the safety of her room.

"*Whose?*" It was Phillip's voice and it reached inside on a bellow as Castle held the door open.

Why did her brother have to arrive now? Oh, life was being malicious today.

She heard Richard speaking in a low bitter tone, but not his words. Then she heard Phillip shout once more. "How long have you known this?"

Oh no! No!

Her father was still standing beside the door. He looked at her with accusation in his eyes.

No!

Phillip came through the door as she moved forward. He was angry. His fingers were gripped in fists. "He says you are with child. *Are you?*"

She didn't answer. She couldn't breathe.

Phillip glared, and behind him their father had flushed red with anger. "Well of course you are. Why would a vicar lie?"

She couldn't find any words.

"It is Pembroke's?" her father accused. There was a vicious sadness in his voice. He glanced at Phillip. "I told you."

Then her mother was in the hall too. "What has she done?"

"Is it him?" Phillip said, as though he did not already know.

"Is who, who?" her mother asked.

And now Jenny was behind their mother, looking into the hall.

"*Is it?*" Phillip shouted, as though he needed to hear Katherine admit it.

"Yes." They knew anyway.

"I told you to stay away from him!" her father roared.

"God, Kate, he has been favouring me, is that the only reason?" Phillip breathed.

"What is true?" her mother cried.

"Katherine?" The last was from, Jenny.

"She is carrying John's child." Phillip's voice was bitter as he looked at their mother.

"I'm sorry," Katherine whispered, but they were ineffective words.

"The bastard," Phillip said on his breath, and then he turned and walked back out the door. His anger seemed tamed, but it was not gone. Phillip flew up into the bows quickly and dropped just as fast, but he was up in the bows still and their mother knew it too.

"Phillip! Do nothing rash! Don't challenge him. Katherine will be to blame. You will not risk yourself for *her*!"

Phillip stopped, turning his anger on their mother "For *her*? If you had cared for *her* a little more, perhaps she would not have turned to John." Looking back at Katherine, he said, "Do not worry, I will sort this." Then he was gone.

Panic rising, Katherine gripped her skirt and turned in the opposite direction. She would not see either Phillip or John hurt because of her.

Her mother's accusation ringing in her ears, Katherine fled back into the parlour, and when she reached the French door, her fingers fumbled to free the lock.

"Katherine!" her father called from the hall.

She heard him coming as the lock clicked loose, and then she was gone.

She ran across the garden and through the back gate onto John's land, with her skirt and petticoats clasped in her hands and held above her knees. She ran and ran, tearing across the deer-grazed grass, racing Phillip to Pembroke Place. He was in the curricle, but the route by road was much longer.

~

A noise came from downstairs, someone shouting. It was growing louder by the minute. "Where is that bastard? I know he's here! Tell me!"

Phillip. This was John's final justice. He'd have done no less for Mary.

"Where are you? You bastard!" The cry now came from the hall. "Is he upstairs? No! Get off me!" Some poor footman must have been thrown aside.

Why on earth had Katherine told?

But John was not going to hide from this. He went to the sitting room door and yelled into the hall. "Let him up!"

His hand shook as it swept through his hair.

God. He had not yet dealt with the pain of her refusal. He'd felt battered and beaten to have bared his soul, only to be turned away. Damn, how could he ever match up to her bloody perfect vicar? He was flawed and chipped and broken in half. How had he ever thought she would favour him over her saint? He'd shown her his worst side. Taken her to the folly and… He should not have done it. He'd been in her body, for God's sake…

Well, he would never be there again.

He waited silently in his private sitting room, listening to Phillip storm along the hall.

"You son of a bitch!" Phillip flew through the door on a whirl-wind of anger and gripped John's collar in one hand. The next John knew, he was on the floor and blood trickled from his nose and lip.

He moved to stand but Phillip kicked him down.

John lifted his hand to ward off another blow, but did not fight back. Sometimes they'd fought as children. John had always won.

"I trusted you!" Phillip yelled. "You were my friend! How could you do it to her?"

John moved to climb to his feet, but again Phillip's heel struck his shoulder and knocked him back. He deserved Phillip's anger.

"You took advantage of her! You bastard! You knew she was defenceless! I hope you rot in hell for what you've done!"

230

John said nothing, merely letting Phillip's tirade run. What was there to say? It was true. He would be saying the same if Phillip had done this to Mary. The only thing John could not understand was why Katherine had told?

"Phillip! Phillip!" John's heart leapt in his chest as Katherine's cries carried from below and then from further along the hall. "Phillip!"

She was running; her footsteps pounded on the hall rug.

Phillip turned and John rose.

"Phillip!" She burst into the room like sunrise breaking over the earth and her eyes spun to John. He felt a new hope bloom inside him, like a flower opening.

She looked at Phillip, panting hard as her eyes dropped to his clenched hands. "Stop it." Her voice was accusing as her gaze lifted to her brother's. She was struggling to catch her breath, and her bosom lifted and fell. She must have run all the way from her father's house. Her fingers were pressed hard against her side as though she had the pain of a stitch there. "It was my fault, Phillip."

"I don't give a damn," Phillip answered. "He bears the guilt. He knew what he was doing. You did not!" A hand was thrown in John's direction.

Phillip was right.

"And violence will not solve this, no matter what. Leave him be, Phillip!"

Phillip's hands were still fisted, and glancing back at John, he answered, "It does one thing, it makes me feel better."

John raised both hands, palm outwards. "I'm sorry. I've told her so. I was grieving. I was not thinking straight. So much had changed and—"

"That is no bloody excuse—" Phillip accused.

"It is not, I know. But it happened, Phillip, it happened and she has her vicar now."

Phillip glared at John. "She has finished it with the vicar, she will not have him, but you are taking her. You are making this right. Do you understand, I don't care what you are or who you are, you might be the bloody king and I'd make you have her!"

The only words of Phillip's diatribe John heard was that she had refused the saint. His gaze flew to Katherine. She was pale and still panting, and sweat had made her hair cling to her face.

Her eyes met his. They did not say relief. They did not say rushing towards a happy ending. "Katherine?" he said, even though Phillip was still railing.

She shook her head and denial forged its expression on her face. She had not come to say yes to him.

She moved suddenly and gripped Phillip's arm. "Leave it, please, Phillip, let it be."

"Let it be, Katherine? It cannot, be. You are with child. I am not giving him a choice. He has to take you!"

"With child?" Shock burst inside John, as Phillip's gaze turned to him.

"You did not know?"

"No! I did not know! Katherine?" John moved towards her but she stepped away, painting him as the damned monster again.

"I will not have Katherine shamed!" Phillip barked, as though he didn't know what else say.

But John was no longer interested in Phillip. Katherine was carrying his child, and she had been planning to marry her vicar regardless. "Katherine?" Why had she not told him?

She turned as if to leave. But he was not letting her. He caught her arm, holding her still, as he glanced back at Phillip. "Give us a moment." When Phillip did not move, John lost his restraint. "I said, leave us! We need to speak."

"If you hurt her," Phillip snarled.

"He'll not hurt me, Phillip," Katherine whispered, though she looked terrified, no matter her words.

As soon as the door shut, John let her go. "You have to marry me…"

"Your offer was made on a whim of jealousy, why would I wish for an arrogant, selfish man?"

"You are wrong, Katherine. I visited Phillip last night to tell him I was going to offer for you, I only found out about you and your vicar then. I asked you because I love you. I'm sorry you do not believe it, but you have no choice now, you will marry me."

Her chin tipped up and her blue eyes flashed. "Will I?"

"Katherine, how can you wish otherwise? You cannot deny me my son or daughter, and them me. We both know what it means to be without our natural parents." The floorboards had become quicksand again. "Why did you not tell me?" His voice carried accusation and anger. She'd hidden this from him.

Her chin tipped up higher. "What would you have done if I had, John?"

"I would have supported you."

"How?"

"Katherine..."

"*How?*"

"I don't know what I would have said a few weeks ago, but I would have protected you."

"And I would have been known as a whore and rejected by my family and hated by the people whose love I treasure. It is jealousy and selfishness that brought you back – and now I've lost that love."

"I came back because I love you too much to let you go. My last offer was wrong, Katherine. I'm sorry. But now I wish you to be my wife. You cannot say no. Surely you understand that."

Even though anger still burned in her eyes, dual tears escaped and ran down her cheeks. His fingers cupped her beautiful face and his thumbs wiped them away. His heart aching for her, he leant to kiss her. It had been weeks since he'd felt the pressure of her lips against his.

"John, your lip is bloody." She pushed him back.

He'd forgotten.

Taking a handkerchief from his pocket, he pressed it against his lip. "But you will marry me?" She said nothing. "Say yes, Katherine."

"If she does not say yes, I shall drag her to the damned altar." Phillip stood in the doorway.

He must have entered when John had been distracted by his fumbled kiss.

"Yes," Katherine breathed. John looked back at her. "Yes," she said it again more loudly as if telling herself and not him, "I will marry you."

A firecracker burst in his chest. "Thank you." What inadequate words. "I will make you happy." What an unemotional tone. Reserve was too instinctual to him. He smiled and flinched from the pain in his lip. But she smiled back.

"What now?" Phillip questioned.

John met his old friend's hard accusing gaze. "I have a special licence. I meant to tell you last night I wished to marry Katherine."

"Really?" There was a dubious note in Phillip's pitch.

"Here," John reached into his inside pocket, withdrew the thing and held it out.

Phillip looked at it dismissively as though it proved nothing.

John turned to Katherine. "I'll take you back to town and find a minister."

"And when the child arrives months early…" Phillip stated.

John sighed. "We'll go somewhere out of the way, and I'll not publicise the marriage, so the date will be unclear. I have been in mourning, a quiet wedding will not be noted, but I can do no more, Phillip, my family will know."

Phillip nodded, grimly. "I'll come to London with you, now." Because, John assumed, Phillip trusted him no more than Katherine.

"Let me clean your lip first," Katherine whispered. "Sit down. Have you brandy in here?" John looked at her, surprised she cared. "Where, John?"

"Over there."

She took the handkerchief from his hand, and walked away to douse it in brandy.

"Sit," she ordered when she turned back.

He did, occupying the chair he'd used when searching the ledgers. Now he was searching his damned soul. How could he not even have thought of the possibility she might be with child? Because he was spoilt, arrogant and selfish. She was right. He did not deserve this woman's consideration.

Her gentle fingers dabbed the cloth against his lip and it stung a little, but her touch made his heart ache more, and he watched her face.

She was to be his duchess. She would not find it easy. She wouldn't have a clue how to go on. She would need his support. He could not be selfish anymore.

"He's got a valet and a house full of footmen to do that," Phillip grumbled.

His valet wasn't here, though, and John preferred her attentions.

Her gaze lifted to his as she finished, and she blushed. His heart bled for her and he stood, still holding her gaze. "I suppose I ought to change. You will not wish to marry a man with blood all over him."

She did not reply. Of course, she did not want to marry him at all.

Katherine watched him go, then her gaze swept about the sitting room. Crimson damask decorated the furniture and draped the windows, and even the ceiling here bore paintings of semi-clad women – the muses – while the walls were coated in gilded leather. It glowed in the daylight and it would sparkle in candlelight, which would complement the glossy satinwood furniture.

The room was sumptuous and beyond anything she could have imagined, and this place was to be her home soon. She could not absorb it.

She heard Phillip approach and turned expecting to be berated, but instead he hugged her and she hugged him.

"You could have told me", he whispered to her ear as he let her go when John came back.

John had changed clothes, and she could not help herself, remembering the torso those clothes hid. Was he really going to marry her?

Chapter Thirteen

The sensitiveness in John's heart as he looked at Katherine during their carriage journey back to town was akin to that in his lip. How could he have attributed his feelings for her as lust?

She was silent and avoiding his gaze. He and Phillip were silent, too, all sitting in corners, poles apart, east, west and north.

John longed to touch her, even just to take her hand. She'd said she no longer loved him earlier. He hoped it wasn't true. He had been all the things he despised to her, though. He could hardly blame her if she did not.

Phillip suggested they use a church in Cheapside. He said the vicar there could be trusted to keep the marriage secret.

John gripped Katherine's hand and held it tightly when they alighted, leaving Phillip to make the arrangements. When the vicar came to greet them, he was accompanied by his housekeeper, who would be their second witness. "Have you the licence?"

John nodded and retrieved it with his free hand, not letting go of Katherine's.

"Thank you. Come this way."

They were led into the church and stood before the altar.

John's heart began to pound as the enormity of what they were doing struck him. This was a lifelong commitment.

Katherine gripped John's hand, holding on so that she did not fall, holding on to receive his strength. But she didn't have the courage to look at him. They hadn't spoken in the carriage. All his professions of love had already fallen into silence. But he was about to marry her.

She was terrified. He did not love her and she could never live in his world.

The vicar opened the service as though he was speaking to a full church, and Katherine remembered Richard, left behind and hurt by her, as she had been hurt by John.

She felt like weeping – on her wedding day.

She looked up at John, because she needed him to look at her, but he was watching the vicar. The coloured light from the stained glass glossed his black hair.

She stood on the side of his swollen lip, and his cheek had a lump, which was dark purple. The vicar must think this a forced match. But John had come to her before he'd known of the child. At least she knew his offer was not forced.

This would have been so different if he had waited two more days. She would have been married in a church full of people, with her father there as well as Phillip. But then she would have married Richard, not John… Her father didn't even know she was getting married… He'd be wondering where she was. They hadn't sent a message before leaving.

"Katherine Spencer, I…" John's ducal voice echoed about the church and he looked down at her at last, his hand holding hers more tightly, "…in sickness and in health…"

Promises, promises.

She met his gaze but did not trust him, he was no longer John, and she barely knew the Duke who stood before her with crystal-clear unfathomable eyes.

He spoke as an orator, announcing his words with authority. This was the façade behind which he hid the young man he was. It was a barrier of steel armour people could not pierce, to ensure they never saw the man beneath. The man who was human, who might love and could feel fear and pain and vulnerability.

But which was true; the man who'd shown all those feelings at her father's house, or this man?

The other, her heart told her, she must remember even in this man he was there, beneath. But she was afraid of the Duke. He'd hurt her.

"Now, Miss Spencer, say after me…" It was her turn to make promises. He'd promised to honour her, she had to obey.

When it came to exchanging a ring, John did not have one, and so he took a gold signet ring from his small finger. It was not overly loose. He had long, artistic, slender fingers.

Yet still her finger curled to hold it there when he let her hand go.

I am going to be his duchess. How could she be? This Cinderella ending did not feel like a fairy tale. It felt like a nightmare.

"I now pronounce you man and wife."

It was like living in a dream. She was watching the scene from the rafters above.

John gripped her shoulders and kissed her temple when she did not lift her face, but then he reached for his handkerchief because his lip had split open again.

He took her hand once more when they moved to sign the register, but even that grip was impersonal now he was the Duke.

He wrote John Harding in the book, with no title, and she wondered if the vicar even knew who John really was.

Phillip and the vicar's housekeeper signed as witnesses.

Then she knew for certain how little the vicar had been told when he took her hand and said, "Felicitations, Mrs Harding."

She wished she was merely Mrs Harding. If she were merely Mrs Harding she would be happy, because then *he* would just be John.

Sheer terror beset her when John said outside the church, "I'll take you home now, but I ought to warn you, my family are there, my parents and the children are staying with me for a while. Mary made her debut recently."

Phillip then said, "I'll leave you here. John's groom will have taken my curricle back to the mews. I can make my own way back."

John nodded with a matter-of-fact manner, while Katherine felt her lifeline being cut.

"Phillip." She hugged him tightly, not knowing what to say. She could hardly ask him to stay. She had a new life to begin, and yet she felt petrified at the thought of stepping into it. How could she do it? It was one thing to have dreamed of being with John. It was another to achieve it. "Phillip," she said again before letting him go. She felt like a limpet clinging to a rock on the beach, holding back against the tide. John was the tide, shifting and unsteady.

Phillip kissed her cheek and whispered, "I will call on you tomorrow to see how you go on."

She nodded and tried to smile but could not; instead she bit her lip.

When she took John's hand to climb into the carriage, she remembered she had not one stitch of clothing with her, only what she wore. She was a ragtag, bastard girl, the illegitimate daughter to a dairymaid, and now his duchess. What on earth would his family think?

He said nothing to her as they rode through the London streets. He appeared in his own world, looking out the window. She longed for some sign of John, a gentle word or gesture, but John was in retreat behind the Duke. She supposed he must be concerned about taking her to meet his parents too. He could not have told them he'd obtained the licence, nothing he'd said implied he had.

The horses' hoof beats rang sharply on the stone as the carriage rocked across the cobble.

She longed for her bedroom at home, to be sitting in the window seat with her mending, in a life she knew.

The houses on either side of the street grew grander. She felt too uncomfortable now to look at John. He'd paid her no attention. Then she recognised the streets from their journey on the day of the funeral and felt trapped. If she obeyed her instinct, she would leap from the carriage and run. She did not. But she clasped her hands and held them together in her lap. She did not even have her reticule or a bonnet or a pelisse. What on earth would his family think?

At least the opulence of his townhouse was not a shock when the carriage drew up outside it.

The carriage rocked as a footman jumped down from the back, and then the door opened. The house door opened too when the footman helped her down.

Katherine recognised the butler, who stood at the top of the stairs.

Her heart pounded. John alighted after her and offered his arm. The action looked purely instinctive, not intentional. Still, she clung to it, feeling his solid muscle beneath the cloth of his coat.

He was dressed entirely appropriately in gloves and hat and coat. It would make the state of her undress only more remarkable. John's fingers covered hers on his arm as they crossed the threshold and the butler's gaze skimmed over her attire, from her uncovered head to her worn half-boots.

She could have cried she was so glad of the reassurance John's touch provided. She looked up at him, but he was facing the butler. "Are my mother and father at home, Finch?"

"Lord and Lady Edward are in the family drawing room, Your Grace."

"And Finch…" John added, as the man bowed far less deeply to her than he had done to John, "gather the staff in the library in half an hour. I will speak to them shortly. I need to introduce the Duchess of Pembroke."

The man did well to cover his shock, she would swear his mouth nearly fell open but his lips closed tightly instead, yet his nod at John was clearly a slip before he recovered himself and bowed more markedly again. "Certainly, Your Grace." Then he turned to her. "Welcome, Your Grace."

"Thank you." Her voice was steady despite her fear. She must set

John's staff an example from the beginning if she was ever going to cope. She'd learned that with the Sunday-school children. The thought made her wish to laugh nervously. The butler would feel insulted if he knew she compared him to a child.

When they climbed the stairs a moment later, John said quietly, "Are you bearing up?"

She glanced at him, and for the first time in four hours, she saw John in his eyes. Her fingers squeezed his arm, but she didn't answer, she was not quite sure what would come out if she did.

"You'll manage, Katherine," he stated on such a down-to-earth note she found her voice.

"I'm glad one of us thinks so." He laughed and she felt a rush of relief sweep in like a wave over her limpet-like self but it was a comforting feeling.

She smiled. He smiled in return, only to open his split lip again. He reached into his pocket for his handkerchief.

As they walked along the landing she could hear conversation and laughter, it grew louder the further they progressed. The laughter sounded boyish but it was punctuated by the occasional girlish squeal. Her heartbeat thundered.

When they reached the open door the sound came from, he stopped and tucked the bloodstained handkerchief back into his pocket. Then his arm dropped from beneath her hand.

She felt bereft for an instant, but then he took her hand and gripped it tightly as he'd done at the church.

She remembered at last how strained his relationship had appeared with his family the night she'd conceived their child. She felt sick as they entered, but straightened and lifted her chin.

"I've brought you a surprise," John stated.

The room was huge. Over half a dozen times the size of her father's parlour. It was decorated in pastel greens and yellows, with gold gilt edging and magnificent plaster cornices and mouldings on the ceiling. It was hardly less grand than the state rooms downstairs.

John's father was kneeling on all-fours, forming a climbing

frame for the younger children. He carefully spilled John's younger brothers from his back onto the floor and knelt up. One of the girls tried to climb on his shoulders then, but he steadied her and stopped her climbing. "Look, your brother's here." She looked at John then looked away as though he was of no interest.

The two older boys were playing a game of chess in one corner, Robbie, the elder, looked up and rose.

John's mother held John's youngest sister on her lap as she sat in between two of the older girls, who were busy sewing samplers, and five-year-old Georgiana was on the floor with a tiny china tea set spread before her.

Mary was not here.

"What did you do to your lip, did you fight?" Robbie challenged from across the room, in a surprised yet awed tone.

All the children looked.

Obviously his mother and father must have noticed the state of his face, but had been too polite to say.

Katherine smiled, looking at the children first. Then she smiled at his parents but her smile felt stiff and awkward.

His mother was looking at John, but then she glanced at Katherine and smiled uncertainly, rising and passing Jemima onto one of the other girls. "Kate, it is indeed a surprise."

John's father was crossing the room. "Kate?" It was a welcome and a query.

John's fingers gripped hers almost painfully tightly. "Mama, Papa, Katherine and I are married."

"Married?" His mother sounded surprised, and hurt.

"John!" His father's expression was disbelief and reprimand.

Katherine wished for a hole at her feet she might leap into but John's firm grip would not have let her jump.

"I'm sorry," his mother said then. "That was very rude of me, Kate. I mean to say, welcome to the family, I wish you well. I am pleased." She sounded anything but pleased. "It is just a shock," she added. Then she looked at John. "Why did you not say? When were you married?"

"Today," he said quietly. "We needed to keep it understated for a reason, Mama." He took a breath then concluded, "Katherine is with child."

Katherine felt herself turn crimson as his mother turned pale. "John." It was a scolding voice.

Not a single nerve or muscle in John's face indicated any discomfort, but he did not look at Katherine and she knew he had slipped back into his ducal armour. She clasped his arm, but he did not respond. Then she was forced to let him go as his father embraced him.

It was only a cover. She heard him whisper by John's ear. "That was badly done, son. Very badly done."

She longed to tell them this was not his fault, as his mother clasped Katherine's hand, and then kissed her cheek.

Afterwards, his father did the same.

They must be thinking ill of her.

"Still, explanations can wait," his father said as he let Katherine go. "Congratulations, welcome to the family, Kate, Your Grace, *daughter*. Or should I say welcome to the rabble."

She bit her lip, feeling the heat of a blush again. "Thank you, my Lord." She was about to curtsy deeply, then remembered she should not now. Now people ought to curtsy to her.

"Just Edward, Kate," he answered, smiling. Then he looked back at his offspring, "Children, come and meet your new sister."

She had always liked John's father and mother. She thought they'd liked her, too, though they could never have thought she might one day be their daughter-in-law.

The next ten minutes were overwhelming as the children surrounded them and the girls wished to know what she had worn. They had not heard John say they were only married today. They asked what flowers she'd had. What bonnet she wore, if her dress was embroidered? So many questions she evaded with foolish comments like, "I was far too excited to remember."

When the chaos subsided, John's mother whispered, "Call me Ellen, Kate, and ask me anything you wish."

Katherine nodded, more grateful than she could say. But then John's fingers braced her waist. "I asked Finch to gather the staff downstairs, Mama. We should go down, Katherine." Oh, she only wished she was at least suitably dressed.

"They are angry," she said as they left the room. His arm was still about her.

"Not because it is you, Katherine, but because I married without telling them, and because of the child. Do not fret over it. We are going to be judged. We can do nothing about it except ignore it. We are going to have to bear the storm."

When they reached the top of the stairs, he let her go but then offered his arm in a formal gesture.

She glanced at him and saw him clothe himself in his ducal armour.

A footman in the hall opened the library door when they stepped from the bottom stair.

She looked up at John and saw his eyes were diamond-hard when they entered. She had faced his family with John, she was doing this alone.

The room of people bowed and curtsied, and her new status struck hard. Her heart pounded as she bid people rise and was then introduced to each by the butler. She felt an utter fraud, and when the housekeeper asked to meet with Her Grace, to discuss the running of the house, Katherine felt like laughing. She had the order of this house, of Pembroke Place, of... Lord, she did not even know where John's other properties were. She would have to ask Phillip, she would not embarrass herself and ask John.

A footman came into the room. "Your Grace, forgive me, but this urgent message arrived."

John took the letter as Katherine asked the housekeeper how the staff were ordered below her. Perhaps it was a standard thing and Katherine ought to know, but she felt the need to ask something and it was all she could think of.

"Damn," John cursed behind her. She turned. "Sorry, Katherine," he whispered. "I'm afraid I need to go out."

Go out…

"I have business I need to discuss. I'm sorry," he said again. "You'll have to stay here. Go up and speak with Mama, she'll help you settle in."

Katherine's mouth fell open, but she closed it again before it had chance to gape. "I'd rather lie down," she responded. "I get tired…" She could not face his parents alone. He seemed to have forgotten all he'd told her of how little he got on with them. She would sleep and then he'd be back.

He looked into her eyes and there was a flash of John somewhere deep within them. Then he turned away and looked at his butler. "Finch, have one of the maids take Her Grace upstairs to the Duchess's chambers, would you?" He looked back at her.

She thought he would kiss her. He did not. She still longed to be held, but he did not do that either. "I cannot say how long this will take, Katherine, I will be back as soon as I can. Goodbye." He nodded at her, still in his ducal skin, and then he left her among his servants and disappeared into the hall. She could hear him being given his coat, hat and gloves.

"Your Grace," the butler said, and for a moment she was confused because John was in the hall, but then she realised Finch was speaking to her. "If you will follow me?"

She nodded, ridiculously feeling as though she should curtsy. John's staff would laugh for weeks if she did something so gauche.

She heard the front door closing behind John as she stepped into the hall.

~

John's head was swimming as he climbed the stairs. Wareham had disappeared. Harvey's men had lost him before he'd reached

Dover. They'd no idea where he was now.

Harvey had written to John as soon as he'd heard, asking John to come and make a statement to a magistrate.

John had ended up presenting evidence for hours. The magistrate had made him repeat things numerous times and asked God knows how many questions, as a clerk had sat next to John scribbling it all down. But now, with the help of the militia, messages had gone out to search all ports.

John looked at a clock on the landing. It was nearly midnight. It was far too late to join Katherine in bed, she'd be sleeping.

A fine wedding night this!

"John?" John turned and faced his stepfather, who stood at the bottom of the stairs leading to the next floor.

"Yes."

"May I speak to you a moment?"

John sighed, "If you wish."

Edward led John to the family drawing room. It was empty. His mother and Mary had retired then, which meant John was probably right about Katherine.

One candelabrum was left burning, presumably awaiting his return in case he wished to dally in here on his wedding night. As if that was likely! And yet here he was. Perhaps his servants knew him better than he knew himself!

"Your mother is upset," Edward began.

Too mentally exhausted for this conversation and feeling belligerent, John answered, "She has no need to be, it is Katherine who has good cause. She is carrying the child."

"How far gone is she?"

"Almost three months."

There was judgement in Edward's eyes, they both knew three months made it the night of the dinner party at The Place, and Edward would also know John had not been near The Place since. "You'll not be able to hide it for long."

"We know. I am not going to publish the marriage and leave

247

the date obscure. There is good reason for it to have been quiet because of my mourning."

"You sound like your grandfather, all matter of fact."

"Do not preach to me, Papa, remember I know the truth about a certain parlour in a gambling den…" John lifted his eyebrows.

"I am not preaching," Edward growled in a low voice, "and if you dare raise that again, I might forget my principles and strike you. Besides, I simply want to say the mistake has been made and we will support Katherine."

"The mistake? It was *no* mistake."

"John—"

"I mean it, Papa, I love her. I took too long coming to the point, yes, but I'd acquired a special licence and I'd travelled down there to offer for her before I knew of the child."

Edward stared, then set a hand on John's shoulder. "Well then, I am glad for you, and I will tell your mother how things stand."

John breathed out, only then realising he'd held his breath. "Would you ask her if she will discuss with Katherine what must be done? I would be grateful… Katherine will need help."

His father nodded and then left.

John retired, and in his rooms, he went to stand at the connecting door leading into Katherine's chamber. His fingers settled on the door handle as he listened for any sound.

There was none.

His forehead rested against the cool solid wood.

He was making a mess of things already. His marriage was barely hours old and he'd failed her again. He should have been here. He'd thought it a hundred times as he'd repeated and repeated his statement, but he hadn't been able to get away.

How many times in his life would his duty come before her and would she be able to understand?

~

The next morning, after a good night's sleep, John felt in higher spirits when he reached the long sunny room in which he normally ate breakfast. He felt excited, anticipating the sight of Katherine like a lovesick fool.

He'd had some business letters to read and reply to before he'd come down, so no doubt she'd nearly finished eating. His mind began to wander through ideas of what to do with the day.

He looked first at Edward, who was sitting nearest the door, and nodded. Then his gaze swept over the other occupants, searching for Katherine. She was not here. His heart dropped in his chest.

His mother rose. So did Mary, with far less decorum, as she launched herself at him and hugged him tightly. "You sneak, marrying Kate in secret. I will never forgive you. I may not invite you to my wedding in return."

He tapped her beneath her chin as she let him go and stepped back. "You will. You're too much of a show-off. You'll want everyone to gloat over your brother, the Duke of Pembroke. Where's Katherine? Has she eaten?"

"You are not the only duke I have as a relation, I have uncles too, and I have no idea where Katherine is, I haven't seen her."

"She has not come down?" John looked at his mother.

"No, and Kate did not join us for dinner last night either." His mother's pitch held a censorious tone. "Esther said Kate was not feeling well. She is still unwell this morning. Have you not seen her?"

The implication in her last words was explicit – he *should* have seen Katherine.

He'd made it obvious he'd not spent his wedding night with his wife – and not doing so was clearly very wrong in his mother's eyes. It meant Katherine must be feeling the same, surely.

His exuberance ebbed instantly. "Mama, would you send for a doctor? I'll go up to her."

"John," she said, catching his arm. "Has she any clothes with her? Esther said there was no luggage."

He was such a fool. "No, we just came away…"

"Well, tell her please I have organised someone to call this morning to take measurements and bring patterns. She will bring some readymade garments which can quickly be adjusted to fit, too."

"Thank you, Mama."

"Go on, go up to her then."

John kissed her cheek first.

There was no response to his knock on Katherine's sitting room door.

"Katherine, it's John!"

Silence.

He entered anyway and walked through her sitting room and dressing room. They were both empty and showed no evidence of occupation. He found her in her bedchamber, though he'd heard her presence from the dressing room. She was kneeling on the floor doubled over a chamber pot, retching.

"*Katherine.*" He was on one knee at her side in an instant and holding her loose hair.

She was wearing the dress she'd worn yesterday – well of course she was, she had nothing to change into.

He also noted the bed was hardly disturbed. She'd slept on top of the covers and probably in her clothes – waiting for him. *Will you never learn, John?*

"Leave me alone," she whispered, sitting back on her heels and holding a cloth to her lips.

The contents of the chamber pot was nothing but bile, she'd clearly not eaten anything last night or this morning.

John rose and took the pot. He left it in the dressing room then returned to her.

"Please, John, I'd rather you just left me." She climbed up onto the bed and lay down.

She looked tired. She had lain there and not slept then.

"I don't wish you to see this."

"I do," he answered, walking over to a jug to pour some water into the wash bowl beside it. "Here, wash your face, I'll send for some ginger-infused tea and dry toast, Mama swears by that remedy, it should help settle your stomach."

"Please, John…"

"Katherine, I got you into this mess, what kind of man would I be if I turned away from the unpleasantness of the outcome?"

"A normal one," she stated, accepting the damp cloth he offered.

He laughed at her quip, wondering how the girl could joke even now. He took the cloth away from her again. "Lie down and rest."

Once she'd done so he discarded the cloth and went over to the bell pull to ring for a maid.

A knock wrapped on the bedchamber door in scarce minutes. John opened it and whispered his requirement to Esther rather than letting her in to disturb Katherine. They were carried out instantly. The dressing room door clicked quietly shut as a maid took the soiled chamber pot.

John moved and leant his back against the mantle, watching Katherine on the bed. Her eyes were closed and one arm loosely covered her face. Her body was still slender; he could not yet see any rise in her stomach. He supposed the only clue was the buttons which pulled taut across her bosom where her breasts were fuller.

A few moments later and Esther was back with the tea and toast and another maid entered bearing a clean chamber pot.

Now the servants knew how things stood as well as his parents.

John asked for it all to be set down near the bed and then bid them leave. Both maids bobbed copious curtsies before disappearing.

"Does it never bother you?" Katherine asked from the bed, lowering her arm and opening her eyes.

He went to smile but stopped when it pulled the scab on his lip. "Does what bother me?"

"All the supplication; they bow and scrape at every turn. It is driving me mad already and I've only endured it for a day."

He laughed quietly and moved closer. "Why do you think I hid abroad so long? I could lead a normal life there. But the answer is you get used to it and then by and large you ignore it. Now sit up and eat a little." He gathered some cushions from a chair and set them behind her back so she could recline, then passed her the uninviting toast and moved the ginger tea within her reach.

He walked about the bed and occupied the far side, slipping off his shoes and then lying down on his back beside her.

One hand rested beneath his head and he raised one knee. He remembered lying in numerous fields talking with Phillip in this position as a boy. He looked up at her and watched her nibble a small piece from her toast.

"It will go away soon if you're lucky."

"What?"

"The sickness, it usually improves after three months, or it always does for my mother and my aunts, although I believe sometimes it can go on. I've sent for a doctor."

"Why? It's normal, you just said so."

"Because," rolling to his side, he bent his elbow to prop up his head on his palm, "I wish to know that you and the child are healthy. It will stop me fretting if I hear a doctor say so. Mama said you were ill last night, too."

"I did not like to go down on my own."

"So you were not ill?"

"Can you call too nervous ill? If so, I was ill?"

"It was just my family, Katherine. You know them, and Mary would have been there." *But you were not* – he saw the answer in her eyes.

He sat upright and slid back up the bed to sit against the pillows beside her. "I was remiss to leave you alone, Katherine, I know, but my business meeting dragged on for much longer than I expected, I'm sorry."

She said nothing.

"It was midnight when I came home. I presumed you'd be

252

asleep. I thought it best not to disturb you, but Mama indicated it was probably a poor choice. You did not sleep, did you? You were waiting for me."

She put the plate down and then reached for the tea and sipped it. He'd had them put sugar in it already so he needn't fuss with pouring and so on.

Her back was to him as she drank, giving a non-verbal answer to his questions.

John folded his arms over his chest and looked up at the bed's canopy. "My mother has arranged for a modiste to call in a while. She will sort out a new wardrobe for you. I know you did not bring your clothes, but even if you had they would not befit a duchess and I will be damned glad to see the last of your blue spencer."

"Still trying to buy me, John?" she answered, sitting back against the pillows with her toast again.

"It worked with the bonnet," he said humorously. "And the dress."

"But now we are married and you have no need for further coercion."

"Yes, but I still want you willing," he teased. Then he sobered his expression. "I honestly thought I was being considerate last night. I'm sorry. In future, sleep in my bed, then there need be no decisions about whether I come to you or not."

"And I am to simply forget we did not share a bed on our wedding night?" Ah, he had really hurt her then.

"And here was I thinking you'd refused my offer yesterday when you had a choice. It implied you did not want me in your bed, Katherine."

"I did not say no to marrying you. I said no to marrying this…" One hand lifted, indicating the room. "And because I did not want a man who did not really want me."

He shifted at that, turning to lift her plate from her hands. Then he leant across her and put it back onto the chest before cupping her cheek.

His gaze met hers; azure seas. "I want you. I love you. Will you believe me?"

"No." Her eyes burned blue fire.

"God, woman. What have I married?" His gaze fell to her lips a moment before he bent and kissed them, soft and warm.

It took her a few moments to respond, but she did, her lips brushing against his as his fingers cradled her jaw.

Desire, love, a strong protective instinct, respect and lust warred inside him, overwhelming his senses. He let his tongue sweep across her lips, and she parted them, turning into him, her fingers reaching to his hair and his waist.

Her touch was intoxicating and for a while he let them both enjoy the moment, but it was not the time for this, not with the doctor about to arrive and her stomach still delicate.

Pulling away, he smiled and removed her hand from his waist and instead pressed it against his groin. "I want you."

She made a face at him and pulled her hand away.

"I only wish there was time, darling. But there is not, not with the doctor coming and the modiste, and then I'm afraid the rest of my family will descend en masse. I've written to everyone to inform them of the wedding so they will all call. I have also changed my mind and decided to put *something* in the paper. Just to say I have taken a wife quietly due to my mourning, I shall not mention the date but I hope it will reduce rumours. However, when society hears, Katherine, they will also all descend on our door, probably tomorrow, or perhaps the day after."

She'd paled, so he reached for the sweetened tea and handed it to her.

"So soon," she whispered.

"I'm afraid so, darling."

"I have nothing to wear."

"You will have by this afternoon. There are some positives to being a duchess which outweigh the bowing and scraping. The modiste will have some dresses sorted for you in hours and I will take you to your first ball tonight and show you off."

"You think I am worth showing." Her pitch was self-mocking.

"I do."

A knock struck the door. "Your Grace." It was Esther. "The doctor is here."

John smiled as much as his scabbed lip would allow as he glanced at Katherine. "Do you want my mother to attend you?"

She nodded and at last smiled in return.

He hoped he'd won some ground back. He just needed to be consistent now and keep it.

"I'll send her up."

~

After an overwhelming day, Katherine found herself sitting in John's plush state carriage in the evening with her fingers woven through his as their joined hands lay on his thigh.

His mother, father and Mary sat opposite.

John was looking out the window, watching the dark streets dashing past. He looked outrageously handsome, dressed in his formal black and white evening clothes. They suited his complexion, a perfect foil for his jet-black hair and pale skin.

He'd been solicitous all day, hovering by her as the modiste had measured and suggested colours and patterns, making suggestions if he had a preference. He'd also spoken to the doctor privately.

Even in the afternoon John had stayed by her side when all his aunts, uncles and cousins had called.

In large, his family had been kind, greeting her with congratulations, although she'd heard John challenged by some of his uncles.

They said he'd taken a high risk.

The rest of that conversation she'd missed because John had deliberately moved away, taking his uncles with him into a huddle across the room. She'd watched them whispering in urgent tones which she couldn't hear, but John had said nothing about it to her.

When Phillip had called amidst the large family gathering, she'd had little chance to speak to him, but on leaving he'd kissed her cheek and whispered, "I take it he is looking after you. Are you happy?"

She'd nodded. She was, but it was a tentative happiness. She felt as though the ivory tower she was living in would shatter at any moment.

Phillip then whispered reassurances to her, telling her John could love her, before he promised to call again tomorrow.

After dinner, in her room, she'd found the dress which the modiste had altered to fit for the evening. It was a shimmering yellow satin and it fitted tightly to her waist, with a low bodice. The short sleeves draped from her shoulders and the heavy material in the skirts hung flat across her stomach and flowed like water as she walked, caressing her thighs, while the bodice embellished her figure, defining it. Small seed pearls were sewn in patterns over it, and it was edged with gold embroidery.

The dress made Katherine feel like a goddess. After Esther had dressed Katherine, and put up her hair, leaving occasional spirals loose, the image in the mirror had been a beautiful stranger's.

When John had entered her room, his eyebrows had arched upwards and his smile had lifted in approval. Then he'd given her a pearl necklace consisting of three strands. Now it lay heavily about her neck in a constant caress. He'd also taken her fingers and removed his loose ring, before replacing it with a simple gold band and another ring with a single large diamond.

"That is more appropriate," he'd stated, but she'd refused to let him keep his signet ring because it was her wedding ring. She'd tucked it into her bodice to stop him taking it.

He'd laughed.

Her own gaze turned to the dark window and she saw her reflection. The light from a single lantern burning inside the carriage glistened on her blonde hair.

She felt like Cinderella tonight; her childhood dreams felt as though they'd come true.

When the carriage halted before the Earl of Derwent's town-house and the carriage door opened, she saw it was raining. The pavement glistened in the streetlight, turning it gold.

John's father climbed down first and helped Mary and John's mother descend. Then John turned to her and drew up the hood of her new cloak, carefully protecting her hair.

"How are you faring?" he whispered with the air of a conspirator. "It has been a long day. If you feel as though you are flagging let me know."

"I'm well, just terrified," she whispered back.

"You will be fine. If you can manage those children in Ashford, you can manage the aristocracy. We are not much different. Bear up, girl." At the last, he gripped her hand and pulled her with him as he stepped out of the carriage.

"I'm sure they are not like children," she answered as her foot touched the carriage step, although she remembered thinking it of his servants yesterday. She held his hand more firmly.

"If I recall, you told me I was spoilt…" he said to her ear as she stepped down.

"You *are*," she stated. Then she smiled. "But now I am, too."

He laughed. "If not already, you will be. I intend spoiling you rotten for the rest of your life. Come."

She laid her ivory silk glove on the sleeve of his ebony evening coat.

Chalk and cheese, that was herself and John – Duke and dairy-maid's daughter. Or perhaps it ought to be diamonds in comparison to cheese – he with his hard exterior and she with her soft, susceptible heart.

They climbed the stairs but as they did the muscle in his arm beneath her fingers tightened and he straightened marginally, dressing himself in his ducal armour.

She glanced at him as they crossed the threshold and saw his jaw had set and his expression was unreadable. His eyes had lost the laughter they'd only just shared and become hard. It was the Duke of Pembroke beside her, not John Harding. Not the man she'd married and not the man she loved.

Her heart raced.

If she must do this in isolation, she didn't know that she could. John had been so solicitous throughout the day she'd felt capable, but she wouldn't feel so without him.

As if he sensed her hesitation, his fingers pressed over hers for a moment.

They entered the hall. He carefully lifted the hood from her hair and untied the ribbons of her cloak then took it from her shoulders before passing it to a footman.

"Your Grace." Another footman bowed low and then they were led across the black and white marble floor to the open doors, from which an orchestra's music spilled, along with the sound of many voices.

"Brace yourself," John whispered as she caught the first glimpse of the swirling colours of many dancers and the bright shine of huge chandeliers throwing sparkling light about the gigantic room. She'd never seen anything like it. Nothing could be as grand and beautiful as this. It *was* a scene from her fairy tale.

"The Duke and Duchess of Pembroke!" a man in royal-blue uniform called beside them.

As they walked into the room, Katherine could see many heads turning and then the sound of voices seemed to merge in a wave of whispers.

The room was suddenly airless.

Ignoring the attention, John faced the Earl and his wife, their hosts, who greeted John and then Katherine, once John had made the introductions. Katherine saw the Countess glance at the bruise on John's cheek and then her gaze skimmed over Katherine from head to toe, as if to say, who is she?

When they walked further into the room, the conversation grew louder, and again numerous people glanced their way.

"Are they talking about us?" she breathed.

His fingers settled over hers on his arm again. "Ignore it. They'll be bored of the topic in a week or two."

The room was packed, but people seemed to move aside for John.

It only served to point out that John had not only been significantly senior to her in Ashford society, he was also senior to many of these people.

John did not stop but carried on until they reached his mother and father, who stood at the edge of the room in the far corner.

"Mary, is already dancing," his father stated.

John's gaze spun to the dancers. "With Framlington, he's an out-and-out rake and a fortune-hunter. He's made no secret of it in the clubs. I'd warn her off."

His father's gaze swung to John. "You're certain."

John just lifted his eyebrows.

"You are going to have to write that list you promised me, of everyone I need to keep her from."

John laughed.

"*Pembroke?*"

John turned, and still holding his arm, Katherine turned with him. She faced a gentleman bearing a woman on his arm. "Katherine, let me introduce you to the Duke and Duchess of Leinster."

The procession of introductions from this moment forward was constant, Dukes, Earls, Marquesses, Barons. Over half the room approached them. Her head was spinning with names and faces when it finally ceased.

"You're popular."

Katherine jumped as John's Uncle Robert leant between them from behind.

They both turned and John's arm fell from beneath her fingers. Instead, she gripped his elbow.

"But then this is a novelty," his uncle continued. "A duke setting up his nursery before he is even thirty. My God, it's a miracle."

"Stop teasing them," Robert's wife, Jane, interjected, holding his arm with both hands.

"You were the one who said it was a crime to marry her in secret so we couldn't make a fuss."

Jane laughed. "You were not supposed to tell them that."

John smiled, but it looked forced because he maintained his ducal façade. "I apologise for depriving you, Aunt Jane."

She struck his shoulder with her closed fan, "You are not sorry at all—"

"Of course he is not," Robert interjected. "He is the hottest topic in the room. Everyone has been trying to prise the details of who Katherine is from us. How are you enjoying life as society's latest curio, Katherine?"

"I've barely had a chance to breathe."

"Or dance, I suppose. Come along then, let me get you started, if you'll allow it, John?"

John nodded. But Katherine hated leaving him.

His uncle was kind, though. "Congratulations, Katherine. I think you are just what he needs," he said as they joined a set. "However, I do not doubt it will be difficult."

She did not respond. She'd no idea what to say.

At the first movement in the dance, which brought them close, he spoke again. "If you need any help, *ask*. Jane can advise you. She's experienced society's fickle wrath herself in the past."

Katherine smiled. "Thank you."

"John can be hard work. He has his problems, I know, Katherine, but you'll mellow him."

The dance steps separated them for a while but when they came together again, he said, "You'll do. You'll do very well."

When the dance ended, he bowed courteously and then took her back to John. But it was like the introductions, there followed a stream of gentlemen asking her to dance.

It was different from an assembly at home; at least there she

260

knew people. She didn't know anything about these men bar their names, and they continually asked questions. Where was she from? What was the name of her family? Where had John been hiding her? She did not answer and she did not like any of them. Most of them flirted with her as though she was not even married.

Curio, Robert had said; she felt more like fresh cattle at a market.

Then a waltz began and the man who'd danced with Mary earlier, Lord Framlington, stood before her. She accepted him out of politeness. Even if John thought him a risk to Mary, a fortune-hunter could be no risk to her.

She learned very quickly she was wrong.

"Pembroke is dull. Perhaps when you tire of him you might think of me…" he whispered seductively in her ear, as they made a turn. "I would be willing to warm your bed if it is cold."

"I will never tire of my husband, my Lord…" Shock and insult made her pitch sharp.

"But there is much to be said for variety, my dear, and your husband knows it, look, see, he's speaking with my sister, an old flame he probably wishes to rekindle."

Katherine glanced at John. He was talking to a beautiful dark-haired woman, who rose to her toes and whispered in his ear. He gripped her arm and whispered something back.

Katherine felt pain grip about her heart.

John leant down to whisper to Lady Ponsonby. "Go away, Elizabeth. I am not interested. I will never be interested." He gripped her arm to set her away.

She seemed to think his marriage an amusing game and was casting dice to win him back.

John looked at Katherine.

She was dancing with Framlington for God's sake, Elizabeth's younger brother. John felt manipulated as Katherine glanced at him and then looked away, blushing. "Have you deliberately deterred me, so he might dance with her, or distracted her so you might annoy me?" She followed his gaze back to Katherine, laughed, and then simply walked off.

John stared at Katherine, incensed. She had heard him say Framlington was no good.

Framlington's palm was splayed on Katherine's slender back and it slid a little downwards.

For the first time since he'd returned to England John had actually been enjoying an evening, because Katherine was here, but now she'd done this. Before John even realised it, he was in motion, ignoring onlookers and surging through the dancers. It was fortunate for him, and Katherine, the dance came to its natural end. He'd have made a spectacle of them both if it had not.

He looked daggers at Framlington when he reached them. "I'd already made a note this evening to warn you off – I do not want you dancing with my sister – and now I see I must also warn you off my wife. Just so that you know, Framlington, hunting my sister is pointless, I would not agree the match and never pay you her dowry, and if you touch my wife again, I'll kill you."

The man just smiled, bowed and walked off, his retreat as silent as his sister's. Which implied it was no retreat at all.

John gritted his teeth more firmly, to prevent his mask slipping, and gripped Katherine's arm, then half dragged her from the floor. She was not happy with him but then *he* was not happy with her.

He did not stop moving until he'd led her into the card room and there he drew her to one side of the door. "Please tell me what you thought you were doing? Why did you dance with him?" His voice was a harsh whisper.

"I didn't think it would harm. I'm hardly prey for fortune-hunters. How was I to know he'd proposition me?" She was bristling too. "And you are making things worse!" Her gaze spun pointedly to the card room.

He glanced back across the room, and saw people staring.

His eyes turned back to Katherine. She was flushed and angry.

Damn, he'd become so used to hiding his feelings he'd forgotten she could not, and Lord, he did not wish her to. But nor did he want his wife to become fodder for men like Framlington.

Suddenly the anger in her eyes turned to doubt. "He said it was his sister you were speaking to…" *Ah bloody hell.* "He implied you were having an affair with her."

Damn. Why did this have to come tonight? "Not here, Katherine."

"Why were you whispering with her?" The question in her voice had a razor-sharp edge, and it carried. More heads turned their way.

"It was nothing, Katherine."

"Nothing?"

"It ended years ago and I am not talking about it here."

"Then take me home and tell me."

"No, Katherine." An exasperated breath left his lungs. He could not. "Not when the entire room will believe there is something wrong. Go back and dance and smile, or people will talk about you more." *Damn.*

He noted the glint of tears in her eyes as she pulled her arm free from his grip and turned away.

Hell. The expletive was followed by others in his head as he watched her walk away.

Unsure what to do, he followed, only to see her leave the ballroom and hurry to the privacy of the retiring chamber. He'd made a mess of the second night of his fledgling marriage.

~

Katherine weaved her way through the throng of guests, refusing to look back as she fought to stop the tears from falling. She was so out of her depth. This was John's world and she didn't fit. She didn't understand these people and their debauchery.

In the hall, she turned to a footman to ask for guidance and he directed her upstairs. John's mother's maid was there and Katherine sat down to let Esther check her hair, simply seeking time to pull herself together.

She'd embarrassed John and he was angry because of it, but if everyone in the room knew about him and Lord Framlington's sister then surely John's whispering in the woman's ear was an equal embarrassment for her.

Katherine closed her eyes.

It was no wonder John had thought nothing of asking her to meet him in the tower if this was the world he lived in.

She opened her eyes. She had two choices. One was to let this world beat her. The second was to fight. She felt a surge of determination. She could rescue John from this life. He hid from these people. He did not hide from her. Surely she was the only one who could rescue him then. She was going to fight. She was going to save him and not let him be like these debauched, selfish people anymore.

"All done, Your Grace," Esther stated.

Katherine stood. "Thank you, Esther." She felt much better, she felt in control again and she ignored the other women in the room who were staring at her. Let them stare, she was his duchess now.

When she left the room, she hastened back to the ballroom. She understood why he'd insisted they stay. But she would much rather they were alone and not among all these false, affected people.

Her mind raced with plans as she neared the top of the stairs, thinking of how she must speak to his servants and take charge of his house, and force her courage for tomorrow when people would call. She was not going to let him down, nor let these people think less of her… She was going to make John trust her and encourage him to end his part in this charade and simply be himself. She could not take him away from these people, but she was going to stop him being like them.

A woman blocked Katherine's path.

"John's *young* Duchess?"

Katherine's heart pounded. It was the woman John had whispered to. Close up, Katherine could see she was much older than John but still beautiful, and she had an allure that said she knew she was. She had huge brown eyes and dark hair.

"Pretty. Where did he find you?" Her casual voice had a hard edge, and Katherine had a feeling their chance meeting was no accident.

"Forgive me, I do not remember being introduced. Excuse me." Katherine moved to walk around the woman but her arm was gripped.

"Perhaps not, but we have a mutual experience, we have both been in John's bed, only I was there before you, in fact, I was his first, I broke him in. So you may thank me for his skill. But be warned, he will tire of you. I—"

Katherine did not stay to hear anymore, she pulled her arm free and walked on, mentally ranting over the woman's poison. These people played with one another for fun while they hid behind their expressionless faces. They were heartless and shallow. They didn't seem to care who they hurt. She was not going to let John be like them anymore.

She glanced about the crowd in the ballroom, but could not see him.

Mary and his parents were dancing.

She was saved by Eleanor.

"Katherine. You sly thing, marrying John. I'm so sorry we could not call earlier. Harry insists I rest in the afternoon if I am to go out in the evening, and the Earl of Derwent is his distant cousin so I could not cry off tonight. Oh, I cannot believe you and John managed to keep this secret, and more fool I, I even let him deceive me into sending that dress and thinking nothing more." Eleanor's fingers touched Katherine's elbow. "You may tell him I am disgusted with him for not at least inviting family to the wedding. How did he court you? Did he shower you with flowers, or was he lax? I shall tell him off if he was lax."

Eleanor led Katherine to a loveseat, while throwing question after question at her, and once they were seated, side-on, Eleanor raised her open fan so they might gossip without their lips being read. "You must tell it all, I am dying to know…"

Katherine knew so little of how to live in John's world – she could not lie to Eleanor, though she was sure John would. "Promise me you will say nothing, not even to your family…"

Eleanor nodded.

"I am with child, John's mother and father and Phillip are the only people who know…"

Eleanor's eyes widened. "The cad, what a rotter… And he made me give you that dress... Oh, I'll—"

"It isn't what you think, really. He'd finished everything and it had not gone so far. The dress was an apology for beginning something which could have no end. Only I did not wish it to end. I went to him. But swear to me you will say nothing…" It felt so good to be honest.

Katherine went on to explain everything. She told Eleanor about Richard, John's proposal and Phillip's outrage, and then she told her about that woman too.

Eleanor wafted the fan casually, hiding Katherine's distress, and when Katherine finished, Eleanor gripped her hand.

"I think John loves you, I would believe him. He says nothing lightly, Katherine. He may have a hard exterior but he's caring and principled. He'll do and say nothing unless he believes in it. Harry constantly complains that John will not be swayed to vote one way or the other in the House of Lords. Trust him, Katherine…"

Looking across Katherine's shoulder then, Eleanor lifted her voice and stood up. "*John.*"

Katherine looked back and stood too, as he crossed the last few feet to join them. He was so outrageously handsome, even with his austere, untouchable look.

"Timely," Eleanor stated mockingly. Then she struck his sleeve with her closed fan, having snapped it shut. "You are a bounder, cousin. You had better look after my friend."

"She is my wife," John answered, "of course I will."

Eleanor's fingers touched the scab on his lip then the bruise on his cheek. "And you deserve these."

"Thank you." His pitch was bitter.

"You're welcome," Eleanor chimed. Then she smiled at Katherine and dropped a little respectful curtsy. "Good evening, Kate, call on me whenever you wish and I shall definitely call on you. In fact I shall speak to Harry about asking you both to dinner." After that she kissed the air beside Katherine's cheek and then disappeared.

Katherine dropped back down on to the loveseat and John took the other side. He did not sit as she and Eleanor had done, though, but leant back and crossed his arms, looking at the room.

"You've told her everything, I assume."

"She is my friend."

His pale-blue gaze turned to her but she saw John in the depths of it. He sighed. "I—" She didn't know if he was going to apologise, berate her or explain – she didn't give him chance to speak.

"I saw that woman. She spoke to me."

His face flushed and his jaw tightened to hold his indifferent mask and once again his eyes turned diamond-hard. "Not here, Katherine, wait until we are home."

"Then take me home. I wish to speak." She was not going to let him set her aside.

He held her gaze in silence for a minute and then sighed. "Very well, if that is what you wish."

~

Katherine seated herself in the far corner of the carriage and longed for darkness to hide in, but John's servants were too fastidious to leave the internal lanterns unlit and so a low light illuminated John as he climbed the step behind her and slid into the corner diagonal to where she sat.

She watched him as the carriage door shut.

He leant back and looked out the window into the darkness, or at his reflection on the black glass, she couldn't tell which. Then his fingers lifted and brushed back his fringe.

A deep emotion of love and longing clasped in her stomach, she sensed vulnerability in him again. It only proved to her that the plans she'd made earlier had to be carried out. He needed saving from himself.

"So will you explain to me now?" she asked, her hands gripping the edge of the seat.

His head turned slowly, and his gaze struck hers, not with its ducal hardness but with intensity, expressing both his irritation and that he deemed the conversation unnecessary. "It was years ago, Katherine. I'm sure you do not wish to hear about it really. Besides, I hardly remember."

"She said she was your first, I think you would remember that."

His lips pursed.

He was her first. She would never forget that night.

"She was my first, yes. It happened in Paris, the summer I left England. She chased me for a week. It is her thing – to break young men in. She broke me. Is that what you wish to know? Or do you want explicit details?" She did not answer the vindictive taunt. "She was the first, but she was not the only," he went on, clearly warming to the theme. "There were many. I had a colourful reputation abroad. I can list names if you wish."

He was deliberately provoking her, she knew, because he did not really wish to speak of this.

"It is what young gentlemen of noble birth do. We are sent abroad on the tour explicitly to sow our wild oats and plough as many furrows as we wish out of the sight of our mamas and the judgement of society. There are whores on every corner at the tourist destinations, even in the arches of the Colosseum. I am mortal and I was young." His piercing gaze bored into her, challenging her to comment or to judge.

When she did neither, a deep sigh left his throat. "I thought I was in love with her, with Elizabeth Ponsonby, if you must know. Now I know it was only ever a youth's infatuation. But when I found her with another man and realised I was nothing to her, I went on a rampage of carnal revenge, behaving just like her. I felt better for it for a long while. It took me years to realise that I was only hurting myself. And still more years to know I never loved her in the first place."

His shoulders shrugged. "She has been chasing me again for a few weeks. It appears I am to her taste once more since I acquired my title. I have already told her once, before tonight, I am not interested. Yet for the sake of her vanity she cannot accept no."

Katherine looked out the window, not really seeing.

"I was one among many, Katherine. Everyone behaved like that abroad."

Does he think that makes it better? "I learned that tonight," she answered, facing him again.

His eyes flashed with anger. "Framlington. He is as bad as his sister. Keep away from him."

"The people you mix with are all false, John. I don't like them." Suddenly her courage of earlier ebbed, her love seemed too sparse to change anything. She needed him to love her back. She realised she was crying.

John moved across the carriage and his arm came about her. "Katherine, I cannot change my past."

Her head fell against his shoulder and she nodded. She knew it. It was just the turmoil of all this sudden change affecting her.

His fingers gripped hers in her lap. "I did not mean to upset you. I have not been with another woman for years, and I never felt for Elizabeth even a hundredth of what I feel for you. Knowing you has proven to me how shallow my feelings for her really were."

A sob left her lips.

"I was alone in Egypt, Katherine. I'm not that person anymore. I will be faithful to you." His pitch urged her to believe him. She looked up at him, and noted the bruise on his cheek again, and the healing cut in his lip.

"Katherine, I love you." She looked into his pale eyes. They shone with sincerity. "Believe me…" They were John's eyes, and they bore the plea she'd seen in the parlour at home when he'd offered for her.

"I know," she whispered in return. But she did not know if he knew how to love. "I'm just tired. Everything has happened so fast…"

He held her gaze, "And you are reliant on a man who has let you down already. He did not come to your marriage bed and now he has introduced you to his former mistress. I'm sorry, Katherine. I want you to be happy but I cannot change the past, sweetheart." He brushed a kiss on her lips, gently.

Her arms reached about his shoulders as she returned it just as gently so she did not hurt his lip. It was an intensely sweet kiss. It was nothing like the lustful, hungry kisses she had shared with him before.

When the carriage finally halted at the door of his, *their*, townhouse, they were still kissing in leisurely devotion.

He pulled away and smiled slightly a moment before a footman opened the door and another set down the step.

John offered his hand, before his footman could, and climbed down first. But when her foot left the step he let her hand go and instead swept her off her feet, whispering, "Another thing I was remiss over yesterday, a bridegroom is supposed to carry his bride over the threshold, is he not?"

She smiled up at him, clinging to his shoulders as he carried her up the steps and into the grand hall. A clock struck twelve somewhere in the downstairs rooms and she looked over his shoulder just to check his coach had not turned into a pumpkin. It had not.

Mr Finch bowed deeply, but John did not set her down, and she was blushing intensely as he crossed the black and white chequered marble floor, speaking over his shoulder to the butler. "Tell Smithson I will not need him, Finch."

The heels of his dancing shoes rang on the marble as he walked, and then he was climbing the stairs with her still in his arms.

"You may set me down," she whispered. "Your staff are watching."

In point of fact they were not, they were doing anything but watching, schooling their faces to a blank as they looked everywhere else but at the stairs.

"They are paid well enough to see and hear nothing, Katherine, and if they dare to gossip they know they'll be dismissed within hours."

When they reached the state chambers, John kicked the door open and then shut it again with his heel. He let her feet slip to the floor when it was shut and then gripped her nape and kissed her once more. His other hand held her waist.

Breaking the kiss after a while, he said, "You're mine, Katherine, I'll not be cuckolded." His pale eyes glowed with the intensity that was all John.

"And you are mine, John Harding," she answered. "I'll not be made a fool of."

He smiled and she knew they had just made another promise to each other as important and as solemn as their marriage vows. His finger tugged loose the ribbon which tied her cloak and it fell to the floor.

She felt breathless. It had been such a long time since the night at Pembroke Place and the hours they'd spent in the tower.

"I already know I am yours, Katherine. I have been since Grandfather's funeral. You are all I think of. I am your slave, darling."

His fingers slipped her dress from her shoulders, leaving the short, puffed sleeves draped lower down her arms.

Her heart thundered with anticipation. All the feelings she had known in the bright tower room and in his shadowed bedchamber flooded back.

As his eyes held hers, his fingers trailed across the top curve of her breasts.

She wanted to touch him but there was a foot between them and his gentle exploration seemed to will her not to breach the

271

boundary he'd set.

"I've missed you," he stated as his hand slid into her bodice.

"Missed my body?" she asked in a husky voice.

"Missed *you*." His fingers slipped free of her bodice and then he moved closer so he could reach around her and undo the buttons at her back. He looked over her shoulder, watching his fingers work as he did so.

She looked up at the ceiling and faced some Greek scene of women lying all about a chaise-longue, dining on fruit.

His lips touched her neck as her dress felt slacker and her breasts seemed to press more firmly against her corset.

He could make her feel such delicious things and she was free to love him without guilt.

Her arms lifted and settled on his shoulders as he bit and nipped at her neck.

He was making no effort to rush, her dress hung open at the back but his hands merely gripped her waist as he kissed her neck.

She kissed his earlobe and his hair and stroked her hands across his back.

A part of her could not believe she was with John again. She was his wife.

His hands lifted and kneaded her breast over the cloth of her gown as his lips came back to hers. The kiss was gentle, by the necessity of his sore lip, but the gentleness was excruciatingly blissful. She felt as if she was drowning in the emotions he induced in her.

When he broke the kiss, she was breathless again.

Holding her gaze, he drew her dress down and, smiling at him, she slipped his evening coat from his shoulders.

He took it off.

Everything in his expression spoke of a devotion and desire that was beyond physical. He needed her. She knew he did. He was letting her in to view all his vulnerability and know him for who he was, letting her know he loved her.

He leant over her shoulder again and unthreaded her lacing.

She began unbuttoning his waistcoat. They then stripped each other systematically and slowly, peeling off layers. When it came to the last, she watched his naked body, sitting on the edge of his bed as her foot rested on his muscular thigh and he rolled down her second stocking.

He kissed the sole of her foot once it was off. Then with one hand still gripping her foot, the other braced against her neck and he kissed her lips once more. She melted inside. His gentleness was sublime. It had not been like this in the tower, nor in his bed at The Place.

"Lie back," he whispered when he broke the kiss. She did, with her legs still dangling to the floor.

He knelt before her and she throbbed there, burning with need and damp heat as he paid homage with his mouth.

If she could simply forget the world beyond his bedchamber, she would have the most wonderful marriage. She was in ecstasy. Her first flood drew close, the wave rising, about to break, but then he ceased and stood and half leant over her and the wave washed away without a crest.

One hand parted her naked thighs wider, and his other hand pressed down on the mattress beside her, and then there was pressure between her thighs where she had only known it once before.

It was not painful. It felt right. Though the sensation of pressure also felt like stretching, it filled her and completed here, the other half of her whole. But it challenged her and overwhelmed her too, to have him there, within her body, where his child already grew.

He was still standing on the floor, leaning over her and pressing into her, slowly, gently.

Her fingers lifted and touched the bruise on his cheek as he withdrew.

John.

His movement expressed tenderness and longing, and a need to relish, but with each movement he gained more depth, pressing a little deeper, urging her legs a little wider.

John.

His thrusts developed a stronger but still slow rhythm. She became breathless again and her fingers gripped his lower arms, while her calves gripped at his back.

She was panting in time with his rhythm and no longer able to see the painting on the ceiling above as her vision clouded. All she could focus on was John, on his face as he looked down at her. The look in his eyes was a caress too.

John.

The pattern he was weaving charmed her senses, assailing them. She had never imagined this could feel as it did. She felt cherished by him, and yet that gentleness drove her wild with need.

"John."

Her fingernails cut into his forearms and her head pressed back into the bed as she closed her eyes and gripped his hips with her legs.

His movement quickened and sharpened. She broke all about him, tumbling over a cliff into drifting heaven.

"I love you," he whispered, increasing his tempo to allegro, moving more swiftly, but there was still a blissful planned determination about it as he delivered these swift, short, sharp strokes, making her pant for more and cling to his shoulders instead of his arms.

He was breathless too, his breathing was heavy and rasping and she could feel and smell sweat on his skin. She liked his smell and liked his body weight coming down more heavily on to her as he neared the end.

"John!" She broke again a moment after his weight fell fully on her and his body clenched in spasm.

His forehead rested on her shoulder.

Her fingers ran though his hair.

When he lifted off her and withdrew, she felt cold.

But he walked about the bed and then pulled the covers down. "Slide in."

She did, feeling tired.

He climbed in beside her, leaving the candles burning, then set his arm about her shoulders and kissed her temple. "I love you, Katherine."

"I love you too," she said, pillowing her head on his shoulder.

"Even after all I have done. I've treated you badly."

"Yes, but love cannot judge. It is why I turned Richard away after you left, I couldn't marry him when I still loved you."

"I am going to make you happy," he said to the air above her, as though it was another vow. "You can trust me, Katherine."

"I am going to make you happy too." Her fingers cupped his cheek, though she was too tired to lift her head. "Be yourself with me. I don't want you to be like the people I met tonight."

She fell asleep.

Chapter Fourteen

"Goodnight," Mary called in the hallway.

Her mother answered, "Sleep well."

The sound pulled Katherine out of sleep.

The Duke and Duchess's suite of rooms extended to the left, and although there were guest rooms opposite, his family used those stretching from the landing to the right.

It wasn't Mary's voice that had woken Katherine though. John had disturbed her. He was breathing heavily, as though he was running, and beneath her palm his skin was damp and hot and his chest muscle twitched.

She rose onto her elbow.

In the candlelight flickering from a stub, she could see his eyes moving rapidly beneath his eyelids. Then he gasped and his arm flailed, pushing her away as he sat up suddenly.

"No!" His cry echoed about the room.

He was fully awake then and one leg hung from the edge of the bed as he sat up, while the other curled before him and his fingers gripped the covers as he fought to catch his breath.

"What did you dream?" She sat up too, holding the sheet to cover her breasts.

He glanced at her as though he'd forgotten she was there and he looked as though he did not quite understand where he was.

Jenny had had dreams like this as a child, disorientating nightmares. Sometimes she'd woken everyone, shouting at shadows.

"Nothing."

She heard a clock chime three after midnight somewhere in the house.

John got up and drew in a deep breath, then he crossed the room to a decanter and poured a glass of brandy, his back to her.

"John?" she said softly. "Tell me what you dreamed. It always made my sister feel better when she spoke of bad dreams."

He turned and the orange light of the flickering candle illuminated him, gilding the firm muscular contours of his chest and limbs.

He sipped his brandy.

"I'm not a child. I told you, it was nothing."

His ducal guard was up again, and his voice was disparaging, it was as though he slipped in and out of his armour without even knowing he did it. It was not nothing, though, otherwise why would he now be on his guard?

She had a feeling he'd dreamed of something which touched reality. He would hardly be scared of imagined monsters, not John.

His hand shook when it swept back his fringe, and he took another sip of brandy. "I'm sorry I woke you."

"John?"

He smiled at her, as he walked back across the room, but it was obviously a false smile. "Honestly, it was nothing, just my head playing tricks."

She made a disbelieving face at him. But he just smiled more broadly. "If you wish to chase away my demons, make love to me again."

The bed dipped as he climbed beneath the sheets, but he made no move to touch her. Instead he slotted the pillows behind him and sat upright against the headboard. His mood had darkened behind his smile. He seemed more like the John of those hours in the tower. He was so hard to read.

"Sit astride me."

Yes, he was the John of the tower, all brooding sexual intensity.

His smile turned wicked as he beckoned her with his fingers. Ignoring his belligerence, she smiled back. She was going to save him from these dark elements of his character. She was going to set him free of his chains and help him to stop retreating into this person who denied human feeling. He *was* feeling.

Her fingers brushed back his hair as she straddled his slender, muscular hips, while the backs of his fingers brushed over her stomach, as though he thought of the child.

She kissed him gently, a kiss of love, she did not let him deepen it but just gently adored his lips with hers as her breasts brushed against his chest and the backs of his fingers drew circles on her stomach.

After a while, though, impatience seemed to grasp him and, his hands bracing her head, he ended the kiss, his pale gaze boring into hers. "Make love to me. I need you to."

Need? She really thought he did need. He looked as though he wanted to escape into her. She would let him do so. She was here for him always now.

As she lifted and impaled herself, she felt his sharp outward breath on her cheek.

Had he been escaping from something when they'd been in the tower room too? He'd said on the way home, he'd lived alone in Egypt. And at The Place he'd said that he felt isolated amongst his family. Had he turned to her then to have someone? No wonder he'd written those desperate letters to her, if that was so. He did need her.

His hands on her hips helped her move, rocking her forward and up, and then down and back, and his breathing was heavy.

The movement began weaving its spell inside her again. It spun up like a wind, gently spiralling and gathering.

Her fingers braced the back of his neck, and her weight was on either shin beside his hips. Her toes curled under to give her more control, guided by him.

He was looking down, watching their joining, absorbed in it.

It felt wonderful to know she could distract him like this, that if he trusted no one else, he was beginning to trust her. She quickened her movement and took the lead from his hands. His grip fell away and instead his hands fell on to her thighs, not clinging but merely feeling and letting her have control.

He was relaxing, and he looked intoxicated as he lifted his head.

Then his hand was at the back of her head and he kissed her hard, once, no matter his damaged lip, before gripping one breast and bringing it to his mouth.

Her head fell back and she worked to please him, lifting and lowering, seeking to free him.

She still fell before him, and when she did, his fingers gripped her hips hard once more and ended the encounter by lifting and dropping her body with hard, aggressive movements until he shattered too.

They were panting and clinging to one another, warm and sweaty again, wrapped in each other's arms, when she came back to reality.

Katherine lifted her head and said in a quiet voice, "When Phillip came today he told me I do not value myself, that I think I am unlovable. He blamed it on his mother and mine, because they both let me down. But he said he loved me, and Richard had loved me, and that you could too."

"I do, Katherine." John's fingers brushed her hair back from her brow. "Why would you think your real mother did not love you?"

"Because she took her own life rather than staying with me. She could not have felt for me, could she?" She heard the heartache in her voice, even after all these years of life with no mother. How could you long for a person you'd never known? But she did. "When we did what we did in the tower, and your chamber, I imagined that I knew her and I could feel a part of her, because I was feeling what she felt."

His eyes narrowed in a look of confusion, but she carried on, wishing to get this out, knowing that if she spoke, perhaps it would cease its hold on her, as if it were a nightmare like John's. And perhaps, if she spoke, he'd speak too.

"When I watched you when I was younger and felt an urge to be close to you, I felt it then too, I rejoiced at the fact I had something of her in me. And Phillip's mother always told me I would fall like my mother." His fingers stroked through her hair. "Sins of the fathers, she preached to me. I *wanted* to be like my mother."

She sighed. "Then I fell with child just as she'd done and didn't understand her at all. How could she have left me alone to face life by myself with no mother or father and no one to love me? I would not have given my child up. I could never do what she did. She didn't love me…"

He held her gaze and stroked her hair again, "And she was probably desolate, Katherine, and terrified and not thinking clearly. She was probably in a deep black hole and did not know how to climb out of her self-pity. She probably thought you would be better off without her—"

"With no one to love me?"

"With a family who could give you food and clothing and a roof. Things would have been very different for you, Katherine, if she'd lived. She would have had to keep working, and not many employers would welcome a woman with a naturally born child to keep. You and she would have probably ended up in the workhouse."

Katherine climbed off him and moved to sit beside him. His arm came about her and she curled into his side, her hand resting on his chest, while one leg slid over his. She wished to climb into his security. But he was only secure in this room, tucked away from the servants and society. She had become a part of his *secret self.* She had not really broken down any of his walls.

His fingers slipped through her hair again. "There is nothing sinful about you, or your behaviour, Katherine, *nothing.* Everyone feels attractions, you were young and growing from a girl to a woman. Of course you would feel something for boys—"

"Not boys," she interrupted, "just you."

There was a slight sound of humour in his throat and his fingers stroked though her hair again. "Then I am very flattered, and a very lucky man to have discovered such devotion, and you cannot think yourself sinful, only in love. I knew it in the summer and I took advantage of it. It was wrong of me. But you saw the world I came from last night and—"

"And you knew no better…"

"I did know better, but I chose to grasp something which was precious. I should have done it honourably, Katherine, I should have courted you from the first—"

"A bastard dairymaid's daughter—"

"A beautiful woman, with a heart of gold, who loves me, when I do not deserve to be loved. A woman who I knew was valuable from the moment I saw her at my grandfather's funeral, when I did not even recognise her… Katherine?" he said, when he clearly realised she was crying, and then he was kissing the crown of her head and wiping her tears away with his thumb. "I love you. If I'm honest, I probably loved you instantly that day I met you in the road, or perhaps it was that first moment when I saw you at the funeral."

"I do believe you love me," Katherine said through her sobs, "but, at the moment, I believe it with my head not my heart, John, my heart is too used to being unloved and insignificant."

"You are not insignificant now either, you are a duchess, and is that not a measure of how much I love you?"

She breathed deeply, wondering how he'd ended up comforting her, when she had begun comforting him.

"We are a pair, aren't we?" he whispered to the air. "Both hungry for love and unsure of it. I think we were meant to be together. I wish I had known it before I went abroad." His hand stroked over her hair again and she felt him looking up at the ceiling beyond the canopy of the bed and felt as though he wished to say something more, but he did not.

Instead, his fingers tilted up her chin and then he was kissing her gently, and a moment later he pressed her back down onto the bed and came over her and made love to her once more.

A sense of complete devotion filled her as he did so. She forgot about everything beyond his bed and his room. Here, she was happy.

~

A gentle knock struck on the connecting door leading to Katherine's rooms.

She woke, curled on her side, with John's weight at her back. She felt sick.

"Stay there," his deep voice commanded as he moved. The knock had obviously woken him too.

He climbed off the bed and she heard him moving about the room but did not turn for fear the sickness would run away with her.

"Come in!"

As the door opened, John appeared on her side of the bed.

He wore a red silk dressing gown and bore a porcelain chamber pot, which he put down on a chest beside the bed.

"Your Grace, I was asked to bring Her Grace's tray early."

"Bring it over here, Esther, please. Thank you."

John took the tray from the maid's hands.

She lowered in a deep curtsy. "Is there anything else, Your Grace?"

"Nothing, thank you, Esther. That will be all."

The maid backed out of the room. She had kept her eyes lowered the whole time, not looking at either of them, deferring. But still the outside world rushed in and formed a wall in between her and John. They would never just be them. There were servants and family and visitors and tenants…

He set the tray down beside the chamber pot and the scent of ginger tea and freshly toasted bread filled the air. She felt hungry.

"Do you want some cushions behind you so you may sit up?"

She nodded and rose carefully so he could set them there.

"You look green." He handed her the plate of toast. "Eat this first then sip the tea. Is it always this bad?"

She nodded tentatively. "Most days."

He sat on the edge of the bed and when she'd eaten a little of the toast, handed her the tea.

She shook her head at him and smiled. "So attentive, John Harding. This was thoughtful of you…" She called him that deliberately, she did not wish to think of him as a duke here. He must have ordered all this yesterday.

His fingers swept her hair off her brow. "Just seeking to make you as spoilt as me so you can stop casting accusations."

She laughed and realised she was actually feeling less sick. Oh, it felt good to have him here – to have someone being kind to her.

Kind? She remembered Mr Wareham.

Could John be kind? Mr Wareham had given his life to John's grandfather and John had summarily dismissed him. "Why did you discharge Mr Wareham?"

She had asked him once at Jenny's party and he'd not answered.

"Where on earth did that come from?" John felt as though she'd punched him in the gut. He did not wish to think of such things here with her. Let his duties sit beyond his bedchamber door.

"I was thinking that it was kind of you to recognise my needs, but then I remembered Mr Wareham, and I remembered that kindness is not always your forte, John."

He sighed. He did deserve that from her, though. "Perhaps not." *Damn.* She may have good reason to judge him badly, but still, that she judged him to be the guilty party, hurt. But her words had let duty invade the room and it gripped a hold of him. He supposed he ought to face it. Much as he wished to, he could not stay with her. Without saying a word, he rose and walked to his dressing room.

Within, he poured the fresh water from the jug into a bowl and commenced his morning ablutions.

But leaving Katherine behind also let the rush of emotion his dream had stirred return. He washed his face. It had been his mother again, outside the carriage, not Katherine, but with her, holding her hand, had stood a small boy, a toddler. John didn't understand it, yet he suspected the child was his unborn son.

Fear set cold and solid in John's stomach as he faced himself in the mirror but he could not look himself in the eyes.

I love Katherine, but can I love my child?

What if I cannot?

Shutting the door to where Katherine lay in bed, he rang for his valet to help him shave and dress. His sudden desire was just to get away, to get out of the house. Now it was time to face his responsibility again he did not wish to feel this emotion and weakness.

~

John returned home early in the evening. He'd spent an hour or two with Harvey going over business and discovering how things stood with Wareham, which was no further forward, other than an ominous report that the man had been seen back in town.

John had eaten at White's and, after that, met his Uncle Robert.

They'd shared a couple of hours in congenial conversation with fellow members of Parliament and discussed the progress of their private business venture.

Finally, John had sought out Phillip and apologised again, achieving a tenuous peace with his new brother-in-law, then he'd encouraged Phillip to accept the role with Harvey and invited Phillip to dine.

They arrived together.

Finch took their hats, gloves and outdoor coats.

"Have there been many callers?" John asked. He felt a measure of guilt sweep in, guilt he'd been determinedly pushing aside all day.

He'd left Katherine and his mother to deal with the matrons of society. His mother was eminently capable, of course, but Katherine...

Yet it would have been odd for him to remain, none of the callers would have expected to see him. Still, he could not escape his nagging conscience, which said he should have stayed.

Phillip was John's peace offering and his shield. He'd run away this morning rather than deal with thoughts and feelings he did not wish to face. Phillip was John's sorry.

"I believe the last caller left half an hour ago, Your Grace, and yes there have been many."

"And my family?"

"In the drawing room upstairs, Your Grace."

John threw a look at Phillip which said, follow, and headed upstairs. His heart was thumping. He had not realised until this morning just how much he cared what Katherine thought. But her judging him poorly over Wareham *had* hurt. Yet he'd no intention of explaining; let her think what she wished, he was not bringing any of his official life into his bed. They were separate things. She had called him John Harding this morning. He wished to just be John Harding with her.

His hand slid along the mahogany rail of the staircase as he climbed.

He hoped she would forgive his desertion. He hoped she would understand when he told her it was not the done thing for him to hover about each day. That he had duties, and it was just not seemly for a duke to hang onto the petticoats of his wife. But he should have told her he was leaving. Yet it had been panic which beat him out the door with a whip.

God, he wished to laugh at himself. He was such a bloody fraud. Here he was pretending he could manage an empire of land and people and businesses, when the thought of a screeching infant, his own, sent him running a mile.

But he just did not wish that child to be unloved, and he felt too like his grandfather now to be sure he could love it.

What if he felt nothing when the child was born? His heart pumped harder.

These were the thoughts he'd run from; he'd not had them beyond the door when he was immersed in business.

He heard his mother's voice, and Mary's, and some of the children's. He didn't hear Katherine's. He longed to hear it. He'd missed her today.

When they entered the room, Mary was immediately on her feet, moving to greet Phillip. John's mother looked up and smiled. Katherine was not there.

John's gaze passed on to his father, who was seated in an armchair, a ledger on his lap as he spun a charcoal pencil in his fingers and followed the columns.

He looked up, acknowledged Phillip and John, then returned his attention to the page.

The boys were grouped about the table behind his father's back playing with an army of lead soldiers that had once been John's.

The girls were all seated about his mother, as though they'd been avidly listening to something she or Mary had been saying. The young ones were on their laps.

His gaze spun back to his mother.

"Mama…"

She smiled, clearly understanding his unspoken question. "Katherine went to lie down. It has been a long afternoon. We've had numerous visitors but she has managed remarkably well. You should be very proud of her, John. I took her into town this morning too. We purchased the accessories and other items she needs. I think I have exhausted her."

"I'll fetch her," he stated, looking at Phillip, and then he immediately left the room.

He wondered how he would be received as he entered his chamber. She was not in his bed. Was that a statement of her feelings?

He didn't find her on her bed either, though. There was a maid there, busy putting the things purchased today into drawers and wardrobes. She spoke to his look of confusion as she bobbed a sudden deep curtsy. "Your Grace, Her Grace went down to the library."

John thanked the maid and retraced his steps. There was anxiety inside him but there was a sense of expectation too, and hopefulness. It was the strangest feeling to have someone he wished to come home to. He remembered feeling so damned arid in the desert and now he felt an intense thirst to be with her.

He passed two footmen in the hall. They bowed.

The library door was left ajar, but there was no sound from within as he crossed the marble floor.

He pushed it wider, passed through and closed it behind him, shutting him in with her and locking out the world as it had been locked out last night.

All he saw of her was her slipper-clad feet swinging from the side of an armchair. Her slender ankles were crossed.

He felt an involuntary smile lift his lips and walked forwards.

When he saw her fully, she was seated sideways, her knees draped over the arm of the chair with one of his sketchbooks spread open on her lap. She was so busy gazing at the pictures she hadn't noticed he'd come in. She turned a page, then must have sensed his presence and looked up.

His arms folded across his chest. "Katherine?"

She moved immediately, guiltily, snapping the book shut and rising impulsively. "Sorry, John, I know I shouldn't be looking…"

He took the book from her hands, "You can look."

"I didn't mean to pry. I came to find a book to take to my room and I noticed it lying on the shelf under your desk. When I saw it said Egypt I was… curious. I'm sorry."

"Curious?" He laughed.

He'd expected a tirade when he got home, anger or silence. Either extreme might have expressed her disappointment in him.

They had been married for two and a half days and he had already failed her four times, leaving her alone the first day, not sharing her bed the first night, displaying the truth of his past last night and now deserting her again today. He felt disloyal and unworthy of her.

"What were you curious about?" She looked beautiful, dressed in sunny lemon-yellow, her hair pinned in a tidy chignon, leaving only a few soft curls to frame her face. But she also looked thin and frail. She had lost weight since the summer. He'd noted it particularly last night. But she'd spent three months without him, frightened and sick, while he had sent her pleading letters saying "love me".

He was an ass. He should not have left her alone in bed this morning, he could have simply said goodbye and told her what he'd planned for the day.

Still, like the stoic woman she was, she'd obviously persisted with the day, without surrendering to feminine paroxysms.

"How did you live? What did you do out there? What did you see?"

"And what did the sketchbook tell you."

"That it is a barren but beautiful place."

"Yes it is."

"Did you draw these?"

"Yes."

"I didn't know you could draw like that."

He said nothing, not knowing what to say as her eyes held his gaze. He'd spent his childhood learning to excel at everything, trying to please his grandfather. He was not proud of any of his skills.

She looked as though she was waiting for him to speak. She was probably hoping for an explanation for his desertion, or an apology, he found neither on his tongue.

She took the book out of his hands, walked across to his desk, set it down and then opened it again, flicking through the pages.

She stopped on one he'd drawn at Karnak, of Yassah beside a huge statue. He'd drawn Yassah in to display the size of it. Seeing the image took him back to that day, the dry heat of the desert and the relief of the area of oases along the Nile, the sounds of local children playing and his men working.

"I like this one," she said. "Who is the man?"

John wished she could see his memories. He walked over, looked over her shoulder and braced his hand at her waist. "It is Yassah. He was a friend out there. I employed him, but we worked together and we had the same way of thinking. The same things excited us. He is still working out there for me. I have been paying for him to continue seeking new tombs. He writes intermittently and tells me what's happening. His letters frequently take my thoughts back there."

She looked sideways, up at his face, but said nothing, then looked back at the book and flicked to the pages at the very back. Pages which had been empty when he'd brought the book home. "Ah." They were now littered with small images of Katherine in various nude and semi-nude poses, mostly memories of their hours in the tower room.

"Yes, ah…" she breathed.

"I couldn't forget you." His hand fell from her waist.

She turned around, clasped his cheeks on either side and drew his head down, then kissed him, gently, minding his still-healing lip.

Then she said, meeting his gaze, "One day will you explain all your pictures to me?"

He felt a frown as confusion stirred. "Yes."

"I don't mind the pictures of me, but put them somewhere safe, John."

He took a deep breath and nodded, wondering what he'd done to deserve this woman. "But no one touches anything on my desk,

Katherine. No one would have seen them. Yet if you feel more comfortable I'll keep them in my – in our – rooms." Then he bent to her ear. "I shall draw and paint you properly, a full nude image."

"No!" She pulled away.

He laughed. "I will hide it away."

"No!"

"We could put it in the tower at The Place and keep the door forever locked."

She shook her head.

"I will draw you, though. I'll make a small portrait of you for myself, but I'll let someone else paint you in a life-size pose and I will put it up in here and take him down." He looked up at the old man, at the painting John had still not got around to removing, and met his grandfather's imperious, judgemental stare.

The old man would have hated Katherine. If he were alive, John would have been standing here receiving the biggest dressing down of his life. Well his grandfather could go to hell. John was very happy with his choice of bride.

He took her hand and remembered his peace offering. Lord, he had forgotten Phillip was waiting upstairs. "I will tell you about Egypt later. Your brother is here."

"Phillip?"

His smile twitched. "You only have one brother, as far as I recall. I asked him to dine with us. My mother said you did well today, she's declared you a success."

"What she means is I managed to resist the urge to insult the pompous women who called to pry and ogle me. Is that called success? Of course there is still tomorrow, and by then I may choose to throttle the lot of them instead. I apologise now if I do, and you are cut because of it."

He laughed and finally found that apology ready on his tongue. "I'm sorry I just disappeared this morning, I had a meeting with Harvey, I—"

Her fingers covered his lips.

"Your mother helped me."

"I'm sorry."

"I coped. Is Phillip upstairs?"

"Yes."

"I'll go up." Her hand slipped from his. He didn't follow as she left. He felt as though she should have shouted at him. He felt guilty. He picked up the book. He'd hide it first and then return to the drawing room.

~

Folly, Katherine told herself, as she had done a dozen times today. *Folly, folly, folly, folly.*

Folly to love him in the first place, *folly* to succumb to his seductions, and certainly *folly* to believe him, but she'd believed him again last night and been enchanted by his attentions, and then he'd disappeared without a word, leaving her behind. Just as he'd done at Ashford.

Catching up her skirt, not hearing him follow, she raced upstairs, her fingers sliding over the warm, silky mahogany.

Seeing his sketches of Egypt had only reinforced again just how different their lives had been. She wished she hadn't seen them, and yet she knew if she was ever to breach the gap between herself and John she had to understand his world, and so she'd dutifully understood when his mother had excused John's disappearance this morning and explained how busy his life was.

Of course he had a life beyond their bedchamber but she longed to lock him away and pretend all else did not exist.

She had shopped with his mother and enjoyed her company, and then faced the matrons of elite society. She'd hated every moment of that, but she had smiled and borne it because she knew eventually these women would be gone and John would come home and they could retire to his rooms again.

Phillip greeted her with a hug and she clung to him for a

291

moment, pressing her cheek to his shoulder and holding onto the feeling of familiarity, when nothing else was familiar anymore.

"How are things?" he asked when they let go of one another.

"Well."

Taking his hand, she then pulled him to a sofa at one side of the room, where they could talk more privately. John's family seemed to respect this and left them to speak.

She told Phillip in a rush about the ball last evening.

When John entered the room a little later, she did not look up.

Nor did she look at him through dinner. He was at the opposite end of the table to her, and Phillip was beside her. She talked endlessly to Phillip, though, and in between courses she gripped his hand.

He told her John had offered him work. He told her their father had written back to him and asked him to watch over her and ensure she was happy, and that Jenny had sent congratulations too.

When they'd finished eating, John's mother stood, and Katherine realised it should have been her role to notice it was time for the women to leave. Oh, she had so much to remember and learn. She finally looked at John then; he was rising out of respect because his mother and his elder sisters had done so. He smiled at her as she stood too, as much as his scabbed lip allowed. She smiled back.

How was she to help him simply be himself when he would be out every day, beyond her reach?

Taking the reins of responsibility from his mother, Katherine turned and led the way from the room, leaving the men to their port and cigars.

~

John walked into the drawing room an hour later. Edward had sent John's brothers up to bed after a quarter-hour. Once they'd gone, the conversation had turned to the developments with Wareham. Thus they'd stayed at the table longer than normal as they'd lost

292

track of time. He'd let Katherine down a fifth time.

He was struck by a domestic tableau as he entered.

Katherine was sitting at his grandmother's pianoforte. It was an instrument on which he'd learned to play as a child. Her fingers ran across the keys with significant ease.

John hated the damn thing.

He stopped just inside the room, motionless, unable to move as both Phillip and his father walked past. It was as though the sound flipped his daytime into the terror of his dreams. The wash of childhood insecurity swept through his veins, confusing his rational mind. *What the hell is happening to me?* he cursed as he forced himself to walk on. *I am not a snivelling child now. For God's sake, stop this.*

Forcing his ill memories away, he crossed the room and took the seat beside Katherine on the stool. His eyes followed the movement of her fingers.

She had a very real skill. He hadn't known she played so well. But even so, the pleasant sound grated on his nerves like fingernails running down a blackboard.

He looked up, searched for the notes she played on the sheet music, and then followed them across the lines. When he turned the page for her, his fingers were shaking.

On the edge of his consciousness he could hear Mary and Phillip talking, and his parents occasionally joining in. The younger girls had been sent to bed too.

He was extremely glad there were no other guests.

Stiffly, he turned the page again, trying to force himself to like the music but it hinted at so many days he had been alone in this house with his grandparents, not understanding how he fitted into the family.

Katherine was absorbed in the music, reading it from the page and transporting it through her fingers into notes. Mary and his parents laughed at something Phillip had said. John felt his muscles contract.

He forced himself to keep breathing and turned the page again. But the tremor in his hands had increased. He was unravelling at the seams once more.

"Why don't you sing for us, John?" Mary called as Katherine's piece drew to its conclusion with a complex flourish she mastered easily.

His fingers fell away from the music to his thigh and he felt an inner panic swamp him. He cursed violently in his head, using every swear word he knew. This was ridiculous. His rational thought knew that. But the problem was there was this other part of him that was irrational and tied up with the damned dream from his childhood. He'd always that thought once he'd known where his mother was, the dream would pass on and these feelings of weakness, inability and unworthiness with it. But no. Life was not to be as kind to him as that.

"Yes, John," Katherine stated, her fingers resting on his thigh.

He gritted his teeth and stood. "Forgive me. There are some papers I ought to review. Excuse me." His gaze reached to his parents and Mary. Then he glanced at Katherine and nodded, before looking at Phillip. "Phillip."

Phillip nodded back and John then left the room, escaping into privacy, where he could nurse his madness in secret.

Katherine felt bewildered as she watched John. He looked upset.

The more time she spent with John, it seemed she understood him less.

She wondered whether to go after him.

"I should be on my way," Phillip stated across the room.

Katherine turned an apologetic smile to him. He was standing, and Mary and John's parents had risen in response.

Katherine stood too.

"John is such a killjoy," Mary stated. "He will never sing, and his voice is the best of us all."

"Mary," John's mother admonished, pressing her fingers to her daughter's arm to silence her. There was something wrong. His mother knew it too.

Phillip came across to Katherine and took her hands, to say goodbye.

"I'll walk down with you," she whispered.

"I'm glad you came," she said, as they left the room.

"Thank John for inviting me."

She nodded. Then as they walked along the hall she asked, "Why does John dislike singing so much?"

Phillip's gaze fell to her as she looked up at him, though they did not stop walking. "It's not my place to say. Ask John."

"But you know?"

"Not really, I only know pieces of his past that would make it likely. I doubt Mary knows the history of it at all, she's so much younger than John."

There was a clue in his words, John's dislike must stem from his childhood.

She accompanied Phillip downstairs but said nothing else. Her mind focused on how to open a conversation with John.

~

John sat at his desk in his private sitting room, his elbows on the solid wood and his head in his hands as he fought the monster of emotion roaring in his head. It was an irrational fear but it was uncontrollable. His head was spinning in a dark pit of pain.

He was not a child anymore, and it shouldn't matter. But it did, *God* it did. The memories and the ensuing pain were unbearable. It was as though he was ten again, driving away with his grandfather in that damn coach and leaving his mother and all happiness behind, as though someone had ripped his innards out.

Pull yourself together. But he could not. The unfeeling ice cold wouldn't come.

Thinking of his grandfather and himself as a small boy, he

remembered craving some sign, some slight signal of connection or approval, and gaining none.

The image slipped to the horde of his younger brothers and sisters, with whom he could achieve no mental or emotional connection.

What of his child?

A bitter lancing pain pierced his chest and he sat back with a groan of despair.

Katherine stood at the door to the room. He'd thoughtlessly left it open. She was watching him, wide-eyed and hesitant.

It was dark, no candles burned. But silver moonlight seeped through the curtains, bleaching the room to white and black. Shadow and light. That was himself and Katherine. She was the light.

His lack of comment obviously gave her courage. She stepped into the room and walked towards him. "What is it, John? What's wrong?"

"Nothing." He would not humiliate himself by admitting to a pathetic childish weakness.

"It is not nothing now, any more than it was nothing last night when you woke."

His lips twisted in a distasteful expression, yet the knot of anxiety was already easing within him. He shrugged. "Nothing important then…"

"No?" Her eyes were dark in the lowlight.

God, I love this woman. The grace of her movements, the pitch of her voice and her understated beauty were all a balm to his battered, jaded soul.

She stopped before him and her hands clasped his face. She had such a soothing, gentle touch, and her hands were warm and took a hold of his senses. She leant and kissed him.

His eyelids fell. Her kiss was like a cold compress pressed on a graze. It healed his pain.

He took a breath and opened his eyes.

She *had* been angry earlier, he'd realised that over dinner when she had barely looked his way. She'd just concealed it, for whatever reason. But her anger was deserved.

His fingers gripped at her hips, and looking up, he met her gaze. "I am sorry about this morning."

"You are getting very good at saying sorry, John, but you cannot really be sorry if you repeat what you have already apologised for." She was right, of course, but there was no way he was prepared to discuss the turbulence currently inside him, not with her, not with anyone.

Her thumbs brushed across his cheekbones and his gaze fell to her stomach. He laid his cheek against where their child grew – another infant who would be hungry for love. Perhaps the child would never receive it from him.

Her fingers slid through John's hair and his breath fractured. He wished he could cry but, of course, such sentimentality had been physically beaten out of him a long time ago.

"John?"

He shook his head, he didn't want to speak. "Just love me, Katherine." His words were brisk and harsh.

Her fingers stroked through his hair as he kissed her stomach through the fabric of her gown and his hands slipped to her buttocks. He could smell her sex through the layers of cloth. She was aroused already. "Undo your dress," he whispered, looking up and meeting her gaze.

His hands had begun working up her skirt.

Between orders and assistance, he rapidly stripped her while he only removed his evening coat. At the last he removed her shoes and stockings as her feet rested on his thighs one by one and her hands gripped his shoulders.

He took pleasure in the relief of commands, seeking solace in the return of control and influence.

Once she was fully naked and vulnerable, he looked up and met her gaze again, smiling. One bare foot still rested on his thigh. His fingers ran upwards and over her knee, then they slipped under her thigh and ran along the inner surface. When he reached her juncture, his thumb pressed against her while his fingers entered and began teasing her senses.

Her grip tightened on his shoulders and her gaze held his. He somehow knew she understood. She knew he needed to play master. She was letting him, as she'd let him in the tower room, which meant she was mastering him, and not the other way about.

He didn't care.

His fingers worked with more determination, claiming all of her attention, and her eyes closed and then her head fell back and she was panting. He watched her, lost in her as she was lost in what he did.

When she came, he used his mouth and tasted her, and once he was satisfied, he stood and lifted her onto the desk, bid her undo his flap and took her like that – he dressed, she naked – driving into her as she sat on the unrelenting desk and clung to his neck.

Katherine knew he was escaping into her again. She relished him turning to her for comfort, even in this form. It was a pattern she had recognised now. She simply gave – *and received*. Oh yes, she received in equal measure to what she gave.

His hands braced her hips and the force of his thrusts had her spinning into ecstasy; she felt dizzy and disorientated.

Her fingers gripped his neck, lacing at his nape as the torrent of his emotion washed over her, and she bit her lip, holding back the cries of pleasure and sighs which ached to be free of her throat when her heart raced and her skin grew over-hot.

She opened her mouth, she couldn't resist any longer, and fractured cries left her throat. While he drove her senses mad, pleasure singing, humming coursed through every nerve.

There was aggressiveness to his claiming, anger and bitterness, as there had been in the tower room that second time. His was a violent, desperate love, but it was love. She really did not doubt it, not at all anymore. She had seen the image of herself through his eyes and she looked beautiful in those sketches of her naked. She did not believe she really looked like that but he thought she did.

She broke again and he fell with her, his muscle locking as his seed spilled into her.

He kissed her hair, her brow. She stroked his head and neck.

"John," she whispered. He didn't move but she heard his breath suddenly crack and her hand caressed his cheek only to feel the damp line of a tear.

Instantly he withdrew and turned away, securing his flap, and then his shirtsleeve swiped across his face.

When he turned back, there was no sign of emotion. He'd shut her out again and set up his ducal walls between his feelings and her.

She sensed he wished to let her in, but did not know how.

She felt as though the two of them were drifting alone on a desolate sea.

"Shall we go to bed now?"

She nodded and then found herself caught up in his arms, her clothing was left strewn about the sitting room for his servants, *their* servants, to find and pick up.

She felt treasured in his firm grip though, cradled.

Once he'd set her on the bed he undressed in silence, intermittently glancing at her as she moved beneath the covers. *He loves me*, she thought, watching him. *He does love me.* Alone in his rooms there was nothing wrong between them, everything felt right.

When he was naked, he picked up the lit candle which burned on the mantle and put it down beside the bed. Her eyes followed his movement, admiring every line of his anatomy.

He slid beneath the covers then reached for something on his side of the bed. The candle flickered as he turned back. "I thought we could look at this." It was his sketchbook. "I'll explain the pictures to you. Perhaps one day I'll take you there. But not about Europe though, Katherine, it holds too may ghosts for me."

She stared at him, wondering if it had been ghosts haunting him last night, and this evening. His grandfather had been a hurricane force in Ashford. She supposed growing up as his heir would have been difficult.

She moved closer to John, not asking any questions, but just letting him speak.

Chapter Fifteen

John jogged downstairs thinking of Katherine, whom he'd left in the care of her maid, dressing. She'd been smiling. She'd seemed happy.

They'd been married almost a week now and he'd not let her down in any way since the third day of their marriage. Things were settling into a normal way of life he'd never thought himself capable of.

In the day he went about his business, be it personal, parliamentary or state, and in the evening when he returned home Katherine was here.

He looked forward to the evenings, to her warm welcome, her bright voice, and her smile.

She was rubbing off on him too. He smiled more frequently and laughed in her company. He'd even found himself laughing in a conversation in White's yesterday. The twins, his Harding cousins from his father's family, who'd no previous acquaintance with Katherine, called her his current hobby because John spoke of things she'd said and done so much in male company. That pleased him. It was true. She was never far from his conscious thoughts and always in his subconscious.

After their first ill-fated attempt at socialising, John had prescribed a thorough dose of their own company until Katherine had had chance to settle into her new life.

In the evening he closeted her away while his parents and Mary went out.

He'd told her the stories of his sketchbooks and one evening he'd taken up pencil and paper and drawn her in several poses. But the honeymoon period had to end sometime. He couldn't keep hiding her away. He'd obligations to his title. Tonight was going to be the night they ventured out again.

He had an invitation to the influential Devonshire ball. At least it would be no shock to Katherine now.

She'd endured a week of acerbic observations, as the women of his society had called here to pry and prise information from her. They wanted to know her past. The question seemed to be on the lips of every man who sat in the House of Lords, as well as that of their wives and daughters, and beyond. He'd been asked countless times for her family name and urged to tell where he'd found her. He'd given no answers. He didn't intend to. Let them salivate over the mystery and never know.

John strolled into the breakfast room smiling, happy himself, but immediately he entered, Edward stood. John's smile fell. *God, what is it now?* His father's face was grim.

Edward picked up the folded paper and held it out. "John. You may want to read this in the library."

"What?"

"Come," Edward gripped John's arm and turned him about, handing him the paper. "Page four."

Frowning, John opened it and turned the pages as they walked across the hall.

"This paragraph," Edward stated, pointing to a published letter as they stepped into the library. Edward closed the door behind them as John read.

The letter was from an anonymous writer, denouncing the new Duchess of P as a commoner, a *natural* – which inferred illegiti-mate – dairymaid's daughter. The author claimed to know both

302

parties intimately and could attest to the truth of this statement.

John just stared at it. He knew the author. *Wareham. The bastard.*

The man had been silent as the grave since his disappearance, but now this. *Damn!* Why had he had to strike at Katherine?

John folded the paper again and looked at his father. There was nothing John could do. It was the truth.

"Your Grace," Finch knocked.

"Come!"

The door opened and Finch appeared bearing a letter. "The Devonshire's footman delivered this a moment ago, Your Grace."

"That was quick," Edward said dryly.

John took it and broke the seal. It was what Edward expected. "Katherine is uninvited yet I am still welcome. Devonshire is petitioning me to vote with him on a bill he's presenting in the House of Lords, so of course he does not wish to offend me, but asks that I understand the sensibilities of his wife."

"And so," Edward stated, "do you intend to give in, or do you intend to fight?"

But it was not about what he wanted. It was Katherine who would be hurt. "Is she strong enough?" Edward asked.

"I think so."

"Of course if you do not fight it, the longer-term hurt will be worse, there is the child too, John. You say Devonshire wants your vote, how badly?"

"There is considerable risk his bill will not pass, many are publicly against it. He's charming us all to get it through."

"If you took Katherine do you think he would turn you away?"

John held his father's gaze. It was too hard to know for certain, yet there was a possibility Devonshire may feel too uncomfortable if she were there in person. It was a risk, but if they won this first battle the new war to have her fully accepted might be half-won before it even really began. "Possibly not."

"Discuss it with her. She is the one who should decide. In the meantime I'll have your mother send word to your aunts. If the family arrive en masse it will be harder for the Devonshires to make a scene."

John nodded. *Hell.* Katherine would not welcome this. She did not need this pressure now, but the thought of Katherine not being accepted was untenable.

He thanked Edward and, still holding the paper, headed back upstairs.

She was in her dressing room, sitting before the mirror, while Esther pinned up her hair.

She looked a perfect picture as she turned and half of it tumbled back down onto one shoulder.

When he commissioned an artist to portray her, perhaps he'd have her painted like this, half his Duchess, half his wife.

He bid Esther leave and Katherine's blue eyes widened.

As soon as Esther had gone, Katherine stood and said, "What is it?"

He took her hand and led her into the sitting room, then bid her take a seat.

She did not. "Just tell me what is wrong," she pressed, as he opened the paper, and folded it back.

He gave it to her. "There."

She read the words he pointed out in silence, her colour blanching. He could have protected her from this but somehow he knew she wouldn't thank him for it.

When her eyes lifted back to him, he passed her the Duke of Devonshire's letter. She read that in silence, too, then she took a deep breath. "So," she stated, looking back up, "I am not going." She gave him the letter back. "Never mind, his wife is as a supercilious cow."

He laughed. He wanted to hug her. His father had asked if she was strong enough. Of course she was. Yet the members of the false and fickle society he belonged to had long memories when they wished. What Edward had said was true. If unchallenged, this behaviour could affect their unborn child and others Katherine conceived. It needed to be quashed now.

"I wish to take you anyway. If you'll brave it?"

"What if they won't let me in?"

He shrugged. "They may not. The only way we will know is if we try."

"And if they do not?" Now she showed her insecurity. He lifted his hands and she slipped into his arms.

"Then we'll both come home without making a fuss, but we will have made our point."

"This is important to you, isn't it?" The vibration of her voice seeped through his morning coat. Trust Katherine to think of him above herself.

He kissed her temple. "It is, yes. I have state duties to fulfil which will be hard to do if society rejects you, and it will affect our children too, Katherine. I want to fight. If Devonshire lets you in, it will set precedents for others." Of course, the same applied if Devonshire did not. "I want you accepted. Do you agree?"

She nodded against his chest as he stroked her hair. No matter her initial condemnation, he knew she was terrified.

~

Katherine held the firm muscle of John's arm through the fabric of his evening coat as they queued, awaiting an introduction to the Devonshires, gradually moving up the stairs.

"Set your smile and keep it." John's voice carried a little.

"That is easy for you," she whispered back. "Sadly not for me."

John's Uncle Richard and his Aunt Penny stood behind them, and beyond them were all John's influential aunts and uncles. The family was showing its solidarity.

Katherine felt guilty for marrying him; she did not even know if his family approved of the match. They surely could not.

The autumn night was chill and the fires in the huge hall in which the stairs were set had not chased the cold away. Katherine shivered. They climbed another two steps and John's fingers covered hers on his arm.

They moved another step. The door to the grand hall was only feet away. Her heart was pounding. She prayed she would not faint. Then they were there. The Duke looked his discontent, while the Duchess of Devonshire's cold accusing gaze passed to Katherine then lifted to John. Katherine felt John's Uncle Richard, the Duke of Arundel, step closer behind her.

"Devonshire," John stated to the Duke, who was the first in line. John held forth his hand.

The Duke hesitated.

Katherine gave a shallow curtsy regardless, still gripping John's arm.

The Duke looked at his wife, then back at John and then over Katherine's shoulder at John's Uncle and his other family beyond.

Her fate and that of their children hovered on the brink. In or out. Katherine could feel the moments ticking by, even though she could hear no clock.

The Duke glanced back at his wife and then once more at John. "Your Grace."

He accepted John's hand and Katherine felt relief crumble her determination like a wall falling. She clung to John.

John passed the Duke and bowed to the Duchess.

She visibly bristled while Devonshire clasped Katherine's hand for an instant and bowed over it.

Afterwards, Katherine bobbed the slightest curtsy at the Duchess, who did not respond, and then John swept Katherine away over the threshold and across the ballroom.

Her heart was pounding.

John smiled in a self-congratulating way.

His Uncle Richard caught them up and set a hand on John's shoulder, then whispered something into John's ear.

When they entered the ballroom, immediately whispers passed about the room in a wave, but no one turned their backs. Katherine understood, from what John had said earlier, that this was due to the Devonshires' assumed acceptance. If people cut her now it would insult their hosts too.

The first notes of a waltz reached above the gossip and John walked on towards the centre of the room, claiming the ground they'd won.

She'd never danced with him.

Her heart was still racing and she felt a little lightheaded and faint as he made the frame of the dance and his expression was set as she faced him. It gave her no comfort at all. She felt isolated by it. He was in his ducal persona once more, shutting out the opinions of the room. Only it also meant he was shutting out her and she'd grown unused to it. Over the past week he'd been himself at home, not the duke. He'd told her story after story of his adventures abroad. He'd been considerate and attentive, even amidst his family. He'd been open, never blank and cold. She'd convinced herself he'd changed.

He had not changed.

As they began to move, she watched his face. Was who he was with her an act – if outside the house he was still like this? Which was his façade? Which the lie? But of course this was the lie; this hard shell he set about him.

His hand at her back and hers on his shoulder, he held her gently, but formally, as her gaze turned to their audience, the people standing at the edge of the room, darting from one group of people who were staring, to another.

"Ignore them," John commanded.

Her heart raced. "I am not like you, I cannot," she answered, meeting his diamond-hard gaze.

Despite her discomfort, his appearance affected her. She loved this man, with his chiselled features, his pale all-absorbing eyes, and her fingers itched to run through his jet-black hair. She wished they were at home in bed.

A smile hovered at the corner of his lips suddenly, but he didn't let it take.

Was it just for show or was it real?

"Letting people think they affect you only encourages their vindictiveness, Katherine. They are like vultures pecking at a corpse if you show weakness." It was for show, then.

"I don't understand this world."

"Who does? Not I, nor them. The biggest mockery of it is that behind closed doors many of them behave without restraint. The Oxfords, the Devonshires, Melbourne, they all have illegitimacy in their lines. It's an open secret everyone ignores. And two generations ago, the Devonshires' great-grandmother travelled with what they deemed '*The mist*', a profligate pack of children, the family's by-blows, delivered of their servants and paramours. Yet *they* hold up their heads and condemn you, the two-faced—"

"John," she whispered, pleading his silence.

"I'm sure the moral of the story is clear. It has something to do with planks and specks," John finished, turning her past a group of whispering matrons with a flourish, his cold gaze casting condemnation.

"You scare me, like this."

His gaze came back to hers. "I am trying to scare *them*."

"Well I wish you would not. I wish you would simply be yourself." Why must he be such a paradox?

His gaze narrowed. "As I said, Katherine, let them know you're vulnerable and they'll be picking over your bones in seconds."

"So, what does that matter? You said you do not care for their good opinion."

"I do not care for it but there are occasions on which I need it. But what I care for least is for them to know me at all. So no, I will not be *myself*, as you put it. Let them think what they like but they'll not challenge me nor denounce you because I will not give them ground." The muscle in his shoulder and his hand tensed more as he spoke and he spun her more aggressively into the next turn.

"Are we arguing, John? I feel as though I am dancing on a battleground, with hostilities from all sides."

The tension ebbed from him instantly. "You know how to play me, don't you. Perhaps it's you I should fear. Very well, if you do not wish me glaring at them, we will have to take another tack and make friends."

He performed one last spin as the music drew to a close, then it abruptly ended and gripping her fingers, he set them on his arm before leading her to a group standing at the edge of the floor.

She faced another facet of John then. He moved about the room charming and ingratiating his way into conversations and constantly passing them to her, insisting she be included. It was cleverly done. He was a formidable force.

What is your opinion on this, Katherine? Have you heard of…? Did you see…? Would you…? He refused to let anyone ignore her.

It was what he'd done at her sister's come-out too, only then she hadn't realised the ruthlessness of his behaviour.

She never wished to be on the wrong side of John.

His family clearly recognised his ability too, for none of them attempted to come to his aid, though she saw them occasionally looking John's way.

They must all be confident in John's ability to manipulate, persuade and disarm people.

After an hour of this artistic assault, John led her back to the family group.

They had occupied one corner of the room as though they had put tents against the wall of a castle. All his aunts and uncles and cousins were gathered there.

Depositing Katherine into the care of his aunt Jane, John whispered, "I have had my fill for now. We will start again after supper. Do you wish for a glass of punch?"

She nodded and then John disappeared with his Uncle Robert.

His family just seemed to ignore his cold moods.

"How are you bearing up, Katherine?" his aunt questioned.

"Well enough, considering I'm in the hands of a demon. How does he do it? He controls people on a whim."

His aunt laughed, "I believe he's learned that skill from the cradle, but I've only known John since he was about fourteen. He had a serious side even then, though, at times."

"He can sulk like the Devil," Katherine stated, smiling at his aunt.

"Yes, well, his black looks are a bit of an art. Still, he is equally charming, and let us not forget powerful and wealthy, so who cares?"

Katherine laughed. She could hear the affection in his aunt's voice, it was not condemnation.

She said more seriously then, "He can be domineering, I know, dear, but *you* have mellowed him a little, Katherine. He is much less affected with you and he seems easier in himself. Robert says people have commented on the change in him in White's. I know it is early days but we all have great hopes for you both."

Great hopes.

Jane touched Katherine's arm. "I know this is all new to you, but you will grow accustomed to John's life and his ways, I dare say. Things will settle. John is John, no matter his mood, underneath he has a heart of gold."

"I know," Katherine whispered, "I just wish he was not so cold in public."

"Defence," Jane answered. "I have done it. It is easier to pretend you do not care for anything or anyone. When you have high standing, there are people who wish to cut you down. He is very conscious of his responsibility. He wishes to prove himself capable and if he shows any weakness he thinks he will not."

Katherine met his aunt's extraordinary emerald gaze.

"Give him time to adjust – give yourself time," Jane concluded as John and his uncle returned. Then she briskly changed the conversation. "My friend, Violet, is holding a charity event tomorrow. She's raising funds for an orphanage in White Chapel. Would you like to come, Katherine?"

Katherine accepted a glass from John. He met her gaze, answering her question before she asked it, "You need not ask me, Katherine. You may do as you will."

Stupidly, even his lack of interest hurt. He had never once asked what she had done in the day, or shared what he had done, for the past week the nights had been theirs, but the days... Well in the days, she understood now, he was the Duke of Pembroke and he wished her to be his duchess. Oh she couldn't bear it if the evenings became the same, if all she'd have of John Harding was a single hour or so when they went to bed.

The shallow foundations of her marriage rocked.

A horrible thought sprung into her head. What if all that pinned them together was their physical bond? What if his love was still only based on sex? After all, if he did not care what she did in the day, did he care for her at all really?

Her hand trembled as she sipped her drink.

He'd given her the impression he'd let her into his life. He had not. He was still holding back. He'd only put her into a niche in it. She had her corner of it. Or perhaps, her shelf. He would put her upon it in the morning and take her down at night.

He must sense her discomfort; he was watching her while continuing a conversation with his aunt and uncle. Proof, if she needed it, of how easily he could manage duplicity.

The notes of a second waltz caught on the air.

"Shall we?" John said, holding out his hand.

She accepted and asked, as soon as they moved into the open space where people danced, "How do you spend your days, John?"

His inexpressive face said nothing, but his eyes told her he thought the question absurd.

Still, he answered as they began dancing. "On business, planning and reviewing with Harvey, or in the Houses of Parliament, or visiting my club to discuss parliamentary affairs with my peers." His voice belittled her interest.

His father spent most days at home, but of course he did not

311

have a seat in the House of Lords, and yet John's uncles did, and even they occasionally called with their wives in the afternoons.

"Does your business take *all* day?"

"Where is this leading, Katherine?" He spun her.

"What did you discuss today?"

His eyebrows lifted slightly. "Who sent that letter to the press, if you must know, and how to respond."

"How will you respond?" She only wanted to know because she wished to know how much he'd tell her.

"I'm sure you do not really wish to know."

She had struck the boundary already then. He was definitely drawing lines. She was not even his duchess really. She was just the mistress he'd married.

"Clearly not." She responded in a cold voice. He did not bite and answer, instead the conversation sank into silence.

~

During supper, and after it, John continued his assault, guiding Katherine to participate in conversations, ensuring she was not excluded.

She acted the model wife, smiling and nodding, and talking when he gave her an opening. Yet, despite his success, John felt as though he was failing. She was bitterly angry with him, he knew it, and yet she hid it perfectly. She had learned how to set a smile tonight and hide her emotion, and now he wished she could not. Her fingers held his arm, but it was a forced touch. She was not seeking his support and there was no caress in her touch.

He felt her coldness keenly and when others began asking her to dance again, he watched her while he continued talking.

She looked into the men's eyes, attentive and smiling and jovial, yet he knew beneath it there was a brittle disgust of these people, *and him*. He was forcing her to emulate what she hated, making her more like him, when he didn't even like himself.

312

This is what he had wanted of her earlier, but now it grated on him. *More fool you, John Harding.* It was stupidity to bemoan it. He could hardly now tell her not to do it. He would only highlight the fact that *he* would not cease doing it, and that was the reason she was angry with him.

Yet her honesty and openness were the things which had captured his heart.

Which was it to be, which was best, to hide one's emotions and be accepted and respected by these people, or just to be oneself and tell them all to go to hell?

That was what he would prefer for her.

But for him?

He could not walk away from this life, could he? He had a duty to fulfil.

"You cannot show weakness. You must be strong, Sayle, else people will make a mockery of you. They'll walk all over you, boy, if you do not show them who is master." God, he had heard that and similar words of dire warning from his grandfather so many times.

It irritated him still further that the men dancing with Katherine were all rakes, because anyone wholly respectable was reserving judgement in the current circumstances. Any other time he'd turn them away, but tonight she needed all the support she could get. Yet he knew these men thought her good game. The history of her birth had only piqued their interest further and they'd all willingly cuckold him, just to knock him down a peg or two. His grandfather was right in that.

To drown out his irritation and condemnation, he began plotting again. He would have his mother and his aunts take Katherine calling.

Let her assault the matrons of society in their homes.

In the carriage on the way home, he and Katherine were silent, while Mary, who didn't know about Wareham's letter, excitedly reviewed the night.

He supposed it was a blessing no one had excluded Mary too.

She could have been caught up in it. Thank heavens she was not.

His thoughts drifted to Wareham. The man was out there in the dark streets, somewhere. John had agreed with Harvey that they would hire three dozen more men to find him. John wanted the man off his mind.

His eyes turned to Katherine. Her lips were pursed and her chin up.

Bloody hell! He knew the storm would break when they got home. Would they ever achieve an evening in society without her finding fault with him?

John climbed out of the carriage first when they arrived, and handed his mother and Mary down, then Katherine.

He kept hold of her hand and led her to the door as his father followed.

Inside, he took his leave of the others and then walked Katherine on to their rooms in ominous silence. When he shut the door and the world out, he turned to face her. "Now, pray tell me what is it you are riled over exactly?"

She did not speak as his fingers worked loose the knot of his cravat. John turned to a decanter. Once his cravat was loose, he tossed it over the back of a chair, then poured himself a port. He took a sip, then put it back down and took off his evening coat, which he threw over the chair, too.

Sipping from the glass again, he undid his waistcoat and left it hanging open. She was still silent. He turned and faced her, intensely annoyed. But casting her a dismissive look, rather than shout, he moved to occupy an armchair before the hearth.

She was watching him. She was supposed to be his solace, his supporter. He was not supposed to receive condemnation from her, not in his own home.

He leant back in the seat and raised one ankle to the other knee. Then, regarding her sternly, he lifted one eyebrow, another affectation he had picked up from his grandsire. "If you have something to say, Katherine…?"

She walked past him and took the chair opposite, staring at the fire now, not him. "Spit it out then. Have a go at me, girl. You're obviously dying to."

She shook her head at him in answer, got back up and walked away.

Bugger. She probably thought he'd follow. He did not. He was in no mood to play bloody lapdog. He did not even look as he heard the door to the bedchamber open. She'd be fleeing to her rooms.

Katherine considered retiring to her own rooms, but she did not. It would be cowardice to do so. Instead she undressed quietly, and not even wishing to leave for a moment in case he came in and locked her out, she borrowed one of his shirts to wear as a nightgown.

John didn't come in. She did not go back to him either. There was no point in talking to him. Dressed in ducal armour, he was in no mood to listen.

His diamond-hard stare had threatened retribution and she'd no patience for him when he was like that. It was wiser to withdraw.

Eventually she fell asleep.

When she woke, John was in bed beside her, and he was breathing heavily, dreaming.

She listened for a moment, hearing his breath fracture on a sudden gasp, and then he was awake, sitting up and turning to sit at the edge of the bed, panting, before sucking in air and then letting go a single long breath. She touched his back. It was damp with sweat.

He pulled away. It was probably deserved after she had cut him earlier.

"John?"

He leant forward and rested his head in his hands, obviously battling the images of his nightmare, while rain rapped on the windowpanes in a low rhythm.

After a moment, he stood, and then moved across the dark

room.

"Where are you going?" she whispered.

"Downstairs," he growled as she watched him pick up his dressing gown, only a shadow in the darkness.

She slid off the bed in pursuit, and reached him before he got to the door, hugging him, wrapping her arms about his midriff and pressing her cheek against his back.

He stilled for a moment but then his hands pulled hers loose. "Leave me alone, Katherine."

The words were harsh but his tone was wounded.

"John, what is it? Tell me?"

He sighed, but didn't answer as he slipped his dressing gown on.

She moved and barred his exit.

"Katherine."

"No, I'm not letting you go until you tell me about your dream."

"I'm sure, you don't care." He moved to pass her.

She blocked his path again.

"Katherine, just get out of the way..." There was vulnerability in his voice, it was unusual for John. He was still discomposed, and he was running because he did not want her to know it disturbed him.

She hated being shut out.

It was too dark for her to see his face clearly but her fingers lifted anyway and found his cheek. "Don't go downstairs. Come back to bed."

"So you can scold! I presume you're still waiting to ring your peel, although for the life of me I cannot see what I did to deserve your ire. I spent the night defending you."

He *was* hurt then, and that was why he'd retreated behind his cold, cutting façade earlier.

Her suspicions grew as her fingers fell from his face, sliding the length of his arm to capture his hand and tug him towards the bed.

"Come on, John, come back to bed." She moved, trying to pull him with her, but her arm and his just stretched wider. He didn't

316

budge, just sighed.

She tugged him more gently.

He moved.

She climbed on to the huge bed, kneeling and looking up at him as she still held his fingers and his attention.

The mattress sunk as he sat and then he rested back against the headboard, leaving his fingers resting in hers.

"Was it the same dream?" Her question was cautious. She was still unsure of her ground with John. He could just as easily get up and walk out instead of answer.

His fingers let hers go, but they lifted to her cheek and then they were in her hair, pulling her forwards.

He kissed her. It wasn't lustful. It was as though he was clinging to her and anchoring himself. When the kiss broke, he held her tightly. "I hate arguing with you, Katherine. Must we keep doing it? You are the one person I truly trust. I feel as though I have no foundation when you are angry with me."

"Then if you trust me, tell me what your dream was about."

She felt him shake his head.

Her fingers pushing against his pectoral muscle, she broke the embrace, looking at his dark silhouette.

A gust of wind threw rain at the windowpanes.

"You can trust me."

"I know that." She heard a catch of emotion in his voice.

"This is me, John."

"I am not afraid." The response was a deep rumble, and the words seemed an answer to himself.

Her brow furrowed. "John, just tell me. If you do, it may even go away. I am presuming it is the same dream. How long have you had it for?"

Sighing, he looked up at the canopy of the bed. "Years, sometimes it goes away for months, and at other times it haunts me every night."

Her fingers dropped to lie at his stomach, resting on his silk dressing-gown. "What is it about?"

He sighed again and one knee rose.

She watched him, her bottom pressing down on her heels as she knelt, while his arm rested on his bent knee. He was silent.

She said nothing, somehow knowing he was gathering courage, and drawing on the anonymity of the darkness.

"I am a child, about ten years old. My mother has recently married Edward. They'd fetched me from Eton in the middle of the night. We'd fled halfway across the country to escape my grandfather. I do not remember seeing my mother before then. I'd lived with them for two weeks. It felt like a dream. I, like any other child. Like any other family. I'd begun believing it was real. Then one morning my grandfather appeared, angry as hell and spitting fire – if a man can achieve that when he has the presence of stone. I had not escaped him. He took me away, and they let me go. In the dream, I'm that boy who looks from my grandfather's carriage, watching my mother run after it and cry out…"

His breathing was ragged when he finished the story, fighting emotion he sought to hide.

She didn't know what to say.

"It is ridiculous, isn't it? I know. A grown man with the fears of a child. But it never goes away, and when I wake up I feel like I did then all over again, lost, alone and unloved."

"You were not unloved, they love you. All your family are fond of you, look how they rallied about you tonight."

"I know that," he whispered, his voice bitter, "in my head. But in my soul… No. My soul remembers all those empty years when my aunts and uncles tried to fill the gap my mother had left, and failed. She left a hole in me, and it remembers the old man's coldness and nothing else. If you knew the things I did to please him, to make him like me, even if he would not love me. I was a pathetic child. And then he sent me away to sing in the chapel at Eton, out of sight and out of mind, to toughen up, truly alone."

His fingers were shaking as they dropped to grip hers.

"I know where she was now." His words fell into the darkness between them as the rain hammered against the windowpanes. "He'd taken me from her, after my father died. Disowned her and left her to starve. He told me, like everyone else, she was dead. She prostituted herself to survive. My grandfather was a heartless bastard. And do you know what makes it worse? He made me the same as him. I don't want to be, but I am. I cannot be myself. You told me I was spoilt. I was not spoilt, I was beaten until I bent to his will, and now I don't know how to straighten up again."

Katherine hugged him and kissed his cheek. "That's not true, John. You're not like him, not with me."

The weight of his palms rested on her hair and her back as, outside, the wind cast the rain at the windows, whistling through the cracks in the frames.

"The dream has changed," he whispered to her hair. "Before we wed, the woman chasing the carriage became you, and now a child is there, our child. What if I cannot love the child, Katherine? What if I cause my son or daughter the pain he caused me? When my mother married Edward, I was glad to have a father, I looked up to him and loved him, and Mary, she was a novelty, as was Robbie, but by the time the others came, I was already disengaged. I look at them now, my brothers and sisters, and there is no feeling. What if I feel nothing for my own child?"

She pulled away, her fingers framing his face in the darkness. "You said yourself Mary and Robbie were new to you. You haven't connected with the others because by then you were not at home. Your own children will be new to you, and you will not be away from them, you will bring them up, share their lives. So you will not feel distant because you will not be distant."

His hands gripped hers and squeezed her fingers.

She realised then he had not only been closing himself off from her at times, he'd closed himself off from their child too.

"John, I believe you love me. You will love our child."

A breath sucked into his lungs as his fingertips tentatively

319

touched her stomach.

She moved and straddled him as his knee slid down to allow it, and her fingers framed his face, giving him the anchor she knew he needed as she kissed him.

His fingers slid up her thighs underneath the shirt she wore, reaching to cup her buttocks as he broke the kiss. "You are wearing one of my shirts."

"I did not wish to leave this room in case you thought I would not sleep here and locked the door."

He laughed. "I would not lock you out."

"You shut me out at the ball, John."

"And that is why you were angry…" She felt his muscle tighten again. "I wasn't shutting you out. I was shutting *them* out…"

Another gust of wind thrust the rain against the window.

"And holding me at a distance too. I wish to be your friend and your helpmate as much as your wife, John—"

"I've told you more than I've told anyone. I told you about Egypt, about Elizabeth and now my grandfather. Believe me, I never thought I'd tell anyone what I've just spoken to you."

"I know. But still you only tell me and show me what you wish, John. I realise now you weren't shutting me out, but yourself in. You let me see what little you choose, as though I am placed in some compartment of your life until you deem to visit it. I feel as though half the time I am standing at a window looking in at you."

She took a breath. She had to tell him how she felt. "You will not speak of your business with me, as though it would be beyond me. Thrice you've told me I would not want to know. I have asked; does that not tell you I do? You avoid me in the day, because God forbid anyone may think you put me first. Or do you do it because you do not like my company unless we are in bed? In the evening, on the two occasions you've taken me out, you set such an expression on your face that people wonder why you married me. They certainly do not think you happy, nor in love. Which, considering my birth, leaves only indecent possibilities." And of course there was still the yellowed, fading bruise on his cheek to add weight to that view.

She stopped, but only to draw another breath. "I was propositioned thrice tonight, by men who think you too cold to warm my bed…"

His fingers clawed on her back.

She sat back, freeing herself from his hold.

"That part of you *is* like your grandfather. It is as though you wear a ducal shroud. I want you to share everything with me and let others see beneath your mask. I want them to know you love me and that you are caring and kind. You must show yourself, if you do not want to be like him."

He sucked in a deep breath.

She knew he was angry again. She could feel his irritation.

Pushing her aside, he then climbed from the bed, and, without a word, walked out of the room.

She did not call him back, or try to prevent him from going. He needed to hear what she'd said. He had just told her he suffered with nightmares because he could not be who he wished to be. He had demons to deal with that were far greater than her.

But she was right and he knew it.

She heard him stop within his sitting room and then turn back.

"There is a new rule in this marriage, Katherine," he said from the door. "You are not to dance with anyone without my permission, understood."

She didn't answer and he didn't wait for her to. It was a ducal command.

He slammed the door.

Her hand covered her stomach. He could love the child, she knew he could, but only if he allowed it, and he had a stubborn vein of iron running through his soul.

She prayed he would allow it. He'd married her. She had to believe that given time he would make the right choice again.

~

When Katherine woke, for the first time in days she lay in an empty bed.

She missed him. She had become used to him silently setting the chamber pot next to her and then bidding the maid enter.

A second knock struck the door.

Katherine called the maid in, sitting up.

The bed felt strange empty, there was only the indent of his head in the pillow to say he'd been there.

The maid set down the tray she carried and turned to leave.

"His Grace?" Katherine asked tentatively.

"Is out riding, Your Grace. The Duke left an hour ago."

As luncheon loomed he'd still not returned, and Katherine fretted. Yet neither his mother nor Mary seemed to think it odd.

When his Aunt Jane arrived to accompany them to her friend's fundraising luncheon, Katherine was in turmoil, terrified she had pushed him too far, but she hoped the social event would distract her.

It did.

After luncheon they were shown about the orphanage, to view the children at their desks, working on slates. They were well fed, clothed and cared for, but they lacked a mother's love. Something she and John both knew could affect a young, helpless soul.

In a room full of children at their lessons, Katherine stopped to sit with a girl. John's aunt and mother kept going, following the group, as Katherine lingered, listening and learning about the children's days.

When they came back for her later, Katherine knew she was in love with all of the children here, and the charity which kept them. She had found the thing to fill the void in her marriage. But just handing over sums of money would not suffice for her. She would come here and help during the day, when John shut her out. She would have love and a place here, to avoid the sense of loneliness.

When the other ladies bid each other farewell, returning to their carriages, Katherine turned to Jane and Ellen. "Would you mind if I stay a little longer? I wish to speak with the matron about helping more significantly. I don't wish to delay you."

Looking at her in earnest, Ellen hesitated. "I'm not sure, Katherine. I don't like leaving you. Why not come back tomorrow? I can come with you then."

"We are committed tomorrow; we are to go to the Duchess of Arundel's. I can stay alone. You may send the carriage back, or I can hire a hackney. One of the grooms can wait with me."

Ellen smiled, "Who is teaching who how to go on, Katherine?"

"You are teaching me, and I am very grateful. But I can manage to hire a carriage and get home without support."

John's aunt Jane smiled too.

Gripping Katherine's forearm, Ellen smiled more broadly. John had inherited his blue eyes from her, but hers were never cold. "You do please me, Katherine. I know John can be a trial, but you are very good for him."

Katherine smiled too, but felt tears in her eyes. "I wish him to be happy."

Ellen's smile fell and her fingers tightened on Katherine's forearm. "He is stubborn. I just hope he can make you happy too."

Oh dear, his parents knew how things stood.

Blushing, Katherine saw the torment John was in was not his mother's fault. It was his grandfather's. Ellen loved him. Yet Katherine also knew the only person who could reach him now was her.

Once the others had gone, sitting in a small office, Katherine discussed the things she could do to help, agreeing to read and play with the children, teach them their letters, and perhaps invigorate their everyday lives with the occasional trip to a park or museum to help them flourish.

She spent a good hour with the matron. It was nearly four when she finally stepped out onto the pavement with John's groom.

Two children barrelled around the corner and collided with her.

She caught the arm of the younger boy. "Stop. What's this?" She saw fear in his eyes as he looked up.

"Miss, let me go, I gotta get 'elp for me Ma. She's 'avin' a baby, an' it ain't goin' right, Miss. She said come an' beg 'ere f'r the midwife. She needs 'elp, Miss."

There was no time for thought. Katherine, thrust her reticule at the groom, ordering him to go immediately with the eldest boy and get a doctor. The youngest she bid to hurry into the orphanage to find the matron, certain the staff would help until the doctor came. Katherine could find a carriage by herself. She was hardly a cosseted female, and Finch would settle the amount when she reached home.

Having watched the groom hurry off around the corner, Katherine turned around, only to find herself looking up into a familiar face. "Mr Wareham?"

He lifted his hat and bowed slightly. "Miss Spencer, what a fortuitous surprise. What brings you to town?"

Swallowing back shock, Katherine nodded and did not correct his use of her maiden name; he obviously had not heard about her marriage. She did not wish to upset him by telling him she was now John's wife. "I am visiting my brother. I was just looking for a hackney."

"Well it's very remiss of him to leave you unescorted. Town is not Ashford, nor Maidstone, Miss Spencer. Allow me." He lifted his arm.

Katherine looked at it uncertainly. She did not really know Mr Wareham beyond a very slight acquaintance, and yet he was a gentleman who'd been in the employ of the old Duke for years. Surely she could trust him. "Thank you."

She laid her fingers on his arm.

He started walking. "If I recall, you promised to join me for tea that day in Maidstone…"

A vacant hackney passed them at a brisk trot. Mr Wareham

made no attempt to hail it. But his head was turned towards her.

"Where is your brother's office?"

She told him, watching another hackney pass.

Her heart began beating harder, but it was silly fretting, there was nothing odd in his behaviour. It was just because she knew John had treated him badly and she felt guilty, though it was not her fault.

"You know, there is something I've long wanted chance to discuss with you, Miss Spencer. Now would be a good time for that cup of tea, and then I could explain. I will accompany you home afterwards."

"I need to be home by five…" When she met his gaze she realised his eyes were very similar to John's. It would do no harm, she supposed. Perhaps she could help Mr Wareham understand John's dismissal wasn't personal, just John dealing with his grandfather's ghost. "…But I shall have enough time."

He led her along several streets, turning and turning again until she was thoroughly lost and had no clue which direction the orphanage or home were. He spoke about Ashford society as they walked and then his move to the city. Apparently he had a mother here.

His arm dropped from under her hand when they reached a tea shop, and then his fingers gripped her elbow.

A few other people were seated at tables.

Seating her first, he called for tea before sitting opposite and regarding her through narrowed eyes.

The delicate scent of tea hovered in the air.

"I knew your mother, Katherine," he stated as his pale-blue gaze held hers. Katherine only just stopped her mouth from falling open, but her heart thumped.

The tea was set down before them.

He filled his cup and then lifted the lid of the teapot. It dropped back down with the sharp sound of porcelain striking porcelain. Then he poured hers. She added milk and sugar, not knowing what to say. He watched her but said nothing. The hard look in his eyes reminded her of John again.

She sipped her tea. As soon as she had drunk it, she would go. She took another sip while Mr Wareham stayed silent.

The buzz of conversation rose in the room, becoming almost deafening.

"I know…" Mr Wareham began, but she couldn't hear properly and leant forwards to listen. "…This will be a shock to you, Katherine, but I wish to tell you that I am your father…"

Katherine stared and the room shifted on its axis, then swayed like water.

She had never known who'd sired her. Now this man… He'd lived within a mile of her. She had passed him numerous times in the street and he'd never said a word. Until that day in Maidstone…

She couldn't speak. Inside her, there was a gaping hole where there ought to be joy.

He drank his tea as though he'd just said that it looked as though it might rain and nothing more.

His hard eyes, too like John's, were watching her.

She sipped her tea, but her arm and the cup felt heavy.

She took another sip before putting it down, wishing to simply leave. She desperately longed for John. But how could she leave hurriedly now, when Mr Wareham had just made such a declaration? She could hardly just say thank you and goodbye.

So what do I say? The question spun about in her mind and seemed to get lost.

She took another sip of tea.

Mr Wareham watched her, apparently awaiting her response.

She did not have one and the room was shifting again and swaying a little.

Her eyes turned to the broad bay window of the shop and the street outside. She did not feel well. She needed John.

A chair scraped and she turned to see Mr Wareham rising, though he was blurred.

He caught her arm and helped her rise.

She was dizzy, weak and confused. She opened her mouth to speak but found no words as he whispered reassurance in her ear and his voice echoed in her head. Then she was being steered from the tea shop and they were out on the street.

She couldn't make her mouth move to say she wished to go home. Her lips were numb and her feet heavy, but she felt pain from his grip on her arm, and fear. This was not right. *John!* The cry rang in her head but it would not come from her lips.

Mr Wareham stopped by a door only a short distance from the shop they had left, and then he withdrew a key from his pocket. She collapsed the moment the door opened, falling onto wooden boards. Then she felt him lift her. Her limbs were heavy and numb. She could no longer see him, her vision was entirely black, yet she could feel herself being carried upstairs. He must have put some drug into her tea.

~

When John returned it was six o'clock. He knew he'd left it far too long, he ought to have come back for luncheon to dine on his humble pie but it was not a meal he relished.

He'd ridden off his demons in Green Park, early, racing across the lawns in dawn's light, fleeing his feelings, just as he'd done in Egypt.

After a good hard ride he'd burned out his ire and started to think, rehearing everything Katherine had said, and listening.

It didn't take much thought to know she was right. But letting people see who he really was, was something he did not care to do. So instead of going home and apologising, he'd ridden on to Harvey's offices.

Harvey was certain Wareham was in London again, and probably using a false name, which meant they'd only trace him by sight.

John had drawn a sketch and copied it over and over for each group of men who were searching.

In the afternoon John had joined one of the search parties, knocking on doors and asking at inns. But as the sunset had painted the sky a bright pink, he'd realised it was beyond time to go home. He couldn't delay his apology any longer. It had to be made. He'd do anything to avoid losing Katherine. Even make himself vulnerable before society, though he wasn't sure he was capable of it.

But if she needed him to change to be happy, he'd try. She was the only part of his life he was sure about. The only part he wouldn't let change.

John climbed the steps to the front door, which Finch held open, then passed off his gloves, hat and riding whip, leaving his grooms to lead his stallion away.

"John." Mary was passing through the hall. "Have you been out all day?"

He smiled. He supposed he was in trouble with all the women of the house. They'd sympathise with Katherine. No doubt his mother would have a few choice words to add to Katherine's.

"I was busy," he answered, about to ask where Katherine was. But before he could, a clatter of horses' iron-clad hooves and voices came from behind him through the closing door. Turning, he saw Harvey on the steps as Finch reopened the door. Behind Harvey, four men sat on horseback, and John's groom was still hovering with his own mount, as though someone had bid him wait.

John's eyebrows lifted, "What is it?"

"We have him," Harvey stated, suddenly grinning broadly, and lifting the papers he carried.

John's jaw set with the anticipation of revenge, and looking at Mary, he said, "Go and fetch Papa. Have him come down, and tell him to hurry."

Clearly absorbing the urgency, she nodded, caught up her skirt and hurried off.

Turning back to Harvey, John asked, "How? Where?"

"The clue has come from his past, Your Grace, I…" Harvey stopped suddenly and looked at Finch. "We should speak in private."

John nodded, turning towards the library, blood pumping in his veins for haste, as a footman rushed ahead to open the door.

Once they were within, the door shut, and John said, "Well?" in a deep hard tone. He was seething with hatred.

"We traced his mother. She is here in London. One of the men visited her. Wareham has been calling there. She didn't know he'd been dismissed. Nor that he was stealing from Your Grace or the previous Duke. When she was told, she broke down. The former Duke is Wareham's father. Mr Wareham was born before the Duke's marriage."

John's gaze fixed on Harvey, *Good God!* The old man was a fraud too. If Wareham had been born in wedlock he would have been heir. "My grandfather supported this woman?"

"Yes. And funded Wareham's education, then employed him. Yet it cannot have been enough recompense. We've found a landlord who rented a room to a man looking like Wareham a few days ago. He recognised the image Your Grace drew. We are on our way there. I thought Your Grace would wish to come."

"Yes," John's pulse raced.

A knock struck the door.

"Come," John called.

"John?" It was Edward.

"Harvey has found Wareham. Apparently he is Grandfather's bastard. Do you wish to come?"

Edward's eyes widened as his right hand curled into a fist. "Of course. Let me change." Edward turned to leave just as Finch knocked on the open door, the two nearly colliding.

"A young lad delivered this a moment ago, Your Grace." Finch held out a folded piece of paper. John's gaze dropped to it. "The child was told to bring it to the front door. He said only the Duke of Pembroke was to read it."

"Is he waiting on an answer?" Walking forward, John knew it was from Wareham.

He took the note, as Finch replied, "No, Your Grace, the child ran off."

John felt a sword slip into his stomach as he unfolded the paper.

I have your wife.

The air left John's lungs.

"John?"

John heard Edward, but he couldn't respond. His body was paralysed.

Katherine?

"John?"

His father was at John's side and John thrust the note at him and looked up, forcing the words from his throat. "Is Katherine not at home?"

"No, she—"

"We have to go," John looked at Harvey as Edward looked down at the note and paled. "Give Lord Edward the address. He can follow."

~

The mattress Katherine lay on was solid and uncomfortable, filled with straw.

Her eyes opened.

The bed was iron-framed and stood in the corner of a small room. It smelt foul, damp and mouldy.

A single square window in the opposite wall showed her it was dark outside. She'd no sense of time. How long had she been here? It could be days. She remembered the tea shop and leaving there... Panic tumbled through her. It rolled in her stomach and whipped at her nerves, stealing her breath away.

Pain burned her wrists and ankles as she tried to move. She was bound and the rope cut into her skin.

She tried to swallow but there was a cloth in her mouth. The gag hurt her throat.

John!

Tears trickled from her eyes. She felt so sick.

Footfalls crossed the room and then a chair scraped. She tried to turn but it was too difficult.

I am going to die. No one knew where she was. No one knew she'd left with Mr Wareham.

"You are awake, then."

She twisted her head to see him.

He sat in a chair a little behind her and leant forwards. His eyes were so like John's. His fingers brushed her cheek then pulled away.

She did not understand.

"You failed to mention when we met, Katherine, what I knew…"

What?

"You married that arrogant boy didn't you?"

John? This was because of John?

Mr Wareham stood then. He towered over her.

Fear lanced her body, like a sword splitting her in half, and again she tried to swallow to ease her dry throat but the foul-tasting cloth only made her gag.

He turned, then walked away, crossing the room to a table.

Terror prickled her skin, lifting goose bumps across her arms.

He turned back and in his hand was a short knife.

Katherine tried to speak, forgetting the gag. Nothing but a muffled, urgent sound escaped. He showed no sign he even heard it as he walked towards her, holding out the knife.

Her heartbeat pounded in her ears.

"It is not your fault, I know, Katherine. But he has taken things from me and so I should take things from him…"

Her stomach clenched and she retched against the gag. *John!* He didn't even know where she was.

331

Mr Wareham sat on the bed beside her stomach and she thought of the child. Her child. John's child. She was suddenly terrified Mr Wareham might know. He could do anything to her… She did not want to lose the child…

The blade's tip slid across her bodice and pressed gently over the position of her heart. Did he intend killing her?

The knife lifted and so did his eyes. They came to look at hers as the knife then drew a line across her cheek without cutting.

He'd said he was her father, she was sure she had not dreamed that.

He laughed and then smiled, a sly tormenting smile, and ran the knife beneath her chin across her throat.

She knew her eyes were wide, as confusion and fear gripped harder. *God help me. Save me!*

He stood up again then and walked back across the room to the table. She watched him as she might a wolf who stalked her.

This time when he turned back he held a gun and smiled. "I am undecided what to do. What do you think shall hurt that boy most?"

He is mad. He is utterly mad.

John pulled his stallion to a halt outside the address they'd been given, slid his leg over the saddle and dropped to the ground. Harvey and the other men did too as the man beside John pointed to a door.

The place was a slum and the cobbles beneath John's feet were slippery with human waste as he ran across them, ahead of the others.

Bystanders stopped to watch them with avid mistrust.

John slammed a fist on the door. It jolted. But knocking was only warning Wareham they were here. What if he ran?

John stepped back and instead smashed a heel against the wood, over and over until the damn thing gave, crashing inward. When the wood splintered, John shouldered it aside to get through, then raced upstairs to the upper room Wareham was meant to be renting.

Time had suspended. It hung in limbo. John could hardly breathe and his heart could not beat until he had Katherine back. He did not think. He could not. What if he was too late?

The handle of the upper door twisted in his hand and then opened inwards.

What faced him hit him like a fist in the gut.

Katherine was tied and gagged, lying on a bare mattress, and Wareham stood over her with a pistol in his hand. It was aimed at her forehead.

"Stay away." Wareham's gaze struck John's.

John hesitated only two feet within the door as behind him the sound of the other men carried into the room. In a moment a pistol was aimed over John's shoulder and the man beside John said, "Put the gun down." Wareham didn't move.

John looked down at Katherine.

She was extremely pale and her eyes wide, the bright blue looking to him, screaming *help me*, and tears stained her cheeks. Wareham's pistol quivered.

The man behind John came further into the room, and another entered.

Wareham could not shoot them all with one gun. But what if it was Katherine who took the bullet?

Another man came past John with a gun trained on Wareham, while the others moved further around.

John's gaze lifted to Wareham's face. This man was his uncle, his mother's half-brother, and he was about to shoot Katherine, who bore no blame. John's grandfather held that. *Katherine.* "Katherine is nothing to do with what has occurred between you and I, leave her be."

"And leave you with everything you have taken from me."

"His Grace has taken nothing, Wareham." Harvey stood behind John, now.

John could literally feel Wareham's desire to turn the gun on him. He willed the man to do it.

The first man into the room was now almost behind Wareham and out of his view. The second was five feet to the side of John, and now a fourth man entered, and a fourth gun was trained on Wareham.

His jaw taut, John held Wareham's gaze, he'd always thought it like his grandsire's, now he knew why.

The man behind Wareham lifted a finger in warning, and then he moved. The room broke into bedlam. Wareham instinctively swung his head to look back, but as he did, John saw his finger tighten on the trigger.

John moved, his only thought to save Katherine. His shoulder struck Wareham's arm just as the gun went off, and then John fell onto her as the room filled with men, who captured Wareham and pinned him down.

Lifting off Katherine, John touched her face, his heart pounding. Her eyes were wide with fear. Behind him there were cries and shouts as Wareham fought for freedom.

There were enough men to handle him. John did not look back. Someone offered him a knife.

He looked down to free her wrists... *God... Oh God...* There was a hole in her spencer, at her shoulder. The bullet. It had entered beneath her collarbone and... Suddenly ice cold, he rolled her forward. Her arms were tied behind her and she winced with pain.

There was blood on the mattress, and the red stain on her back was spreading as he watched. The shot had passed through. *Oh God.*

His hands shaking, he used the knife to slice through the rope, and once her arms were free, he lay her back and dropped it, then stripped off his coat. The scarlet stain had spread across her shoulder in the front too, and into her blonde hair. She looked at him, her gaze a plea.

"Your Grace." Harvey was at John's shoulder.

"She is wounded." John replied as he set his coat beneath her shoulder, hoping to keep the wound cleaner. Then he began untying his cravat, his fingers still shaking. Harvey bent to pull the gag from her mouth. It was obvious she was wounded, John needn't have said it; her pelisse bore a huge vivid scarlet stain now, and it was creeping outward all the time.

The bluebells in her eyes gleamed and when the gag was out a sob left her throat and then she was crying as one arm lifted, while the other tried to but could not. She flinched.

"Lie still, Katherine," he whispered as his stomach turned over. The blood continued to spread, drenching her clothes, his coat and the mattress beneath. *Lord, help me.* He worked his neckcloth free, unwinding it hurriedly. Once it was loose, he used it as best he could to stem the blood, pressing the rolled-up pad of cotton on the wound, and looked up at Harvey. "Your neckcloth, too, hurry."

John felt like ice inside, cold and frozen; he did not even care what was happening with Wareham, though he could hear the man being dragged away.

Someone cut Katherine's ankles free as Harvey handed John his neckcloth.

John swapped it with his own, looking into Katherine's eyes. She was a sickly white. "Katherine, stay with me. I'll get you home." Her eyes rolled upwards even as he spoke, but her blood still pulsed beneath his hand. She'd fainted. At least she would be free of pain.

John looked over his shoulder. "For God's sake, Harvey, get me a hackney! I need to get her help!"

"John!" Relief swept in as John saw Edward enter the room. Only now did he remember how every time he'd needed help as a child, Edward had always been there. "Katherine?" Edward's gaze had turned to her.

"A bullet has gone through her shoulder. The wound will be dirty. There is nothing here to clean it…" John felt despair.

"I have the carriage. You take her. I'll bring a surgeon." John thanked God for his father's logic. Edward had always been

335

profoundly pragmatic no matter what trauma beset them.

"She'll live, John," Edward whispered.

God, I hope so! I pray so. Her body was limp and heavy when he lifted her. *She cannot die!* He would promise anything to God to persuade Him to let her live.

In the carriage, John held her close, cradling her head and shoulder and trying to stop the ruts in the streets from jarring her as he felt the blood now seeping through his shirt.

He willed his driver to hurry, holding the strap so they did not slide about as they rushed. Her breathing fractured and grew shallow as they took a corner too sharply, and his heart pounded. He should have been the one who was struck.

When the carriage drew to a halt, he couldn't move without hurting her, and his anger and frustration built as he waited barely moments for the groom to come. It felt like hours.

As he carried her in, his mother and Mary came into the hall.

Mary cried out when she saw the quantity of blood now over him as well as Katherine.

"A bullet, Mama," John said, looking to her for help.

"Take her up, I shall have boiled water, liquor and linen brought up and I'll send for a surgeon."

"Papa has already gone to find one."

She nodded as John moved, and then disappeared below stairs. Mary rushed ahead of him opening doors, including the one to Katherine's chamber, when he reached it.

His feet felt too heavy to move, and his heart like marble in his chest. He'd promised they would always share a bed. Yet now was not the time to protest, her bed was closer. If she died, he'd die too. He couldn't live without her. He would not.

"John." His mother was at the door behind them. "Leave her with me, and you can get out of those bloody things." But it was Katherine's precious blood he couldn't change.

His mother's hand brushed his arm. "Go, John, change, otherwise you will frighten her when she wakes."

His eyes turned to Katherine. She lay limp and unconscious.

He'd failed her. He'd left her this morning and let her get hurt. His hand was shaking as it brushed back his fringe.

"I will look after her, John," his mother urged.

"Where is the patient?" A man's voice echoed along the landing. The surgeon.

Mary rushed from the room. "Here!"

His mother gripped John's arm. "Go, let the doctor clean her wound. I will stay with her. If she wakes I'll send for you."

He nodded, then bent and kissed Katherine's brow before pressing his cheek to hers. Her skin was cold and clammy. Whispering to her ear, he said, "I love you. I won't be long."

The doctor entered when John straightened, feeling a shudder reach into his bones. "You must do everything necessary to save her."

John was numb inside when he left the room, hollow, and yet on the edge of that emptiness was a husk that he knew was about to break.

His father stood on the landing.

"How is she?"

"Living but unconscious." The words sounded hard, as though he did not care. He did care. "I am going to change." But he needed a drink first.

Edward briefly gripped John's arm. "She'll survive."

John felt pain leak into his eyes. The numbness had passed and now he was in agony. This was his fault.

Not really knowing where he walked, just walking, John went downstairs to the library.

His stride was long as he crossed the floor, the thread of his sanity slipping further through his fingers as he walked. In the room, he poured a brandy, and as he sipped it he saw a mental image of Katherine, in the chair, looking through his sketches. *I wish to be your friend and your helpmate as much as your wife.*

He hadn't wholly trusted her... He hadn't told her about

Wareham. He'd shut her out when she'd asked. He didn't even have a reason why, it was just his habit not to share things.

Clutching the edge of his desk, he let it take his weight, the thin husk of his control cracking and emotion surging in. He wished he could weep, he longed to weep, to cry and have this out, but the ability to shed tears was beaten out of him.

Instead, anger filled the void of despair. He blamed himself, true, but there was someone else…

His head lifted and his fingers gripped tighter around the glass. He stared at the portrait of the old man and sipped the brandy. Its heat slid into his veins as hatred did too.

That devil had disowned and left his mother for dead because she'd eloped with a man he did not like. That devil had sired a son out of wedlock, a far worse sin, and harboured him at Pembroke Place. Living life as though he was pure of sin, when his heart was dark as jet beneath.

Disgust, revulsion and anger swelled and pulsed. The last vestige of John's sanity slipped and drawing back his hand John threw the glass at the picture.

The brandy smeared his grandfather's face.

It did not ease John's rage. With a growl, he swiped the contents off the desk. Items shattered on the floor. Then he turned to the mantle and saw the hunting statues his grandfather had loved. Striding across the room, he grasped one and threw that at his grandfather too. It tore the canvas. He threw another, growling as he hurled it.

Then he picked up a vase the old man had had shipped from Florence and thrust it at the floor. It shattered.

"John! What the hell is going on?" His father was at the open door.

John's chest heaved with heavy breaths when he turned. "If he was alive I would kill him."

Edward shut the door. "When he was alive I often wished to. But destroying his things is not going to help Katherine." Edward crossed the room.

John felt ten again, helpless. "I cannot do this." The desire to weep washed over him once more.

"You can, and you will. She needs you."

"I let her down. We argued last night and I walked away. She asked me to tell her why I'd dismissed Wareham three times. I did not tell her. I considered it nothing to do with her. We argued because she hates me shutting her out. She wants me to rely on her. She cannot rely on me…" John looked up at the ornate ceiling. "I cannot live without her."

His father's footfalls came closer. "This is not your doing. It's Wareham's, and if Katherine is to recover, she needs you, and she is not the sort to lay blame, John."

Edward gripped John's shoulder. "You will get through this, and your marriage will become what it ought. People take time to learn about each other. But Katherine is right. It is not just her you close yourself off from. I know it is from a need to be strong—"

"Because I am not strong… If people saw this, and knew me…"

"They would see a man who loved his wife. There is no harm in that. Look at your Uncle Richard or Robert. Do they hide their affections? Do they hold people distant? Are they seen as weak? It was too late for your grandfather to change when he discovered how much he had hurt your mother. It is not too late for you. Listen to Katherine. She's good for you…"

Edward's grasp firmed. "Now, go and change. The servants will clear this. You will want to be ready when Katherine wakes."

I wish to be your friend and your helpmate as much as your wife…

John gripped Edward's arm.

Edward embraced John briefly, then let him go again. "No one doubts you, John. Look how you have managed. You are respected. Focus on being happy now and making Kate so."

John met his father's deep blue-grey gaze. "I will try."

"As I once told your mother, I do not accept trying. Trying is not good enough. *Change.* You can."

339

Their gazes held, as though Edward cast a gauntlet at John's feet.

John picked it up and nodded agreement before turning away. His birth father could have loved him no more than Edward did.

~

John stripped and washed, then returned to Katherine's bedside; his clean clothes carrying the scent of starch and rosemary.

He wore only a shirt and trousers, he had not had the patience to tie a clean neckcloth and he was in no mood to be fussed over by his valet. He felt raw inside.

He looked at his mother when he entered the room.

Katherine should be in his bed, not here.

"She is not conscious," his mother said. "But the wound has been stitched and the doctor said her heart seems strong. She just needs time."

He looked at Katherine. Her head rested on the white pillow, her skin was paler, if that were possible. She'd lost a lot of blood.

Loose blonde curls framed her face and her light-brown eyelashes rested on her pale cheeks. She'd been bathed and dressed in a nightgown.

She'd have scars to remind them both of this, scars which would remind him he'd failed her.

He moved a chair beside her bed as his mother told him all the doctor had said.

The child seemed unharmed and Katherine was to have fluid whenever she roused. It all washed over him. He just wished her to open her eyes and speak.

Sitting, he took up his vigil. "You may go, Mama, I'll stay."

"You need not sit with her alone, John." Edward had probably already reported John's earlier tantrum.

"I would prefer it, Mama, she probably cannot hear me but there are things I wish to say."

His mother nodded then, and leant to press a kiss on his

340

forehead, her fingers brushing his cheek. "She'll get well." *If there was any justice in the world…* He was not convinced.

He looked at Katherine. The door clicked shut.

John gripped Katherine's fingers, which had been resting on the covers. His thumb stroking across her palm, he pictured the colour of her eyes, fiery with anger and then bright with need in the light of the tower room. *Katherine.* "I'm sorry. I'll not hold you away again. I am going to change. *Live* and help me change…"

He closed his eyes and leant on the bed, pressing her cold fingers against his brow as he prayed, making a deal with God. He'd give up everything, anything, for her.

~

"John, you have to eat. Katherine would tell you the same," his mother pressed.

"I am not hungry." John's eyes stayed on Katherine. He'd spent hours during the night pleading and begging with God to let her wake, to let her live. Nothing had changed.

There was a knock.

"Enter," his mother called.

"I've brought you some plum cake and coffee, John." It was Mary. "I knew you would refuse to come down." She set the tray she carried on a chest at the bedside. "Has she changed?"

"Her colour is better." He glanced up, but only for an instant.

Mary smiled. Sympathy and concern in her eyes. "Phillip is downstairs, he's only just received Papa's note. He wishes to see her."

John looked back again. "Send him up."

As Mary left, John squeezed Katherine's fingers gently, then let go and stood. He moved to poor some coffee. That he was glad of; it would keep him awake.

Phillip looked shocked and pale when he came in. "I only just heard… How did it happen?" He took the chair John had vacated, lifting Katherine's fingers, and then he kissed them, his hand shaking.

"I'll leave you alone," John's mother said.

John was looking at Phillip when the door shut. "Do you want anything…" John indicated the tray.

Phillip shook his head. "Just tell me how?"

John explained Wareham's past and then told Phillip about the note, and where and how he'd found Katherine. Then he spoke of her injury.

"What was she doing there?"

"My mother and aunt left her at an orphanage she'd decided to sponsor. The groom accompanying her was tricked into leaving her alone. Wareham must have been following her. I should have realised he might go after Katherine." His coffee cup was empty. John set it down. "I cannot bear the thought of losing her. I don't even care what happens to Wareham… let him rot in a jail."

"She's a fighter," Phillip responded. "She will survive, if only to make your life hell for putting her through this."

A laugh cracked from John's throat, a broken sound of pain. Instantly Katherine groaned and moved to sit up, her hand slipping from Phillip's.

Within a moment, John was beside the bed, leaning past Phillip and resting his fingers on her clavicle, gently pressing her back. "Katherine stay still, you have been hurt."

When she lay back on the pillow, his hand dropped to take hers. Her fingers tightened around his grip and his heart beat harder with relief, hope and love, as his thumb brushed her hand.

Her eyelids flickered open.

"Katherine." He smiled, but then it slipped as he remembered the last time they'd spoken and all that had happened since. *What must she think of me?*

"My shoulder hurts."

"I know, darling. The bullet hit you. You have stitches. It tore right through your shoulder. You will need to take it easy for a long while."

He could see her memory returning, flashing behind her eyes. "Where am I?"

"Home. *Safe.* Wareham is gone and Phillip is here."

Tears glittered in her eyes as she looked beyond John for her brother. Of course she wished to see her brother over *him*. Phillip had never let her down.

"Katherine," Phillip leant forwards, John straightened and stepped back, letting her hand go once more so Phillip might take it.

She reached out. "Phillip."

"John and I have let you down. I knew about Wareham, too, Kate, he'd been stealing from John. We should have told you…" Foolish that Phillip had no hesitation in honesty and apology with his sister, when John thought himself stronger and had been unable to speak to her with any honesty for months. When he had finally done so, he'd walked out rather than hear her advice. He'd never liked being challenged; it was another scar his grandfather had cut.

I am arrogant. He did not deserve this open-hearted woman.

John saw her hold Phillip's hand tighter. "Mr Wareham said he is my father. Do you think he is? Why would he—" *Good God, that would make them cousins… It—*

"He lied." There was anger in Phillip's response as he silenced both Katherine and John's thoughts. "He can only have said it to be cruel. Do not believe it."

Phillip knew who her father was, John would swear it. His voice had held too much conviction. John watched them. Certain he was right. But Phillip had always said no one knew.

John glanced at Katherine, frowning. She'd not noticed Phillip's odd reaction.

"I must go, Kate, I'm sorry." Phillip stood and then leant to kiss Katherine's forehead. "I'll come back soon. Do as John says and rest."

John moved out of the way, but he was dumbfounded by Phillip's sudden haste. He'd not long come.

Phillip said goodbye, shaking John's hand, then his heels echoed on the wooden floor as John turned to Katherine, unsure what to do or say.

"I'm sorry, John." Just like her brother the expression of emotion came easily to her. She cried then.

He sat beside her and held her hand, while his other wiped her tears away. "You have nothing to be sorry for." He lifted her hand, kissed it and then pressed the back against his cheek.

"I should have known you dismissed him for a reason, but I felt sorry for him. I didn't think…" She started crying again.

His thumb stroked her hand. "It is not your fault. You asked me at The Place, and here, and I did not tell you. I did not wish to. You are my escape. I came to you in Ashford to get away from my arguments with Wareham, and my duties."

Unable to look at her, John's head bowed with the weight of guilt and he held the back of her fingers to his forehead. "I used you, I suppose, Katherine, terribly. It is I who am sorry, sorrier than I can ever say." He looked back up and faced the blue eyes which had enchanted him from the moment of their first reunion.

"I should have told you why I laid him off when you asked me. What you said the night before last was right, my life is like a Chinese cabinet with a hundred different drawers, I open and shut them depending on where I am and who I am with and what face or knowledge I am to display to the world. I do not put you away and forget you, but yes, I have tried to hide you in a drawer in my life. You are precious to me. You have been from the beginning. I did not want to share what we have with anyone else, so I hid it. But I heard what you said." Her eyes implied she did not believe him. "I promise you, Katherine."

"I went to an orphanage—"

"I know."

"I liked it." Her eyes lifted to the canopy above the bed. "I am going to work there in the day, when you are not here." She glanced back at him. "The children have so much love to give,

John, and they need someone to give it back."

Because you think me incapable of it. Had he destroyed his marriage? He sighed and rose, still unable to discuss his feelings easily: he was *unchanged.* He had to change.

"You ought to eat and drink something. You lost a lot of blood."

She nodded and he moved to ring the bell.

"Don't leave."

He looked back. His desertion the other night had truly hurt her. "I am only going to ring for a maid." Her eyes filled with tears again.

I have to change.

He pulled the cord, then came back to the bed and sat beside her, holding her hand once more. "Can you no longer love me, Katherine? Have I killed what you felt for me?"

A little choking sound came from her throat as she tried to sit up and then she winced.

"Shall I fetch you some laudanum?"

"No, I just wish to sit upright."

He fetched more cushions from chairs around the room to prop behind her back, then carefully helped her sit. "Better?"

"Yes. Why did you not come home yesterday?"

He sat down. *Be honest, John, change.* "Because I was avoiding this conversation, I knew you were right and I am too arrogant to simply admit it. I am a fool…"

She smiled at his self-mocking tone before wincing from pain. "I wish you would be like this outside the house."

Well this was going to be his biggest challenge. "If I must be different outside the house to keep your love, Katherine, and to make you happy, I shall be." She just looked at him.

"You do not believe me, do you?"

She shook her head. "You have promised before."

"And not changed… I shall this time, and you must recover. So I can prove it to you."

345

~

John had spent two days with her, making sure she ate and drank, while Katherine made sure he ate and drank, too.

He'd slept beside her, refusing to leave, even when his mother or Mary offered to stay with her in his stead.

She was glad.

She needed him. She felt vulnerable, all shaky inside, and she could not stop thinking of being tied on that bed every time she shut her eyes. In her sleep she heard Mr Wareham say he was her father over and over.

John had been holding her when she'd woken from one dream. She'd been crying. He'd said nothing as his warmth and the solidity of his chest had calmed her fears.

His desertion the day it had happened had affected them both, though, it had changed things, and although they were together, they were not. There was a ravine between them again. She dare not trust what he'd said about changing, and he seemed to be wary, knowing she no longer trusted him.

She clung to the time they had now, knowing it was rare, knowing it would not last. Here, in private, he was everything she wished him to be. This privacy, this John, was precious.

When the morning of the third day came, the doctor agreed to her attempting to get out of bed and John left her so she might wash and change.

It felt awful to be without him. It felt as though it was an end.

~

Katherine's absence rankled inside John like a canker. But he'd agreed to let his mother help her dress, and left her.

When he returned, she was paler.

Walking to where she lay against the pillows, atop the bed, he said, "I'll carry you."

346

"I can walk. It is my shoulder that's wounded not my legs."

He smiled, noting with a feeling of warmth that if she was berating him she was feeling better. "Very well, but you will take my arm, and you are only going as far as your sitting room today." She gave him a half-smile, which clearly accused him of being domineering, but conceded, sliding to the edge of the bed, while lifting her hand.

He took it, but her fingers gripped over-tightly as she rose. "My head is spinning."

"Let me carry you."

"No." Her determined gaze met his.

"Very well." Swallowing back his irritation and his need to cosset her, he pressed her fingers to his arm. He liked it when she turned to him for comfort. He did not like it when she turned away. And here was a lesson to him. Is this not what Katherine had complained of the night of the last ball? She liked him turning to her, too. "Ready?"

She nodded but her smile stiffened.

"It hurts?"

"Like the devil," she whispered.

"Do you want to take another dose of laudanum when you are settled?"

"No," she answered with revulsion, "it makes me feel sick and too sleepy and I fear what it does to the child."

John's mother intervened in their *tête-à-tête* "Get settled then, and I'll get you some sweet tea. Mary can read to you, too, and that will distract you."

John walked Katherine into the other room and saw her into a chair, then stepped back and let his mother and Mary fuss, begrudging their presence. He'd become too used to being alone with Katherine; he was not ready to share her with others yet.

"May I see, Kate, Mama?"

John turned.

Georgiana, one of his much younger sisters, stood at the

347

sitting-room door.

At his mother's and Katherine's agreement, she came in, carrying a rolled sheet of paper.

"Mama said you were poorly, Kate. We drew you a picture to make you feel better." John watched his mother's gaze soften, and Katherine's too.

"That is very sweet of you, Georgie," his mother said as his young sister handed the paper to Katherine.

"It is lovely," Katherine exclaimed, as she unrolled it, "thank you, Georgie, and thank your sisters."

"David wanted me to bring the spider he found and put in a jar this morning, but I told him you would not want it."

Laughing lightly, Katherine shook her head. "You're right, I would not. You may tell him I appreciate the thought, but I do not like spiders."

John laughed and it brought Georgiana's attention to him. Stiffening her spine, she curtsied, looking meek and nervous, and then she hurriedly disappeared.

The truth could not be more obvious, Katherine had won over his siblings' hearts already, while *that* was the effect he had on them. He scared them. *As you were terrified of your grandfather. It is your own fault. You choose to be like him.*

But he did not want his son or daughter running from him like that.

Sighing, he moved to see how else he could help Katherine, but before he reached her side there was a rap on the open sitting-room door.

"Kate?"

Edward.

John turned.

"Phillip is here, he is waiting in the hall. He's brought your father to see you." Edward hesitated, as though he sensed some undercurrent. "I wasn't certain you'd wish me to send them up."

When John turned back to her, she was looking at him and

348

she lifted her hand.

He caught it in reassurance. "Do you wish to see him?"

"You'll stay?" Her eyes were wide with insecurity. This was not going to be an easy meeting. She had not seen her father since the day they'd married, when she had run to John.

Squeezing her hand, he answered, "Of course." Then he looked at Edward. "Send them up," before glancing at his mother. "Can you send for that tea too, but leave us. I think this conversation would be better private."

As his family drifted away, John fetched Katherine a footstool.

When Phillip and her father arrived, the tea tray was on their heels. John bid the maid pour and asked Phillip and Katherine's father to sit.

Neither man did. Instead they hovered on their feet, her father's hands clasping behind his back, while Phillip's clutched his gloves.

John remained on his feet too, watching them, trying to gauge what was going on.

The maid passed a cup to Katherine. The other cups were left on the tray, none of them accepted.

After bobbing a deep curtsy, her eyes looking to the floor, the maid disappeared.

As soon as she was gone, Phillip spoke. "Father has something to say to you, Katherine." His words were terse. John looked to Mr Spencer as she did. He straightened defensively, but the look he gave to Katherine was apologetic.

"I am sorry, Kate. I should have told you this long ago, but I could not find either the words or the moment. Phillip said Mr Wareham told you he was your father. He is not. I know, because, I am."

The china in her hand wobbled, rattling, and John moved, hurriedly bending to take the cup and saucer from her fingers. He set them aside.

The little colour she'd regained had faded.

He set a hand on her shoulder, though he was as shocked as

she was. He'd had no idea.

Her father pressed on, his eyes darting between Katherine and John. "Your mother was not my choice. Our marriage was arranged. We were no happier then than now. It is no excuse, I know." He glanced at Phillip, and then back at Katherine. "I was fond of your mother, Katherine."

"She took her own life," Katherine breathed.

"She had lost her position, she was—"

"Alone, Papa, you had left her alone." Katherine sounded horrified by the revelation. John pressed his hand more firmly on her shoulder.

"What could I have done? I was married, Kate. I gave her money…"

"You could have not touched her," Phillip growled.

"Hindsight is no good." Her father threw at Phillip. Then he turned back to Katherine. "I cannot change what happened. But your mother and I took you in, and I raised you as my daughter."

"*I am your daughter* and you never told me."

"I'm sorry."

This man had left her suffering and he'd known how isolated she'd felt.

Spencer blushed.

John looked at Phillip. "You knew?" He felt angry with Phillip too. It seemed everyone in Katherine's life had let her down. John would not do so again. She deserved better than this.

Phillip's gaze met John's. "Since I was fifteen. I worked it out, challenged him, and he confessed." He looked at Katherine. "I've always wished you to know, but it was not my place to speak. I couldn't hurt you."

"At least I know why Mama hates me, now," Katherine whispered.

"She does not hate you. She hates what you came from," her father answered. "Phillip has pressed me to speak of this to you for years, but I have never had the courage. I was your father anyway. Was I wrong?"

"Yes, you were wrong." Katherine stood, with a clear urge to express her disappointment, but something held her back, probably her dignity. She had a lot of that, more than any of them in the room. "You let her treat me as though I am nothing, when I am yours... I want nothing more to do with her. She has never been like a mother to me. I wish to see Jenny again, but I will never call on you, or invite Mama to visit us... Unless she is willing to come to me and say that she is sorry."

"I am sorry, Katherine. For us both. But the wrong is mine."

"Yet Mama judged me for it..."

John had kept apologising to her, too, *but sorry was not good enough*, John saw it in her eyes. Putting things right, treating her as she deserved, that was what should be done. She was the sort of person who just kept giving while people took. John was going to give back to her now.

He moved forwards.

"I think you have said enough for today."

Spencer's gaze flew to John's face.

John looked at Katherine. It was her choice. She nodded.

"Let me show you out."

"But—"

"You may call again tomorrow, when Katherine has had a chance to think and decide if she wishes to maintain any connection with you."

"Your Grace—"

"No complaints. Let Katherine rest."

"I will speak with you again tomorrow, Papa, if you stay in town." Again, Katherine gave. She always would, because compassion was embedded in her soul.

He looked back at her. "You may have some time to speak with Phillip, while I show your father out."

Their journey downstairs was littered with warnings, as John made it clear Spencer was to recognise Katherine openly, and as John spoke he heard the words himself and knew he must do the same. He had built up the courage to marry her, but not the courage to show the world he loved her. He would show them now.

~

The room was dark, almost black, the day had been grey and the sky beyond the closed curtains must still be cloudy, hiding the moon. It was chilly too, the fire having burned itself out long ago, but John's presence warmed Katherine.

He lay behind her, his body moulded to hers, one arm across her waist. His other arm lay above his head.

She felt his breath stir her hair.

He'd spent the day with her again. It was two weeks since her abduction, and he'd been present ever since.

He'd only leave her if she bid him go, and he never left the house.

He had changed. The looks from his family suggested it too. His aunts and uncles all smiled when they saw John hovering at her elbow. He even carried out his business at home and mostly in the same room as her so he needn't leave her.

She snuggled back against him.

What was happening was wonderful but… She was terrified of what would happen outside the house. He'd always been attentive here, but outside…?

She'd grown too used to this John. It might break her heart if she faced his ducal reserve again. A tear streaked down her cheek. Her shoulder still hurt, but her heart ached more, unsure whether it dare beat or not. Phillip, her father, everyone she thought had cared had hurt her… A sob escaped her throat.

John's hand pressed against her stomach. "What is it?"

Katherine rolled onto her back, and looked over as though she might see him. She couldn't, it was too dark. "I'm afraid."

"Of what?"

"Of everything and nothing, John. I am just in a blue mood."
"Why?"

She began crying again and he kissed her cheek. She felt his love, but it only made her cry more.

"Hush, Katherine, what is it?"

Her fingers gripped in his hair, holding him close. "I am afraid of losing this. With my father I… I just cannot… I cannot go back to how things were, John."

"Your father—"

"Not my father, *you*, I do not wish to lose you."

"You shall not."

"But you cannot always stay here, we cannot keep hiding here forever, and when… You are all I have."

"And you are all I have, and you are going to have to trust me. We understand each other, Katherine, like no one else can."

He kissed the tip of her nose and then her lips.

"Your aunt Penny asked if I wished to attend her at home tomorrow afternoon, your uncle will be there."

"And you wish me to accompany you."

"Yes."

She felt like crying again, because she had been so terrified of asking.

"We will go then."

He brushed another kiss on her lips.

They'd not made love once since her abduction. But now his fingers slid to her hip and began sliding up her nightgown. "Do you wish to…"

She nodded. She did. It would ease her fear to have this physical connection again. She had always felt closer to him when they were united like that.

"Do not be afraid, Katherine, I swear to you I will be different now."

~

It was another two weeks later that John's new demeanour was put fully to the test.

Katherine had attended three separate afternoon entertainments in his company, during which he had sat silently beside her most of the time, smiling, but in a way which still seemed to say nothing of what was on his mind.

Yet he had not been cold, and at times he had participated in conversations, but most of the other guests had been members of his family.

This was their first ball.

It was the Earl of Gladstone's Christmas ball and the weather had kindly deemed to dress the evening in a seasonal fall of snow. It coated the pavements, roofs and cobbled streets. They'd had to wait in the carriage for an age, watching the large white star-like flakes falling and she knew John was looking at it, longing for it to cease, no matter how beautiful it looked. Tomorrow the family were to travel to Pembroke Place, to celebrate the yuletide there. John was longing to retreat there, he had admitted as much last night.

Her fingers were clasped beneath her fur-lined cloak, and John's gloved hand clutched her waist as they were admitted into the warmth of the grand hall. Katherine glanced up at his face, his lips were tight and his expression was not set, but neither were his features mobile. If his face set in its old mask when they had been out previously, she'd lifted her eyebrows when she'd caught his attention and smiled. Then he'd smile in return, forcing his features to relax. It was like sharing a secret with him as she'd see his eyes glint with understanding.

His family were wary of the fragile changes in him too. They often commented to her on how different John was, but no one said it to him, and his mother watched him with a look of happiness and fear.

Once, Katherine had seen his mother standing outside the nursery silent and looking in. Then Katherine had heard John. She'd walked up and looked past his mother to see John on the floor with his young brothers. They had been playing with an army of lead soldiers. Something had caught hard about her heart when she saw him smiling at the boys.

Soon, this would be John with their son, or daughter.

It was as though he was discovering himself again. He had started going out again, to his club and the House of Lords, and to meet his businessman. But when he came home he talked about where he had been and what he'd done, and he did not stay out all day. He'd even taken her with him to visit his man of business, where Phillip now worked, on two occasions. Once, they'd called on one of John's peers too, so John might discuss some bill, while Katherine had sat with the man's wife. She *was* a part of his life now, but tonight was the final test.

John was nervous, she knew, and uncomfortable. He'd been silent over dinner and on the journey here. She unclasped her hands and caught his as it slipped from her waist. He looked down and smiled as a footman stepped forwards to take their outdoor clothing.

Afterwards, they were offered warm punch. Its sweet scent filled the hall.

"Ready," John asked once she'd had a drink.

She shivered in her sleeveless dress. "This fashion is not suited to winter."

He laughed, and then his white-gloved fingers briefly rubbed her arms to warm them, careful not to hurt her shoulder, which was still terribly sore. "We'll get you dancing then. That will warm you up."

She nodded. Though with her arm supported in a velvet band hung from her neck to hold her shoulder steady, the only dance she was probably capable of was a waltz.

"Come on." His fingers gently gripped her arm and he led her to the receiving line.

Katherine glanced up at his profile. He was so ridiculously handsome.

He looked down and smiled.

"I love you," she whispered.

He bent to her ear. "I love you too."

"Pembroke, you look pleased with yourself. Marital harmony, I suppose?" They were Lord Gladstone's opening words.

"Damn, I am rumbled," John stated. She knew the Earl was a close acquaintance of John's. "Pray, do not expose me."

"Too late old chap, you've done that yourself, the word's already loose. Everyone knows she's broken you. The smile you bestow on your wife says you're smitten."

John scoffed, his expression turning to a look of self-disgust, but he did not raise his mask. "Am I that obvious?"

"Yes." The Earl laughed.

John laughed too, "God help me then, I'll not deny it."

The Earl's arm lifted, and his hand patted John's shoulder. "Never mind Pembroke, I'd rather be in your shoes than some others. Your Grace." He bowed to Katherine and then she and John moved on.

"That is it then, my reputation is in shreds," John whispered into her ear. But his voice was light and humorous.

She glanced up. "Does it upset you?"

His pale-blue gaze held hers, sparkling and open. "No, Katherine, let them gossip. Your smile is worth my reputation."

"I prefer Lord Gladstone's view of it anyway."

John's smile broke wider, as his fingers caught hers. "Come on, they are starting a waltz."

She saw Eleanor, who was now heavy with child.

Katherine's fingers touched her own stomach. Her condition was beginning to show. She wondered if she would become as large as Eleanor. That was partly why they were going to The Place. John had said they would stay there over Christmas only, and then move on to one of his more isolated estates. He was having The Place decorated once they moved on. He'd told her it was to dispose of his ill memories once and for all.

"John! Katherine!" Eleanor called before they could move

among the dancers. She approached with her husband, who gripped her elbow, smiling in the fashion of a proud expectant father.

"You look well," Eleanor said to Katherine first, and then glanced at John. "You too. What has she done to you? You are actually smiling!"

John laughed and smiled more, the sort of smile he kept for their private apartments. "She has made me happy."

God, he did feel happy – happy and not uncomfortable at all – when he'd feared feeling stripped naked by the exposure of his inner self.

"Well, Amen to that," Eleanor replied, before gossiping to Katherine over something.

John spoke with Nettleton for a moment until the other couple left to continue their circuit of the ballroom.

It was too late to begin the waltz, which was a shame; he had been looking forward to spending more time with Katherine here. He was determined not to argue with her, and not to let the company disturb him. He was determined to stay relaxed.

"John?" He felt himself stiffen instantly, and turned. Elizabeth Ponsonby; could the woman not learn that no meant no?

She smiled her hollow seductress' smile. It did not entice, it only revolted.

Katherine's fingers wrapped about John's forearm, gentle and precious. He felt them wrap about his heart too and the ice inside him melted. He actually found the smile he had become accustomed to in the last weeks lift his lips. "Elizabeth."

Katherine was facing Elizabeth too.

"What is this, a show of marital bliss? How sickening. It shan't last."

Katherine pressed against him in what he knew was a gesture of claiming, and he treasured it, treasured her willingness to hold by him. "It shall," she answered in a matter-of-fact voice, and then she looked up at him, giving him a cue. He smiled down at her, knowing his love burned in his eyes. He did not give a damn if others knew. He wished them to. "Shan't it, John," she whispered.

There was no one else in the room but her as he looked into her eyes. "It will last," he answered as his hand lifted to touch her chin and his lips lowered to hers. He was not even thinking of what he did until he'd done it, and then he realised ... He had just kissed his wife in a ballroom full of his peers... And then he remembered Elizabeth.

He laughed when he straightened, still holding Katherine's gaze, not quite believing himself and how happy he felt. When he looked back at Elizabeth it was with a dismissive humour. Her presence no longer made him bristle. He really did not care whether she was there or not.

She must have seen what little power she had over him now, because she merely gave him a proud, indifferent look and walked away.

His fingers cupping Katherine's chin, John kissed her again and then they both laughed.

"Let's play a hand of cards or two, as your shoulder prevents us dancing."

A wide, broad smile caught in her eyes and parted her lips before she nodded.

John remembered the weight of loneliness he'd felt at night when he'd lived in Egypt, a year ago, and the dark stark memories of his childhood, which had not bothered him for weeks. Everything seemed lifted from his shoulders, and all the darkness gone. He did not expect to ever have the dream again. His mind did not need to look back. It had the future to look to now and the birth of his child.

When he turned to the room, those around them were staring, and when he and Katherine walked away, fans and hands were raised and whispered behind. He searched for anger and bitterness inside him and found none. None.

He didn't give a damn what others thought, not anymore.

Epilogue

Leaning over the cradle, John watched his son gurgle to himself, in a happy one-sided conversation. The infant's eyes glowed with pleasure. John smiled.

Paul Harding, the Marquess of Sayle, lifted his arms, reaching in John's direction.

John picked him up. He was heavy. At six months he was a chubby, hearty, healthy child.

His fingers grasped John's hair.

John caught the boy's hand and carried him to the window to look out over the grounds of The Place.

In the distance, he saw the folly tower. "All this will be yours one day, Paul. But for now, it is just your playground. I will not let you take its weight too soon, not as I did." John kissed the child's head and felt love fill his heart as he smelled his son's sweet, childish scent.

"So this is where you've run off to. Everyone is waiting for you downstairs."

John turned to Katherine, his smile broadening as he lifted Paul high and tossed him upwards then caught him, making the boy giggle.

"He's supposed to be sleeping," Katherine charged, but beneath the accusing words was a note of amusement.

"He'd woken."

"Because you were watching and disturbed him."

"I was checking to see he was comfortable."

"And waking him so you had an excuse to take him down and show him off."

John grinned.

She came closer. "You will spoil him, John."

"With love, yes… always."

She shook her head, her smile saying it was not worth the battle. "Spoil him, if you will," she murmured, stepping closer, and then she rose to her toes and kissed his cheek, before kissing Paul's head.

"Then may I bring him down?"

Her eyebrows lifted, "You are incorrigible."

"I dote on him, and I dote on you. There is no need to be jealous. There is space in my heart for you both."

She smacked his arm, laughing a little, but then her expression changed and the depth in her eyes increased. "There must be more space though, John."

His brow furrowed.

"I am only a few days late, but I am never late and the signs are already there…"

One arm holding Paul, his other arm drew her close. He could not comprehend the sudden rush of joy inside him.

"Oh, Katherine, that is wonderful."

She smiled up at him when he let her go, tears shining in her eyes. She wiped them away.

"I love you."

"I love you too."

A year and a half ago Katherine could never have imagined this. John had been so far above her and now she was his equal.

John cupped her nape and brought her lips back to his. "I do not just dote on you both. I am besotted by you both, and I shall be with every other child we have."

360

He was very open now, but even so, moments like this were precious; John still held elements of himself just for her, well, for her and Paul.

"Come on." His fingers fell to grip hers. "Let us go down. Mama and Papa have not even seen him since they came, but I am not sharing our secret, we'll keep it ours for a little while, shall we?"

"Yes."

When she had watched him in the lake so long ago, she'd known the quality of this man, but she'd had no expectation, only dreams and longing. Now all her dreams had come true. It was beyond a Cinderella story.

Printed by Amazon Italia Logistica S.r.l.
Torrazza Piemonte (TO), Italy

59978482R00211